RAPHAEL

THE KAIYO STORIES

BOOK II

Keep Enjoy the Adventure!

Cliff

CLIFF COCHRAN

ISBN 978-1-64569-666-7 (paperback)
ISBN 978-1-64569-667-4 (digital)

Christian Faith Publishing, Inc.
832 Park Avenue
Meadville, PA 16335
www.christianfaithpublishing.com

This story is a work of fiction. Names, characters, businesses, places, events, locales, and incidents are either the products of the author's imagination or are used in a fully fictitious manner. Any resemblance to actual persons, living or dead, or actual events is purely coincidental.

Printed in the United States of America

Remember…be as wise as snakes and as blameless as doves.

—Matthew 10:16 (Open English Bible)

CHARACTERS

McLeod

1. Dean McLeod: Fifteen-year-old son of Sam and Susan McLeod
2. Gracie McLeod: Ten-year-old daughter of Sam and Susan McLeod
3. Kaiyo McLeod: Two-and-a-half-year-old adopted grizzly bear, son of Sam and Susan McLeod
4. Libby McLeod: Seventeen-year-old daughter of Sam and Susan McLeod
5. Sam McLeod: Rancher, husband of Susan and father of Libby, Dean, Gracie, and Kaiyo
6. Susan McLeod: Rancher, wife of Sam and mother of Libby, Dean, Gracie, and Kaiyo

Gibbs

7. Aliyah Gibbs: Friend and neighbor to the McLeods and mother of Kate and Jack
8. Jack Gibbs: Fifteen-year-old son of Gunner and Aliyah Gibbs
9. Kate Gibbs: Fourteen-year-old daughter of Gunner and Aliyah Gibbs
10. Steve "Gunner" Gibbs: Friend and neighbor to the McLeods and father of Kate and Jack

Specials (extraordinary creatures)

1. Annag: A Sobek
2. Aylmer: The Aurochs
3. Benaiah: The Watcher, a.k.a. Rimmy, friend of the McLeods
4. Dohv/Dovie: The black bear
5. Eli: Kaiyo's bear father
6. Goliath: Very big grizzly, mentor of Kaiyo
7. Haydar: A Sobek
8. Jana: Kaiyo's bear mother
9. Kaiyo (McLeod): Two-and-a-half-year-old adopted grizzly bear, son of Sam and Susan McLeod
10. Lavi: A mountain lion
11. Tracker: Wolf, friend of the McLeods

Animals (ordinary)

1. Cali: Susan's palomino quarter horse
2. Chevy: Jack's quarter horse
3. Duke: Gracie's pony, buckskin Welsh Cob
4. Hershel: Sam's horse, a bay with a blond flax mane and tail
5. Humphrey: Sam's mule
6. Jet: Libby's horse, black with a white patch on her face
7. Luke: Danielle Klein's dog
8. Major: McLeods' guard dog (a mix of large German shepherd and Carolina dog)
9. Moose: McLeods' guard dog (a mix of Argentine Dogo and Anatolian Shepherd)
10. Peyton: A huge Shire horse, chestnut brown
11. Rosie: A young alpaca
12. Solo: Dean's horse, slate blue dun mustang

Spirits

1. Meginnah: Cherub
2. Raphael: Archangel

Other humans

1. Alan Osbourne: Major, Park County Sheriff's Department
2. Bill Adams: USFS ranger
3. Cindy Rich: Veterinarian
4. Danielle Klein: Child abducted by the Sobeks
5. Duane: Criminal camper, boyfriend to Stephanie
6. Ed Hamby: Captain, Montana State Patrol
7. Emma Garcia: Wyoming State Patrol Officer
8. Justin Martinez: Sergeant, Madison County Sheriff's Department
9. Kent Thomas: USFS ranger
10. Kurt and Linda Tompkins: Sarah's parents
11. Lee Tuttle: Sheriff, Madison County Sheriff's Department; wife, Ellie
12. Lowe Brigham: Game Warden, Montana Department of Fish, Wildlife and Parks
13. Landon Haldor: Hiker, friend of McLeods
14. Robin and Chris Klein: Parents of Danielle Klein
15. Sarah Tompkins: Rescued victim of demonic possession
16. Stephanie: Criminal camper, girlfriend to Duane
17. Troy Stahr: Captain, Madison County Sheriff's Department

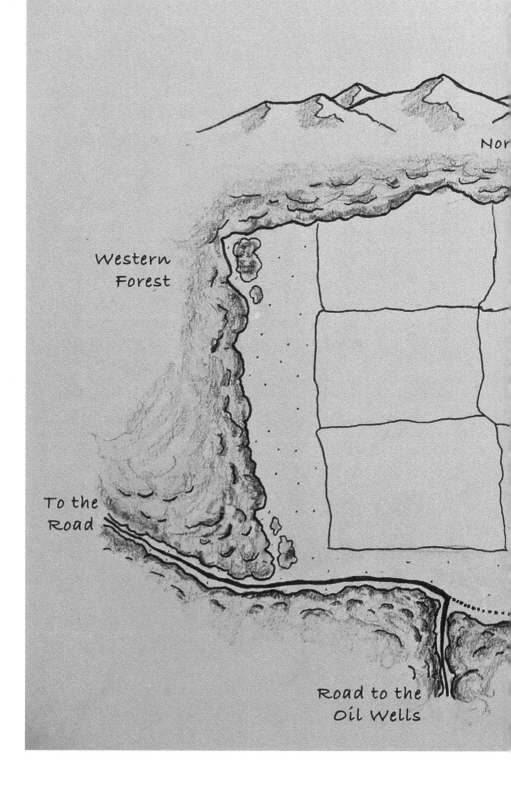

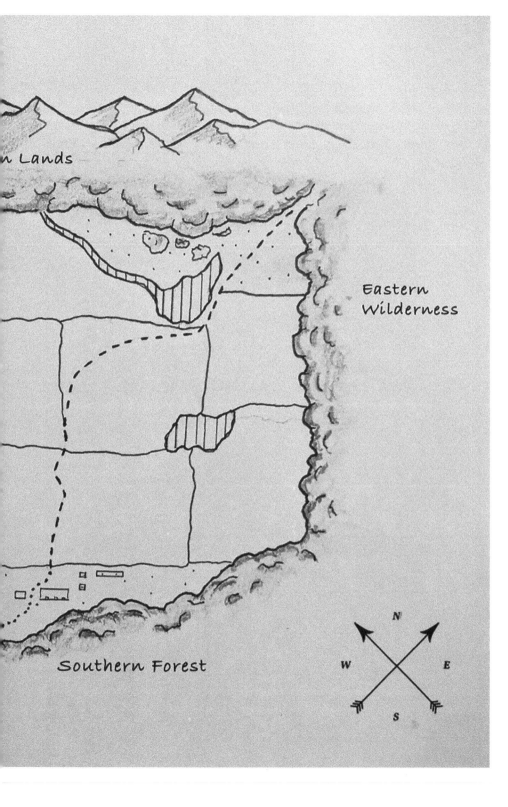

Lands

Eastern
Wilderness

Southern Forest

N

W   E

S

ACKNOWLEDGMENTS

Thank you to so many readers of Kaiyo—The Lost Nation who loved the story and encouraged this sequel. To my children, Brooke, Bin and Lily, having you as my BearWolf Books partners is a dream come true. Your art, your creativity, your market savvy and your love for a grizzly bear named Kaiyo makes it all much more fun. To Kriss, my wife and business partner for so many years, well, every day you still take my breath away. It's all been a wonderfully grand adventure. And, your tireless editing and encouragement made this story possible. To God, thank you for not giving up on me. You didn't have to keep knocking on my door, but you never stopped. When it's time for me to come home and after we finally embrace, I sure would like to meet your bears.

INTRODUCTION

GRACE

There are many creatures that have patrolled the earth. Most of them were born here, but others come as visitors. Some of the visitors are our friends, and others just want to be left alone. But sometimes, some of them want to take and destroy. They are the evil things that go bump in the night—and sometimes by day. But we have learned.

My little brother is a grizzly bear named Kaiyo. Kaiyo opened our eyes. And this is his story.

PROLOGUE

ADAM'S CRY

My children know little of what we lost, and their children know almost nothing. If they knew, they would hate me. And they would be right to do so. They know even less of my father. Though I am old, I remember him. He was our Abba. He walked and laughed with us. He was beautiful.

We needed no faith because he was with us. We did not suffer from doubt or the guilt that now accompanies our doubts. Abba gave answers to every question, and we knew no fear. Best of all, he loved us. Whenever he saw us, he showed his joy. We had everything.

Everything but gratitude.

From the beginning, the serpent planned to separate us from Abba. That's what he does, and he is good at it. He watched us, and he watched our eyes. We had only one law and complete freedom in all other things. But whenever we saw the Tree, he noticed our gaze. When our curiosity changed into desire, he was ready.

Had we known of his plans, I would have cast him out of Eden. He knew that. Instead, he told us only what we wanted to hear. Like all the animals, he talked to us freely. He often spoke wisely and truthfully. He masqueraded as the most prudent of all the creatures in Eden. After a time, he poisoned our hearts with subtle deceit. When we wandered near the Tree, he was waiting. Our gratitude to Abba had long before waned. We wanted to take what wasn't ours. When we did, we lost everything.

I remember our paradise. It has been so many years. My mind and my body have slowed. That wasn't my father's plan either. Pain was only to warn. Now, it is my grim companion in life, and every day sees more of it. Our kind now wanders the world as pariahs from creation. The beasts of the earth, like those in Eden, were once our friends. But they have lost their understanding, and they speak no more. We once had every creature, both in Eden and on earth, as a friend. They were much like us, and Abba loved them as well. But the animals were just a little lower than us, and because of that, they were afflicted by our sin. My sin.

The earth's creatures are cursed, and violence is with them always. We once received their love and companionship, and we loved them in return. Now, we receive their fear. They wisely run from our presence. They do not know why they fear us, but a distant memory reminds them we are the root of all that went wrong.

We almost lost our God, and we surely lost our paradise. But Abba says our redeemer lives, even now. I don't know him, but someday, I will. As for now, Eden, with its vast waters and endless lands, still thrives. The creatures of Eden, our friends, were not cast out. Abba's grace allowed them to stay behind. Their children still roam its expanse. We have broken their hearts, yet they miss us still. They are near, but I cannot find them. They are hidden from my eyes.

PART 1

BACK TRAILS

QUESTIONS—DEAN

Sometimes, I do what I am doing now. I watch him. He is holding so much back from us. For me to call this bear and the whole situation here a mystery is true, but I really don't like the word mystery; it invites lazy thinking. But try as I do, I cannot get past the questions. Who is Kaiyo? Why is he here? What is he? Because he sure isn't a normal bear. And, to me, the most important question is where did he come from? There are answers to each of those questions, but the answers keep eluding me.

HOMES—KAIYO

My kind and most of mankind are alike in a lot of ways. But a big difference is my kind knows we belong to two countries. It's not complicated—in fact, everybody, man and beast, once knew. But these days, most people just focus on their earth country; they're almost oblivious to their other country, but not my kind. We get it, at least most of us do.

A few years ago, when I was just a cub, I was rescued by my human family. I love them. Later in the same year, when I was a yearling, I was rescued from my ignorance by a wolf. It was the same wolf, Tracker, who took me to a different country. It's my first home. I have been back home five times since then, and I will go back again in a few weeks to continue learning.

I am Kaiyo, and Kaiyo is my only name. Tracker has another name he was given at birth, but he hasn't used it, and I don't know it. The name Tracker suits him well.

I have another home, and it is in this world. It's my second home, and it is precious to me. We just call it *the farm*. When I am with my human family, I am happy. With them, I can be what I was made for. I am made for my family. But I am not their servant as one thinks of animals. I am too much like them, and they know it. Still, I am not quite their equal. The whole thing is easier lived than explained. And we both have enemies; we always have plenty of those.

BACK TRAILS—SAM

When Libby was an infant, we lived in a cabin on the farm. Our current house had not been built yet, and our farm was much smaller than it is today. With money always being tight, Susan and I would often hunt to put meat on the table. But with Libby joining the family, I would often go into the Eastern Wilderness and hunt alone. If people know where you are going and if they know when you are coming back, hunting alone is not necessarily a terrible idea. Hunting with others, though, is far safer.

But we had no choice. Elk season was in full swing, and the grocery bills were hard to pay. We needed meat, and the meat of an elk rivals good beef in flavor and texture. I left our cabin and rode east toward elk country. Elk were common, but we had decided not to ever hunt within a few miles of our property. In case of an emergency, I wanted elk, deer, and other tasty wildlife to feel comfortable and safe around the farm.

I left late in the morning because I wanted to camp and be in position to hunt the next morning. If unsuccessful, I would spend another night out and hunt the following morning and then start home. The day started out beautifully. I rode my two-year-old horse, Hershel, and we pulled my old pack mule named Humphrey. Humphrey wasn't fast, but he was stronger than most horses, and he liked nice days. Typical of Montana, the sky was a vivid blue, and the air was crisp. A light breeze was in my face, and I felt good.

That day, we made about fifteen miles, and by early afternoon, I found a flat area to set up camp. Everything was nice until the next day. That was when I met two dangerous strangers named Duane and Stephanie.

I left my beloved state of Georgia because I felt called to come here. I still love Georgia, but I learned that everything good and worthwhile about Georgia can also be found here. The West has always been a magnet to those who wanted to build something for themselves, and that was what I wanted to do. Unfortunately, the West was also a magnet to awful people who wanted to steal from the builders. With people so spread out, often in remote areas, predatory people knew they could get away with murder.

Montana also attracts people who are best described as travelers. Some are good; some are terrible. They ride horses or motorcycles, they hop trains, or they just walk from here to there. This couple looked like travelers.

I had spent most of the morning hunting to the south of my campsite. I saw plenty of deer and a few antelope but no elk. I had seen elk in the area before, but on that morning, I didn't even see any recent tracks. Hunting season has a way of changing an animal's habits, and I guessed the elk had moved to thicker cover. So that was where I would go.

After breaking camp, I was on the move again. The trail I was taking ran generally east to west. This area had open grasslands, roll-ing hills, and large and small patches of timber that usually clung to the slopes. After a few hours of riding, I came up on a couple as they were breaking down their camp. They were camping along a low ledge overlooking one of the area's year-round, clear water creeks. It was a pretty spot except for them messing it up. Both of them were dirty, and their camp was trashy. I hate that. But they did have two horses that looked well cared for so that worked in their favor. I was in a hurry and didn't much feel like talking, so I tipped my hat and moved on.

Not thirty minutes later, I spotted them riding fast on the same trail I was on. I didn't really want company, but my Southern roots are deep. I would be friendly.

"Hey, rider. Hold up," yelled the man.

I pulled off the trail and waited. Like many in Montana, I kept a pistol on my hip. I made a point to take off the strap, and I placed my hand close to the butt of the gun. I usually carried a .45, and this trip was no different. It's not the biggest or most powerful handgun in the world, but for most things, it's big enough. They rode quickly, and it was obvious to me they were not experienced riders. But they had good gear. They reached me, and both were smiling.

They introduced themselves. Duane was older than me. He was a thick man with deep-set eyes. He looked to be more powerful than fat, though. He hadn't shaved in days, but who did when they camped? Stephanie was younger than Duane, but she was gaunt and appeared unhealthy. She looked like she had once been pretty. She wasn't that day. Both looked to be in their late twenties or early thirties, and everything about them told me to be careful. They said they were headed east and would enjoy some company. I said little, but I gave them my name and agreed out of courtesy to ride with them, and we headed out together. Immediately, I sensed these two were big-time trouble. As if on cue, Duane started bringing his horse over to ride to my right, and Stephanie pulled hers to my left. That wouldn't do. So I lied.

One thing I have learned in life is a lot of people are scared of Southern country folk, sometimes with good reason. Southerners can be particularly mean fighters. They also speak in a way that annoys folks. Truth be told, I still am a bit of a Southern redneck; I'm just bilingual. Anyway, I gave them a dose of Southern.

Each region of the South has its own sweet sound. Even people in the same town can have different accents too. It all depended on upbringing, education, and the way neighbors and friends talk. I gave them a backcountry, South Georgia sound. That accent has always sounded good to me, but it definitely has a hard, country edge. For some, it's probably like nails on a chalkboard. At the very least, I had a little fun.

"Naw, we cain't ride like this," I said as I pulled back on Hershel's reins. I smiled as I said it, but my eyes never smiled. "You, see, I cain't but barely see out of my right eye. I got hit hard there by a swinging liquor bottle, and now, I'm nearly blind in that eye. So y'all need to ride to my left, so I can see you both when we ride. There's no sense in conversin if I cain't see who I'm talking to. So you two ride ahead, and I'll pull up on the outside next to Mr. Duane, here."

With that, I slowed up, let them pass, and came around to the right of Duane. They didn't say it, but they obviously didn't like it. It kept me out of their reach, and it kept my gun hand free. We rode that way for another twenty or so minutes. They talked the whole time and were overly friendly. They asked way too many questions, and I spoke only rarely. Sensing it was time to ditch those folks, I simply said *goodbye*, waited for them to get past me, and headed north toward a range of low, wooded hills three or four miles away. I did that for two reasons. One is that I wanted to get away from those creepy people, and second, the area was close enough to where I intended to hunt, and I knew it well.

Periodically, I would look back to see if they were following me. Knowing if I was being followed was, and still is, a key to my survival out here. Wolves, grizzlies, and mountain lions are known to follow hunters and campers. The wolves, I was not so worried about, there weren't many in those days, and they almost never killed people. Grizzlies were an issue, but any mountain lion that follows is up to no good. While I watched out for them too, I was far more concerned about my former trail mates.

Just before I got into the forest, I pulled up behind a mess of tumbled boulders. I grabbed my binoculars and climbed up on one of the bigger rocks, and after a few minutes, I saw them. They were several miles away, but Stephanie's horse was mostly white, and unless it's snowing, it's near impossible to be stealthy on a white horse. Duane rode a mouse-colored horse that blended in beautifully with the sedge grass. But they were probably banking on the notion

I wouldn't be suspicious and watch my back trail. They should have known better.

I quickly got back on Hershel, and the three of us headed into the hills. I made my trail obvious. A horse and a mule make a lot of tracks. To make things even easier, I broke branches, and threw an apple core behind me. Humphrey snorted and tried to turn back to eat it, but that wasn't the plan.

Deep into the forest I rode. I loved this place, and the northern slopes and meadows were filled with elk. I kept riding north and stayed in the forest. With the long afternoon shadows beating back the sunlight, I came to a ten-acre open meadow. There, I set up camp at the far end of the meadow. First, I led Hershel and Humphrey to a small creek so they could drink; then, I led them back, unpacked both, and staked Humphrey in the grass. I unsaddled Hershel, but I kept him handy.

I set up my small tent and even built a smoky fire. Then, I ate and stowed away my gear. When it got dark, I put out the fire and waited in my tent until I got my night vision. A person's pupils will quickly contract in bright light, but eyes take much longer to adjust to darkness. Impatient people can miss much because they simply don't wait to see in the dark. Sometimes, that can be fatal. So I stayed in my tent for another half hour. The whole time, I scanned the surrounding meadow. As expected, my vision steadily improved, and I was able to start seeing a few elk at the far end of the meadow. I mostly looked south though, because that was where my stalkers were.

Seeing in the dark takes a little skill. The way the eye is designed, there are more light receptors on the sides of the retina than at the very back. That means when it's dark, looking straight at something may be the worst way to see it. A good woodsman always looks at and then around things when it's dark. In the dark, looking just to the side of what you want to see is the best way to see it.

I followed the movement of a cow elk as she grazed near the southern wood line. If Duane was watching me, he would probably be there. I chose this place because the wind, though light, was coming from the south. If he was still in those woods, the elk would know it and soon. Keeping an eye on the elk, I made sure I had what I needed. After another twenty minutes, the cow elk continued to graze. It was time.

I stepped out of the tent and gently closed the tent flap. I mounted Hershel bareback to avoid the inevitable creaking sounds of his saddle. He didn't know what we were doing, but he was young and smart, and he enjoyed moving. We turned south and headed into the forest on the west side of the meadow, parallel to my prior path. After another mile or so, I smelled the first hint of wood smoke. I wasn't surprised, and I kept heading southward up a good-sized, thickly wooded hill. As I reached the crest, I could see to the bottom of the other side of the hill. Through the thick trees, I could see the flickering light of a campfire.

We McLeods believe the best defense is to act if trouble is at hand. Doing nothing invites more trouble, and I wanted no trouble. Unfortunately, trouble was following me. So I dismounted and tied up Hershel. Then, I took off my boots and put on a pair of moccasins. I had about forty-five yards to get there, and I needed to walk silently. It's practically impossible to do that in boots. We still keep moccasins with us whenever we camp for this very reason.

With the moccasins on, I was able to slide through the woods and slip up on the couple. They were sitting around their little fire and enjoying the flames. That was their second mistake. Their first mistake was following me. But, by staring into the fire, they robbed themselves of their ability to see beyond the light and into the darkness. They were night-blind. It was not an unusual thing; people who feel safe are rarely alert for danger. Also, it's hard not to look at fire. Fire mimics spirit and looks alive. While fire is not alive, it's almost hypnotizing. Because of that, I was able to creep up close and remain unseen.

Hiding just out of the glow of the flames, I avoided looking directly at them or their fire. I listened as the two casually discussed killing me and stealing my horse, my mule, my guns, and my gear. If it were the Old West, I would have simply walked up to the fire and shot them both. There's not much difference in guilt between a murderer and one who is in the process of attempting a murder. But the times are more complicated, and killing someone, even potential killers, invites enormous problems.

Still, I had to deal with the issue of two well-armed people who were conspiring to kill me. So instead of shooting them, I stood up, walked out of the darkness, and strolled into their camp and confronted them. To say they were shocked was an understatement. One second, they were alone, and the next second, they were staring into the face an intruder with a gun. They were typical jackals, and they were scared. They both started talking a mile a minute. I let them speak for a few minutes until I told them to shut up. I kept my formerly used Southern accent and smiled a lot. They were caught, and they were terrified.

I told them I knew what their intentions were. I also told them I had no plans to be a victim. They thought I was going to kill them. Their plan was to kill me, so it made sense that my plan was to kill them. I had no such intentions, though. First, I went over to their gear and took their two rifles. Then, I took two pistols I found in their tent. The couple stayed put; I never took my .45 off them. I was pretty sure one or both of them were still packing guns somewhere on them.

I asked if they had any other weapons on them, and they both profusely denied they had any more guns. They said I had found everything. My grandfather was a lawyer, and he once told me that liars always lie. He cross-examined liars for a living, so I trusted him on the issue. So I ordered them to strip to their underwear and to take off their boots. I had to. People stash knives and guns in their clothes, and I didn't want to end up dead. Duane protested loudly, but I simply smiled and told him I'd kill him if he didn't. Because he was a murderer and he thought little of killing others, he, no doubt, thought I would. She didn't doubt it either.

They were fortunate to have been wearing long underwear. It's common attire when spending outdoors out here, especially in the fall. In fact, I was counting on it. I didn't want anyone to think I was some weird creeper. When all but their underwear was stripped off, I had them step back and away from their clothes. The old adage that most people don't look good in their underwear was true here. They both looked bad. She was boney thin and showed the signs of some sort of drug addiction. I made Duane take off his shirt too. Duane just looked like a fool.

It was cold, and the slight breeze soon had them shivering uncontrollably. I then took their clothes. I kept their money and their wallets. I also kept the two small pistols they had concealed in their pockets and had somehow forgotten to tell me about. Even though I wasn't surprised, finding those additional weapons angered me more than I suspected it would. I spit out commands for them to throw more wood on their fire until it was roaring. Then, I ordered them to throw their clothes in the fire, including their boots. They started to complain loudly, but I wasn't faking my anger. They quickly obliged. Then, I threw all their extra clothes and their backpacks in the fire. I kept out a blanket, their horses' saddles, and their horses' saddlebags. I needed those.

With a burning stick from the fire, I walked over to their tiny tent and took it and their bedding and lit it all on fire. The couple's mouths dropped like anchors, but they stayed in place.

They say clothes make the man. That may be true, but nakedness usually robs a person of all false pride. And it did for them. Duane, standing barefooted and in only the bottom part of his long underwear, started to cry. So did Stephanie. They both looked ridiculous. I only felt contempt for them.

I waited a few minutes to be assured their clothes and boots were thoroughly burned beyond use. Then, I spoke the truth to them. I ordered them back to the ground and stood over them. They looked like the fools they were. But they were still dangerous vipers.

"I should kill you both, but that wouldn't be a very Christian-like thing, now would it?"

The couple quickly agreed, so I continued. "But I never have been a very good Christian, and I depend on God's good graces all the time. So if I decide to kill you, I really think God would forgive me, especially in this situation. As far as I know, my killing you would be an act of godly justice. There's not much difference in you killing me or conspiring to kill me. But I'm not positive of that, and if not, I really don't want to add your deaths to my rather long list of sins. Unless I have to."

"So here is what I am going to do. Tonight, as you shiver in the cold, be content knowing I will have your horses and your guns. I left a blanket for you so your misery will be tempered. You have ruined a hunt for me, and I do not appreciate it at all. You also still want to kill me and keep my stuff, and that won't do. So, in the morning, take the trail to my camp. You have already scouted my camp, so I know you can find it. There, you will find one of your horses and my only can of bear spray. The only reason I am leaving that with you is so you can protect yourself from a hungry bear or lion. And as you make your way out of here tomorrow, just know I will be watching. Tomorrow, head straight to the first lawman you see and turn yourself in."

Then, I ordered them to saddle their own horses. I took the horses, loaded their saddlebags, and slipped back into the forest to where I left Hershel. With their horses in tow, I headed back to my camp. Not wanting to tempt fate, I immediately packed up my gear and loaded up Humphrey, and we left into the darkness.

I rode all night and stopped from time to time to watch my back trail. Other than riding through darkness, which I don't like doing, I made good time. When I got home the next morning, I called the new county sheriff, my old friend from Georgia, Lee Tuttle. Tuttle came over and took possession of the couple's guns, saddlebags, saddles, wallets, and money. A deputy later came towing a trailer and got their horse.

While Tuttle was at our house, he made a few calls, and a chopper was sent to find them. Soon, his deputies spotted the couple from the air, riding together, nearly naked, on a white horse, out in the wilderness. They were arrested shortly thereafter. We found out later that one of the pistols I took from them belonged to a camper who was found murdered in his tent in Wyoming a year before. The other guns were all stolen, so were their horses and tack. That solved several unsolved cases, and it supported my testimony at their trial about their attempt to murder me. I have always prayed those vultures would repent and get to know Jesus. I doubt they will ever get out of prison.

And that is why we always watch our back trails.

HOME—DEAN

Sometimes, it astonishes me we have a two-and-a-half-year-old wild grizzly living with us. Well, he lives here at least most of the time. From time to time, he vanishes, sometimes for weeks on end. We have no idea where he goes. We have tried to track him, but he always manages to lose us. It's like a game to him. At first, he would leave with a wolf who would visit here from time to time and sometimes take him away. We named the wolf *Big Bad Wolf* at first, but it was obvious he thought the name was childish. He made it clear he liked the name *Tracker* when we suggested it. I wouldn't be surprised if Tracker was his real name just by the way he acted.

The wolf is even stranger than Kaiyo, but we love him too. When Kaiyo was young, we hated seeing the wolf stroll onto the farm, but after a few abductions of Kaiyo, we came to learn our little bear always intended to come back and live with us here.

In a normal world, the simple fact that Kaiyo does live with us here defies all understanding. He weighs well over three hundred pounds now and is freakishly strong. He is also getting bigger and stronger every day. He can easily run as fast or faster than our two dogs, Moose and Major. He once broke the neck of an elk who refused to leave our fields. The elk tried to challenge him. That was a fatal mistake.

Last spring, Kaiyo stormed into a pack of wolves who were trying to kill Moose. It would seem only crazy people would live with such a creature and love him. And so we McLeods must be crazy. In fact, only crazy people would let their ten-year-old daughter sneak up and jump on a grizzly as it sleeps in the grass. But my mom and dad treat it as a spectator sport.

It's another early summer morning, and Gracie leaves the kitchen and tiptoes down the back-porch steps. Slowly and silently, she pads through the dew-laden grass. I see the bear lift his head and spy Gracie coming at him. I see him pretend to be asleep. Gracie gets close, runs, and leaps onto the bear; and she is immediately hidden by his enormous arms. She screams in laughter as they complete another morning ritual. Mom and Dad and my sister, Libby, leave the window and walk back to the kitchen table, all chuckling. It never gets old to them—or to me. And mystery or not, I know I love that bear. And I know Kaiyo loves me right back. I also believe he is here with us for a reason. My job is to figure it all out. And sooner or later, I will.

We live on a farm in western Montana. We have tried to give it a name, but the names never stuck. We just call it *the farm*. Some people call this God's country, but it takes tough people to live in it. It's even tougher to farm it. But we do. And for all my fifteen years plus three months or so, it's all I have known. Fortunately, I am tall for my age and stronger than normal. Mom said my size and strength are from her pure Viking heritage. Dad says it comes from his Scottish highlander roots. Knowing his family and Mom's family, I think the strength part is Viking-related. The good thing is speed, size, and strength come in mighty handy when working a farm. Farmwork is hard and dirty, and it can smell awful, especially now it's summer. In short, it sounds bad, but it's wonderful. It's wonderful for many reasons.

Farm work proves that there is an unbroken link between life and filth. A missionary in Guatemala once told my dad, "Where there's life, there's filth. If you want life, you will have filth."

When Dad told me that, it changed my view of the farm. I cannot love the many lives on the farm and hate the filth; filth is just a small part of it. I don't like it, but I cannot be surprised by it. People have to deal with filth, and so they either move it or use it. That's farm life. I know I cannot have the horse without the poop. My job is to remove the poop; the horse is well worth it.

On this morning, I was grabbing my cap and jacket to get started when the phone rang. Having the landline ring when you live in an area that doesn't have great cell phone coverage is normal. Libby is a pretty, seventeen-year-old, and she has a lot of friends. Most of them are girls, but a few older boys have been calling for a while too. Dad wasn't very happy about that development, but it's been going on since before we met Kaiyo. He's used to it now. He doesn't like it, but he's used to it.

Mom and Dad have a solid business with the farm and the oil wells, so they get calls all the time from suppliers of everything a farm needs and from the buyers of what we grow or make. But calls at such an early hour were rare. Dad took the call, so I headed on out to the main barn. Libby hollered out she would join me there in five.

We have several barns and more sheds, but the main barn is the only one we call *the barn*. If I looked straight out the back of the house and past the courtyard made by the driveway circle, I would see the big front doors to the barn. In the winter, the barn seems far away; in the summer, it seems to be just a few steps away. In truth, it's about a hundred feet away. Inside the barn are some amazing horses. There are also two areas set aside for chickens and guineas. They are not at all amazing, but they do taste good when Mom or Dad fries one up.

Among several jobs, Libby and I have the responsibility of mucking out the stalls of our six horses and keeping them watered and fed. Last year, Dad got Gracie a beautiful buckskin Welsh Cob gelding named Duke. A Welsh Cob is a large pony. In fact, they're bigger than some horses. Duke is smart and very gentle. He's fast, strong, and a capable jumper. Gracie was turning into an excellent rider too.

Some people think a ten-year-old is too young to ride, but that's just not true. The ancient Mongols made sure their three-year-old boys could ride by themselves. For them, learning to ride and fight was often the difference between life and death.

I am proud of Gracie. Several times, the three of us have taken our horses and gone into the Eastern Wilderness. We don't tell Mom, but I think she knows. Dad is a good tracker, and he has noticed our little trips. He just tells me to be careful and to be smart by using what I know to be true.

I notice a lot of people tell their kids what not to do. And sometimes, that's the right thing. Little kids need to know not to touch fire or to play with mean dogs. But knowing what not to do is never the same as knowing what to do. So Dad will tell us to "be smart, use what you know," while another parent might say to their kid, "Don't do anything stupid." They both mean to say the same thing, but the message is totally different. One kid focuses on doing the smart thing, while the other one focuses on not being stupid. Not being stupid is a mighty low standard.

Anyway, since I was the first one in the barn, I led the horses into their pasture. It's easy. I get Peyton, our enormous shire horse, out first and then open the other stalls, and the others will follow us out of the barn and into the pasture. Our dogs, Moose and Major, were already in the barn. Dogs like daily routine; it seems to make them happy for some reason. Moose and Major are the perfect farm dogs. Both are big, but Moose is really big. Major's nose is better, and Moose is stronger. Major is a serious dog, while Moose is a happy-go-lucky dog, even though he's dangerous to some animals and to a lot of people he doesn't know. The farm really wouldn't be successful without them. Their job is to make sure the deer, elk, and black bears don't eat the crops. They are good at it too.

Kaiyo usually joins me, and today was no different. When we first brought Duke to the farm, it took Duke several weeks to get used to Kaiyo. I sure didn't blame him. Kaiyo could smell a little stinky from time to time, and he was definitely a meat eater. He was big, and he had a swagger about him. I think every animal out there except Peyton and a few steers would have been afraid of Kaiyo.

Anyway, each day, either Libby or I would take the horses out of their stalls and take them out to pasture, and Kaiyo would usually take the lead. Duke was a smart horse, and he figured out Kaiyo wasn't there to eat him. It was Kaiyo's friendship with Peyton that eventually won him over. Sometimes, Kaiyo will join the horses and graze on the grass of the horse pasture. They're usually joined by Rosie the alpaca. Rosie would follow Kaiyo everywhere if we let her. She and Kaiyo used to play when Kaiyo first joined the family. She jumps over her fence to join Kaiyo when he grazes with the horses. Friends who visit are always surprised to see that sight.

When I got back, Libby told me it was Sheriff Tuttle and Captain Stahr who had called. It seemed another hiker was missing. That was the third one this year. I suspected the Sheriff's Department probably needed help to find him or her.

Just about each season, Dad gets asked to go into the Eastern or Northern Wildernesses to find a lost hiker or two. In the winter, he has searched for lost snowmobilers and cross-country skiers. In the fall, it's usually a hunter who gets turned around and lost. Spring can be a terrible time for hikers. The weather can go from hot to freezing in hours, and rain or snow is always a problem.

It was late June, and this year, we had already helped find two other lost hikers. Like anybody who gets lost in the wilderness, they were lucky to be found alive. Once again, Kaiyo came to their rescue. He found them when the captain's dogs could not.

From Monday through Friday, we have Gunner Gibbs come and help us on the farm. At first, I called him Mr. Gibbs, but he didn't like it. He wanted me to call him just Gunner, so eventually I did. Gunner is top-notch, and he works steady, and he enjoys hard work. I think Dad saw Libby growing up and me getting involved in sports, and he knew he would need help.

Several years ago, Gunner and his family came into our lives at the right time. His son, Jack, is my best friend. We both go to the same school and play football there. I think Jack has a crush on Libby, but it's not reciprocated. Fifteen-year-old guys rarely get the pretty, seventeen-year-old girl. Libby thinks Jack is cute, but that is about as far as it goes.

Gunner's daughter, Kate, is not quite a year younger than me, and she's a very pretty girl. I noticed her the moment I saw her a few years ago. Grown-ups will sometimes say odd things to me like, "Now you're a teenager, you're going to start liking girls."

Seriously, I have no idea why grown-ups say such dumb things. The truth is, I can't remember ever not liking girls. They have always been interesting to me. Kate was different. She was a better kind of different. It's hard to explain, so I won't. But I say all this only to explain that Gunner didn't work on Saturdays or Sunday except during planting or harvest. During those times, we all work the weekends. And today was a beautiful Saturday, and Dad wanted to talk.

WILDERNESS—SAM

This hiker was actually pretty good. A lot of them put no more thought into a wilderness hike than they do a short hike around their town's park. Once a hiker enters the Eastern Wilderness, a cell phone becomes nothing more than a clock and an MP3 player. Convenience stores become cherished memories. Years ago, Dean, Libby, and I watched a line of hikers walk across a grassed meadow with each of them listening to music on their headphones. They didn't even notice the berry bushes they had just passed were concealing a good-sized, male grizzly. We watched the bear as it watched them. He probably thought they were as dumb as we did. We had to go out of our way to intercept them and give them a brief survival course. Those types of hikers are usually the type we have to go find.

Not long ago, there was a group of teenage boys and girls from some cities on the West Coast who were made to walk about twenty-five miles in an area close to Yellowstone. Their path was through known bear country as part of some ridiculous, self-confidence training exercise. They were given nothing for self-defense except a two-way radio. That was it. It was as dangerous as it was absurd. For some other crazy reason, they weren't given any bear spray. Each hiker should have had a can.

As you can guess, they ran into a cranky grizzly about halfway through, and with them being inexperienced and defenseless, they ran. They were told not to run, but staring down a grizzly with only fists is a lot to ask of anybody, much less some green teenagers. I understood. They were unprepared and inexperienced, and bears can be frightening. The bear caught and mauled two of them severely and then simply wandered off. Heck, if they were taught to make some simple spears out of saplings, they could have stood their ground. A bear rarely would complete an attack against twelve spearmen, acting together.

We were the first on the scene, and after the two torn-up, bloody kids were airlifted out, we escorted the rest back as they completed their *walk* in the wilderness. We met their frantic parents in the parking area at the beginning of the trailhead. I felt sorry for the coach who put the whole thing together. He was a desert wilderness expert who had no real experience with grizzly country. The poor guy was devastated. I could only imagine the legal troubles he has been facing ever since.

But, like I said, this hiker was pretty good. His name is Landon Haldor. Landon is a twenty-two-year-old who was already an experienced hiker and hunter. He appeared to have done everything right from the beginning. Before he left, he had checked in at the National Forest Service ranger's cabin and filed his plan. The ranger there reported that Landon's pack was well stocked with a tool kit style of knife, a seven-inch hunting knife, a hatchet, fifty feet of para-cord, a tarp, fire starters, a small tent, clothes, and a bedroll with some other helpful odds and ends. He had plenty of food and a cheap but effective water filtration straw. He also had two cans of EPA-approved bear spray with him. The ranger had known Landon for several years, and other than a crazy penchant for hiking the wilderness alone, Landon had proven himself to be a careful and thoughtful woodsman.

Two years before, I met Landon briefly while riding the Eastern Wilderness looking for stray cattle. The breaks and draws out there often hold wild cattle or horses. I'm not interested in the horses, but the cattle are there for the taking. Landon was sticking to a well-marked path and was headed to the parking area about fifteen miles away when I rode by him. It was time to take a break, and a nearby creek was perfect for Hershel. He joined me, and we introduced ourselves. He told me he was originally from North Carolina. His mom was Cherokee, and he was born at the Indian Hospital in the mountain town of Cherokee, North Carolina. His dad was of mostly European descent. He looked like a mix of the two but by the way he had mastered the Eastern Wilderness, he acted more like a Cherokee. He was strong when I saw him, and the ranger confirmed he again appeared in top physical shape.

The sheriff told me Landon had missed his return date by eight days, and his parents and friends were panicking. A number of his friends, experienced hikers themselves, had gone out on their own or in small groups to look for him. They all came back empty-handed.

I don't blame them; who wouldn't try to save a friend? But good hikers, even good outdoorsmen, aren't necessarily good trackers.

Outdoorsmen, both men and women, are often good at spotting wildlife and recognizing sign. Sign means things like tracks, prints, or scat. But tracking is the next level up. Sign is used to track, but trackers need to think like the animal or person they are tracking. And that is much easier said than done. Rarely can somebody find a set of tracks and walk up on the creature that makes them. Tracking is as much about interception as it is pursuit.

His parents had given Captain Stahr some clothes of Landon's, and the captain had put them in my mailbox. Susan went and got them and met me on the back porch. There, we had a family meeting. Kaiyo, Libby, and Dean came out of the barn, crossed the courtyard, and joined us. Gracie rode on Duke and stayed in the saddle. She was young, but she was made for the saddle.

It was time to find him or what was left of him.

Ghost—Susan

Gracie was probably my most difficult child. I don't mean in the sense she was at all disrespectful or engaged in improper behaviors because, for the most part, that was rarely the case. What I mean is she was relentless. When she wants to do something, she simply doesn't look at my *no* as anything other than the first round of a one-sided negotiation. And she doesn't go about it like Dean either. Dean goes straight for the reasoned argument to present his case, and he enjoys a complicated set of negotiations. He's a master at using leading questions. Gracie's not like Libby either. Libby seems to generally understand her own self-imposed boundaries, and she can lay out a good argument too. Libby can be emotional, but she understands emotions are not to be trusted.

Gracie, on the other hand, seems to always have us on the defensive. To her, nearly every boundary we establish is arbitrary, and it is our responsibility to defend those boundaries. She's always been that way. So I knew that when I told her that she would not be going out on the search to find the lost hiker, she would not accept it. Sam and I would deal with it, but I was preparing myself for one disappointed ten-year-old girl. Truth be told, I didn't want to be left alone here. I am a mom, and I would be plagued with worry if all five of them left and got swallowed up in the Eastern Wilderness, even if it was only a two-day trip.

I was inside, looking out my kitchen widow. There was the little huddle that made my family. My husband and my four children were looking at some clothes and a map. Gracie was on her pony listening to her dad and siblings talk and look at the map. She preferred to stay on Duke. I think the height increase for a little girl was a bonus. She was also a natural rider. She took after me in that talent. I used to love to ride, and I was pretty good. I have a few rodeo medals to prove it. In fact, I still do love to ride. Out here, being a good rider can save your life, so we made sure the kids could ride at an early age. But Gracie was a natural, and she took to riding like a young otter takes to water. She was made for it.

I redirected my gaze to Kaiyo. Everybody was looking down, but Kaiyo was staring intently at Gracie. He loved her, but this time, his expression was a concerned one. That may sound odd with me looking at the face of a grizzly bear. But living on a farm and observing body language and reading the expressions on the faces of animals can become second nature. The hard part is understanding what was observed. Animals aren't people, and they don't think people thoughts. Assuming an animal has kind, humanlike feelings might get you killed. Cows and pigs can look quite content in one moment and then show pure aggression in another moment. That being said, we understand that the way an animal places its ears or stares or paws at the ground is pure communication. With all that, Kaiyo has always been different, of course. First, Kaiyo was my son, and he has been from the day he came here. Second, his expressions were far more understandable. Like all my kids, I could read Kaiyo like a book.

I followed his gaze as he looked toward Gracie. She looked surprised, as if she heard something. Her head swiveled as she looked about the courtyard. Clearly, no one else was hearing anything. She looked quickly from side to side and up. Nobody else looked startled or surprised. They were all discussing their plans. Gracie then hopped off Duke, tied him to the porch railing, climbed up on the back porch, and marched inside. Kaiyo followed her in. She came to me, and she looked like she had seen a ghost.

Then, she said, "That man, the hiker, he's lost, and he's scared. He doesn't know how to get home."

I looked at Gracie. "How do you know that, sweetie," I asked.

Gracie looked at me for a second. "I think he just told me," she said.

2

INTO THE WILDERNESS—SAM

If we knew where we would be going, I probably would have Dean or Libby take one of our UTV's to carry our provisions. But we were clueless where Haldor went, and in that case, horses are superior to anything with wheels. Horses can go a lot of places UTVs cannot, and I was guessing that when Haldor got lost, it wasn't on a nice flat trail or on a cleared logging road. We had ended our gathering, and I headed into the barn. Kaiyo and Gracie had gone inside, and Libby and Dean followed me into the barn. We had to head east, and that is still beautiful, wild country. Our property makes up a very small portion of the western edge of the Eastern Wilderness. Wild country surrounds the farm, but the Eastern Wilderness is special. It's vast, and there are no towns out there. It's home to buffalo, antelope, deer, elk, moose, wolves, and bears and nearly everything else. I could ride for days without running into anyone else. There aren't many places like that, and I love it.

The Eastern Wilderness is made mostly of national forests mixed with a dozen private holdings. Some of the private lands are ranches, and some are privately held lands dedicated to preserving vital ground for grizzly bears and other big game animals. Those private land owners who have preserved their lands will be looked at by future generations as true American heroes. The human population here in America will continue to grow, and that is just a fact. I'm not planning on leaving, and I want an economy that grows, and I want farms that feed us. But I'm still concerned about wildlife and carnivores.

The role God gave each of us is to be good stewards of the lands we have. Instead of complaining about the effect of humans on our wild lands and demand the government restrict private property usage, the folks who buy property and set it aside for wildlife are truly doing the right thing. Most of the private property out here is owned by friends or by organizations we happily support. We all may not see eye to eye on politics, but we agree on this cause. We also have informal agreements that they can come across our lands and we can go across theirs. Still, courtesy calls are appreciated and a good practice if you don't want to get shot. Since we didn't know where Haldor went, Susan and I called all the land owners to give them a heads up. They all knew about Haldor's disappearance, and they wished us well.

Ever since Kaiyo got here a few years ago, we have become accustomed to accepting weirdness. For many years now, I have been a Christian. So I have long been convinced there is something vast and amazing beyond our three-dimensional life here on earth. In the last few years, however, I have become used to brushing against things most would find to be unbelievable. Kaiyo has verified our belief that there is so much more to learn. So when Susan and Gracie came in to talk, I was prepared. At least, I thought I was.

I heard Kaiyo bark at me. I don't mean he barked like a dog, but it wasn't a growl either. I was used to it. Short of using the King's English, that bear was a master at communicating his intentions. I turned, and he led Susan and Gracie into the barn. Libby and Dean figured something was up. Kaiyo was acting like a herald. Susan gave me a glance that clearly said something like *pay attention*. I knew it was no time to joke. I really thought Gracie was going to ask to come with us, but I was wrong.

"Dad," Gracie said, "I think something is different about this hiker."

I looked at her. "Okay," I said. "Why do you think that?"

One thing about Gracie was she was a very tough ten-year-old. That's why we were all surprised when she broke into tears. Her tears didn't let up. She was weeping deeply. In between her tears, she tried to talk, but she couldn't. Frustrated, Gracie screamed as she clenched her fists. It shocked us all, but by screaming, she seemed to settle herself down.

With watery eyes, she began to speak. "Dad, I was on Duke and listening in to y'all's plans to find the lost hiker."

We may live in Montana, but I still speak Southern, and my kids have picked some of it up. The word *y'all* was firmly in their vocabularies. She kept talking.

"While I was sitting there, I started hearing a man calling for help. At first, I thought everybody would hear it. But nobody seemed to hear anything. He sounded frustrated and really scared. I remember him saying, 'Help!' 'How do I get out of this place?' 'Let me out.' Then, he said, 'Help me, little girl. Help me!' And then I couldn't hear him anymore. When I looked around, only Kaiyo seemed to notice. He was looking right at me."

Well, this was new territory for me. Like I said, we are far more open now to supernatural stuff, but this one was very strange. One thing I didn't do was question whether Gracie was telling us what had really happened. I have doubted Gracie before, and I was proven wrong. Besides, at only ten years old, Gracie was capable. I looked at Kaiyo. He had a worried, confused look. We all looked at him. He stared into the ground for a few moments before he rambled over to the rack of saddles. He gave his little bark and stared at us. His message was clear. It was time to saddle up and go.

Saddle Up—Libby

Because of the weirdness surrounding Gracie, this trip to the Eastern Wilderness took on a whole new sense of urgency. Finding lost hikers is serious business, and when needed, we jump on the task. But this one was clearly different.

Gracie knew she couldn't go with us. I expected her to complain about that. She's physically strong for her age and has become a very good rider. But she didn't complain. She took Mom's hand and told us they would get busy making our packs. Mom winked at us and smiled. She and Mom then turned around and walked out of the barn. All of us, even Kaiyo, stopped in our tracks. Gracie has never volunteered to make our lunch or to help us put our packs together. If I had any doubt about Gracie's story before, I no longer did. Gracie was serious about finding that guy. We all got busy.

The barn became a blur of disciplined action, except for Kaiyo. He wandered out of the barn and into the grass where he stretched out in the sun. "Must be nice," I told him.

Kaiyo chuckled, but he stayed put. Dean had already gone out to the horse pasture to get our horses. My horse was Jet. Jet was black with a white star. She was both quick and fast. Hershel was Dad's horse. He was probably the smartest of the horses and still the fastest too. Hershel was a beautiful bay with a mane and tail that looked like blond flax. He and Dad have had many adventures together. Dean's horse was a slate blue mustang dun named Solo. Solo was part horse, part mountain goat. He could go anywhere and climb hills most horses couldn't. I was sure Solo would come in handy on this trip. Peyton, our enormous shire horse, was also coming because we needed him to carry extra supplies and because we hoped to find that hiker. Depending on how we found him, either the hiker would get on Peyton's saddle or his body would be bagged and strapped to Peyton's saddle. Either way, we were going to find him, and he was going to come back home.

Jack Gibbs had called Dean earlier and asked if he could come with us. Jack was a good kid, a great athlete, and a terrific student. Having him join us seemed like a good idea. He was a bit of a cut up and was always fun. I loved his attitude. Last year, Gunner had bought a couple of horses for Jack and Kate. Both were sorry riders at first, but they practiced a lot, and they both became good riders. They ride the back trail to and from our houses frequently. Kate was probably a little better than Jack, but he was more than good enough. And besides, we were just going to find a lost hiker; it wasn't a steeplechase.

Dean brought the horses back, and they were soon saddled and readied for travel. Alongside each saddle was a scabbard. Dean kept a 12-gauge shotgun loaded with slugs. It's capable of bringing down anything that's out there if it's not at long distance. I would be armed with a 270-caliber rifle. A 270 round is not the biggest bullet around, but I'm a good shot, and I can hit something at a very long distance. Dad had a short-barreled Marlin lever action. It was like a small cannon, but like Dean's shotgun, it was not for long distances. Because we were only interested in self-defense, those weapons were just fine.

For the most part, our horses like to get out and have an adventure. Well, that's not always true. Most of the horses aren't fans of bad winter weather except for Peyton. He enjoys bitter cold and deep snow. With it being June, the temperatures would be nice, and the horses sensed our excitement.

All of us went in and out of the house to get what we would need for a two-night excursion. Two tents, a few extra shirts, a change of clothes, toothbrushes, mosquito nets, blackfly hoods, and a few other things were about all we needed. We had to travel light. Also, each of us had bug spray, bear spray, our guns, and some extra ammo.

Some of our cousins live in the Deep South. In the summers there, it can get buggy. I have spent a lot of time in Georgia, South Carolina, and Alabama; and the mosquitoes, gnats, and flies can be awful. But most Southerners tend to think we are bug-free in Montana, and that's just not true. We have a lot of the same thing. We even have snow mosquitoes. Dad tries not to use insecticides unless he must. All around the pastures and barns, Dad uses traps of every kind. He has even built sandpits and fenced them in as homes for a type of wasp that eats horseflies. Horsefly traps are placed wherever we have livestock. Some look like pyramids suspended over a big black metal beach ball. They work, and they need to. Horseflies and deerflies can be brutal on cows, pigs, and horses. They also spread terrible diseases.

My prayer is we don't run into blackflies. My Southern cousins don't know about them. These horrible creatures can literally make animals go mad. They are tiny, and they fly into the eyes, ears, and noses of anything that breathes. And their bites hurt. We had a typical winter and spring, so we had to be prepared for them. Wishing for a real dry spring is a bad idea for a farmer, but at least, it helps with the blackfly problem.

We also needed to be careful about the bigger things, like bears. Every few years or so, somewhere in Canada or the United States, a black bear or a grizzly drags some poor camper out of their tent and kills them. Sometimes, they're eaten too. That would just be awful. We usually can rely on Moose or Major or both to provide an effective early warning system. They don't like bears except for Kaiyo and a giant bear we call Goliath. Those two bears are Specials. The rest can't be trusted.

Three years ago, Dad and I took a trip into the Eastern Wilderness. I was fourteen, and it was my second overnight trip into the wilds. During the night, a grizzly probably caught our scent and decided to check us out. We had ridden hard that day, and we slept soundly. So did the dogs. That grizzly bear was casually nosing around the camp when the dogs woke up. I'm not much for cussing, but when that happened, the only way I can describe it is to say that all freaking hell broke loose. The dogs went from asleep to vicious, howling banshees in about a second. That poor grizzly was unprepared and tried to fight, but those two dogs knew how to keep the bear on the defensive. One would keep him occupied, and the other would circle behind and give the bear's backside a savage bite or two. It was loud, but that bear cut and ran after just a few minutes. He turned and flew into the darkness. The dogs turned to us and looked proud. Dad congratulated the dogs and winked at me, and we all went back to sleep.

It doesn't always work that way, though. Grizzlies can be startled, but if they are prepared in advance, dogs don't scare them very much. Grizzlies are about as fearless as any creature out there. They are cautious, but that shouldn't be interpreted as fear. Grizzlies will think nothing of killing and eating a dog. Grizzlies often chase wolves away from their kills, so they are accustomed to canines. Still, dogs have a sort of foolish bravery that wolves do not. A dog, even though not as strong as a wolf, will wade into fights that wolves wisely avoid. For us, that headlong, foolish, dog bravery was a good thing.

Having Kaiyo joining us was a mixed bag. He's big and very fast, but being somewhere between two and three years old, he's still cubish. Compared to the average male grizzly out there, he's on the small side of medium. A three-hundred-pound grizzly is smaller than even many of the male black bears out here. Being different, he's also people-style smart. Intelligence often leads to arrogance, and arrogance is dangerous. So far, though, we haven't seen any of that in him. But, as a male grizzly, he's a target for other male grizzlies out there, and they would try to kill him if they could. Travelling with people, dogs, and horses, though, confuses the other bears. We confuse a lot of people too.

Anyway, it was time to leave. We led our horses out of the barn and into the courtyard. It was time to say goodbye to Mom and Gracie. Mom and Gracie came, and we gathered together and prayed. We pray a lot, and we do it because it's a good idea to do so. Dad and Mom prayed we would find the hiker and come back safely. We prayed for the hiker to be alive too.

Just then, we heard a diesel pickup truck coming down our long driveway. The sound of a diesel is easy to identify, even at a distance. After a few minutes, we saw Gunner towing a horse trailer. While we were waiting for them, Dad went on over to Mom, and he spoke to her quietly. Mom was obviously worried about our task. I saw Dad put his arms around Mom and gently kiss her on the cheek. He then leaned over and picked up Gracie and kissed her cheek too. The three of them were all bunched together. Geez, it looked like we were headed to war instead of going to look for another lost hiker. Dean and I stood by our horses while the dogs paced in anticipation. Kaiyo had pulled himself out of his slumber and was eying the approaching Gibbses. Kaiyo liked the Gibbses, Gunner especially.

They came in a small swirl of summer dust and parked by the back courtyard next to the barn. Kate hopped out of the front of the truck, threw back her long hair, and looked right over at Dean. Kate was a tall, pretty, fourteen-year-old, and she and Dean had been something of an item for a while. Everybody knew it, but I doubt those two knew we knew. Dean looked back at Kate and smiled his goofy smile. Kate apparently liked it.

Jack had exited the truck, and he and his dad were already leading his horse out of the trailer. When Gunner bought Jack's horse, he knew what he was doing. Jack's horse was gorgeous. Brown with white socks, Jack's horse was a tall quarter horse named Chevy. Mom's horse, Cali was a quarter horse too, but Cali was almost a full hand shorter. Chevy was faster than Cali, but Cali could cut quicker. Both were excellent cow catchers.

Jack led Chevy over to Dean. Chevy was already saddled, and Jack's saddlebags were full. Jack also had a can of bear spray holstered to him, and he had his 12-gauge shotgun in the scabbard. I was pleasantly surprised to see Jack so well prepared. Jack handed Dean a few things and hit him in the shoulder. They both laughed. There's a lot about boys I don't much understand; the hitting thing is one of them.

Dad and Gunner spoke briefly, and Gunner handed Dad what looked to be a flask of whisky and a few other things. After a quizzical look from Dad and a few words from Gunner, they both laughed. Dad and Gunner never mix guns and alcohol, so it was odd. Gunner then went over and said hello to Kaiyo. Those two, for whatever reason, were very close. In no time, they started wrestling and play fighting. Again, males are just different.

I hugged Mom, and I could tell she believed this trip was different. She gave me what she called as *lectures one through forty-two.* That was her way of saying *be careful.* I bent over and hugged Gracie. Gracie smiled and told me to "find that poor boy."

Boy? I thought we were looking for an adult.

I turned to see Kate talking to Dean. She looked worried too. He was obviously telling her he'd be fine. He spoke with her and walked her to her truck. There, Dean shook Gunner's hand, and they chatted for a minute. Before Kate got in the truck, she passed by her dad and went right to Dean and kissed him hard right on the cheek. She then held his face in her hands and planted a big one square on his fifteen-year-old, puckered-up lips. Dean turned bright red; Gunner frowned. Kate turned to her father, looked at him, and gave him a *Yeah, I just did that!* look. She climbed in the truck and said, "Let's go."

Gunner looked to Dean, then to Dad, and then to Mom. Then, he sighed, looked defeated, and waved to us. He got behind the wheel, started his truck, circled the courtyard, and headed home. Dean was still red-faced. Jack laughed. Dean wheeled around and headed to Solo.

"It's time to go," he said loudly.

Everybody was acting so strange. What was going on here? We were going out in nice weather, well-armed, and with some great animals. Kaiyo was coming too. I really thought we would be back by the next morning. I thought to myself, *What could possibly go wrong?*

QUESTIONS—DEAN

We hadn't been riding long, the farm was barely behind us, and Kate was on my mind. I had to admit, Kate's kiss was as nice as it was unexpected. I couldn't quit thinking about her. Geez, she was pretty. There were other pretty girls at school, but Kate had some stuff to her. She was more mature than Jack, but that wasn't saying much. She was also tough. My mind started drifting to some wonderful thoughts of me taking her on some day trips alone into the wilderness when I shook my head and forced myself to focus on what we were doing. But it sure wasn't easy.

Jack rode up next to me and said, "Next time you kiss my sister, my dad and I are going to kick the crap out of you."

That brought me back to reality. Jack started laughing and gave me that two-fingered *I'm watching you* gesture. I just started laughing right back at him. You just got to know Jack. He could make a rattlesnake laugh. His face was capable of a thousand expressions, and he used them with skill. He was the best friend anybody could have. It was too bad Kate was his sister, but he'd just have to deal with it. And I would have to be mighty sick for Jack to have a chance of taking me on. That just made what he said even funnier. Still, I wouldn't cross his dad, Gunner. In the past, Gunner spent a lot of time on the wrong side of the law, and he was a true, long-range sniper in the Air Force. He is the best shot I have ever seen. I was glad he liked me.

Eventually, we all started focusing on the business ahead. Riding in a car for a long time is tiring. Riding on a horse for the same amount of time is even more so. Even at fifteen, riding a horse makes every joint noticeable. I was used to it because I ride a lot, but it was a little like football practice. Even though I was accustomed to hitting and getting hit, there is no question my body noticed. Pain is hard to ignore. The saving grace of all of it was that riding, like football, was a challenge. And sometimes, it was a lot of fun. Today was fun even though we were probably looking for a dead guy.

I love my family, and I loved where I was. The Eastern Wilderness is a beautiful mix of vast grasslands, mountains, canyons, and forests. And it's enormous. The Bible talks about creation revealing the glory of God. I never really understood what that meant until Dad told me to just replace the word *glory* with the word *obviousness*. And out here, God's creation pointed to his obviousness. It fact, it screamed it out. There was beauty in every direction. There were also plenty dangers out here, but we were prepared for most of them. Nothing is worse than getting waylaid by some rookie mistake. I felt like we were good. Dad seemed confident, and that helped.

A few hours' ride from the farm, we came to a pretty, meandering stream. We called this area the Elk Pen. A lot of streams out here are seasonal, and in the summer, they can go dry—not this one. Kaiyo loves this place. After this much walking, he had probably built up an appetite. We all stopped and watered our horses, while Kaiyo headed upstream with Major in tow. We left Moose at home to watch over Mom and Gracie. He didn't like being left behind, but protecting the farm is what he does.

The horses quickly drank their fills, and we walked them across the stream and staked them so they could relax and crop grass. Peyton spent a little more time in the creek; hydrating that huge body of his took longer. When he was through, he joined his herd and started grazing. We had a strong breeze, and that kept the biting bugs away. For horses, being free of biting insects was nothing short of a miracle.

The four of us plopped onto the grass and watched Kaiyo swat a few fish out of the creek. He somehow had learned to chase the fish upstream and then muddy up the water downstream. Quickly after that, he ran on the creek bank past where the fish hid, and then, he came crashing downstream at them, chasing the frightened fish toward the shallower, muddy water. The fish panicked, swam into the shallows, and were blinded by the murk. In no time, he had tossed out five fish, each around two pounds. He gave Major a fish, and he kept four to himself. Jack just kept saying, "Amazing. Freaking amazing."

The old phrase *hungry as a bear* is rooted in truth, and Kaiyo was always hungry. In fact, about the only time Kaiyo gets a little crabby is when he's really hungry. They ate quickly and joined us.

We gave the animals and ourselves another half hour to rest. While we did so, we talked about trying to get to the hiker's last location. Dad laid out the options.

"I think this guy is either dead, lost, or disappeared on purpose. I doubt he's kidnapped. If he's dead, there's nothing we can do but find a body. If he's trying to disappear, well then, I don't want all of us wasting our time. I am still betting he's just lost. Also, Gracie's vision or dream or whatever it was tells me he's not dead, and he didn't run away."

Dad looked at his map. "So we are about sixteen miles west of Blankets Creek. That's a fast piece of water, and the rangers don't think he crossed to the east of it. At least their searchers found no evidence of him being over there. That means Haldor got lost somewhere between here and Blankets Creek and then went either north or south. His last set of tracks were found about a mile west of Blanket's Creek due east of here."

"Which way was he going? North or south?" Libby asked.

"He was walking north," Dad said. "And according to the sheriff, he was probably running when he made those tracks. Unfortunately, when his friends poured into that area to find him, they made tracking him impossible. We won't be able to track him, so somehow, we have to make some assumptions about where he was going to find him. I think the first assumption is he got a lot farther north than the searchers went."

I thought about that. It made some sense. "Then that means we need to ride northeast and try to cross his path several miles from his last track, right? And hopefully we can find something helpful."

"Well," said Dad, "we have a few thousand square miles to find him, and we won't ever find him without a plan. And that plan is as good a one as any other."

Dad smiled, looked at us, and said, "Saddle up?"

Even Jack and Major knew what that meant.

I watched my dad, and I could see his age was getting to him. He still had the determination and drive that he always had, but as he slowly picked himself up off the grass, it was obvious the long ride had consequences. Poor thing, it must be tough being forty. I couldn't imagine being that old. I was already in the saddle, and somehow, I caught Dad's eye. He looked at me and said, "What are you looking at?"

I smiled. "Do you need me to come over and help you climb up on Hershel? Maybe give you a boost? I can tell it's kinda tough on you. You know, it's been a long, hard ride, especially for an old man like you."

Dad and I have been verbally sparring for years. He's pretty good at it. We enjoy poking fun at each other. But we need to be careful. When I was really young, like ten or eleven, I started in on Dad, and he trash-talked back and said something that made me cry. I can't even remember what it was, but Mom took Dad outside, and they had a *discussion*. I watched out the window, and it looked like a mostly one-sided discussion. Dad tried a few times to say something, but he was totally on the defensive. Libby joined me at the window, and we just started laughing. Dad looked like the dog who pooped on the rug. It was fun to watch. Head down, shoulders slumped, he just looked miserable.

Anyway, when Dad came back in, he apologized, and we set up some ground rules about the back and forth. He told me we couldn't get too personal because that can hurt. Also, we can't be disrespectful or trash-talk in front of others. They just wouldn't understand. And we couldn't allow ourselves to get offended easily. I knew what he meant. From then on, our skins got thicker, and life went on.

Dad looked at me, hopped up on Hershel with surprising ease, and smiled. Then, Dad said, "Cute, Dean. I think you're about thirty-five years premature on that. And by the way, I'll be riding into my eighties, and you'll probably be riding a desk somewhere, getting soft."

"Never!" I said.

"We'll see," Dad smirked.

"Burned!" said Jack.

Libby laughed. Geez. He got under my skin, and he didn't even insult me. He was so good at this back-and-forth stuff. What he said also scared me. I didn't want that life for me.

Dad then put on his serious face. "Okay," he said. "From this point on, we need to be on our toes. We are headed north. This is where we don't often go, and there are places we've never been. If we're lucky, we'll link up with Goliath."

Kaiyo and the rest of us, even the dog, looked up at the mention of the giant grizzly bear. Goliath was a close friend of the family, and he was like Kaiyo. When I say that, I mean Goliath was smart like us. It's a long story, but a few years ago, Goliath tried his best to kill me. So, before he could get to me, I shot him in the head. I thank God all the time I just grazed him and didn't get in a better shot. Goliath is an amazing creature.

Dad looked over at Jack and said, "Jack, if we do see Goliath, be careful with Chevy. They don't know each other, and Chevy will be frightened. Chevy can run like a rocket, and I wouldn't blame him. Goliath is a beast."

Jack said that he would be careful. Unfortunately, Jack and the word *careful* don't go together, so I was sure Jack would forget. We rode hard to the northeast for a few more hours. We were probably about ten to twelve miles north of where Haldor's last tracks were seen. Dad stopped and looked around.

"Listen up," said Dad. "We are many miles north of where the last of Haldor's searchers have gone. Whether or not he's dead or alive, I suspect he once went this way. From here on, until we find something, I want Major and Kaiyo with me. We will tack back and forth into the wind trying to catch the hiker's scent. Libby, you and Jack go about fifty yards to my right. Dean go about fifty yards to my left, and y'all keep your eyes peeled for anything. Remember, look for anything that's not ordinary."

I think Jack was thrilled with his assignment. Dad knew what he was doing. Jack would take a bullet for Libby, and Dad always wanted to make sure his daughters were safe. As for Jack, he didn't have a chance with Libby, and Dad knew it. Libby was definitely safe. And Jack had to be somewhere.

I took Solo off to the left and quickly checked our back trails. Checking to see if anybody or anything was following us was a matter of survival out here. Bears will follow humans, and so will wolves. But we were usually more concerned that some person might be following us. It has happened to Dad before, and if he didn't have a habit of checking his back trail, he would have been killed and left to the scavengers.

Libby rode off to Dad's right, and Jack did the same. I kept my eyes peeled to the ground and at the surrounding landscape. Kaiyo took the lead, and Major stayed with Dad. There was no question Major was extremely loyal to Dad. Moose was loyal to the entire family, and Major did love us, but he always preferred to be with Dad. We were used to it; that's why Major didn't come with me, even though having him with me might have been helpful. He has a good nose.

People often don't understand that Montana is really dry. We usually only get about sixteen to seventeen inches of rain a year. Of course, we do get about five to six feet of snow, but that doesn't translate into five to six feet of moisture. The colder it gets, the deeper the snow, but the actual amount of moisture doesn't change. In the Eastern Wilderness, we were mostly in short grasslands interspersed with dry creek beds. Mountains seemed to be everywhere, some closer, some farther. Antelope lived out here, and so did elk. There were whitetails, and the mule deer could be found at the higher elevations. Moose lived wherever there were creeks or ponds. And there were bears and wolves. Unfortunately, where we were, it was dry out, and dry hard ground doesn't allow much for tracks or for scents. After an hour of looking and riding generally north, I had nothing. But Kaiyo caught something.

Footprints—Sam

I watched Kaiyo far more than I watched Major. The nose of a bear is vastly superior to the nose of a dog. We had been searching for some time, heading north-northeast when it became obvious Kaiyo was picking up a scent. He ran past Jack and Libby, and Major ran off and fell in line behind him. Hershel seemed to know what I wanted to do, so he broke into a canter, and we quickly caught up to Kaiyo and Major. By this time, both Kaiyo and Major were running east toward Blankets Creek.

This creek's source is deep in the mountains, and it always runs wet. In June, it runs quickly as the snow on the mountains continues to melt. Over the years, it has carved out a wide floodplain that was filled with thick willows and with mud deposits left from the recent late-spring flooding. Kaiyo found some tracks and gave his roar. Libby was first on the scene. She quickly hopped off Jet and walked over to the tracks. We all dismounted and carefully followed.

"They're his tracks," she said.

The tracks here were clear. They were of a human who wore about size twelve hiking boots. The tracks had the same pattern of Haldor's boots. Being an avid hiker, Haldor bought several pairs at the same time, and his parents had given Officer Brigham photographs of the tread patterns of his extra boots. They matched. Haldor had strayed far off from the hiking plan he filed at the ranger station forty or so miles south of here. But we already knew that. People had scoured the area that was in his plan. It made sense he wasn't there; if he was, they would have found him. So we were close. We still didn't know if he was dead or alive, but by the looks of the tracks, he had passed this way about a week before.

Dean came up and took Hershel's reins. I took a can of bug spray, bear spray, and my rifle. We had done this before. "Dean and Libby," I said, "I'll go into the willows with Major and Kaiyo, and we'll try to follow his tracks. Be on watch for anything I spook out of the willows."

Libby and Dean warned me to be on the lookout for moose and bears. I knew to do so, but it was good advice anyway. Right now, both bears and moose had their cubs and calves, and they were nasty mean when it came to protecting their youngsters. Today, we weren't hunting, so before we plunged into the brush, I whistled loudly to advertise our presence. I can whistle louder than most people. It's loud and fully annoying. Kaiyo understands why I do it, but the dogs hate it. The horses don't seem to care.

I put my fingers to my teeth and whistled. As suspected, we heard the crashing of some large animals running away from us. Good. Kaiyo looked at me with an approving glance. It looked like Haldor headed into the willows directly toward the creek. Other than those tracks, that was about all we had to go on, but that was enough.

I followed Kaiyo into the thick brush all the while calling out Haldor's name. I didn't really expect to answer, but it alerted animals to our presence. Animals hate surprises, and surprising the big ones is not smart. And we did get some bugs, but we at least had a breeze that kept them off-balance.

Kaiyo and Major were working a trail, and I trusted them. The ground was swampy, and the brush was thick, but we soon came to a wide stretch of open, silty, mudflats. The mud covered a twenty-yard-wide strip that hugged the western edge of the creek bank for about a hundred and fifty yards. The flooding must have been impressive. By the looks of it, some of the flooding occurred within the past two weeks. Major raced over to flats and let out a short bark. Kaiyo wandered over and nuzzled Major. That caused Major's tail to wag as if it were me who praised him. I made my way over and saw what they were looking at. In the mud, we found tracks. Haldor's were there, and so were other tracks. And they told a story that started out looking hopeful.

This part of the creek was somewhat open, and I needed Dean, Jack, and Libby here. I whistled twice, and Libby returned a single whistle. So did Dean. I guess Jack couldn't whistle. We had a way of communicating that worked out here, and I had just told them to come to me. Kaiyo hustled back into the brush along my back trail. Major stayed with me. In short order, he returned leading Jack, Dean, and Libby on their horses; and they brought Hershel and Peyton along. Seeing Peyton and his size always made me glad he was on our side. His huge hooves spread out his weight, so he was able to walk through the marshy area nicely.

I explained what we were looking at and hopped up on Hershel while I was talking. I needed the extra height to help me understand. At the same time, Dean dismounted and stood over the tracks.

"Well," said Dean, "He was still going north. I wonder what he was thinking."

He started walking in the direction of the tracks and said, "Big wolf tracks are here too. Really, really big ones."

Kaiyo was already sniffing the tracks, and so was Major. Then, Major's tail started to wag. We all knew, but I asked Kaiyo, "Is that our wolf friend?"

Kaiyo nodded to say *yes*. Jack gave out a loud, "Woo-hoo!"

Libby loudly said, "Yes!"

The wolf is Tracker. He is a family friend now, but we got off to a rocky start when he became a part of my family's story years ago. He visits us frequently, and it's always great to see him. Major and Moose adore him. He seems to be a mentor of sorts for Kaiyo. Tracker and Gracie are also very close.

The wolf is one of the Specials. We only know of three others. Kaiyo, Goliath, Tracker, and a watcher we named Rimmy are the Specials. Rimmy once saved my life. These four are special because they look like animals, and they can act like animals, but they think a whole lot like people. Oh, and apparently they're Christians too. At least I think they are. That may sound strange, but our whole experience since we met Kaiyo has been entirely strange, so why not? From my point of view, if an animal could think like us, then his or her being a Christian is a perfectly valid choice. It still required some getting used to.

Over the years, Dean has been learning to track, and he loved it. At fifteen, he was already better than most of the older outdoorsmen. It wouldn't be long before he would be better than me. Dean started following the tracks. "He was following Tracker. That's doesn't sound right, but it's true. Why would anyone want to follow a wolf? Especially a wolf as scary-looking as Tracker."

Tracker was an impressive wolf. As far as wolves go, he was huge. I suspect he weighed in close to three hundred pounds. He was strong and fearless. Landon Haldor had to be crazy to follow Tracker. While I was convinced that Tracker was safe around my family, I doubted that such a courtesy would be extended to others, except the Gibbses. And this young fool was following him.

He was also way off the path he told the rangers he would be sticking to. Dean got back up on his horse, and we slowly started following the tracks. With the tracks in some old mud, following Haldor was easy. Because some of Haldor's tracks were over the wolf's tracks, it was easy to tell who was following who. In tracking, that's not always an easy thing, but even a novice tracker could figure this one out.

For the next hour or so, we followed the tracks as they went in and out of the mud patches. Occasionally, the willows and brush forced us into the creek, but the creek was wide, so our horses had no problem with it. Kaiyo and Major played in the creek and checked out the banks on each side. It seemed like the wolf and the hiker went out of their way to walk in the mud. It made sense. Walking in the mud is easier than walking in the brush. Dean would call out changes. We believe the wolf knew he was being followed because we could find areas of concealment, like a fallen tree or thick brush, where it appeared he crouched to watch his back trail. But that's about all the tracks told us. Of course, these occasional mud deposits had the tracks of nearly all of the other animals that lived in the area. We saw the tracks of black bears and grizzlies, wolves and coyotes, moose, elk and deer, and all sorts of rodents and smaller mammals. We even saw antelope tracks where the brush gave way to open prairie.

The sun was starting to get low in the sky, and we decided to get clear of the creek and set up camp. These forested floodplains are both animal hideaways and animal highways, and camping in such an area invites trouble. As long as we were not hiding, it is far better to set up camp out in the open. The land on the east side of the creek led to open prairie, so we turned our horses to the creek to head that way. When we did so, we crossed another mudded area. Suddenly, Dean stopped, handed the reins to me, and was off his horse. Whatever he saw, Kaiyo and Major were right behind him. Dean ran north another twenty yards, stopped, and looked around at the ground. I saw the hair on Major's back go up.

"What do you see?" yelled Libby.

"Trouble," said Dean. "I think we got a watcher following Haldor."

3

The Quiet—Libby

That was bad news. In fact, it was awful news. We were hopeful we could find the hiker alive, but this complicated things. Watchers aren't usually good things to have around. People call them bigfoot, booger, sasquatch, and a thousand other names. A few years ago, four of them kidnapped Dad and then tried to kill and eat him. At least we think they wanted to eat him. We're almost one hundred percent sure killing him was something they planned to do.

Rimmy is a watcher, and he's a friend of the family, but the watchers that live in the forest to the south of the farm are unpleasant. Rimmy helped Dad escape as some of the rest of us came to Dad's rescue. It was dramatic, but it was pretty scary too. We don't know why Rimmy helped Dad, but it seemed Kaiyo living with us had everything to do with it.

We call them watchers because in years past, the dogs would occasionally go to the southern edge of our farm, near our house, and growl. They wouldn't charge into the thick Southern Forest, but they would stay put and stand their ground. Sometimes, we would be watched for hours. It was thoroughly creepy, and Dad would not allow us to enter the Southern Forest. Now that Kaiyo is with us and now we know what's out there, we are watched far less often. Neither Dad nor Kaiyo put up with it. If we're lucky, one of the watchers is

Rimmy. Then, the dogs don't growl at all. But the average watcher is a killer of dogs and maybe a lot worse.

I am sure of this, though. If I ever went camping where watchers might be, I would keep an eye out for any kids of mine. Watchers are smart and are way too strong to be ignored. We have been thinking that watchers may have been responsible for a lot of the disappearances that occur in the country's national forests and parks. And there are a lot more disappearances than most people think.

So the tracks showed that a watcher was around. That complicated things. And it added an element of danger I didn't look forward to. Anyway, we didn't have time for all that, the sun was going down soon, and we needed to set up camp.

Dean mounted back up, and we all walked single file eastward across the creek. With the exception of Major, nobody had any trouble crossing the creek. Major was smallest, and the water was moving downstream quickly. Fortunately, the water was only about eighteen inches deep, but Major walked straight into a deep hole, and he plunged in over his head. Kaiyo was right there, and he reached out with his right paw and kept Major from going downstream. In a few moments, Major was safe, and he crossed safely to the east bank. He practically leaped up on Kaiyo in gratitude. Describing that bit of hardly noticed drama is so hard. To have a grizzly calmly save your dog and then think nothing of it is an amazing miracle. I looked over at Dad. Major is his dog, and he saw it all. He just looked at me and said, "That's not something you see every day, is it?"

No, it wasn't.

The horses and the animals hauled themselves up and over the creek bank, and we walked another seventy-five yards. There, we stopped in an open grassland of short sedge grass and pine grass next to a single ponderosa pine. We knew the drill. All of us dismounted and got to work. Jack staked the horses so they could safely graze without getting tangled up. I got to work setting up one tent, while Dean set up the other. Dad dug a shallow firepit and gathered firewood. When Dean and Jack were done, they helped me finish setting up camp, and we all went and got more firewood. The rule is that there's never enough firewood. Getting firewood out here was simple if the snakes stay away. That's why we made sure we had enough. Gathering firewood in the night is not only hard but also scary. A snake can look a lot like a stick, and there's other stuff out in the dark that's not real pleasant too.

Fortunately, in June, it doesn't get dark until almost ten o'clock, and it starts to get noticeably light around five in the morning. The days are warm, and at night, it's in the forties. That's sleeping weather.

Right around dark, we got the fire going. It was time to eat. Dad always had the cooking duties, which on trips like this included something calorie rich for Kaiyo, dog food and meaty leftovers for Major, and sandwiches or MREs for us. Jack brought sandwiches and beef jerky. Kaiyo was given a couple of rich, marbled steaks that were not trimmed of any fat. At his age and with the walking he's done on this trip, he probably needed 25,000 to 35,000 calories just to replace what he burned today. So, in addition to the steaks, Dad gave him a side of homemade bacon. Kaiyo shared some of that with Major. Gracie made and packed for Kaiyo eight enormous peanut butter and jelly sandwiches, and Dad gave Kaiyo two of them. And that was enough.

The beauty of our meals was it was easy, and we didn't cook anything. Cooking smells are like bear bait. We burned the butcher paper that held the meat, and the smell of the rest of our food probably wasn't strong enough to attract any bears. We spoke for a while about what tomorrow would bring as we all got sleepy. The four of us humans grabbed our firearms and bear spray and said our good nights to Kaiyo and Major. We love that bear like a brother, and Dad considers Kaiyo his son. Jack and his dad are crazy about Kaiyo too. Fortunately, Kaiyo didn't want in the tents, and we didn't want him in either. He's still a bear, and that means he smells like a bear. And, when he sleeps, he makes a lot of noises, and some of those noises are disgusting.

Then, five of us prayed. We prayed for the safety of Landon Haldor and for our own so we could get home soon. With the fire down to a few flickering tongues of visible flame, Dad and I went into one tent, and the boys in the other. Usually, the boys stay up talking and laughing, but not tonight. I think we all just climbed into our bags and quickly fell asleep.

The first time I woke up was because we all heard something cross the creek and come our way. Major started barking, but whatever it was kept coming. Kaiyo obviously had enough, so he let out a rather respectable roar. Whatever it was turned and ran back through the creek and into the brush on the west side. We all laughed. It was probably another grizzly bear, but it could have been anything big. Single dogs aren't very frightening to most animals out here. A deer or an antelope would be scared, but that's about it. A dog with a grizzly bear as backup is totally different, I guess. We all were asleep within minutes.

Dean woke Dad and me up sometime around two in the morning.

"Do you hear that?" he said.

We both stepped out our tent and strained to hear. What we heard sounded something like static in the distance. Dean described it more as a buzzing sound, while Jack said it sounded like a downed electrical wire. Kaiyo passed us and went out into the darkness of the open space and roared. A different kind of roar, deep and throaty, the kind that rattles your insides, answered him from the other side of the creek. Jack's eyes were wide, as were mine. All of us instinctively reached for our firearms. But then, after a few minutes, Kaiyo passed us and went back to the camp and lay back down. We followed him.

"Everything okay, Kaiyo?" Dad asked.

Kaiyo nodded, grunted, and fell back to sleep. We watched as Major curled up next to him. And the static sound went away.

"I think we're into something entirely new tomorrow. I don't know what it means for Haldor or if he's even alive," Dad said. "But expect to have some more of the mystery about the Specials revealed."

"Dad?" Dean asked. "Whatever roared back there, do you think it's a Special?"

"Yep, and I bet Kaiyo knows him. As for now, we need sleep."

Dad and I went back in our tent, while Dean and Jack headed back to theirs. Poor Jack; he was a little shaken up.

I had a ton of questions, and my heart was still beating fast. I didn't think I could fall asleep, but I was wrong. We were all back asleep in just a few minutes.

When I woke up, it was early. The sun was still below the eastern mountains, but I heard Dad outside, and I smelled wood smoke. If you have never camped, waking up is one of the best parts. I sat up and stretched and pulled on my coat and my boots. I could see my breath. Dean and Jack had already woken up. I was the last one in a tent. I heard the guys talking in low tones, and Kaiyo was making his growly sounds. When I unzipped the tent, I looked out into the early light of dawn, and about ten feet away, I looked right into a huge pair of eyes staring back at me. I jumped back out of instinct.

"Go dogs!" he whispered loudly. And then he laughed!

The Quest—Dean

"Wait for it. Wait for it," I whispered to Jack.

I heard Libby rustling inside the tent. Dad was waiting and watching. So was Kaiyo. And of course, Jack was. Poor thing, he was smitten with Libby, and there was nothing—absolutely nothing— that he could do about it. Major was off inspecting a ground squirrel.

For the most part, God gave girls higher voices, so I should be okay with it, but that high-pitched scream of a joyful girl can practically pierce eardrums. And this time was no different. She opened the tent, glanced outside, and screamed. Then, she came out of the tent like she was shot out of a canon. Rimmy was sitting on the ground, and she ran right into him. Even sitting, he was taller than she was. He wrapped her up in his massive, thick, apelike, long arms and laughed out loud. We watched and enjoyed the fun.

Libby asked him a dozen questions in rapid fire order, but he just looked back at her in amusement. The questions were like

"When did you get here?" and "Was that you who tried to come into our camp last night?" and "Were those your tracks we saw?" and "Was that you who roared at us last night?" and "Where's that hiker?" Then, she got to, "So how have you been?"

He answered none of those questions, of course. She looked at him, and then, she just broke into her own laughter. "Oh, Rimmy, we sure have missed you."

Rimmy hugged her again, and then, he grabbed her under the shoulders with his huge hands and gently stood her up. Then, he stood. He had to be six inches over eight feet tall and weigh at least eight hundred fifty pounds. Rimmy was impressive. Dad pulled out some snacks. He tossed Rimmy one of Kaiyo's peanut butter and jelly sandwiches. Both man and beast love those peanut butter sandwiches. Kaiyo got a sandwich, and Major got dog food. We humans got beef jerky, which was fine. I'm never hungry in the mornings anyway. I added wood to the fire as we waited to warm up.

Jack and I moved the horses further out so they could graze on fresh grass. We stood in the gloomy light and looked east. Far off to the east was a range of mountains that temporarily hid the sun from view. I had never gone that far, but someday, I would. The eastern slopes of those mountains had some beautiful places to ski too.

I took in the scene. Looking toward the sun always casts everything in dark shadows. If the sun is to your back, that's when the colors come alive, and everything comes into stark focus. But I was waiting for one of the best parts of the day. I looked to my right, and Kaiyo had joined me. Jack was to my left. I heard the others by the tents and then listened to the sounds of the wilderness. For anyone that listens, the wilderness is not quiet. The wind was heard in the trees. The creek could be heard from here. Birds of every type were making their morning noises. Some jays were busy around the camp, a few magpies were making their raspy sounds not far off, and I even heard dippers over toward the creek. Dippers are weird birds. They look like gray robins, but they live in and around creeks. They swim and dive into the rapids and even walk along the bottom of the creeks. But their call is nice.

Soon, we saw the first glimmer of the sun. If you have ever been up early enough to watch the sunrise, it's always a treat. And it's surprisingly fast. First, there was the light behind the mountain range; then, a piece of the sun was visible between the peaks. In moments, the sun just shot up and over the far mountaintops. Reds and pinks, purples, and yellows were all over the sky. It was wonderful. And amidst the sounds of the wilderness, I heard a wolf cry out off to the north. Hearing wolves out here or even at the farm was normal stuff. So I paid it no attention. But Kaiyo did. Major barked and ran over to us. Rimmy walked over and howled like a cow trying to sound like a fire truck siren. If he wasn't right here, I would be convinced some human hoaxer was trying to trick us. It didn't sound like any animal I was used to. In the distance, the wolf answered. Jack was not used to Rimmy at all, and he was close to freaking out. I hit him in the shoulder and told him to get a grip on himself. He hit me back and said he was just fine. It was time to go.

Libby was already tearing down the one tent, so Jack went over and helped her, while I took ours down. Dad brought back Peyton to load him up. Rimmy waved goodbye, got on all fours, and double-timed over to the creek, crossed it, and disappeared in the brush and willows. He hated to be caught out in the open. He was okay if it was dark, but the sun was now up. The shadows were still long and dark, and the gray morning mist was slow to leave, but for Rimmy, that was too much light. He watched us from within the woods. Kaiyo did what Kaiyo usually does. He lay in the grass and snoozed. Major found Dad and stayed close to him.

I brought back our horses. Each of us saddled our own mounts, Libby too. I like that in her. Libby doesn't deny that men are usually stronger than women, but she pulls her own weight. If she wanted help, she would ask for it. Her horse, Jet, wasn't a small horse, and Libby was only about 5'4". That meant she had to lift a forty-five-pound saddle up over her head and do it in a way that didn't hurt Jet. It's easier said than done, especially since she didn't have a mounting block to step up on. We have them at home, and they're handy.

She had a method. First, she put the pad on Jet and then a blanket. That was the easy part. Then, she hooked the right stirrup on the saddle horn so it didn't swing and whack Jet. The girths were tied up with the saddle's conchos. Then, she grabbed the saddle, got her center of gravity directly over her bent knees, and lifted and swung the saddle up with a full-body twist to land on the highest point of Jet's withers. That way, if the saddle was off a bit, then she could shift the saddle back with the direction of Jet's hair to the right place. The rest was easy. She checked the placement, and then, she cinched the girths. Only spending time in the weight room or working a farm can give a typical girl the ability to toss a saddle around without hurting her horse. And Libby did both. I'm proud of her.

I'm two years younger than Libby, but I'm already at least eight inches taller than she is. I'm also a lot stronger. But she was the one who taught me to saddle a horse when I wasn't so tall or very strong. Nowadays, though, I just lift my saddle and gently lower it on Solo's back.

Jack was already done saddling Chevy, and he got busy cleaning up the camp. Jack always pulled his weight, and he was quick at nearly everything. Dad had already saddled Hershel and was saddling Peyton. Because Peyton is so tall, and his saddle is right at sixty-five pounds, Dad used basically the same method Libby did.

The wolf called again from the distance, and Kaiyo heaved himself up. He looked at us and barked and started walking north. Major waited for Dad, while the rest of us closed camp. Jack put out the fire, while I stacked the unused firewood for the next camper. Then, we mounted up and turned our horses northward. I suppose each of us were wondering what was in store for us. I was curious.

Because Gracie heard Haldor cry out for help, I knew the whole thing was going to be on the weird side. Except for Kaiyo, we have never had any of the Specials help us to find a hiker. Their attitude toward mankind seemed to be hands-off. Why they cared about Haldor was beyond me but apparently, they did.

We rode north by northeast and parallel to the creek for an hour. The banks of the creek were wooded with cottonwoods, aspen, and all sorts of willows. We skirted around a large beaver pond where a large cow moose and her calf were munching on lake weeds. She didn't care about us, but she paid attention to Kaiyo. Kaiyo was leading us, but he stopped and watched them for a few seconds before moving on. Kaiyo enjoys eating, and the look he had was the kind a predator has when it's in hunt mode. Sometimes, Kaiyo kills animals by himself; sometimes, he finds them already dead. Fortunately for my parents, the local game warden brings Kaiyo road-killed deer, moose, and elk. He loves it, and the meat shouldn't go to waste.

Anyway, when we broke camp, it was just barely after sunup, and it was cold. But the sun started warming us up, and the four of us soon shed our jackets and tied them off to our saddles. The terrain had changed from mostly grassland to forest as we kept climbing up into mountains. As we continued upstream, the creek turned into a series of noisy but beautiful rapids and falls. We kept climbing and held close to the east side of the creek, while Kaiyo led. We saw Rimmy walking parallel to us on the other side of the creek about fifty yards away. He only feels comfortable in the forest. This was the first time we saw him since he left camp this morning. We knew he was usually nearby because sometimes we could hear him. I think he was guarding us, but I didn't know from what.

We climbed up a steep, wooded slope that presented no problems for Solo. Solo was a mountain pony and had great balance. Solo was made for this. Peyton had some trouble, but he was strong. He placed his hooves carefully and just sort of bulldozed his way up. Hershel, Chevy, and Jet made it up too, but not as gracefully as Solo. When we popped out on top of the slope, we came into one of those beautiful high, grassed valleys that just happen in the Montana mountains. Surrounded by wooded slopes, the valley was a sight to see. Beavers had dammed up the creek sometime in the past, and the old forest in this valley died from the long-gone floodwaters. There were still some dead trees sprinkled throughout the valley, but the huge valley floor was now fully grassed over, and there were patches of wild flowers too numerous to count.

Libby and I gasped at the beauty. Jack tipped his hat back, while Dad sighed, and we all took it in. Kaiyo was less impressed; he kept going. Major waited for Dad, of course. At the far end of the valley, a small herd of bison was bunched together grazing. Bison are not supposed to be up here. They say the only bison in Montana are in Yellowstone and in a few of the parks. That was wrong, and we have always known it. There's a decent-sized herd in the Eastern Wilderness that lives closer to the farm. No one talks about them because a lot of folks would try to exterminate them. Some say bison carry diseases that could kill cows. That may be true, but we've never seen it on our farm. Elk carry the same diseases, but nobody gets too bent out of shape about them. Seeing the bison here was an unexpected treat.

We also saw about twenty elk grazing a few hundred yards off to our right. There are lots of elk around here; seeing them was not unusual. They were grazing too, but they kept their eyes on us. We saw a few mule deer, but the grass was high enough to conceal most of their bodies. I'm sure there were more; we just couldn't see them.

Sitting here seeing this hidden valley, it was easy to understand why people love Montana. But Kaiyo was having none of it. He barked at us. When I say bark, it's more like a growly "grolf" or "haufff." But there are no words for that, so we stick to saying *bark*.

Kaiyo was in a hurry. We turned west and then north to get on the west side of the valley. We crossed the creek and found a path through the trees. Sometime a long time ago, when this valley was fully flooded, the lakeshore was here, and the animals had made a path alongside the edges of the lake. We took to it and kept riding north. I saw Rimmy higher up on the hillside to our left. The land to our west was a moderately sloping series of hillsides that climbed back away from the valley for quite a distance before the slopes got too steep. The forest was open with frequent rock outcroppings and rock walls. Somehow, Rimmy had passed us. He was standing among some weathered rocks and was watching our back trail. I'm glad somebody was. Kaiyo was now in charge, and he was in a hurry. From his perch, Rimmy watched as we all rode past him. He glanced at us, but he kept his eyes to the south along our back trail. We assumed we were being followed.

After another forty-five minutes, the trail took us back out of the forest and onto the valley edge. Once we were back in the open, we stopped at a small brook that was flowing out of the mountains to our west and into the valley. It ran fast and was irresistible to our horses. The area here was damp and muddy, but the creek ran fast and clean. We let Major and the horses get their fill, and then, we took the horses a dozen yards into the valley to graze. The grass was thick and tall enough to brush their shoulders.

After a few moments, Kaiyo came to us and barked. He wasn't happy with us, but the horses were in grass heaven. It was everywhere, tall and thick. To them, it was like going to an all-you-can-eat steak house when you're hungry. The horses didn't want to leave. Dad looked at Kaiyo.

"Come on, Kaiyo," Dad said. "The only thing these horses have had to eat was the dry grass around the camp this morning and yesterday. Other than that, they haven't eaten. Let's give them half an hour."

Kaiyo knew not to cross Dad unless it really mattered, so I guess it did. Kaiyo shook his head from side to side and barked. He even growled at Dad.

"Are we safe here, Kaiyo?" Dad asked. He cut to the chase. "Because if we're not, we'll get back up on those horses and follow you. Are we in danger?"

Kaiyo just looked frustrated, and he moved his snout slightly from side to side. That answered a few questions. The first thing was obvious. We were safe. The second thing was Kaiyo was still in a hurry.

"Wrong question, Dad," Libby said.

Dad looked at her, smiled, and said, "Fire away, Libby."

Libby turned to Kaiyo. "Kaiyo, I know Dad wants us safe, but is there another reason for us to hurry?"

Kaiyo jumped up and made it obvious we needed to get moving. That was fine with me. It was still early, and our horses were tough. We could find grass later. Maybe. But for now, we needed to leave. Kaiyo turned and looked up the slopes to the west. Dad did give the horses another five minutes to eat, but they weren't too happy to leave. That must have been some good grass.

We mounted up and left that beautiful, unnamed valley and began our incline into the forested hills. I promised myself I would come back here someday. But right now, we needed to keep moving.

Pay Dirt—Kaiyo

My dad was acting like we were on a picnic. I know Dad was concerned about the horses, but we needed to get moving. Those horses were a lot stronger than he believed. Everybody knows that horses like tall green grass, and so did I, but it was time to get out of there. First, Tracker has been waiting, and he's not a patient wolf. Second, we were being followed by those who wanted to kill the hiker. I was not sure exactly what was going on, but I could tell this was a bigger problem than just a lost hiker. And whatever was going on with my sister's vision, well, that's new to me too. I would just have to figure that part out later.

We walked steadily up the long gentle slope of the mountain. We tried to stay near the stream, and because the forest was open, we made good time. We could see the valley below us about 1,000 feet lower. The trees were a mix of pines and firs spaced about the landscape. I didn't know how high we were, but the tree line was still far off. The area was rocky, but there was enough undergrowth, dirt, and soil litter that the horses could easily keep their footing.

After another hundred yards, we saw Tracker through the open woods. Even though we were the closest of friends, his size always surprised me. My sister called out, and the horses got wind of him. Their attitudes immediately improved, and they picked up their pace. Well, not Jack's horse. Chevy didn't know Tracker, and most horses don't like wolves. His was no different. Jack held back and let my brother and sister race on. The slope flattened out, and we could see him standing on a low boulder near the stream. He had the look of a king. Libby and Dean and their mounts passed me and raced on over to Tracker. Dean let out a whoop as they sped by. My dad rode up next to me, and the three of us walked up together.

After my brother and sister and Dad traded quick greetings with Tracker, Jack dismounted and tied up Chevy. Jack then ran up to Tracker and gave him a hug. Tracker's tail wagged. Jack then stood back, and after a few moments, Tracker directed our attention over toward a low, rock overhang that jutted out of a slope off to our right. Sheltered by the rock overhang, a cave was formed that was darkly shaded. A roar came out of the cave's darkness that scared only Chevy. It was a ferocious roar, to be sure. And nearly anybody else would have been terrified, but we knew the owner of that roar. As expected, Goliath stepped out into the morning's sunlight. Goliath was huge. I knew that, but every time I saw him, I was surprised. It made me happy knowing I would be just as big as Goliath someday too.

The younger humans ran over to Goliath and hugged him and talked fast. Dad stayed with me, and we both noticed Tracker watching the woods around us. I asked Tracker what was going on. Dad, of course, had no idea what we were talking about. He couldn't understand us. But he trusted us, and that was all that really mattered. Dad got bored and wandered over to Peyton and got some things out of his saddlebags, and then, he went over to Chevy to reassure him everything was okay. Tracker and I both noticed.

"You have a great father," Tracker said. "Don't ever forget that."

I laughed at that. "No way I would do that. And Dad understands me and you too. I don't quite know how he does, but he does."

"I remember," said Tracker.

After a few moments, I asked Tracker why we were here. "Kaiyo," he said, "that hiker tried to follow me home."

Tracker let that sink in. "In fact, he's slippery. I didn't even know he was following me until the end."

That was, to me, impossible. Tracker was always super careful. "How could that happen?" I asked.

"Good question," said Tracker. "In fact, he probably followed me for miles, and I never knew he was there. He stayed out of sight and was always downwind. He was good. He's a mess right now, though. He's been through a lot."

"Yeah," I said. "It looks like a watcher was following him too. How far did he get?"

"Almost inside," said Tracker.

I was stunned. How that hiker survived was a mystery to me. He should have been dead the moment he got close. "Are we supposed to kill him?" I was serious.

"Hah," laughed Tracker. "That was my question, but Raphael told me to get him to your family for safe passage. Right now, he is a marked man. Some of our more powerful citizens haven't heard from Raphael yet, and they are determined to kill him. He is, though, for some reason, important to the Master. So he must live. Benaiah knows all of this. That is why he has come to help your family."

Rimmy's real name is Benaiah. Dad named him Rimmy when Benaiah rescued him from other watchers a few years back. Benaiah is an old Hebrew name. David, the famous king of Israel, once had thirty freakishly strong and talented fighting men. The Hebrew Benaiah was incredibly strong for a human. He killed a lion, which was impressive. He was also the chief of David's bodyguard. So the name fit. Benaiah knows Raphael and is a very trusted guard. I suspect it was Benaiah who followed the hiker.

Tracker continued. "Kaiyo, not many of us know about this. It is your responsibility to get him to your farm home to safety. But when you get home, you are wanted back immediately. Raphael wants to meet with you."

Now, I was the terrified one. "What? Why?"

For a moment, Tracker looked disappointed in me. Then, his face turned soft, and he looked at me and said, "Kaiyo, the first thing Raphael will say to you is not to be afraid. But as to why he wants to meet you so soon, well, he didn't say."

Tracker always knew when I was scared or nervous, but this time, it was obvious. He was okay with me not being grown-up yet. I was going to respond when we heard a human, a man, call out from the cave.

"Help me! I'm in here… And there's a bear!"

I turned back to Tracker. "Go say hello to Goliath, and let's get that young man out of there," said Tracker.

I ran to where Goliath was standing with Libby, Dean, and Jack. Dad joined me. They finished greeting Goliath, and they passed me on their way to see Tracker. The guy in the hole sounded off a few more times, but he seemed okay. He could wait. I jumped right into

Goliath. He was so big. He was at least three times bigger than me. Goliath covered me in one of his massive paws.

"I have missed you so much!" he said.

For the next few minutes, we talked quickly back and forth. We hadn't seen each other in almost a year. Last summer, just for fun, I went out and visited with him for a few weeks. Back then, I was still a smallish bear, so I brought Moose with me. I just missed Goliath and needed some teaching time. Goliath knew about the wilderness and how to live in it, and he taught me many wild bear skills.

For the second time in the last few minutes, Dad was looking a little bored with our conversation. He had no idea what we were saying, of course, but he was patient. After a few more moments, Dad cleared his throat and asked Goliath if he could go in. Goliath nodded, and the three of us went in to go get the hiker.

I had a lot on my mind. I was thinking that getting this guy home would be a challenge. I also didn't know what to think about Raphael wanting to see me. Who was I to get any attention from him? That troubled me, but it was really amazing too. As scared as I was, I couldn't wait.

Rescue—Sam

I never know what the Specials say to one another when they communicate. They obviously understand my English. To me, it sounds like growls and whiny sounds. I used to try to figure it out, but they use a language I cannot begin to piece together. So I'm getting used to standing there like a third wheel.

The three of us turned and headed into the cave's darkness. Goliath went first, and Kaiyo followed him. I was last. The overhang was a little low, so I had to stoop. Goliath kept his head low, but Kaiyo had no problems. We walked for about twenty paces, and any light from outside had disappeared as we turned a corner. The ceiling also raised itself, and I could stand. I turned on my flashlight.

"Is that you, Haldor?" I called out.

"Yes! Yes! It's me! And be careful. There's an enormous bear somewhere around here."

I chuckled, but I understood. Goliath is a terrifying creature. There was literally nothing out here that could defeat him. Except for a random poacher with a high-powered rifle, Goliath had nothing to fear. He weighed over 1,300 pounds, and when he stood up, his head could rest on a basketball rim. So he was scary. But Haldor had to also understand Goliath hadn't eaten him yet, and there was probably a reason.

"Don't worry about the bear," I yelled out into the darkness. "He's with me."

Haldor yelled back and said slightly sarcastically, "Well, why doesn't that surprise me?"

I directed my flashlight to the sound of his words, and soon, I saw him seated in the inky darkness. He squinted in the face of the bright beam of the flashlight. I adjusted the beam, so the light diffused, and it showed him and his little cave prison. He looked like he had been through an ordeal. His clothes were dirty, and they hung loosely; he had a hungry look. He also had some cuts and scratches about his face and arms, but they looked to be healing up. His eyes were sharp, though.

"Ready to go?" I said.

"Yes, sir. I am," he said. "But what about the bears? Do they know not to kill me?"

I walked over to help him up. "Oh, I suspect they do. The big one doesn't take orders from me, but we're close friends, so I think you ought to be okay. His name is Goliath. And the other bear here is my son, adopted of course."

I heard Kaiyo give a chuckle. It sounded more like a snort, but I understood it. "His name is Kaiyo."

Haldor looked at the two bears and said, "Good to meet you, Kaiyo. Thank you for not killing me, Goliath. I was thinking you might have wanted to do that."

When I reached Haldor, I handed the flashlight to Kaiyo. He put it in his mouth and played with the light by shining it everywhere but where I needed it. Who doesn't like flashlights, especially kids? Anyway, I'd had enough.

"Really, Kaiyo?" I said. "A little help?"

Kaiyo laughed his growly laugh as he turned and gave us some light.

I leaned over and extended a hand to Haldor and helped him to stand up. He was shaky, but he got to his feet. "Thank you," he said.

"Well, let's get you home," I said. "My name is Sam McLeod. We met a few years back. The rest of the team is outside waiting. I bet you're ready to see your family and your friends."

"Yes, sir. I am. And I miss them," he said. "And I remember you. But what I really want first are some answers. And some food. Any food you can share would be really great. And water. Water would be nice. And please, let's get out of this cave. This is like the second, most creepiest place I have ever been in."

"No worries," I said to Landon. "We'll be out in a few moments."

We turned, and I was helping him out of the cave, following the light of the flashlight that Kaiyo seemed to be playing with again. Rather quickly, we saw natural light streaming through the cave opening. We didn't have far to go.

"So, Landon"—I said—"I'm just curious. What was the first, most, creepiest place you have ever been in?"

Near the opening to the cave, it was light enough to see. Kaiyo had wandered on out, and Goliath was walking right behind us. When I asked Landon that last question, he stopped, looked at me with a slightly embarrassed look, and said, "If I told you, you would think I was insane."

I looked right back at him and said, "Try me. But first, let's get you squared away."

Landon walked out to a sight that should have caused anybody a double take. Waiting for us, we saw Tracker next to Jack and Dean who was holding Major by the collar standing off to our left. The horses were loitering behind them, but Peyton's bulk was obvious. Rimmy had joined the group, and he was standing off to our right. I saw his shoulders and head, but that was all because Goliath was walking past us on the right. When the enormous bear fully passed us, that's when we saw my daughter. She was standing next to Rimmy, but it looked odd. Libby is only about five feet, four inches. Rimmy is over eight feet tall. To me, it looked funny. To Landon, he saw something else. I saw my daughter. He saw a truly beautiful girl, and it stopped him in his tracks.

I leaned over. "Don't even think about it," I whispered in Landon's ear.

"Oh yes, sir," he whispered back.

But I think he lied. His eyes only slowly left her, and all the time, Libby was looking straight back at him. Libby was looking at him while betraying no emotion. But I knew Libby. She was interested, but she was in control.

I had to break the tension. "Libby," I said, "can you bring Landon some water? Dean, Jack, let's get him something to eat to hold him over."

My children broke into action and headed to the horses. Tracker came over and sat in front of Landon. The young hiker looked at Tracker and said, "Again, thank you."

Then, he laughed and said, "It would have been better if I knew the big bear was your friend. I was certain he was going to kill and eat me. And thank you for bringing these people to me."

Tracker's tail wagged. Landon waited for a moment. Landon looked at me. He looked confused. "Do you know this wolf?" he asked. I nodded. "Does he ever talk? He talks, right?"

Landon's voice quivered. He looked seriously concerned, like he was concerned about his sanity.

"Well, no," I replied. "At least he's never spoken to me. But trust me, Landon, I know he's very, very different from any other wolf I have ever seen. In fact, we call Tracker, Rimmy, Goliath, and Kaiyo the 'Specials.'"

I looked at Tracker and said, "Maybe someday Tracker will talk to me too."

Tracker just looked back at me and said nothing. Landon looked enormously relieved.

I motioned to Rimmy, and Rimmy waved back. Rimmy was busy being our bodyguard and keeping his eyes on the woods. "Anyway, there are only four of them that we know personally. I suspect there are some others, but I don't know where they come from."

Landon nodded and whispered, "Well, I can tell you there are tens of thousands of them, maybe more. And they all talk, and some of them hate me."

He let that sink in.

I looked at Tracker. "Can he tell me what happened?"

Tracker nodded. "What about the rest of the family and Jack?"

Tracker seemed to smile, and he nodded again. "What about to others, our friends, like the folks who already know about Kaiyo and Goliath?"

Tracker thought about that for a few moments. Then, he nodded. Well, I was curious, but I needed to know my boundaries. "Can he tell anyone else, like his own family?"

Tracker shook his head side to side, and he looked deadly serious. So there it was.

"You get that, Landon? Whatever you went through, the only people you can tell are either here or at my farm. Do you get that?"

Landon looked at me and said, "Mr. McLeod, I am serious. I really don't know what happened to me. All I know is I went where I wasn't supposed to go, and I saw some things I probably wasn't supposed to see. And I was almost killed several times because of it. I really don't want to share it with others, your family here being the exception. First, no one would believe me, and second, I owe my life to the wolf here. If the wolf says *no*, then it's no."

I looked at Landon. "Well, it's a *no*, but I will want to hear everything. It's afternoon already. We will camp where we camped last night and go home tomorrow morning. You will need food and some real rest."

Dean, Jack, and Libby had returned with food and water and had caught most of our conversation with Tracker. Libby handed Landon a canteen even though the nearby brook was probably clean enough to drink from. Landon took it and looked at her, but he quickly looked away. He pulled on the canteen, and I could see Libby stare at him and look at his filthy clothes. Libby was not starstruck or giggly; that's not her style. But she studied him. He knew she was watching, and it obviously made him nervous. Instead, Landon looked at Dean.

"Have you eaten lately?" Dean asked.

"No, nothing. No food or water for three or four days, maybe," said Landon.

That surprised me because anybody who goes that long without food can survive somewhat easily, but surviving that long without water would be nearly impossible, especially to be in the shape he was in. He should be at least nearly dead or severely dehydrated. But there he was, a little gaunt, but otherwise, he was fine. I was looking forward to hearing where he was.

Dean shared glances at us. "Okay, we're going to start a little slow with you. You've been gone longer than you think. So we don't want you throwing up while we ride away from here, so let's start with an apple. And let's sit you down."

Landon sat and was surrounded by two bears, a wolf, and the kids. Dean slowly parceled out some chocolate-covered peanut M&Ms and then a protein bar with extra protein. Kaiyo and Goliath got some of the M&M's too. Rimmy had drifted back in the woods, ever our bodyguard. Landon ate everything handed to him as he thanked the Specials for saving his life. It was obvious to us he was trying to figure us out too.

I pulled out a flask Gunner gave me and sprinkled a piece of gauze with its contents. Libby raised an eyebrow. "It's mouthwash mixed with grain alcohol. It's definitely not for drinking. In fact, anyone who drinks it would get mighty sick. But it kills germs, and it can be used to help start a fire. This stuff kills even the worst of germs, the kind doctors can't stop."

Libby looked pleased with the answer. She knew we never mixed guns and drinking, so the presence of the flask must have confused her. I handed the wet gauze to Landon and told him to wipe down and clean the cuts on his arms and face.

"So"—said Landon as he was tending to his scratches and cuts—"how do you guys fit in? I mean, I met you, Mr. McLeod, a few years back out in the wilderness. But here you all are rescuing me, and you guys are probably the only ones who would believe I'm not crazy. And you are friends with the Specials. How does that happen? And why is there still trouble? Why does it look like getting home will not be so easy?"

Those were good questions. Libby obviously agreed. "Great questions, but with all due respect, that's none of your business."

Landon looked like he'd been hit in the face. To look at her, people might underestimate her because of her beauty, but Libby is pure steel. On top of that, she was piling it on thick.

Spies: Libby

I'm not going to lie—Landon Haldor was cute. He had a great smile and better shoulders. Landon was powerfully built, but he had a terrific laugh and twinkly eyes. He also was showing respect to the Specials and to us. He certainly was no whiner. Still, I knew little about him, and his asking questions of us was not going to happen. And besides, he was too old for me. Well, maybe.

"Landon," I said. "Look, I don't want to be rude with you being in the poor shape you're in, but you aren't going to be asking any questions of us, at least for a while."

Dean sat back and was enjoying this. Jack looked confused. Dad was giving me plenty of rope. He winked at me, so I kept going. "Yesterday morning, because nobody could find you, the authorities asked us to find you or your lifeless body. We dropped everything, gathered our camping gear, packed our horses, slept out in the wilderness, and did what no one else could. We found you. And we still have to get you home. And on top of that, we all believe we've been followed for some reason. So that means we are expecting trouble. Right now, we need to get off this mountain and get out in the open, back to last night's campsite. So can you ride a horse?"

"Yes, ma'am," said Landon. "I mean, yes, Libby. I can ride a horse."

Poor thing. I guess he expected his rescuers to be more ecstatic about finding him. "Good, because you'll be riding the strongest animal in Montana."

Goliath snorted at that, and Rimmy harrumphed from within the woods. "Okay!" I said loudly. "He's the strongest horse in Montana."

I looked at Dad, and Dad asked us to circle up. Everybody but Landon knew what to do, but he complied. Here we prayed. Time was too short not to pray, and we knew we had some opposition. Dad prayed for protection, Jack prayed for speed, and Dean prayed for courage. I gave thanks for finding Landon alive. Then, Rimmy prayed. I have no idea what he said, but it was powerful and beautiful, and whatever it was, he meant it. Tracker was moved to a quiet, low howl, while the bears put their faces to the ground and groaned. Then, we were done.

We all looked back at Dad. Dad wiped a tear from his eye and said, "Thank you, everyone. That was beautiful. Now, let's get off this mountain and head back. If we have no problems, we can get back to the campsite well before dark. So, saddle up!"

It was obvious Kaiyo, Goliath, Tracker, and Rimmy were pleased to leave.

Landon was still a bit weak, and Dean had to help him get up on Peyton, but once up there, Landon smiled big. "Oh man," he exclaimed. "He's enormous. I'm so high! The saddle is just huge. Amazing!"

He was right. Peyton was big. And he was sturdy.

We formed up in a tight double diamond. The inner diamond had Landon in the middle, Dad up front, Dean to the left of Landon, and me to the right. Jack fell behind us. The outer diamond had Tracker up front, Goliath next to Dean, Kaiyo next me, and Rimmy fell back behind the group. Major wove in and out of the group. We rode this way for the next twenty minutes until we got to the floor of our beautiful valley. And that was when things got scary.

The valley was empty. No bison, no elk, and no deer. It was just quiet. I think we all got the creeps because nobody talked about the horses eating the juicy grass. Even the horses seemed eager to keep moving. And that's what we did. Keeping to the right side of the valley and on the same trail we took on the way in, our diamond flattened out. Tracker stayed up front, and Dad fell in behind him. Dean pulled up behind Dad while Jack, Goliath, Kaiyo, and I followed Landon. Rimmy had taken to the wooded slopes to our right. He eyes seemed to be following something in the deep grass of the meadow. Rimmy was not panicked, but he was watchful.

We were walking quickly, and what took us forty-five minutes to walk the length of the valley on the way in took us just less than thirty minutes on the way out. We all bunched up at the top of the steep downward slope that made the south edge of the valley. Dad told us to circle up.

When we did, Dad said, "Rimmy and I have each been watching our back trail. It is obvious we are being followed. So here's the plan. No more diamond formations. I want y'all to stay bunched up and mix it up as you head down the slope. I'm going stay back and watch the back trail to see whatever it is that's following us. If you stay bunched up, I probably won't be missed."

Dad looked over at Kaiyo, Goliath, and Tracker. They all seem to agree with the plan. Rimmy had joined us, and he agreed too. Dad then told us to head on out and to go ahead and to start setting up camp. He was going to stay hidden here or on the slope.

Dean immediately protested. "Dad," he said, "if we are being followed, you and Hershel are going to stand out like sore thumbs. I am just guessing we aren't being followed by people, right?"

Dad was familiar with Dean's cross-examinations. Dean was born conversing in the Socratic method. He knew that the one who asks the questions controls the conversation. Dad asked his own question.

"Well, Dean," Dad said impatiently, "we need to know what's following us. What would you recommend?"

Dad walked right into Dean's trap. "It's simple, Dad. You have to agree you are our leader here, right?"

Dean looked at everybody but Dad. He looked at each of us. "Right, Tracker, Goliath? Kaiyo? Jack? Rimmy? Libby? Dad's the leader, right?"

We each nodded in turn. We had no choice. He was right. Landon just looked on like the outsider he was.

"We have no time," Dean said. "Dad, we need you to lead the operation and get Landon home. Take Solo and give me the walkie-talkie. If it's okay with Rimmy, then Rimmy and I are going to slide over the slope, and we will hide. When we rode past a few hours ago, I saw several dense thickets of skunkbush about thirty or forty yards down the slope from here. From my spot, I will tell you what we need to prep for tonight. Rimmy's scent and the skunkbush will hide my own scent. No offense, Rimmy. And besides, Dad, there's no way we could keep Major from following you, and either he will give up your position or he would get hurt himself."

Dad looked like Dean's idea was a nonstarter, but Dean was right. "He's right, Dad," I said. "It's a better idea."

Dean looked at us and didn't wait for Dad to interject. "All right, folks, let's all push down the slope, and once I get over the edge, I'll slide off Solo and make a bolt for the thickets off to the right. From in there, I ought to be able to see whatever follows you guys. Keep moving. And, Dad, keep the walkie-talkie on channel four. I'll try to give you an idea of what we see. Tonight, Rimmy will bring me back to the campsite if it's safe. I'll take my 12-gauge, some extra shells, and some bear spray. Rimmy, is that okay with you?"

Rimmy nodded. He loved stuff like this. Dad started to protest, but he quickly gave in.

"All right," Dad said. "Landon, when Dean leaves, I want you on Dean's horse. Whatever followed us yesterday was used to seeing Peyton riderless. Dean, if you can't talk, just double-click. I don't want to respond and give up your position, so I won't verbally check back in. If you get compromised, get the hell out of there. Rimmy, if you have to, save him like you once saved me. Can you do this?"

Rimmy smiled and softly said, "Go dogs."

Dad laughed and gave out his orders. We all crossed the creek; and then, one by one, we turned away from the valley; and single file, we headed over the edge and down the long-wooded slope. It wasn't long when we saw Dean grab his shotgun and his backpack and slide off Solo. From there, he ran at top speed into a thicket next to the creek. Once he was in the skunkbushes, I truly couldn't see him. Rimmy was right with him, and he went past Dean and disappeared on the other side of the creek. Landon quickly switched horses, and we never slowed down.

The slope was steep, so we would ride from right to left, then down, and then back again. Doing that is slower but safer. Landon was right behind me in line, and he asked if he could at least ask one question. I laughed and agreed.

He cleared his throat and said, "So who's the little girl? Is she your sister? Seriously, I cried out for three or four days when I was trapped, and she's the only one who heard me. I saw others, but she heard me immediately. Were you in the group with her? Everybody's faces were blurry but not hers. We'll that's not quite true. I saw Kaiyo clearly too. None of it made sense, but I was in a world where nothing made sense, so I didn't second-guess it. So is she your sister?"

For the next fifteen minutes, I described Gracie to Landon. It's an exercise everybody ought to do. The more I talked about her, the more I realized what an awesome little girl she was. I tended to take her for granted, but I realized I was missing an opportunity to have a terrific sister. Several times, Goliath would snort his approval as I spoke.

"Landon," I said, "Goliath here once tried to kill Gracie, but it was Gracie who was the first of us to forgive him and truly love him. Dean and Dad wanted to give Goliath another chance, but that wasn't true forgiveness. Gracie embraced Goliath and practically sang her forgiveness to him. Right, Goliath?"

Goliath huffed and nodded his head. He loved Gracie dearly.

By this time, the slope had started to flatten out, and the trees started to thin noticeably. We saw no wildlife, but we were a pretty big outfit; and we had two grizzlies, an enormous wolf, and a big dog with us, so I wasn't much concerned.

Landon then asked if she had some sort of special powers that allowed her to hear him. Several of us laughed. Gracie definitely had some special powers, like her temper when she had to wake up too early. Everybody knew about those powers. But when it came to special powers, Gracie had, up until that moment, been thoroughly normal.

We descended the slopes and headed for flatter country. It wasn't long before we came to a point where we could see the lone ponderosa pine that hovered over our old campsite a mile or so away. Shadows were long, but because the site was out in the open and on a slight rise, it was still well illuminated in the sunlight. We were tired, and it was inviting for sure. The horses and the animals involuntarily picked up their paces. I was fine with that. Just then, Dad's walkie-talkie got a double-click from Dean. Dad stopped and double-clicked back. We all bunched up around Dad. Within a few seconds, Dean's voice was whispering. Dad turned up the volume.

Dean was still whispering, but we could all hear him. "Dad, you got tag along. I think we'll be okay, though. Other than some hawks that are keeping tabs on you, it looks like the only thing that's following you is a small black bear and a bull. It looks like one of the hawks just flew by and gave them a report of your location. I think we've been overconcerned. Over."

Well, that didn't seem too bad. We certainly couldn't be too worried about a cow and a little black bear. At least it didn't seem bad until Landon spoke up. "He said that he would trample me to death or worse. And it's a huge beast. And he's got a bad temper." Landon looked at Dad and said, "Ask Dean if it's tremendous, black, and with horns that point forward."

Dad looked at Landon and said, "Yeah, we have a lot to learn from you. Once we get settled in, let's all hear what happened, okay?"

Without waiting for an answer, Dad double-clicked the walkie-talkie. Dean was able to respond, so Dad asked Dean what the bull looked like. Dean described what Landon described except for the size. Dad asked if he still saw them. Dean whispered back that he did, and Dad asked how big the black bear's ears and eyes were. We all knew what Dad was doing. The bigger the bear, the smaller the ears and eyes. The question was whether Dean was judging the bear's size by assuming the bull was normal sized or vice versa. If the bear's ears and eyes were big, well that meant the bull wasn't all that big.

Dean whispered back and said, "I was wrong. Yeah, little ears, little eyes…real little. So that little bear is a big black bear, and the bull is bigger than any I have ever seen. It's bigger than a bison, maybe a lot bigger. It's almost Peyton big, and they're headed off your way. I'll stay here another fifteen minutes to see if that's it, and then, we'll head on back."

Dad signed off, and we all looked at each other. All we knew was we were being followed by a big bull with a temper and a black bear, and both probably happened to be Specials. I wasn't worried; we had Goliath, Tracker, Kaiyo, Major, and guns for protection; and that would be plenty. There was nothing left to do so we headed to the campsite.

Within another six or seven minutes, we were riding into our prior night's campsite. We still had a couple of hours or so of sunlight, so camp setup would be easy. Everybody, especially Landon, was looking forward to getting home the next day. Each of us took off our horse's saddles and saddlebags and then got to work setting up camp. Jack led each our horses and took them to the creek, one by one, to water them. On the way back, he staked them so each one had good grass to eat. Jack was a good rider, and he was so good to the horses. All the way down to the creek, he talked to them in soothing tones. The horses trusted him.

Dean radioed Dad and whispered, "Dad, I got trouble, and it's not the bull. I need prayer from everybody, and I need it now. Guns won't work."

Back Trails—Dean

About fifteen yards after we all headed down the slope, I slid off Solo and ran through the woods another thirty-five yards and crashed into a deep thicket that was running parallel to the east side of the creek. Rimmy ran past me and on to the other side the creek to stand guard. I got nestled in and hid myself. I put my backpack in front of me and propped my shotgun up on it. Unless somebody was standing in front of me or was on his knees and knew exactly where I was, I was hidden and out of sight. I was not worried about Rimmy at all. He's big, but he's a master at hiding—all watchers are.

I was able to watch as our team moved down the steep wooded slope. They looked careful but unconcerned. I was able to watch them until finally they were out of sight. Shortly thereafter, I saw what appeared to be a black bull and a small black bear come over the slope as they kept their eyes on my family far down the hillside. I had a hard time understanding what was going on, but I needed to report back what I saw. The whole thing was odd because I've never seen a bull and a bear work together. But they were clearly together. The small bear would listen to the bull, and the bull would listen to the bear. It was obvious to me they were Specials.

Just because they were Specials didn't mean they were good. I cannot tell whether a Special is on our side or on the other side or on their own side. Because of what happened to Dad a few years ago, we know some, maybe most, of the watchers are clearly on the other side. Goliath wasn't on our side for a long time either. Thank God he is now.

I was able to radio Dad and let him know what was following them. Dad got back with me and asked me to recalibrate the size of the bear. Sure enough, I had misjudged the size of the bull because I thought the bear was a small bear. Any woodsman knows how a bear can look big, but if the ears and eyes are big, then the bear isn't. Bears' ears don't grow much, so as bears grow, their ears seem smaller. A very big bear will have ears that are less pronounced, and it will have very small eyes. I made a rookie mistake and quickly corrected it. With that adjustment, it was obvious the bull was enormous, and I reported back to my dad.

I was comfortable in my little hiding place, and I wanted that enormous bull to get some distance, so I stayed and kept a lookout. I gave a low whistle and heard a reply from Rimmy. I had more than enough daylight left, and I was being guarded by perhaps the strongest beast in Montana besides Goliath. I should have felt secure, but I unconsciously started to feel a growing sense of dread. After a few more minutes, I became aware of my feelings. I felt like running, but I knew to lay low and out of sight. I heard Rimmy grunt behind me. He felt it too. Like a fog rolling in, there came on both of us a thick feeling of oppression, and I became frightened. I hadn't felt that way in years. I have learned whenever I feel oppression and dread, it's almost never my imagination. Usually, it comes from being too close to evil, and sometimes, it's demonic.

Then, as I peered through the skunkbush boughs back up the slope, I saw the source of my dread. When I saw them, it was clear we were in danger. But part of me was curious, and I knew better than to fear demons. I didn't think that I could be both scared and curious, but I was. They seemed to glide from the valley floor to the edge of the slope. Well, at least one of them glided. That would be the demon thing. The other one was natural. I had no doubt the natural one was a Special. We had seen that teamwork before. That way, the evil twosome was quite capable in both spiritual and natural worlds. Demons cannot stand to be in the presence of a nearby praying Christian, but prayer has no immediate effect on flesh and blood. If a bad guy wants to shoot you, praying is a lot less effective than return fire. On the other hand, shooting at a demon is a waste of time.

The creature was an ordinary mountain lion. It was on the big side, but still normal for a mountain lion. It looked powerful, but its friend was far more threatening in appearance. In general, demons are spirit unless they possess a human. By possession, a demon gains a vehicle to enjoy and use. I am sure plenty of people have been killed because their demon possessor threatened others. Shoot the body, the demon just leaves. I also learned not to expect movie-style special effects. They don't do that. This demon was apparently possessing the body of some poor young woman. She looked young, maybe in her late twenties, early thirties, but she could sure use a cut and a curl. She looked a lot like a long-term meth addict. My heart broke for her.

The two were probably following the bull and the black bear. At that point, I whispered back to Rimmy to start praying and to keep his eye on the lion. I then prayed hard that the demon would have no power over me or the poor human it was using. I radioed Dad to get some prayer backup. That demon immediately felt the sting of prayer, and she shrieked in anger and pain. Then, she pointed my way and ordered her mountain lion to get me.

I was only about thirty-five yards away, so it took the big cat a few quick seconds to close the distance. At some point midway in his charge, I could tell he saw me in my hiding spot, and that was extremely unnerving. I was ready to pull the trigger when a split-second later, Rimmy leapt over me and backhanded the lion like it was a house cat. The lion had no time to react, and it was knocked unconscious immediately. It flipped over several times in the air before it hit the ground. It just lay there like it was dead.

I crawled out of the bushes and thanked Rimmy. Then, I poked the lion with the tip of my shotgun. It was breathing, but that was about it. Basically, lights out, nobody home.

Not far away, the demon lady shrieked again, but she stood her ground. Her fists were clenched to her side, and she looked like pure evil. I'm not sure what was coming out of her mouth, but I was betting it was some sort of attempt to curse us. It sounded like some ancient language. This was new ground to me. Both Libby and I had dealt with demons before. When we prayed, they screamed like crazy and left the area. Easy-peasy. But this one was digging in, and it showed no plans to run away. I didn't know what to do.

Unfortunately for the demon, it picked a slender lady's body to call home. I thought about it for a few moments and realized we really didn't have any good options. That thing just kept hissing and spitting out major cuss words, some in English and some in some other language. Finally, I looked up at Rimmy and said, "Let's catch her!"

Rimmy looked at me like I had lost my mind. "Come on," I said. "Go get her and bring her back. We'll take her to Dad."

Rimmy needed some convincing. He shook his head vigorously. "Rimmy, that thing is going to cause us some trouble down the road if we don't get it. Now, please, go get her. And besides, it's just a girl. You ought to be able to take down a tiny little lady, but I guess if you're scared, I understand. She does look a little nasty."

Rimmy snarled at me. I had to be careful here. Rimmy's type have short tempers. I was also sure he knew that people who are possessed are capable of feats of superhuman strength. And capturing a demon would be a first-time thing for both of us.

"Rimmy," I said as smoothly as I could, "have you ever caught a demon before? Have any of your buddies? I bet not. C'mon, be the first to do it. Once you do it, you know the others will be doing it all the time. I can't imagine why you wouldn't want to give it a shot. Be the first. Why, I bet catching a demon is on your bucket list, right? And don't worry. I'll cover you in prayer the whole way."

I was serious about that. Rimmy's eyes went to a squint, and I could tell he didn't have it in him. To be honest, I didn't blame him. Demons are terrifying creatures. So I looked at Rimmy and said, "Now, think about it. Don't you want to save that poor girl's life? We both know that no demon can stand up to Christ. It's a no-brainer. We will all pray over her tonight, and that demon over there will be sent packing, and she will be set free. Otherwise, that demon is sure to get her killed."

That was it. Rimmy looked defeated. He was also probably just tired of hearing me talk, but everything I said was true. I whispered, "If you go get that girl, you will save her life."

Then, Rimmy looked resolved as he turned his bulk to face the shrieking demon standing there in its lady suit. Just then, the demon figured out we weren't going to run away, but we were going to come at it. In a flash, that thing turned and ran back up the hill toward the valley. I'll give her some credit, for a human, she was fast. But few things are faster than a watcher. The moment she turned to run, Rimmy was already giving chase. Predators will be predators, and predators just love chasing prey. Rimmy was quickly upon her.

I turned and grabbed my backpack and retrieved some rope. I could tell Rimmy had caught the demon woman, and she was giving him fits. She was screaming and making cowlike mooing sounds and even roared a few times. While Rimmy was doing his thing, I had to make sure the lion was not going to be a problem. Mountain lions are tough, and their claws are deadly weapons. Acting fast, I tied the lion's front paws securely together and then the back paws together. I had a knit cap with me I used to cover its head. Then, I tied a length of cord so that the front and back paws were pulled together. *He's not going anywhere*, I thought.

I grabbed my walkie-talkie and called Dad. I guess people tend to panic when the last word they hear from you is something like "Dad, I got trouble, and I need prayer from everybody now because guns won't work."

But I did need their prayer.

Anyway, I had to spend some time telling Dad and everybody what happened. He turned up the volume so everybody in the camp could hear. I could hear Kaiyo and Tracker making their growly noises, and Goliath huffed a few times. Jack kept saying, "No way!"

In short order, Rimmy had tossed the demon lady over his shoulder, and was headed my way. She was making a tremendous racket and was cursing up a storm. She hadn't quite given up yet. A couple of times, she got away, and Rimmy had to chase her down and subdue her again. Everybody heard this. Dad was incredulous.

"So are you telling us you and Rimmy have just captured a special mountain lion and a demon?" he said.

"Sort of. Rimmy pretty much did it all by himself."

I made sure that Rimmy heard me say that too. I once heard a smart man say when it came to recognition, *men die for it and babies cry for it.* Watcher's need it too. And I was proud of Rimmy, and he knew it. He probably saved my life from that mountain lion. I am pretty sure that I could've gotten a killing shot on him, but because he was a Special, I hesitated. That was stupid on my part. Rimmy's intervention assured the lion was neutralized.

I told Jack to hurry and bring a tarp so I could wrap the cat. Jack would bring Peyton and my horse. I also needed Kaiyo. Rimmy would head on down and bring the demon lady back to camp. Dad agreed to the plan and told me Jack was already getting his things together.

I turned to Rimmy. The demon lady was still thrown over his shoulder, and she seemed to have tired herself out. I stood in front of Rimmy where only Rimmy could see me.

"Don't trust her," I said. "She is absolutely full of lies. Demons are masters at lying, and the minute she gets you alone, she'll start saying a bunch of malarkey. Keep in mind it was her lying boss who convinced Eve and then Adam to ruin everything. If she tries to talk to you and if it's getting to you, then just take her and beat her brains out on some rocks. It won't kill the demon, but it will have to leave nonetheless."

Rimmy's eyes were huge, and his mouth was wide open. He was aghast. Then, I winked at him, so he knew I was kidding. Relief immediately flowed into the beautiful lines of his amazing face. How Rimmy could look like a pure warrior while also show tenderness was beyond me.

I radioed Dad that Rimmy was coming, and he needed a ton of prayer cover. I also told Dad that sending Tracker and maybe Goliath to meet him on the way would be a good idea. I hugged Rimmy without touching the upended demon lady. He then turned and headed down the slope at a fast pace. When he turned, the demon lady lifted her head and stared right at me. She hissed and cussed like an angry, drunk sailor. I just smiled and waved goodbye to her. That really ticked her off.

In moments, Rimmy was moving fast downhill and was almost out of sight. That poor demon lady was bouncing so fast she started to blur up. She also couldn't get a word out either. He would be out of the forest shortly.

With Rimmy gone, I turned around to look at the mountain lion. With a stick, I pulled off the hat I had used to cover his eyes. He had awakened and was just lying there on his side. I pulled up a log a safe distance from him and sat. When the big cat saw me, he gave me his best angry mountain lion screech, and he started to writhe against his bindings.

Cougars aren't really listed as big cats. That list is limited only to cats that can roar; and only tigers, lions, leopards, and jaguars can roar. Still, this guy was big as far as cats go. A mountain lion is basically an enormous house cat. Their proportions are much the same. This guy was probably about 225 pounds, and no matter their puny voices, he was a big, dangerous cat.

I just sat and stared at him for a few minutes. He kept trying to break free until I finally said, "Please. Could you just give it a rest? You're fooling no one, certainly not me. You have turned your back on God, and it's not becoming of a great cat like you. Yes, I know you understand me. I also know you are aware we are in on your little secret. And I know you are smart. Big deal. You never saw Rimmy until he literally smacked the daylights out of you, and now, you are my prisoner. So quit your struggling and relax. Being smart has only made you a fool."

The cat blinked his eyes and looked at me. I think he didn't like me, but at least he quit his caterwauling. He also quit fighting. "So," I said, "you're a big strong cat. Why in the world would you team up with evil? What's that going to get you? It almost got you killed, and it still might. We just caught your pathetic little master. He…she… it was a joke. And I'm sure you're pals with some bigger, stronger demons, and they probably promised you something. What was it?

What could it possibly be? Did they promise you power? Revenge? Just keep in mind those slimy things lie for a living. Whatever they promised you, just trust me, you will never see it. In a few minutes, you can explain all this to my little brother. He's on his way now. Maybe he can hear you out."

That last statement got to him. Cats think differently than dogs and bears. I had no idea how to deal with a smart one. Even though these types are smart like people, they don't lose their natures. Bears are still bears, wolves are still wolves, and cats are still cats. They aren't people. That means when one goes rogue, they can be exceptionally dangerous. I knew this guy was likely very dangerous.

It wasn't long before Kaiyo came trudging up the hill; Jack was behind him riding Chevy and bringing Solo and Peyton. The cat heard them and screamed out. Kaiyo roared in reply and never missed a step; he just kept coming. The roar settled the cat right down. Jack was on high alert; his right hand never left the butt of his shotgun as it hung in the scabbard. His eyes were pacing from right to left. Jack was a big-time joker, but just then, he looked like all business. When they got close, I looked at them both and said, "No worries. We have the cat tied up, and the demon lady is our prisoner. Lighten up."

Kaiyo growled at me as he walked past me, and Jack didn't smile. I was confused.

Jack looked up at me and said, "Dean, we believe that black bull you saw is real trouble, more trouble for us than the demon lady and your little kitty cat here. Keep your shotgun handy, and let's get out of here quick."

Lavi—Kaiyo

I think Dean's bravery will get us all killed one day. Catching that demon thing was probably a terrible idea. Standing it down and praying was a good call, but having Benaiah catch it was really a crazy thing to do. Where in the Book does it ever say we ought to go running around catching demons and carting them home? Those things are terrifying to everybody except to Dean and maybe Benaiah. He even seemed to be enjoying himself as he ran by us. The demon thing slung over his shoulders gave me the pure creeps. I bet I knew a lot more about how dangerous those things were than anyone else in my family. On their own, they're bad enough, but when they get into somebody, they're hellish.

Anyway, I had a mountain lion to chat with. I passed my brother as Jack filled him in. I was no match for the big bull who was trying to kill Landon. Goliath said the bull was exceptionally fierce, and beating him was no guarantee. When he said that, I was stunned. Nothing was stronger than Goliath. Benaiah was close, but Goliath was stronger. Somehow, we had to get word to the cow and his black bear buddy that all is well. I think I could hold my own against the black bear, but he probably outweighed me by maybe another hundred pounds. That bull had about four thousand pounds on me.

I pulled myself in front of the mountain lion and looked him over. He was lying on his left side with his big paws tied up tight. He was helpless. Dean did a good job of tying him up. The cat's short muzzle was bloody on its left side, and dried blood was still on its snout. But his eyes were sharp and focused. I looked him over. Cats are super strong, and even though I was a lot bigger than him, I doubted my strength would match up. I'm sure he knew that too. I took my time.

Finally, I asked him his name. He just spit at me the way cats do. "So what's your plan?" I asked.

He looked at me oddly. "Seriously, you have a plan, right? We both come from the same place, so you have made your decision. So did one of Abaddon's minions get to you? They worked on Goliath for years, but Goliath figured it out eventually. You might remember Goliath as a big, nasty grizzly living in these parts."

The lion's eyebrows showed surprise. "Yeah, I thought so. So, again, what is your name? Is it like Fluffy or Boots or just Kitty? Those are good names for cats."

I quit speaking. The lion got sullen again and said nothing. He had to be uncomfortable, but he was my enemy, and sympathy toward him was unwarranted. I fully remembered that less than a half hour before, he had tried to kill my big brother. Unfortunately, we didn't have the time to spend with him like we did with Goliath a few years back. "So tell me. What should we do with you, Fluffy?"

"My name is Lavi," he said. "And do with me what you want, cub. I am your prisoner, after all. Now, go away and lick your slave master's boots."

Well, la-dee-dah, I thought to myself. This guy is trying to taunt me. Two could play that game.

"Okay," I said. "If you don't have any ideas, my brother does. He's gonna wrap you in a tarp like a house cat in a towel, and then, we'll drag your ill-tempered butt back to camp. I was trying to be nice, but have it your way."

I was disgusted with the lion. He was so full of pride; it was no wonder that he got bought and fooled by the bad guys. I was sure he fell for their flattery and some vague promises. So I got up and went over to where my brother was. He and Jack were waiting for me to finish.

"Any luck?" asked Dean in a low voice.

I shook my head, and my face must have given away my dislike of the lion. "Let's just shoot it," said Jack in a slightly too loud voice.

He winked at both of us. "Well," said Dean, "I once read cougar meat was really good to eat."

Like a dog wagging its tail, a cougar can't control its ears. Even though he was on the ground facing away from us, his ears were trying to turn to hear it all.

"Let's do this," said Dean. "Let's wrap him. There's no time to waste. But if he resists, then Jack, just shoot him in the head. Then, I might cut out his backstraps and tenderloin, and at least, we'll get a good meal out of him."

Dean was one smooth talker. Nobody was going to shoot Lavi if he was helpless. That would be murder. But the cat didn't know it. So Dean nodded for me to go back to where the cat was lying.

I shuffled over in my bear style and got back in front of him. The lion looked defiant, but I was thinking he was scared. I was wrong.

"Shoot me," said Lavi. "But nobody is going to wrap me up and drag me to some inquisition. I will happily die as long as I am trying to kill the first one of your despicable humans who touches me. I will not be mocked."

"What were you and your demon pal trying to accomplish?" I asked. "Answer it truthfully, and I will set you free."

I could not believe I said it, but I did.

The cat thought for a moment before he spoke. "It's obvious, isn't it? Even to a kept pet like you," he said with his annoying, pompous tone. "My partners want the secret to get back inside. They desire all of it, of course. They already own the earth, and they want the rest. Eden is a big part of it all. So they intend to get information from the hiker who you and your people are protecting. They are curious as to how he did what he did. My job is to provide protection to the interrogators. And that is all I agreed to tell. Now, set me free."

"Fair enough," I said. "I asked you to be truthful, and you were. I thought you were just a low-level thug and a toady, and I was right. Even worse, you're so filled with pride you call your masters your partners. They own your sorry butt, and you are too stupid to know it. If you try following us, one of us will be waiting for you. But I still have hope for you. I look forward to seeing you again."

"I can assure you that you will see me again, cub. Oh, and it will be on my terms, and I will enjoy killing you. Now, let me go, slave."

You know, it just took everything in me to keep calm. What I wanted was for Dean to come over and shoot him or club him and then wrap him up and drag him the two miles or so to camp. Lavi was dangerous, and he didn't have an ounce of grace or gratitude in him. I don't know what crawled up his backside, but Lavi was insufferable and frightening. But I made a deal, and I have been taught by my families, both on the farm and at home, to keep my word. Unlike other faiths, we are told to love our enemies, and we don't get to lie even if it promotes our purposes. Right then, though, I was tempted to renege on the deal and ask for forgiveness later. As a bear in this world, there are lots of dangers to deal with, especially as a young one. But having a smart, former citizen swear to kill me was totally getting to me.

I roared in Lavi's face and told him to bring it on. He would have to hurry, I was growing fast, and his already slim chances of killing me diminished each day. I went over to Jack and Dean. They were watching our discussion.

"That conversation didn't look very productive," said Dean.

Dean's voice immediately made me feel better. "So do we kill him, or do we take him as our prisoner?" asked Jack.

I shook my head at both options and pointed back up the hill. We played a quick twenty-one questions, and in a few moments, Dean realized I wanted to let Lavi go.

"Well," he said, "I trust your judgment. But he's still dangerous, right?"

I nodded vigorously at the question. I understand why we have the language gap, but it was always frustrating. Tracker is so patient, and he somehow always got his point across. I feel like I'm in a constant game of charades. Tracker tells me to *be the bear*. That just means nothing to me.

Dean looked at us and said, "Okay, so this guy is bad news. Jack, be ready to blow his head off if he moves a muscle. Kaiyo, stay right next to me and talk to him if he does something sketchy after I tell him what we are doing. I don't have to let him go. I'll let him know that too."

We walked over to the immobile lion. Dean stood over Lavi and explained what he was going to do. Jack kneeled and put the barrel of his shotgun on the top of Lavi's head. Then, Dean pulled out a fearsome hunting knife to cut the lion's bindings.

"I know you have a tendency toward being stupid because you like hanging out with the bad guys, so I'm just going to tell you what we are doing here even though it ought to be pretty obvious. Against my better judgment and only because Kaiyo wants me to release you, I am planning on cutting off the cords that have you all tied up. So if you move a muscle, my best pal Jack here will blow your brains out. If you somehow duck in time, I will gut you with my bowie knife, and if that isn't enough, you will have to face an angry grizzly while you are dealing with a severe gunshot wound and at least one deep stab to the gut. In short, you have almost no way to win. I am hoping you have at least enough intelligence to figure that out."

Dean was such a good talker. I looked at Lavi and told him to just be still. With a few quick pulls, Dean had cut through the cords. Lavi flexed his paws back and forth, but otherwise didn't move. Dean and Jack slowly stepped back a few feet. Dean then told Lavi to get to his feet. Lavi obeyed and looked at me. He hated me, but I think he really hated what I stood for.

"I look forward to seeing you again, Kaiyo," he said as he checked out his paws.

As he displayed his big, sharp claws, he whispered, "I told you I would kill you, and I meant it. I'll just wait until the time is right."

Geez, Lavi was a piece of work. "Yeah, yeah, yeah. That's a bunch of bold talk from a glorified tomcat," I said. "I can take you down now, and you know it. Move along, and go spray on some squirrels."

I still have no idea why I said that. I was pretty sure Lavi could beat me in a fight to the death. But it would be close. And besides, I knew time was on my side. Every day, I was growing bigger and stronger. Sometimes, I could feel it. It no longer surprised me when I could easily handle a boulder or a tree log that was impossible just a week before. In truth, I almost looked forward to taking on that snotty cat. I had a strong hunch I would face him sooner rather than later. Events later proved my hunch right.

Dean and Jack weren't quite sure what was going on, but they stayed alert. Jack and Dean had their shotguns pointed right at Lavi. With disdain, Lavi snarled and turned and headed back uphill. With two or three bounds, he was out of sight and disappeared back into the meadow. It dawned on me Lavi preferred living to dying, and while that wasn't much of an edge to exploit, it was a weakness. That demon lady probably didn't care as much about living. You can't kill a demon. The only thing killable is the body they've hijacked. Anyway, my goal was to avoid Lavi as long as possible.

"Well," said Dean, "I'm thinking that you and the lion were doing some major trash-talking back there."

Then, Dean got serious. "Be careful, Kaiyo," said Dean. "Cats are killers. They're good at it, and I bet that cat is more experienced than most. I know you have a lot of fight in you, and I'm proud of you, but avoid him if possible. I love you, little brother, so do be watchful, okay?"

Dean knelt and gave me a hug. With a paw, I easily wrestled him to the ground, and we laughed. It was time for us to get out of there.

TRIALS—TRACKER

Goliath and I caught up with Benaiah at the base of the foot-hills, and he was coming at us fast. Few things are faster than a watcher, and he had no plans to stop and talk. We both pulled up and reversed course. We turned and caught up with Benaiah and the demon thing, but we were both in a full out sprint. How was this happening? This was an unexpected problem. Why would anybody want to catch a demon?

While we raced back to camp, my mind wandered. The more time I spent with this family, the more I realized how much I missed their company. I know sin is common to all thinkers, but I almost believe that had Sam and Susan been given a shot at being first, they might have changed our story.

Their children are just like them too. But as good and as loving as they are, they do have a few rough spots. As a family, they are all a little reckless, and Sam and his son Dean are the most reckless. They aren't dumb reckless; in fact, they're both smart. They're just some-times too brave for their own good. And Dean is clearly the worst of the bunch. He has always shown a sort of bravery that is way out of proportion to his age. The Master must have plans for him because he was somehow still alive. My friend Goliath almost killed him a few years ago. Goliath had a different heart back then, and he was one of the most dangerous animals in the world. Dean, of course, tried to get close and shoot him. And now, Dean was bringing us a demon.

As we closed in on our campsite, the possessed woman started screaming. Amid being jostled around somewhat violently, she was saying terrible things about each of us. We have learned to ignore them. Demons want to draw us into their conversations. They mix truth with lies so they can destroy. Their goals are almost always to break up relationships. They want to destroy marriages, friendships, societies, and especially fellowship with the Master. Without relationships, a man in a crowded city is still totally alone. People who are alone are easy for them to pick off. And this particular demon was no different.

When we finally got close to our camp, we saw Sam, Libby, and Landon waiting. The closer we got to them, the more she screamed. Benaiah wasn't slowing down. He was done with her. I could see Sam holding rope and duct tape. Benaiah ran right up to Sam. In moments, Benaiah and Goliath held the demon woman, while Sam tied her up. She was surprisingly strong, and she writhed as if she was in pain, but Sam tied her up in no time. Libby duct taped her mouth too. I was glad. The venom coming out of that mouth was hard to listen to.

Our mission had somehow changed. We had a simple mission, and we just made it harder. Well, Dean had made it harder. But the one thing I know is we are judged on how we handle life. A change in plans, especially an unplanned one like this, is just life. Since we are not in control, I will assume that the Master has plans for both the demon and his poor victim, and all of us here are a part of their two stories. I am honored to be a part of it. Even though I think catching a demon is unwise, we all felt for the poor woman.

She had slumped to the ground and appeared to be asleep. By the looks of her, she was probably a woman of early middle age, perhaps lower thirties. However, she looked like she had lived a tough life, and the life she had while possessed was brutal on her frame. While I could not trust her because of the demon inside of her, she was heartbreaking to look at. If it were up to me, I would cast this demon out immediately. But that is not our role. We were not given the authority to do so. No, that power comes through the Master and can only be wielded by man.

Unfortunately, I knew this type of demon. I imagine Dean was as surprised as anyone when he prayed, and the demon didn't flee. Demons usually flee when bombarded by the prayers of a man or a woman who's a child of the Master. But this one was strong. Just like when Michael was once held up by the demon known as the Prince of Persia, this one did not intend to leave. Rarely have I ever seen a family with more faith, but I knew they would need every ounce of it to conquer this one. If they failed, the woman would probably be doomed.

Dean, Jack, and Kaiyo soon joined us. Once they unsaddled their horses, Jack took his and Dean's horses and the big horse away to the creek for much needed water. From there, he would take them back up the gentle slope past our camp and stake them out for pasture. The big horse I have known for years and his strength and gentle temper are lessons for all of us. I caught Kaiyo's eye and asked him to come over.

Kaiyo is like a little brother to me. He has much to learn, but he is also a very good student. I am proud of him. Raphael is the closest thing we have to a day-to-day ruler, and he sees greatness in Kaiyo. So did I. Kaiyo surprised me with his question.

"Hey, Tracker, you don't happen to know a mountain lion named Lavi, do you? Because we just had a run in with him."

That was not good news. "I do," I said. "And he is a very dangerous lion. He and I have been enemies for years. Did he have something to do with this demon woman here?"

"He did," said Kaiyo. "He was her bodyguard, and he would have killed Dean if Benaiah hadn't jumped in front of Dean and knocked him out.

"And get this," said a laughing Kaiyo. "Dean wanted to wrap Lavi up in a tarp, like people wrap up cats when they go to the vet. Then, Dean was going to drag him home with us. Oh, yeah, that would've been great."

I just rolled my eyes. Dean again, of course. Kaiyo was enjoying himself.

"Anyway, I got to talking to him, and he's just a true piece of work. He's got that annoying voice, and he's so pompous. And, Tracker, honestly, that guy is a Class A hater. He hates humans, and he hates me. We definitely didn't get along. And he said he was going to kill me. He meant it too."

Well, that was some even worse news. "Kaiyo," I said, "Lavi is a killer. And your impression was right—he despises humans. As long as I have known him, he blames humans for everything wrong in the world. He says paradise was ruined by man and the earth has since been ruined by man again and again. He looks at man as a disease. He has proven himself incapable of finding any good in humanity. Because of that, he has declared war on the Master. He does not understand the Master's love of man, so he is filled with resentment. As you noticed, his pride is limitless, and so he became easy prey to our enemies. But, Kaiyo, do not let your guard down. I have never known Lavi to make an empty threat. He would happily kill me if he had a way other than a straight-on, fair fight. He wouldn't win that one, but he rarely fights fair."

Kaiyo nodded; then, he looked at me, winked, and said, "Don't worry, Tracker. I can take him."

I didn't have his confidence, but I appreciated his attitude. "Well, let's stick close to camp, okay? I am worried, and I know you don't want me to worry too much, right?"

I said the last part like it was an order. Kaiyo then looked at me and said, "Seriously, Tracker, I have enough respect for Lavi to steer clear. And I know he's super dangerous. I'll be watchful, I promise. Dean on the other hand, who knows, right?"

Then, Kaiyo turned his attention back to the group. I loved that little bear. Well, he was not so little anymore, but I surely loved him. One day, he would be as big as Goliath. As for the demon, we had an issue, and Sam called for a meeting.

FREE—SAM

Susan has a saying about how to go at things that needed to be done. She always says, "First things first."

The wisdom of that simple statement can easily get lost in the urgency of what we were dealing with. When I get confused about what to do next, it is that statement that often comes to mind. And we had lots to do. We had a bull and a black bear somewhere out there wanting to kill Landon, we had a captured demon that was a booger to get rid of, and somewhere out there was a mountain lion that had it in for us; and if Dean's observations are correct, Kaiyo may be its next target. But if it is indeed first things first, then that demon had to go.

I asked Rimmy to take the demon lady and tie her to a tree about seventy-five yards away from camp and next to the creek. The creek had some nice low rapids there, and it would have a hard time hearing anything from us. Then, all of us except Major stood in a tight circle. We had three huge beasts plus Kaiyo who, at over three hundred pounds, was pretty big too, so the circle was not very tight. Everyone was looking at me.

"Well, Dean," I said, "you made Rimmy bring that thing here. Got any plans to exorcise it out of her."

Everybody turned to Dean. I knew he would have something to say, and I was right.

"Here's the way I see it," said Dean. "That demon there is the type discussed in the book of Mark. Remember some disciples tried to cast out a demon from some poor guy, but for some reason, they couldn't get rid of it? Finally, Jesus had to do it. Remember that? But then Jesus kind of chastised them for not having enough faith. Then, it says that type of demon requires much fasting and prayer. So I figured when I commanded it to leave, this demon was that type, and it didn't split because I don't have enough faith. Seriously, that surprised me too. I thought I was solid, but apparently, I have more pride than faith. You know more faith in me than in God. So I have some work to do."

When he said that, everybody just kinda looked at each other and nodded in agreement. So I looked at the Specials. "Y'all seem to be sure of your faith. Can you do this?"

All of them, by movements in response to my questions, made it clear the Specials were not exorcists. I didn't understand why, but I accepted it. I have just come to learn that when it comes to the Specials, the question "why" is usually unanswerable. So I thought for a moment and said, "Well, you all can pray for us, right?"

The four Specials agreed. I then looked at Libby. "Libby, let's me and you give it a shot. Are you up to it?"

Libby was quick to respond that she was. Landon was standing next to her, of course, and he spoke. "Sam, I think I could help."

"No," I said. "The demon woman down there by the creek had terrible plans for you. I remain concerned for your safety around her…or it. I think Libby and I got this."

Landon smiled, nodded, and stepped back. Rimmy went and retrieved the demon lady and had her sit in the middle of camp.

"Well, Dad," said Libby, "we haven't eaten since breakfast, so I hope this is enough of a fast to get the job done."

"No worries, Libby. We come at this with the faith we got. It ought to be sufficient."

I looked at Libby, and I could see she was concerned. The demon woman had chewed through the duct tape previously keeping her quiet. She was already mocking us and cursing up a storm. And believe me when I say she was saying some of the vilest and most disgusting things I have ever heard. My instinct was to destroy her, but a man led by instinct would be no better than the demon in that woman.

"Pray," I said to Libby. "Ignore her and pray hard."

We walked up to her. Rimmy held her down, but that didn't shut her up. She was shrieking every profanity known to man and then some. Out of her mouth came pure poison. Voices were coming out of her that were not made by that poor woman's voice box. At times, it even sounded like the throaty howls of an angry range bull. The noise was terrific.

For the next five minutes, Libby and I prayed over this demon. We commanded it to leave. We begged for God's help. We laid hands on the possessed woman, being careful, though, not to get bitten. But the demon was only laughing at us. It mocked us, and it mocked God. In doing so, my anger and Libby's became intense. Angry, we prayed even louder. The result was nothing but noise and condemnation from the demon lady. Rimmy was looking at us for direction. I looked at Kaiyo and Tracker for anything helpful. I didn't know what to do.

Just then, my attention was distracted by a hand on my shoulder, pushing me away. Landon stepped up, and the demon lady screamed in terror. She kept it up, while Landon got on his knees and grabbed the woman by either side of her head. Calmly, almost in a whisper, he said, "In the amazing name of Jesus Christ, leave us and leave this poor woman."

The screams of the demon woman abruptly ceased, and the woman passed out. And there was silence. And we all stood there in awe. Libby hugged me all the while looking at Landon like he was superman. I heard the creek and some birds, and I heard Jack whisper, "That was crazy."

Rimmy stood and looked. Goliath came up and sniffed at the woman's body. She was alive. Then, I heard Dean quietly say, "Thank you, Landon."

Tracker's tail wagged slowly. Kaiyo seemed pleased. And I realized, like Dean, I had a pride problem too. I guess the apple didn't fall too far from the tree. It's a whole lot easier being in the club of

Christians than it is being a true Christ follower. I had been taking my eye off the prize. I guess that I had backslid some. Maybe more than some. It's not that my behavior changed, but my focus did. I think I had more confidence in me than in Christ being in me.

I looked at Landon and said, "You knew you could help, didn't you? What made you so sure?"

Landon looked at the ground and then back to Libby. The both gave each other nervous smiles as their eyes locked briefly. Libby looked red in the cheeks. Landon scuffed the ground with his shoe. My tough little girl who had put Landon in his place a little earlier today seemed to have disappeared. Even a blind man could see where this was headed. Anyway, I cleared my throat, which brought them back into Montana.

"Yes, sir," Landon stammered.

Landon took a breath and gave a terrific answer. "Faith," he said, "is a gift of God. In the last week, I have seen some amazing things. I was trapped between dimensions. I was almost killed by a four-faced cherub. I literally talked back and forth to animals, including Tracker here. I saw into another world, and I was rescued by a family of soldiers from both worlds. So when I look around and I see this family, a family of people and animals the way they should be, I see a miracle. And that is on top of many other miracles I have seen, plus a lot more. So you ask why I have faith. I think anybody who did what I did would have a measure and a half of faith, right? Even a fool would come out of this past week with a laser focus on the truth. Life, regular life, did not get in my way like it does for everyone. I have been given a gift. I hope to be able to keep it."

And then, just behind us, we heard the woman start to cry.

Sarah's Day—Libby

When we heard her, I kneeled at her side. She was a thin woman, no taller than me, and she had a haggard face that didn't quite belong on somebody that I was assuming was only in her early thirties. Her hair was a long, matted mess. She had on a loose, long-sleeved flannel shirt, dirty jeans, and old Converse tennis shoes. She was filthy, and she smelled awful. But other than that, she could be any other unfortunate, drugged-out, homeless person. But drugged-out homeless people don't live in the Eastern Wilderness where we were, so she was way out of place.

Everybody was standing over her, and it was a little congested. Gently, I said, "Okay, y'all, let's give this poor girl some air. And if I'm not mistaken, don't we still have trouble with that cow thing and his black bear friend?"

I said that because if it was as big as they say, it might be a bad guy. Also, the lady needed some space, and from her point of view, all she saw besides me was a bunch of males, carnivores, and a watcher standing over her. I assumed that sight was more than intimidating. Everyone dispersed, and Dad started barking out some orders about getting camp ready and needing guards. All around us, Dad, Dean, and Jack saw to it that camp was set up, while the Specials went out as some impressive sentries.

I turned back to her, and we locked eyes. I didn't expect to see intelligence, but I did. I don't quite know what I expected to see, but it was not that. She sat up and pulled her legs up to her chest with her arms around her knees. She broke my gaze and started looking around. She seemed embarrassed while she wiped her runny nose on her sleeve. She looked away for a few moments, and then, she turned back at me.

"I know where I am," she said. "And I know who you are. You're Libby McLeod. That big bear over there is Goliath. He had a different name before he met you. He used to be a friend to my old master before you guys got to him."

She held back a sob, but she started softly crying again. She got a hold of herself again and whispered, "I don't want him to be my master anymore. He's strong, and he's terrifying. But here with you guys, I can't hear him anymore."

In the midst of her tears, she managed a little laugh as she said, "Your whole family here has my old master concerned. He hates you all."

That didn't surprise me. I looked back at her. She was breaking my heart. Her story was awful and unfortunately seemed to have been very real. I was interested in her story. "So," I asked, "you know my name. What's yours?"

"Sarah. Is *sarah* place I can get a drink around here?" she said laughing. "Sorry, that's an old joke."

I didn't laugh, so she continued. "My name is Sarah Tompkins. I went to high school in Helena. I even went to UM for a couple of years. Go Grizzlies!" she said as she weakly pumped her fist in the air.

She continued. "For a while, I was even in a sorority, until they kicked me out," she laughed. "Look at me, hard to believe, right? I'm only twenty-eight, but I look like I'm sixty-eight."

She looked at herself. "Gross. And I'm dirty, and I smell terrible."

Then, in a barely audible whisper, she said, "I haven't seen my parents in a long time."

I needed her to think better, less self-destructive thoughts. I changed the topic. "What size are you? You look like a two or maybe a small four. You're pretty thin."

Sarah was confused. "What?" She smiled. "Why are you asking that?

"Well, I always bring an extra shirt, pants, socks, and underwear. Always. I hate being wet, and crossing creeks is always risky. I have an idea. Let's take you down to the creek and get you a bath. We'll burn those clothes of yours too. For shoes, you can wear my moccasins. It will be a little chilly, but it's summer, so it won't be too bad. What do you think?"

"A bath," she said, "even in a cold creek, sounds terrific." Then, she looked around, "But everybody can see."

First off, I was pleased with the modesty. "No worries, Sarah. I got this."

I called Rimmy over and told him what I wanted to do. Then, I asked him to take a tarp and to drape it so it would shield Sarah from view while she bathed. He easily agreed and got to it. I then went to my overnight case and opened it. There, I always keep a small bottle of shampoo, a bar of soap, and conditioner. We get them free from hotels when we travel. Then, I went to the boys and to Dad. I told them what I knew and that her name was Sarah Tompkins. I also told them what we were going to do and to stay at the campsite. I grabbed my moccasins and walked back to a waiting Sarah.

"Here we go. A flannel shirt, clean underwear, clean jeans, and socks ought to do the trick. And, Sarah, if you aren't grossed out, you will be keeping my toothbrush after I use it in a few minutes."

What did I care? By noon tomorrow, I would be home. "Oh my gosh," said Sarah thankfully. "That would be a luxury. Seriously, you have no idea how nice that will be."

Actually, I did know. Her breath was horrible. I doubt she had brushed her teeth in months. Fortunately for her, her mostly carnivorous diet kept her teeth in surprisingly good condition.

We wandered down to the creek. Behind the tarp was a wide, deep hole of about three to four feet. I sat on a rock while Sarah undressed. She was too thin, but she had more meat on her bones than some super models. She put her nasty clothes in a pile and gently stepped into the flowing water. "Oh geez!" she exclaimed. "It's soooo cold!"

I laughed. "Get in, you witch. Afraid you're going to sink?"

"Hey, you guys were supposed to fix the witch thing!"

By this time, Sarah and I were laughing hard. And the water was cold. "Go on, get in," I said.

She took a minute to get in; then, she took the soap and got to work. She was quick about it, but she was deliberate. While she was there, we talked about her upbringing, and I shared mine. Strangely enough, she was raised a lot like me. Her parents were, by her own admission, great folks and good parents. She described them as not overtly religious but decent and good. It was her decisions though, she said, that led to her problems. She then asked me about my life. I told her what I could, but since she already knew all about the Specials, I really didn't have any secrets to keep from her.

After about ten minutes, Sarah's lips were blue, and she was shivering uncontrollably. She was clean, and her long hair was washed, but she asked for just a few more minutes. She went underwater and came up and looked back at me.

"Libby, you have to experience real filth, both inside and out, to truly appreciate being clean. This water is cold, but it's wonderful too. Look at it, it's clear as glass. And my filth is already downstream. I don't ever want to go back. You'll help me with that, right?"

"It would be my honor, Sarah."

I must admit that last utterance of mine was said with a lump in my throat. I said a prayer right then thanking God for Dean. Everybody else would've left Sarah with the demon. Then, I thanked God for Sarah, and I prayed she would get to know him like we do.

I smelled the beautiful smoke of our campfire. There was still plenty of light, but the sun was getting lower in the sky, and even in the summer, that meant it would start getting chilly.

"All right," I said, "everybody out of the pool."

Sarah climbed out of the creek and shivered in the light breeze. I threw her my towel, and she dried off. She seemed to be rediscovering her skin, so she took her time. I didn't rush her; she'd been through a nightmare. She got dressed and came over to me. Her clothes hung loosely, but they fit well enough. We talked some more as I brushed out her hair. That took some time as it hadn't been brushed in a while. Before her bath, Sarah's hair looked like a dirty gray. I would never have guessed her hair was a beautiful brunette color with natural red tints.

She brushed her teeth and took her time with it too. She drank freely from her bottle of water. Then, she turned to me, and there before me stood a pretty girl.

I blurted out, "Damn, girl. Where were you hiding? You look so much better."

I laughed, and she kept peppering me with questions like "Really?" and "What do I look like?"

I reached in my overnight kit and handed her a mirror. When she saw herself, she burst into tears. "Oh God," she said. "I remember me. What have I done?"

I gave her a hug and waited a few moments for her to pull herself together. "Trust me," I said. "Just remember the thief on the cross. Whatever you did probably wasn't as bad as what he did, and he's just fine."

"Huh? What thief?"

"We'll fill you in later. It's a great story. You'll love it. Hungry?"

"Starving!"

Well, we were out in the middle of a wilderness, but when we walked from behind the tarp, we could hear the gasps. I guess it was sort of a low-rent reveal. Neither of us had makeup, and with Landon around, I was wishing I had brought some. As we walked up from the creek, I could hear Jack whistle. We kept coming up, and the males stepped aside as Sarah walked past them and went straight to the campfire. One by one, she dropped her filthy clothes into the fire and watched as the flames ate away at the fabrics. Lastly, the shoes went in. The soles put out a dark sooty smoke. It all had the look of a sad little ceremony, and I guess it was. Everybody stood aside as she quietly watched the flames. Dad finally broke the ice by going up to Sarah and putting an arm over her shoulders. "Let's pray guys. Come on."

Dad prayed over Sarah and for Sarah to find the freedom found in God's love. He also prayed for protection for the night and for the trip home in the morning. When he was done, Sarah looked at him and thanked him for the prayers and for taking care of her.

Dad laughed his sweet laugh and said, "Well, I'm going to put you to work, so you might want to hold up on those thanks."

Sarah smiled. "Bring it on! And still, thank you!"

Dad looked at me and told me to come with him to get the huge saddlebags we hung off Peyton. He told Sarah and Dean to grab the blankets for sitting and then to get some firewood. Dad and I walked off together. He told me he had instructed Landon to keep his adventure quiet until we got home. I had a ton of questions for Landon, but he told me Sarah hadn't yet earned our trust. She wasn't a Christian, at least not yet, and even most Christians couldn't be trusted to keep Landon's secrets. That made sense; the stakes were high.

Next, Dad and I collected all the food we had left. Everybody had skipped lunch, and everybody was hungry. Plus, we had our three additional, huge beasts to join us at the table.

Dad called for the Specials to join us. Then, he asked us to sit on the blankets while the Specials sat behind us. Major was paying really close attention. He knew what was coming.

"Okay!" said Dad to the group. "We had an amazing day. No question about it. We have been blessed with being a part of helping two people being found even though both were lost in totally different ways. Like the old hymn, they were lost, but now, they're found."

I clapped, and so did Jack and Dean. Everybody gave out some whoops, and even a few whoops came from the Specials. Landon and Sarah looked both happy and embarrassed. We were having a good time. It was like a regular campout. At that moment, I strangely missed Mom and Gracie. I wish they were here to enjoy this part.

Dad continued. "So we have some more good news, but we also have some bad news. Who wants the good news first?"

Kaiyo piped up so Dad pointed to Kaiyo and said, "Good news it is. Okay, tomorrow morning, we are all headed to the farm where Susan will have a feast ready for everybody. There will be steaks, pot roast, fried chicken, mashed potatoes, hash browns, pies, and all the fixins. These two lost children are returning, and they and their rescuers deserve the best. Dean, when we get going in the morning, do you think you can ride ahead and give Mom the good news?"

Dean readily agreed, and Jack said he would go with him. The two bears volunteered as well. "Okay, now for the bad news. As good as were going to eat tomorrow night, tonight will be slim pickings for everybody. Obviously, we didn't bring enough food for everybody, but we believe everybody gets treated equally. So, Libby, let's get started."

Jack came up and placed his five sandwiches and a pound or so of beef jerky onto the blanket in front of Dad. He told us to share them. We had dog food in abundance for Major, so he was first. Dean took him to the side and poured out a good portion for him. He ate greedily. We had two of Kaiyo's big, well-marbled steaks left. Dad cut them in two and handed each to Tracker, Rimmy, Goliath, and Kaiyo. Gracie had packed another eight peanut butter and jelly sandwiches, three of those were originally for Kaiyo. Dad looked at Sarah and asked if she could handle a PBJ. She said *yes*. Landon also said *yes* when asked. Then, Dad gave me, Dean, Jack, and himself a sandwich.

We all ate. Sarah took her time, so did Rimmy. Kaiyo, Goliath, and Tracker maybe took three seconds to eat their steaks. The rest of us ate quickly. Sarah just laughed at how good it was. She pulled bite-sized pieces away from the sandwich and relished each bite. Dad passed around water that had been boiled. It was warm but good.

Then, Dad pulled out four pounds of uncooked bacon and handed a pound to each the Specials. That gave each of them another 2,000 calories. We had another six MREs, and Dad gave each of us a choice between that or a sandwich. Dean and Jack opted for the sandwiches, and Dad handed out the MREs. The remainder of the sandwiches were handed to the Specials. Goliath and Rimmy got the PBJ's made for Kaiyo because they were huge and so were the sandwiches.

After that, we all settled into enjoying our meals. After a few minutes, Rimmy came up and put his hand on Dad's shoulder. "Go dogs," he said lightly.

Then, he laughed and pointed to where he was planning to go for the night. He and Dad communicated, and Rimmy walked away to the creek and to his post. Rimmy always preferred the woods to the prairie, and his being out in the open grassland during daylight was a first.

Goliath got up, wandered over to Sarah, and put his enormous head on her shoulder, next to her face. She cradled his big head in her arms and then buried her face in his fur. She cried and then whispered a thank you in his ear. I guess they both once had the same master, and they uniquely understood each other. Then, Goliath lifted his head and put a gentle but enormous paw on her face, and they just looked at each other for a few moments. After that, Goliath walked past her and over toward the creek. Sarah just looked at me, wiped away a tear, sniffled, and said, "Good bear."

I laughed. She went back to what was left of her meal, looked at it, and gave the rest to Major. Kaiyo went to the creek to join Goliath. There, they settled into grazing on the sweet, green grass that flourished by the creek's banks. Tracker sat with us. I just decided to trust their sniffers and believe we were safe for now.

Jack and Dean went and restaked the horses so they could graze on the new grass. When they got back, Dean plopped on the blankets, looked at Sarah, and said, "Sarah, are you ready to change teams yet?"

"Dean," she said, "I was wondering if anybody was going to ask."

Then, she got serious. "But I am nothing like you guys. I have a history, and my past is really awful. It's worse than awful, Dean. It's disgusting. I am pretty sure your god doesn't want or need people like me."

She wasn't kidding, but she also didn't know Dean.

"Well, Sarah," said Dean, "I am counting on this fact. If you can't get in, then neither can I. Or my dad or my sister and definitely not Jack here!"

Jack hit him but kept quiet. "Okay, you're going to hear the *Reader's Digest* version, okay?"

Sarah nodded. She pulled her knees up to her chest, while Dad went and got a blanket to cover her shoulders. And Dean got started. "Sarah, you probably look at God as people have from the beginning of time. There's also no telling how much crap you've been told. Most people look at God as the rule maker in the sky. They also believe only the good get to heaven. Is that sort of what you think? God loves the people who are good, and he hates the people who are bad?"

Sarah looked at Dean and said, "They told me God plays favorites, and I wasn't one of them…"

"Of course," said Dean. "If they hadn't told you, then you would have said it to yourself anyway. The most dangerous lies are usually the ones we tell ourselves. But you're dead wrong about God. Trust me on this, though. You are definitely not good enough to get into heaven, and no matter what, you never will be."

I knew where Dean was headed with this, but Sarah didn't. Sarah looked at him with a confused face. Dean continued. "But I am not good enough to get into heaven either. None of us are. There aren't enough good deeds in the world to counteract my sin.

Everybody sins. Everybody. You do, Jack does a ton, I do…but only rarely."

Then, he winked at Sarah and said, "The truth is, I sin all the time. Shoot, just yesterday morning, I was having sinful thoughts about Jack's sister."

Jack groaned. Dad looked down and slowly shook his head. Sarah laughed.

"But God gave us his Son Jesus to take our sin. People killed him for it, but he rose from the dead. Jesus beat death so that we could too. It's a terrific story, but the part we want to talk about here is about the thief."

Dean paused and then continued. "So the Romans crucified Jesus between two thieves. They must have been some seriously bad guys because the Romans usually reserved crucifixion for acts of treason. Trust me, those two bad guys didn't just steal a loaf of bread. The Greek word used for them is different than their regular word for *thief.* This Greek word meant *plunderers.* So they were probably like rebellious, murderous pirates who went after something Roman and maybe killed some Romans, and they got caught doing it."

"Anyway, because of a conversation while hanging on the cross, one of the thieves was kind to Jesus and acknowledged Jesus' innocence and his own sin. The thief asked Jesus to remember him when Jesus came into his kingdom. Here's the kicker—Jesus told the thief that he would see him in paradise that very day. Amazing! So, Sarah, while the criminal was up on the cross, how many good deeds could he do?"

Sarah thought for a moment. "Well, none really."

"Exactly," said Dean. "There were no old ladies he could help cross the street. I doubt he ever went to church, and he certainly couldn't while hanging on the cross. There was no money he could give to the poor. He couldn't save somebody's life. Nope, he was what he was—a very, very bad guy. But he put his trust in Jesus. And that was all it took."

Sarah smiled as Dean kept going. "Sarah, God is a god of infinite grace. That's what we depend on. We can never make it on our own. We will always fail. But Jesus will take your sin away if you want him to. But he will never make you do it. It's your choice. And, Sarah, you can be sure of one thing. No matter what you did, even with you trying to be besties with the devil as recently as this morning, all of it combined isn't enough to condemn you, unless condemnation is what you want. Sarah, never, ever confuse your crummy life as a measure of God's love. He's just waiting on you to turn to him."

Dean quit talking for a few moments. Then, he looked at Sarah and said, "So what are you waiting for?"

Sarah looked back, smiled, and said, "Let's do it!"

And right there, under the big Montana sky, with the stars starting to emerge, Sarah met God for the first time. Tears were mixed with laughter and all in abundance. I had always wanted an older sister, and now, I had one. The absurdity of it all—this demon-possessed woman was now a child of God. I know it has happened before, but not in front of me, and it was a beautiful thing to see.

Kaiyo roared. Tracker howled in pure happiness. Rimmy gave his elated response from the woods by the creek. Goliath grabbed Sarah and covered her with his enormous arms. Goliath just groaned. His joy was felt by everyone. Only Goliath could understand what she went through. They both knew the pure, destructive evil of their former common oppressor. And now, they were both free.

Sarah had indeed been lost, but now, Sarah was found.

6

GOING HOME—DEAN

I woke to darkness. Before I moved, I opened my eyes but only barely. I listened. With my right hand clutching my knife just in case, I made no movements to betray the fact I was awake. I heard a few barely audible pops from our dying campfire and then heard the rhythmic breathing of Kaiyo and Major. I could hear tossing and turning from within the tents. Sarah mumbled weakly in her sleep. Then, I heard footfalls coming quickly from the horses, gliding through the sedge and pine grass. With the horses being quiet, that would be Tracker. The horses knew him and liked him.

Years ago, Dad taught me to be careful in the woods. That included waking up carefully. Of course, this time, it was all practice. I was not remotely worried about anything creeping up on me because they would have to get past Major and the Specials. But practicing is always smart. Opening my eyes further, I saw the enormous wolf settle down next to Kaiyo and Major. Tracker had just finished his patrol. I couldn't hear Goliath, but he was sure to be nearby. He was probably getting up too. Kaiyo, on the other hand, would sleep until the last minute.

The night was cold, and Jack and I slept outside. The two girls were in one tent, and Dad and Landon in the other. It made sense because they didn't have to wake up early. Jack and I and the bears had agreed to leave early to fill Mom and Gracie in on the hungry crowd that would be coming. The night was peaceful, and when I slept, I slept hard. But I needed to get going well before everybody else for my warning to do any good. In June, mornings in Montana come mighty early. There's almost enough light to ride by 5:00 a.m., and leaving at that time was the plan. I would have the sun to my back. That's a good way to travel.

I pulled myself out of my bedroll. The night before, I gave Sarah my sleeping bag, so I slept in my bedroll. I had simply slept in what I had on, so I was both warm and ready to go. Jack had done the same thing; he gave Landon his sleeping bag. Once out, I emptied out my boots of whatever was in them, if anything, pulled them on, and stood up. Then, I whispered in the darkness to Jack to wake up. He was already up and rolling up his bedroll.

The night before, Dad and I had loaded up my saddlebags with what I might need for the short trip home and some dirty clothes I could wash when I got home. Jack loaded his saddlebags too. To be honest, I was looking forward to seeing Kate, so I happily accepted Dad's assignment. I hoped to beat the main group by three hours, and that was plenty of time to take on some chores, get a shower, and maybe have some time with Kate before everybody got there.

I also knew we might run into the big bull and his bear buddy. I didn't want that thing going after Landon or Sarah, and I didn't want Libby or Dad to go all hero and try to stop it. The night before, I gave Landon a pair of my clean socks, and I had him put his nasty socks in a baggy and give them to me. They were rank, but I figured I might need them later, and I was right. I made sure they were in my saddlebags too.

We had another fifteen minutes until twilight, so we took our time getting our horses. I didn't want to cross the creek in the black dark; that's just a bad idea. I needed at least a little light. When I got to Solo, he was hard to see. Solo was a beautiful dun. I loved my horse, and he knew it. I brought him an apple and waited for him to finish it. Then, I whispered in his ear, "Let's go home."

Most animals that live with man learn a few words. Solo knew several words, and one of his favorite words was *home*. He liked it so much he didn't fight the bit. Whenever I know I am going to get up early, I try to put the bit in my bedroll or my sleeping bag so it's warm and not so unpleasant for Solo. I did that this time, but I think Solo would have happily chomped on a frozen bit if it meant going home. Home for Solo meant rest and better food. For me, it meant all that plus Kate. The party that was sure to follow sounded nice too.

Jack and I led our horses back over to the edge of camp. We got our horses' pads, blankets, and saddles and quietly got to work getting the horses ready to go. I asked Jack if he needed me to lift his heavy saddle, but all I got in return was a series of whispered, slightly profane insults. We laughed, and it was obvious that we were both looking forward to going home.

Out of the side of my eye, I saw Dad coming at us in the darkness. I kept working on Solo as Dad came up to talk to us. Dad first put a sandwich and a small bag of beef jerky in each of our saddlebags. They were the last of the leftovers. Dad made sure we had our guns, bear spray, some water, and filter straws for creek water. Tracker came up and sat next to us. Goliath and Kaiyo came up too. Dad kept his voice low and told us to be careful and to keep an eye out for the big bull.

Tracker and Goliath indicated it wasn't near here. We all believed the bull and the black bear probably went back to wherever they came from when they saw Rimmy and Goliath and all of us with guns. The likelihood they happened to be going in the direction of the farm was pretty slim too. There is a lot of land on all points of the compass in the Eastern Wilderness for them to be. I wasn't worried in the least. Running into a mother grizzly or a cow moose were legitimate concerns, but that was about it.

"Rimmy is waiting for you two on the other side of the creek. Let him escort you through the woods along the west side of the creek. That ought to only be about sixty to seventy yards. Then, you'll be back in the open. From there, just head back the way we came. If you go straight through, you might be home in three or four hours. I'll get a fire started and let Sarah and Landon get some much-needed sleep. I'll have their horses ready by the time they wake up. We'll probably be leaving around seven o'clock. Because we have two green riders, we also won't be moving as fast, so I expect we'll get home about two hours after you."

I gave Dad a hug, and then, Dad gave Jack a hug. "You know you're family, don't you? You two be careful out there and watch each other."

"Yes, sir," said Jack. "I've known that for a long time. My mom says all of us Gibbses ought to just go ahead and hyphenate our names and add McLeod."

In my mind, I thought adding McLeod to Kate's name would be a good idea someday too. We both hopped up on our horses. Dad reached out and held onto Solo's cheekpiece.

He looked at both of us and said, "Watch your back trails. It's actually a lot easier to do it when you're alone. When it's the four of you, it's easy to get complacent. Be alert. We may not be done with this adventure yet. And, Dean, if trouble comes up, don't protect a Special if it wants to harm you. That mountain lion nearly got you because you hesitated."

"No worries, Dad. We got this," I said.

I was serious, and I wasn't afraid. I was just ready to go. Dad laughed and said, "I fully believe you believe that. Just stay alert, and you ought to be fine. Take the walkie-talkies just in case."

Dad put one in Jack's saddlebags, and the other one, he put in mine. Then, Dad spoke to the bears and gave Kaiyo a hug. He told them to keep a watch on me too. I laughed and shook Dad's hand, and we pulled out into the darkness. It was light enough to see the trees outlined against the sky. In short order, we made it to the creek, and we let the horses and the bears drink their fill.

In a few minutes, I heard Rimmy come up on the other side about fifty yards upstream. We led the horses north and stopped when we heard Rimmy grunt. With Goliath and Kaiyo leading the way, we waded the creek and easily made it to the other side. Rimmy picked a good crossing place. Solo knew Rimmy well, and Chevy had gotten accustomed to Rimmy and Goliath on this trip. Neither were frightened as Rimmy grunted, and we followed. The woods were thick, and it took another ten minutes to pick our way through. Several times, we heard something crash through the woods away from us, but we were not remotely worried; nothing wants to tangle with a watcher and two grizzlies.

By the time we made it to the edge of the woods, it had gotten noticeably lighter. We said our goodbyes to Rimmy and moved out into the open grassland. By now, the light was dim, but we could see though everything looked gray. I knew we could go faster, but until it got lighter, I didn't want to push it; there are a lot of holes that are hard to see in the dark. The eyesight of bears at night is much better than ours, but there was no need to risk injury to the horses. We rode to the southwest at a walk for the next twenty minutes, and then, we picked up speed; the shadows were still long and dark, but we had plenty of light by then. It amazed me how the bears could easily keep up.

Along the way, Jack and I would stop and check our back trail for anything following us. We also talked about a ton of things. He congratulated me for convincing Rimmy to capture Sarah while she was possessed. That took some convincing too. We laughed as we remembered how Rimmy really didn't want to do it. Jack and I talked about Sarah finding God and how amazing that all was. Every time someone comes to God, it's a miracle. Being a part of it is an honor. I knew God had his hooks in her, so if it wasn't me helping, it would have been somebody else, probably Jack, Libby, Gracie, or Mom. I'm just glad I didn't blow the opportunity. I've done that a few times, and I will always regret my cowardice.

We rode at a good clip for another hour with the sun to our back when we approached a rocky ridge that rose up from the flatter grasslands we were in. This rocky peninsula pointed like a fat finger from the mountains of the north into the open grasslands to the south. There were scattered trees on the slopes that increased in number the higher and farther to the north it went. It was basically a ridgeline of low cliffs and half-buried boulders, interspersed with small trees. When we came this way when we were looking for Landon, we had skirted well to the south of here, but we could see the ridge rise up from the plain. Now, the ridge was in our way.

A mile before we got to the ridge, we gathered in a small patch of timber to check our back trail again and to rest the bears. The sun was right in our eyes when we looked back down our trail so if something was following us, it would have an advantage. We dismounted, and the four of us discussed working our way up and over the ridge and through the lusher area to its west. Even though that would have been a more direct route home, we discarded the idea quickly. Exploring is always fun, but we all wanted to get home. Shortcuts aren't always a good idea. We would go around it.

As we were about to ride out of our little patch of timber, both Goliath and Kaiyo huffed. Jack and I immediately pulled up. Kaiyo saw something on the top of a medium-sized cliff on the ridge. I pulled out my binoculars, looked, and handed them to Jack.

"Well, well, well," said Jack. "There's a black bear who seems mighty interested in things our way. Watch him. He's standing and looking. He has no idea we are here. Kaiyo, Goliath, do you think he saw us?"

Both bears shook their heads *no*. I agreed. We came at the right time; the bear was blinded by the sun. But as for us, his black fur stood out nicely. The winds were fickle, and at times, we were downwind and upwind sometimes too.

Jack then asked, "Do you think that's the bear you saw yesterday?"

"Yeah," I said. "He's acting like he has a job to do. He's not acting like a regular bear. The problem is we don't know where his big beefy friend is. But I would bet you he's trying to ambush us. Kaiyo, you got a sniff or two of them yesterday. Is that the black bear from yesterday?"

Kaiyo nodded. Jack agreed about the ambush and added, "If he's as big as you say, then he is bigger than a buffalo. That's a dangerous beast, and for some reason, they want to kill Landon and maybe us."

THE PLAN—KAIYO

I was getting pretty tired, so I was liking our little recess in the woods. The wind was unsteady, but I was getting occasional whiffs of the black bear and the bull. That meant they might be getting whiffs of us too. At least, they couldn't see us.

Dean casually reached around his saddlebags and pulled out a bag of socks. He pulled one out and hung it on a tree. I immediately knew it was Landon's sock. People and bears smell things differently. Dean acted like the socks stunk; I thought they smelled like Landon. Then, Dean asked us if we knew either the bear or the bull. Sometimes, Dean doesn't get it. He must think home is like a small-town zoo, like there are three bears here, a few lions there, and a giraffe. He's wrong; home is huge. The Master created a country and maybe even a world. I have only begun to see a tiny bit of it.

But, to my surprise, Goliath did know the big bull. I guess I owed Dean a silent apology. Goliath looked at me and said, "Yep, I know him. He's a somewhat prideful aurochs. He's got a bad temper, but he's super loyal to the Master. Aurochsen are an extinct type of cattle, and they're big and strong. In fact, a lot of the world's cattle came from aurochsen. The general rule is extinct species are supposed to stay home, but some just can't help themselves. The Master prefers they stay home because their presence over here confuses the nonbelievers. Those folks are confused enough."

That was true. Goliath and I laughed while the two boys just looked at us with confused faces. They didn't have a clue what we were talking about. "Yeah," I said. "I did notice there's a lot more creatures there than here. There are some crazy-looking things there."

"Oh, you haven't seen anything yet!" whispered Goliath. "There are huge bears there that have long legs who could easily take me out if they wanted to. I'm big here, but not so big there. That's one of many stupid reasons I gave myself to leave the first time. Anyway, now that humans have cameras everywhere, it's even more important the rules are followed. Strange-looking animals attract a lot of negative attention really quick. A few flying serpents learned the hard way about that a while back. They got shot up and killed by some cowboys. Anyway, there's a lot less variation of animals than there used to be. I'll explain why later. Or you can ask Raphael."

"What!" I gulped. "You know about that?"

"Who doesn't?" said Goliath. "But right now, we need to focus on the aurochs. His name is Aylmer. It means something like *noble* and *famous* in old English. And he thinks he is noble. He's been warned about his pride, but he's bullheaded. And now you know where that term comes from."

"Well, how do you stop Elmer?" I asked. "He sounds like a beast."

"First of all, he hates to be called Elmer. Second, remember, he's wrong, but he's not evil. He wants to kill Landon because he thinks Landon escaped and is going to reveal some secrets God doesn't want revealed. But Landon never escaped. He was let go. Big difference, right?"

I nodded. "But why does he hate his name? It's nice."

"Because, little bear, it's Aylmer, not Elmer. I can't really tell the difference, but to me Aylmer is harder to say than Elmer. It sounds a lot like the way your human cousins from South Carolina talk."

He had a point there. They can stretch a one syllable word into a three-syllable word without trying. "So can we just talk to him? He's already breaking the rules. He's extinct, right?"

"Sorta," said Goliath. "For most of us, the rules are more like guardrails though some of us don't understand. They think the rules are arbitrary, but they're not. They're mostly in place to protect us animal folk from doing dumb things and getting hurt. But with Aylmer being an aurochs, he basically just looks like a really big cow. He could easily pass for a big gaur or a banteng."

"What are those?" I asked.

"Really big cows," said Goliath with a smile. "Now, let's seek a solution. You are right. We do need to talk to him. Tracker would sure be handy right about now. He's diplomatic. But we are on our own, and we have to put an end to this quickly. Unfortunately, getting his attention is hard. He tends to charge. So, Kaiyo, how fast are you? Can you keep up with the dogs yet?"

Personally, I was almost offended. I can outrun them both. Not by much, but I do it all the time. I told him I could, and the next thing he said was, "Good. Then, you are the bait."

That was interesting. And frightening. I could tell Jack was getting impatient, but Dean trusted us. He knew we weren't just wasting time. Dean told Jack to "simmer down."

Then, Goliath laid out his plan to me. Goliath didn't want anybody to get hurt, but this goofy bull was in our way, and we all wanted to go home. Dad's promise of a feast today had Goliath thinking hard. Plus, he told me it was time to see everybody again. He's especially fond of Gracie. She gave him his first lesson on God's grace, and he never forgot it.

The plan was dangerous. I hoped I was as fast as I thought I was.

BAD BEEF—DEAN

Jack and I watched Goliath and Kaiyo converse for the last few minutes. I got used to having a bear around, but I am always amazed he is my little brother. Watching him talk to Goliath was fascinating too. I had no idea what they said to each other, of course, but it was fun to watch. It didn't take long for me to figure out they were hatching a plan. I also didn't worry I wouldn't be able to understand them when they were ready. Somehow, we always managed.

I saw Kaiyo nod. Goliath came over to me and made some motions. Again, we played some charades, but I quickly understood the big bull was nearby and that Kaiyo and I would be the bait to flush him out. I was also to try to rope him. That would be like roping a big bison, and that's plain crazy, but I trusted Goliath.

I told Jack that killing the bull was the last resort. He learned to rope last summer, so I told him to make a lariat and hide in the woods with Goliath until the time was right. Then, I reached up and grabbed Landon's rank sock I had previously put in a tree and put it over my pommel. Kaiyo and I then strolled out of the woods and made sure the black bear saw us. Hopefully, the bull would get hasty and make a run at us.

The black bear saw us and immediately vanished into the rocks. We walked straight at the ridge and then turned slightly to the south. As if on cue, the big bull stepped from behind a boulder. He was truly one big animal. In fact, he seemed even more enormous than when I saw him the day before. And he was charging right for me.

DOHV—KAIYO

Well, there he was. From behind some boulders out came Aylmer. He was big, but I focused on those horns. Those things came out of his head, curled forward up and over his face and snout, and rose to point directly at me. I'm not going claim I wasn't scared, because I was. It wouldn't even be a close fight. I even think Dean was scared.

I'll give it to Aylmer. Except for a little pawing of the ground, he didn't waste any time. He acted on Landon's sock scent, and he bolted right at us in a full charge. Dean and I turned to run. I didn't look back because I was afraid of what I would see. After a few seconds, Dean and Solo caught up with me. And then, they passed me.

I heard the bull bellowing behind me, and it was close. We ran right past our little patch of timber, and I was praying Jack and Goliath were on the job. I saw Goliath bolt out of the woods, and a split-second later, Goliath ran at top speed smack into the side of the aurochs. Goliath weighed about 1,300 pounds, and he basically tackled a four-thousand-pound beast. All of us heard the hit. Aylmer bellowed, but he was caught by total surprise. Goliath hit him shoulder high, and hearing the hit was my queue. I turned and saw Aylmer fall on his right side with Goliath on top of him. Geez, Goliath did not look big enough to hold Aylmer down.

I saw Dean turn back, and Jack was riding fast toward the writhing, screaming mass of angry bovine. Aylmer was furious, but when I raced in and bit down on his ear, his mood went to pure rage. I had done what Goliath told me to do; I was the bulldog substitute. But weighing well over three hundred pounds, when I bit his ear to hold his head down, he wasn't getting up. And I was holding on for dear life.

Jack had roped Aylmer's back left leg, and Dean tried to throw a rope on Aylmer's horns, but Dean couldn't get a clean toss. Aylmer was playing pure kamikaze, so threatening him with guns wouldn't work. I was biting down on his ear trying to keep Aylmer's head down, and by doing that, it helped keep him off his hooves. Goliath was just lying on Aylmer, so his weight would keep him down. The noise was intense. Dean, frustrated and maybe a little crazy, jumped off Solo, grabbed a loop, and ran up to Aylmer and grabbed a horn. Then, he put the loop around Aylmer's head and neck. Dean was yelling at Aylmer the whole time. Then, he ran back, jumped up on Solo, and walked Solo back until his rope pulled tight. Sometimes, we all wonder if Dean is more than just a little crazy.

Jack had walked Chevy backward and pulled the rope attached to Aylmer's leg nice and tight. If Aylmer did get up, he couldn't use a back leg. Aylmer's head was being pulled by Dean one way, and Jack pulled Aylmer's back left leg the opposite way. It was all over in a few furious seconds. Aylmer was caught, and he was our prisoner.

Not totally satisfied, Dean left Solo again and ran up to Aylmer while he was still forced to lie on his side. Dean had cut a short piece of cord and had tied loops to each end. Dean slid the loops on to Aylmer's front legs and cinched tight; Dean had made a hobble. At that point, I really did think Dean was 100% crazy, but we did need Aylmer to be as immobile as possible. I let go of Aylmer's ear and jumped clear of his horns. Goliath did too. Aylmer was able to do a three-leg stand, but he couldn't go anywhere. He was making a heck of a racket, but he was stuck in place. Goliath walked to his front.

I happened to look at Jack, and I saw that the black bear had gotten too close, and he was watching everything that had happened. At first, I was concerned for Jack's safety; the bear was only about ten yards behind him. I yelled to Goliath and told him I had to cover Jack. I raced to intercept the other bear. He saw me coming at him, and he turned to run; that made me run even faster. I was in a full run, and because grizzlies are faster than black bears, I caught up to him quickly. He was bigger than me by at least seventy-five pounds, but I didn't care. This stalking thing of theirs had to stop.

"Stop, now!" I yelled.

And to my surprise, the bear whirled around and stood, ready to fight, and defend himself. I thought we were going to fight, and I was concerned. When a smaller bear fights a bigger bear, the bigger bear almost always wins. So I was thinking about that. But I'm also a grizzly, and pound for pound, grizzlies are stronger than black bears. I was hoping Dean or Jack could save me if I started taking a whipping.

"What are you doing?" I yelled at the bear. "And why do you want to kill me?"

Just saying it made me mad. The loony ox had tried to kill me, and this bear was his helper. The black bear fell to the ground, and then, I noticed the bear was a *she*, not a *he*. She was shaking in fear, but she was still very dangerous. Well, I sure didn't expect that. I'm not sure what I expected, but it wasn't that. I needed to say so something.

"Hey, there," I said. "You guys want to kill me. I should be the one shaking. C'mon, nobody is going to hurt you."

I was really feeling sorry for her. Then, she looked at me with her angry bear eyes and yelled, "Don't you get it, Kaiyo? That guy got away, and he's going to tell. He's even hanging around a demon now. They will get every detail out of him. Our world is in danger. Why are you helping him? Why have you abandoned us?"

Then, she cried. She cried hard. I admit it; I was way out of my comfort zone. I had no idea what to do. I was thinking I would be better off with Lavi the killer mountain lion than dealing with a crying and still dangerous black bear. I was also super surprised she knew my name, but first things first.

"Okay, if I could prove to you none of that was true, would you hear me out?"

She gave me a tentative, "Yes, I guess so."

I looked over at Goliath, and he was talking to a fully immobilized Aylmer. I knew I had one shot, so I decided to start at the beginning. First, I asked her what her name was.

"Dohv," she said as she was trying to clear up her sniffles. "It's Hebrew for bear. It's pronounced like 'the swimmer dove into the water.' My friends, though, just call me Dovie, like the bird."

"Okay, that's a nice name too. So Dovie," I asked, "how do you know who I am?"

"Kaiyo, you convince me first why I got all this wrong. Then, I'll answer your questions."

Fair enough. I started at the beginning with Dad getting a call that his help was needed to find a lost hiker. I even told her about Gracie's vision. Then, I described our trip and our finding Landon in the cave and our discussions with Tracker when we came out. Dovie sat and listened as I described our being followed by both her and Aylmer and then by the demon lady and Lavi. I also told her about my run in with Lavi. Dovie listened intently as I talked, and she gasped when she heard Lavi's name.

"He's a bad lion," she said. "Keep talking!"

I described Dean and his decision to capture the demon lady. I pointed over to him. Dean happened to be looking our way, and he waved. Dovie waved back. "Yeah," I said, "Dean's my big brother. He's brave, but sometimes, he's irrational brave."

Then, I told her Sarah's story. I told her how only Landon had enough faith in God to cast out the demon. After that, I shared how Dean told Sarah about the thief on the cross. Then, I told her how Sarah found her way to God.

By this time, Dovie was gently crying. "Wow!" she whispered. "You said you would convince me, and you did."

We both looked over to Aylmer and Goliath. They were still talking, but Dean and Jack had let their ropes go slack. They looked bored.

"So, Dovie, how do you know my name?"

Dovie looked at me and smiled, "A lot of us bears know who you are. You're famous. First of all, you have a real human family. We long for the day when the restoration comes. Somehow, maybe because of you being rescued as a cub, you have found a bit of restoration on your own. That is not something adults like us can do. Second, because you're a prince of your clan, even the other bears know you are destined for greatness. Raphael told them that. That's why I was so upset when I thought you switched sides. Betrayal is not altogether uncommon, you know. Even the Master was betrayed."

My mouth was open, and I'm sure I looked like a fool.

"Oh my gosh," exclaimed Dovie. "You didn't know, did you? I'm sorry!"

"Maybe that's why Raphael wants to talk to me," I wondered out loud.

Dovie obviously wanted to change the subject. "Can you introduce me to your friends?" asked Dovie.

And I did. We walked up to Jack as he was taking the lasso off Aylmer's leg. Jack was always a gentleman and introduced himself to Dovie. She liked him. Then, we went over to Dean. Dovie was already impressed with him, and he was a gentleman too.

"Miss Bear," he said, "you are cordially invited to my house where we will feast with new friends. You will be one of those. Can you walk with us? We will be in a hurry, and we'll be leaving shortly."

Dovie nodded vigorously. She and I then went over to Aylmer, and he looked at her. He was truly a big beast. Goliath was there too, and they had finished their discussions. Dean had already removed his hobble and the loop he had thrown around Aylmer's horns. Dovie asked if he would come to the feast.

"Well," said Aylmer, "I tried to kill them, and now, I learn that I should have been protecting them. Who knew? The least we can do is escort them. And you, Kaiyo, I will forgive you for trying to eat my ear off. I guess it was a necessity, right?"

And that was that. We turned west and went over the ridge. They knew the path, and the shortcut put us right back on schedule. Dovie was a good walker, and she never complained. The sun was getting higher, and I was getting hungry when the Elk Pen came into view. The truth is bears are always hungry, and I was well past that. If everything works right and there are no delays, the Elk Pen is only a two-hour slow walk from the farm.

Even for a bear, this place was beautiful. The meadows were huge, and there were usually lots of berries, and the creek had fish in it. But this time, there were bison, and to be honest, when it comes to bison, I'm not a fan. And there were bison everywhere strung out along the creek. That wasn't good.

Dean yelled out, "Hold up!"

We all did. Dean turned Solo around to look at us. "Okay, everybody. We all need some rest, and our horses need water, but unfortunately, that bunch of buffalos got to the creek over there first. So I know we're all tired, but I'm afraid we're going to have to wait for the herd to clear out. And that can take a long time."

I happened to be looking at Aylmer and watched as he smiled. He then whispered something into Goliath's ear. Goliath chuckled, looked at him, and nodded his head. The two of them walked past Dean and Solo and just kept walking toward the herd. We all knew they were up to something. When they got to within one hundred yards of the herd, Goliath roared, and Aylmer let out a howl, and they ran right at them. The bison looked up and watched, and as they kept coming, those bison panicked. They ran this way and that way. They ran over each other getting out of the way. I used to chase pigeons like that at the farm when I was young. We were all laughing so hard. Then, Dean and Jack looked at each other, and as if on signal, they both spurred their horses in a run, and they chased off a few frightened buffalo too. They were laughing the whole time.

As we followed the group, I looked at Dovie. "Hungry? The creek is full of fish."

"Yeah, right," she said. "They're too fast. It's impossible to catch them. I've tried."

"O ye of little faith," I joked. "Come and learn from the master… Goliath."

For the next twenty minutes, the horses drank their fills and then grazed on the grasses next to the creek. Aylmer drank, and he went and laid next to Jack and Dean. I would hear him make cow noises from time to time as he and Dean and Jack communicated. We three bears wasted no time, and we started catching fish. Dovie learned how we caught them; she had a great time, and she ate at least four fish. I had four, and Goliath had six. With a few minutes left, we bears took a dip in a deep part to cool off. Then, we dragged ourselves out and dozed for a few minutes in the sun. It was so nice.

Rested, we got up and continued our voyage back to my farm. I was glad Dovie and Aylmer would get to see my family. I had no idea we were famous.

The time went by fast, and the closer we got to the farm, the happier we felt. Soon, we saw the farm in the distance. Dean and Jack said that they were going to go fast, and we should follow at our own speed. I liked the idea. The two boys took off, and they raced out of sight. We slowed our pace, but only a little as Goliath gave Dovie and Aylmer a few lessons about the farm and about my mom and dad and Libby and Gracie. He also told them that friends of the family, the Gibbses, would be joining us as well as a few lawmen. Aylmer and Dovie were surprised at that. Dovie said that her only experience with lawmen was when she once crept into town and went dumpster diving. She said that the next thing she knew, some fool with a badge shot her butt with a beanbag gun.

"That bean bag felt like I got slapped by a grizzly bear. I was not happy."

"Hah," said Goliath, "that might well have been either Captain Stahr or the game warden. They will both probably join us tonight, and they are good people. Try not to bite them, okay?"

"I'll try," she said.

More—Gracie

It was about lunchtime when I heard the stampede of hooves and Dean and Jack's whooping and hollering as they were headed our way flying past the pastures. I was in the barn and had finished mucking out the stalls and was in Duke's stall brushing him down when I heard the racket.

During the summer, when the horses are usually in their pasture, mucking out the stalls isn't so bad; there's not much muck. We had a storm the night before, so Mom and I brought in Cali, her horse, and Duke; and both had left a few gifts for me to clean up. The rest of our horses were out with the family looking for the hiker. I had already cleaned up the guinea hens' coop and the chickens' coop, and that was always nasty work. But as for cleaning up after the horses, there was only a little cleanup that was necessary. I stopped to figure out if I heard happy voices or hysterical voices. After a second, I heard laughter; they were happy. That's good. That meant they had the hiker too.

I left Duke in his stall and walked out of the barn and into the courtyard. Mom was coming down the back steps, and we both saw Dean and Jack heading our way fast. They skidded as Dean jumped off Solo. Then, he started talking, stopped, and then hugged Mom.

"Don't worry. Everybody is okay," he said breathlessly.

Mom looked so relieved. Dean kept going at a machine-gun pace. "Well, at least I think they're all okay. I'm pretty sure they're fine. Well, they were fine when Jack, Kaiyo, Goliath, and I left this morning. The rest are coming later. Oh, we found the hiker. He's coming, and you'll love him. He's a great guy. I think Libby fell in love with him. Seriously. You'll also love Sarah. Yesterday, she was possessed by a true butt kicker of a demon, but Landon the hiker cast it out of her. It was not pretty. I tried, but I couldn't pull it off. Anyway, we found two more Specials. They're coming this way with Kaiyo and Goliath. We left them about two miles from the east entrance..."

Well, that was all I needed to hear. I was having a hard time keeping up anyway. I raced back in the barn and yelled, "Duke, let's ride!"

He knew what that meant. I tossed on his pad, blanket, and saddle and cinched the girth, and he eagerly took the bit. I threw open the stall door and swung up on the saddle. I hurried to the barn's main entrance, and when I saw the way was clear, I looked at Mom. She and Dean were deep in conversation.

I yelled out, "Mom, I'm going to go see Goliath and Kaiyo."

Then, I lowered my head, kicked Duke, and rode away from the courtyard and down the path. I heard Mom yell out at me, but it was only one of those *be careful* type of things.

Duke was fast, and the big pastures slid by. In no time, I was off our farm and into the Eastern Wilderness. This part was still our land, but it was not farmed, and Dad said it never would be. My mind was wondering who the other Specials were when they came into view about a mile or so away. I was so surprised when I figured out the big one wasn't Goliath. That just made me ride even harder.

THE FAMILY—KAIYO

I saw her first. "What did I tell you?" I said to the rest of us. "She's almost as brave as Dean!"

I looked over at Aylmer and said, "This is the one I talked about. She was the one who showed Goliath what real grace looks like. Her name is Gracie, and it's appropriate. Keep in mind Goliath once tried to kill her. Just watch what she does when she gets here."

Aylmer smiled. We all stopped and waited. It didn't take long. She was riding Duke in a full gallop. We heard her yelling before she got to us. "Goooooliiiiaaathh!"

She came in fast and only pulled up on Duke's reins about fifteen feet away. She skidded to a stop. In one motion, she threw her leg over her saddle, hit the ground running, and leaped into Goliath's outstretched paws. He fell backward as she hugged him tight.

"We missed you Goliath. I missed you. It is so good to see you!"

Sitting on his chest, this tiny little ten-year-old girl grabbed his face and looked into Goliath's eyes. She just stared at him. "But now, you're here, and I love you!" she said.

Aylmer was enjoying all of it. "So this is Goliath, the famous, ill-tempered, killer bear of the Montana wilderness. I hope you know you have somehow won the lottery."

Goliath knew what he meant. He had indeed. Had it not been for Dean and Dad, he'd be dead. But Gracie was the one who probably saved him.

After a few more minutes, Gracie scrambled off Goliath and walked over to Aylmer. She was looking him over. He towered over her. She reached up to touch his nose. Aylmer looked at Goliath and said, "Uh, what does she want me to do?"

"Just lower your head and let her say hello," Goliath replied.

Aylmer's attention was immediately directed toward Gracie as she looked at him. "I know y'all talk to each other and I can't understand any of it, but I know you understand me. Welcome to the farm. I think you'll love it. You'll always be safe here."

Aylmer just looked at Goliath and said, "She's so precious. And you, Goliath, were going to hurt this sweet thing? Seriously, you have come a long way."

Aylmer lowered his big bullhead, and he let Gracie pet his nose.

"Yeah, hard to believe it is true," said Goliath. "But trust me. She can throw a mean stapler."

Aylmer looked from Goliath to me oddly, so I told him I would tell him later.

In a flash, Gracie turned and leaped on me. I was used to it. But I was never tired of it. "Okay, little brother, you're about to meet your match!"

Gracie was laughing hard as she tried to take me down. For a ten-year-old girl, Gracie was strong. We laughed and played for a few moments until she gave up. Then, we stood back up. Gracie brushed off her jeans and went to Dovie and said, "Friends of my little brother are friends of ours. Please come with us and stay."

After a few moments with Dovie, Gracie grabbed Duke's reins and looked at me and Goliath and said, "I'll ride ahead. I am afraid Moose will not like the sweet, black bear. He fights them all the time."

She looked at Dovie and said, "No offense, Miss Bear. I just don't trust Jack or Dean to remember."

And she was off in a cloud of dust headed back to the farm. We started walking again. Aylmer and Dovie both asked why we should be concerned about a dog. I explained how big and how ferocious Moose was. I also explained how great he would be once he got to know them. I told them part of the story of how Moose once saved my life when I went on an adventure to find Goliath so Goliath could save Dad.

Aylmer looked at Goliath dryly and said, "And I suppose you once tried to kill this Moose dog too? Hmmm?"

"Yeah," I laughed. "He basically tried to kill all of us!"

"Okay," said Dovie. "Tonight, I want back story. All of it."

As we walked, I thought of my blessings. There's no doubt I deserved none of the love I received from the McLeods, but they loved me anyway. I am a lot like Goliath. We are savage and still very wild bears, but I also knew we were all meant for a purpose. For me and for Goliath, the McLeods are a part of that purpose, and so is my other home. How everything would all play out in the battles ahead was unknown to me, but the side we had chosen was worthy of whatever sacrifice was necessary. I looked forward to being a part of it all.

Still, Aylmer was right—Goliath had won the lottery. I guess I had too. I miss my bear mother so much, but I had also been fortunate. Tonight, would be a good night.

THE HOME FRONT—SUSAN

A lot had happened in two days. Dean and Jack were tired, but they told me what they knew. Jack excused himself and headed upstairs to take a quick nap and shower up; his family would be coming later. Dean stayed with me to fill me in on everything. He also told me about Dad's promise of a feast. Basically, it would be Thanksgiving in July. And it made sense. Two young people, totally lost but in drastically different ways, were found. I sensed Sarah would be the more fragile of the two just because of what she went through. Landon, the hiker, didn't have to deal with self-imposed shame. He would have to figure out a story, and he would have some explaining to do, but there was no shame. Whatever Sarah went through, I doubt her life over the past few years had been marked by high accomplishment and discipline.

The first thing I did was call Captain Ed Hamby of the State Patrol and Sheriff Tuttle. They were our friends, and both were involved in trying to find the hiker. I got them both on a conference call and told them the good news about Landon. I told them we were also bringing in a missing person, but I didn't know her last name. They asked many questions, none of which I knew answers to. Sheriff Tuttle said that he would call Landon's parents to let them know their son was okay. I told them Landon wasn't to be whisked away because we were going to have a party and two new Specials involved in the rescue would be attending. There could be no strangers and no press, but later that evening, both of them could take him to the hospital to be checked out. Landon could meet up with his parents there too. I invited the lawmen to the party. They agreed to come immediately. I asked Sheriff Tuttle to bring Captain Stahr and to call Lowe Brigham, our friend and local game warden.

As for cooking a feast for perhaps a dozen people and some animals with tremendous appetites, that was easier than it sounded. Except for the bull Dean talked about, everybody liked to eat the same stuff. I would cook a lot of meat, a lot of potatoes, and a bunch of pies. I have learned a lot in the past few years, and there are no real food preferences when it comes to bears or watchers. They are both like enormous raccoons. So if I undercook the meat a little bit or overcook it a little bit, they don't care. They still love it. They're perfectly happy with raw meat too.

As for the pies, they do prefer fruit pies over the others, but they've never sent one back. Giving sugar to mammals is always bad for their teeth, but wherever the Specials go, it seems to fix their health issues. Our veterinarian, Dr. Cindy, once checked out Rimmy, Goliath, and Kaiyo; and all their teeth were in great condition. Tracker refused, but I think he knew it was a waste of time.

Moose's barking alerted me to visitors. I saw the Gibbs' ATV pull up out back. On it were Aliyah Gibbs and her daughter Kate. Kate would be fifteen in January. They parked in the back and made a beeline toward the back door. They were two of the prettiest females I had ever seen. Aliyah's parents came from East Africa. She was tall and classically beautiful. Kate was tall for her age, and she already was starting to look like she was twenty. Dean was totally smitten with her, and he was probably in for a little heartache in the future. Girls like Kate get a lot of attention from older boys, and high school for Kate was a month away. Sam and I have long believed that getting too involved in our children's crushes was a bad idea. Girlfriends and boyfriends seem to come and go. With Kate, it would be more difficult because we loved her. We decided we would deal with whatever happened when it happened. The Gibbses were among our best friends.

Aliyah bounded up the steps and opened the kitchen door. I loved her smile. She looked at me and laughed.

"Jack called and told us some of our old friends and some new guests are coming. Girl, you are in dire need of help! We are here until you make us leave."

Fat chance. I pulled out a bottle of wine, looked at Aliyah, laughed, and said, "First things first!"

And with that, we opened the bottle, poured a couple of glasses, and started working. Kate looked around, and I knew why. She has a beautiful voice, and I love hearing her call me *Miss Susan*. We talked for a minute or so, and then, she ducked out and went straight to the barn where Dean was. Aliyah and I looked at each other; our eyebrows were raised. We decided to give them five minutes, and then, they would have to come out in the open. Fortunately, they returned soon enough.

Gracie had Duke in a full gallop flying back down the path. Duke loved to run. At the top of her lungs, she was yelling something about Moose. Our dog, Moose, was a cross between an Argentine Dogo and an Anatolian Shepherd. He looked mean, and sometimes, he was. He was also the perfect watchdog, and he was very, very protective. Dean told me earlier one of the new Specials was a black bear. Dean and I should have thought about the problems of a black bear being around Moose. Thank goodness for Gracie.

Black bears are amazing creatures, and they're smart. Unfortunately, since they have a taste for beans, corn, and alpaca, Moose and Major have been taught to chase them out of the fields and into the woods that surround the farm. A few times, a bear has decided to stay and fight, and that never worked out well for the bear. Moose and Major can be quite vicious. Over the years, only a few grizzlies have tried to dine at the farm, but a lot more black bears have made that poor decision. So, when it comes to bears, Moose and Major chase away black bears. So Gracie's concern was well founded.

Moose heard her coming, so he was waiting for her in the courtyard. Dean walked to him, casually grabbed his collar, and took him inside. Aliyah and I had already pulled about eighty pounds of beef, elk, and venison out of the cooler, so he was delighted. Gracie pulled up, tied up Duke, and came inside. She immediately ran to Aliyah and gave her a quick hug.

"They're coming," she said with a smile. "And, Miss Aliyah, you are not going to believe the size of the bull coming our way."

Gracie and Aliyah talked as Dean and Kate came in. Dean had already fired up our huge outdoor cooker/smoker. We got it after Kaiyo came into our lives. Even though Kaiyo likes raw meat, he likes the cooked stuff too. Dean and Kate listened to Gracie. They were in great moods just being together. *Beginnings are nice*, I thought to myself.

"She's right, Miss Aliyah," said Dean. "The black bear is a little bigger than Kaiyo, and she seems very sweet. The bull is like a rhino or a smallish elephant. Seriously."

Then, he and Kate looked at one another; they grabbed their platters and back out they went. Dean and Kate were talking a mile a minute. I was happy the first group made it back, but it was the second group I most longed for. I missed Sam. Libby I wanted home too. And Sarah, whoever she was, was on my mind. I decided to get busy.

Revelations—Sam

About an hour after Dean and his crew left, Landon came out of the tent. He scratched his head, looked around, and saw me and Tracker. I stood up, poured him some coffee, and asked if he was up for a short walk. He was.

Tracker came with us as we made our way toward the horses. Once out of earshot from our campsite, I told Landon we still needed to be careful around Sarah. Landon was surprised I would be concerned about her. He wasn't antagonistic; he just seemed like he wanted to know. I looked at Landon and said, "Sarah's been through a lot. I am convinced you did cast out the demon last night, but she's probably pretty fragile, and she'll be that way for a while. When she was possessed, I suspect she would have tortured you to death to reveal what you saw and experienced. I believe she did find God last night too. Of course, she could have been faking it, but I sure didn't get that impression. But here's the deal—you have enemies who think you have valuable information and they are willing to kill you, Dean, or anybody else to get it. Telling Sarah what you know does her no favors, because if you tell her, then she will be a target just like you. Does that make sense?"

Landon shook his head and agreed. "Got it," he said. "I definitely don't want her to have to deal with anything like that. Those are good points."

The truth was, though, I didn't trust Sarah yet. She sure seemed nice, but I have learned trust is something that must be earned. She was, to me, an unknown. Time would tell. I then turned to Landon and asked him what he saw. He knew what I meant. Landon slowed his pace and looked from me to Tracker, and then, he began to speak.

"Well, I was on my hike, and I had made my turn to come back. It was a good trip, but I saw nothing unusual. This area is beautiful, but that's normal, right? I was well ahead of schedule, so I decided to veer from the plan I filed at the ranger station. I was going to follow Blankets Creek north for a day and camp. My plan was to then break camp and go back south toward the ranger station and then home from there. As I was walking and just enjoying being out here, I was about six miles north from my planned route. I took a break on the sunny side of a low hill. The way I was sitting, my body happened to be hidden from the north. But I could see over the top of the little, low hill. That was when I first saw Tracker a few hundred yards away. He was seated on some dry mudflats along the creek's west bank. At first, I thought he was just a plain, ordinary wolf. No offense, Tracker."

Tracker's tail wagged, so I assumed no offense was taken. Landon kept going. "I dug in my pack and got out my binoculars, and when I zeroed in on him, I saw Tracker was being approached by a big bull elk. The elk was real eight-pointer. Huge! The first thing I realized was how big Tracker was. Elk are big, and I guessed Tracker was bigger by another half the size of the biggest wolf I had ever seen. I was right too. Anyway, the second thing I noticed was the two seemed to communicate. I expected to watch a predator-prey relationship play out, but what I saw was cooperation. While I was watching, a raven flew out of the east and landed right by them. The three seemed to communicate with one another, which, at the time, was fascinating. Then, the big elk headed off quickly to the west, and the raven flew off back to the east. I figured I had seen something extraordinary, something that would make a lot of scientific scholarship stand on its ear. And I was convinced Tracker was the key to understanding it all. So, obsessed with figuring out the mystery, I followed him.

"I followed him for the rest of the day. It wasn't easy. I always had to stay downwind, and I had to use the cover of hills, grasses, and trees so Tracker didn't see me. Several times, I sensed he had stopped, and I was usually right. Twice, I saw him watching his back trail. I stayed pretty far away and relied on my binoculars. He never saw me.

"I could tell Tracker was different. Several times, he could've killed a deer, but he looked like he had a purpose, and it wasn't just survival. Anyway, the brush and trees steadily got thicker, and I completely lost sight of him. So I ginned up some courage and ran. I closed the distance and plunged into the brush. I figured that from where I last saw him, he was probably only about two hundred yards away. The brush opened up near the creek's banks into another series of mudflats, and I found his big tracks heading north along the west side of the creek. I moved fast, but I was still quiet. In fact, I somehow slipped past Rimmy, which, by the way, isn't his real name. Neither Rimmy nor I knew I had gotten past him until I was about fifty yards past him. Anyway, when he saw me, he roared his disapproval. I turned around and saw who was roaring, and I knew I was dead. He came after me fast, so I ran."

Landon took a breath. I looked at Tracker. He nodded his head. I looked back at Landon. "Go on," I said.

"Well, right before Rimmy figured me out, I watched Tracker slip away. Literally. Tracker crossed dimensions. He was there, and then, he wasn't there. And then, Rimmy roared. I knew I couldn't outrun him, so I ran to where Tracker disappeared. It was my only hope. And I am still pretty sure that had Rimmy captured me, he would have killed me. Right?"

I thought about that for a few seconds. I looked at Landon and said, "Watchers are definitely dangerous, and even the good ones are frightening. Still, I am pretty sure murder is not something Rimmy would do. But I can't rule it out. He was obviously guarding Tracker."

Tracker growled his disapproval. "No," said Landon. "Rimmy was guarding the entrance, not Tracker."

Tracker again nodded his head. "So what happened?" I asked.

"Well, I was terrified, and I had no choice. The place where Tracker vanished was a spot that looked different. It was a vague, oblong spot about as big as a commercial garage door. It was like I was looking through water. It is hard to describe, but I plunged in. In that split-second, I knew I had totally left Montana. It was like I ran into a dimly lit, thin long brushy field that had opaque walls. It was only about three hundred yards wide but much longer. The walls were sort of like wax paper. I couldn't see out of the walls, at least not at first. And it was sort of a bleak place, filled with shadows and without much color. Again, it's a hard place to describe, but I hid out there for at least a week, so I remember it well. I dared not go back because of Rimmy. I didn't know he was a Special, and I assumed if he was like Tracker, he would have followed me right on in.

"So I noticed at the other end of this field, maybe a mile away, I could see a ridgeline of small hills, and in the middle was a gap. From where that gap was, I saw light glowing from between the hills. The light wasn't just our normal white light. It had colors, and let me tell you, it had all of them. I saw colors there I have never seen before. It's hard to describe, but we don't see but half of the colors that are there. Since I had no place to go and I wanted to see what was making the beautiful light, I started walking.

"There was a clear path that had the tracks of all sorts of animals, so I decided to follow it. Several times as I walked, birds would fly overhead, going in the direction of the gap. Without exception, they all said something like 'You will die.' At first, I thought it was somebody talking near me, but after a few minutes, I became convinced that I heard it from the birds. They were mostly crows and ravens, a few magpies, and some hawks and falcons. I was sure somebody had taught those birds to say things like that.

"I was still confused when I heard a stampede coming fast from behind me. I threw myself in the brush, behind a low tree, as three elk came rushing past. The big bull I saw earlier with Tracker was one of them. He stopped as the others kept going. I was really scared.

Then, he came back, looked at me, and told me I had made a big mistake and I would pay with my life. I was shaking, but I asked him why. He said something about me not belonging there. Of course, I was starting to wonder if I was going crazy.

"So anyway, the big elk rumbled on, and I watched as he entered into the lighted area. Then, he was gone. I didn't want to die, but I didn't quite feel any particular place was safer than any other place. I also wanted to see where the talking animals were going. I was hoping I could meet somebody there who could help me get back home. Unfortunately, what I found was nothing helpful.

"I left the brush, got back on the path, and headed to the lighted end of the path. Several times, some bigger animals came either past me going the opposite way or they came from behind me. One of the bigger animals was probably the big bull who is looking for me now. He saw me and immediately chased me in the brush and said that he would kill me if he could. He also laughed and said I was good as dead anyway. The fact is that he easily could have chased me down and killed me, but he didn't. I figured out he was obeying some sort of rule about killing.

"Once I figured that out, I came on out and walked to the path. The bull just went crazy, and I really was concerned I had wrongly guessed about any rules against killing. He could have easily gored me, flattened me, or both. And, by the way, Dean was right—he is truly enormous. He's bigger than Peyton. He's maybe not as tall, but he's definitely heaver."

I raised an eyebrow at that. Landon shrugged. "Listen," he said, "you'll get to see him soon enough. He's a match for Goliath, so let's hope he is willing to hear us out. Otherwise, we're all going to have to shoot him full of holes. I really don't want to do that, but he is probably a charge-and-kill first, ask questions later, type of bovine. I hope not. Anyway, back to my story."

Landon thought for a moment. "So the bull charged two or three times, but he always pulled up short. He truly had a bad temper, though. Before he left, he said that if I ever escaped, he would track me down and kill me where it was allowed. That statement told me I was right. He couldn't kill me there, and that meant the others couldn't either. That made it not so terrifying.

"Well, I listened long enough to the blowhard, so I told him if I escaped and if he tried something like that, then I would enjoy a few years of free pot roast, hamburgers, and steaks. He understood and bellowed and said that I wouldn't make it anyway. Then, he turned and headed toward the entrance back where I had come from. I also knew if I followed him out, he would be waiting for me on the other side. So I went on down the path in the other direction.

"Despite various animals telling me to go back and others telling me I shouldn't be there, I just kept going. About a hundred yards or so before I got to the gap, I started seeing some skeletons. Several were of people but not ordinary people, they were big, like twelve feet tall. I remembered stories of the Nephilim, and it dawned on me that if something killed those giants, then I was in great danger. Some of the skeletons were of people too. Some were of other things I didn't recognize. So I started praying because my life depended on it. Somewhere, a bubble of courage must have surfaced in me because I kept going.

"In a few minutes, I reached the gap in the low hills. There, before me, down a short path from where the gap opened up, stood miles upon miles of plains, forests, lakes, and rivers. In the distance were more mountains. But what stood out were the animals. Some were quite close, while others were miles away. Do you remember the scene in Jurassic Park when the people just got there, and they saw all sorts of dinosaurs living peacefully in the huge savannah? What I saw was like that except for the different types of animals and the obvious organization of the landscape. There were paths and roads, some cultivated areas, and habitations of all sorts. And there were dinosaurs. Plenty of them too."

At this point my mind was reeling. I had a thousand questions for Landon. Tracker just sat there listening. Occasionally, his tail wagged. All I could blurt out was, "Then, what happened?"

Landon looked back at camp and then back to us. He said, "Well, I just stood there and took it all in. It was beautiful, and it was so incredibly colorful I know remembering it will be difficult. After a few minutes of just standing there, I heard a frightening sound that kept getting louder. From the area below, I saw a multiwinged monster flying my way quickly. I was so scared I couldn't move. It was big, like fifteen to twenty feet tall, and it landed in front of me. I'm telling you the truth—that thing had four faces and four wings. The wings were outstretched and as long as a basketball court, making him look even taller. The faces were those of a man, a bull, an eagle, and a lion. It was a combination of a lot of things, but it was pure terror standing there. And it was totally mad at me."

I could see Landon start trembling and his face got pale. To get his mind off the monster thing, I asked him how he met Tracker. "I'll get to that in a minute," said Landon.

He didn't appreciate my clumsy attempt to change the subject. Landon caught his thoughts together and continued. "I'm going to wrap this story up. Are you okay with a short version?"

I told him I was. We had been out here for a while, and I imagined Libby and Sarah would be waking up soon. It was also time to wrap it up because my mind was already filled with images, thoughts, and questions. I looked at Landon, and he picked up where he left off.

"That thing spoke loudly, but it didn't yell or scream or growl or anything like that. When it did speak, its faces spoke at one time. Somehow, the faces all seemed to be looking at me. It shifted from side to side rapidly, so each face could see me. I'll remember what it said forever. He said it more than once. It said, 'Come closer, child, and you will die. Your bones will be among those of the evil scouts who have lain for centuries at my feet. No one may pass, even the grafted like you.'

"He seemed both serious and capable, so I ran back up into the long, drab path to hide. For the next few days, I hid. I looked for an exit, but nothing came or went. My plan was to follow some harmless creature, like a raccoon or a deer, if it was headed out. That way, if it turned on me on the other side, I would have a chance. I was even willing to risk running into the bull or Benaiah."

I had not heard that name before, so I made a note to myself to ask later.

"But nothing came or went," said Landon. "I was desperate, and I was praying up a storm. I was falling into hopelessness. So I spent my time like a witless fly, groping around the walls, looking for a way out. Every once in a while, I could see something. Then, just yesterday, I saw you and your family standing outside. I think you guys were looking at a map. The view was mostly clear—that was new. I screamed out, and only your daughter heard me. I also noticed you had a bear who seemed to notice your daughter while she was noticing me. Then, I lost sight of you guys. But I was comforted. First, somebody had heard me, and second, I knew your bear Kaiyo had to be like Tracker here. That told me I wasn't crazy, and maybe help would come."

Landon took a step over to Tracker and patted Tracker's big head. Tracker didn't usually like to be treated like a dog, but he was obviously very fond of Landon, and he seemed to enjoy the pat.

"And help did arrive," said Landon. "It started with Tracker. Tracker here wandered out of the pretty place. I watched. He and the monster chatted for a while, and they would look my way from time to time. I was about as far away from the monster as I could get, but I recognized Tracker. I was waiting for him to come tell me I was going to die because that was what all the other animals said.

"I had no place to run, so I decided to leave my hiding place and meet Tracker on the path. If he wanted to kill me, then we would just have it out right there. But, as I learned, Tracker was my helper. So Tracker comes to me and said everything would be all right. That was the first time I knew that I would be safe and that I would be going home. But he did tell me that there would be danger. Then, he said something interesting. Well, I guess anything a talking wolf says is automatically interesting, but what he said was profound. Tracker said, 'Landon, your life will certainly be in danger for a while but only because the enemy doesn't understand. They have been trying to break into this wonderful place from the first day, but our place is not of the world, so the enemy will never have influence here. But remember this. The enemy will try to make you talk, and if he captures you, he will probably kill you in the process.'"

"By the way," said Landon, "how do you know Tracker's name is Tracker."

"I'll tell you on the ride back," I said. "And let's finish this story on the ride back too."

I could see that Sarah and Libby had crawled out of their tent and were milling around. We would give them some privacy, and then, I would make some breakfast. Hopefully, we would be only thirty minutes or so from leaving. My mind was swimming with what Landon was telling me. I really couldn't hear much more. I needed some pondering time. A four-hour ride home would do the trick.

Cat Tail—Tracker

It was good to be going to the farm. We needed to get Landon out of the wilderness to safety at the farm. Landon and Sarah rode Peyton. Libby took the left side, Sam was on the right, and I took the lead. I felt good, so I set a fast pace. Major stayed near Sam. Benaiah followed us, but, as usual, he did things differently. As big as he was, he stayed hidden. He crossed behind us and went into the timbered hills to the north. From there, he kept up with us as we hurried west, though he was always a mile or two away from us.

After about an hour, I looked at Sam and motioned him to go on. Then, I pulled into a thicket to check out our back trail. Sam would know what I was doing. I moved into the brush into a position where I was both hidden and where I had a clear view to the east. Watching back trails always takes patience. Travelers don't like to waste time, so they often miss their own pursuers. A patient pursuer can be a deadly pursuer because they are never seen until it's too late. So, as much as I wanted to stay with the group and get back to the farm, I waited. I was patient. But Lavi wasn't.

There, about a mile away, crawling along our trail, scurrying from rock to brush and staying out of sight, was Lavi. True to form, Lavi travelled alone. Lavi was no coward; he wanted to win. I suspect he was just wanting to know where we were going. He hated us and was gunning for Kaiyo. I am sure he knew he had better hurry; Kaiyo would be more than a match for him soon enough.

The farm was no secret, but Lavi would not know about it. But trailing us wouldn't be hard for anybody; there were a lot of us going in the same direction. Still, we needed to shake this dangerous cat. I quickly turned and raced to catch up to the group. They were miles away, but I was fast enough to catch up with them. I did have to go out of my way at first so that Lavi didn't see me; that took some extra time. When I found the group, Sam was dismounted and studying the ground. This area was near a rocky ridge that jutted southward a good distance. I knew this area well.

I walked up to them at the same time catching many scents. By the look of the ground, there had been a fight and a struggle. There was no blood, but something happened. I left the group and followed more tracks. The story was clear. I saw the tracks of my friends and of a tremendous bull. There were also tracks of a large black bear. And they were walking together. I barked over at Sam. He hopped up on his mount, and the whole team came over. Neither Libby nor Sam appeared frightened or overly concerned. They were curious. I directed their attention to the tracks. Sam looked at them for a few minutes.

"Tracker," he said, "do you think they walked off together?"

I nodded my approval. "Do you think the big bull and the black bear are prisoners?"

That was a good question, but the tracks didn't show anything like that. I shook my head to show that I didn't think so. "Well, good," said Sam. "We are united. Let's go home."

Libby, Sarah, and Landon were obviously pleased. I looked back behind us though, on purpose. Sam understood me maybe better than anyone else, except for Dean.

"Do we have followers, Tracker?"

I nodded. Sam spoke up. "Libby, follow the tracks up and over that ridge. Once we get to the other side, Tracker and I will hang back and discourage our pesky follower. Then, just follow the tracks all the way home. Major will stay with me. Landon and Sarah, Libby's in charge, got it?"

Landon and Sarah laughed. "Mr. McLeod, Libby is always in charge," said Landon.

I didn't quite know what they were talking about, but Libby was strong, so it made sense. We all made our way up and over the ridge, and the three of them quickly rode off. Sam and I carefully walked back. Sam had his rifle and we hid in the boulders. We stayed vigilant, and sure enough, out of a patch of woods a mile or so back came Lavi. He was trotting and seemingly had no concern about being watched. He assumed we didn't watch our back trails. His disdain for us came from his pride. Lavi showed no fear of the McLeods. He didn't know them like I did. I looked at Sam. We waited until he had closed the distance to about fifty yards away. It was time. I stepped from behind a boulder.

Lavi stopped in his tracks. He was motionless except for his tail; the way it twitched, I could tell he was agitated. He had been seen, and his cover had been blown.

"Well, if it's not the great wolf of God, here in the flesh. Your scent, of course, gave you away yesterday. I knew you were with those humans. I thought that was breaking the rules, right? Anyway, you have a prisoner. I want her back. Hand her over to me. She's of no use to you."

"No can do, Lavi. She switched teams last night. She doesn't serve your master anymore. She is free. So either join us or run along like a good little cat and leave us alone."

Lavi thought that over for a minute. "I promised to protect her, and I always keep my word. My employer wants her back. Leave her, and I won't kill the boy. Of course, I still intend on killing his pet talking bear. It's your choice."

That lion's conceit was beyond understanding. At least I knew his plans. I knew he wanted to harm Kaiyo; I had no idea that he wanted to kill Dean too. From what I heard though, Dean had made a fool of Lavi, and Lavi didn't forgive anyone. As for his demands, it is basic wisdom to never negotiate with evil; evil will always lie. Lavi had killing on the mind, and he was never much at telling the truth. Worse, he had started to believe his own lies. He somehow even believed he could beat me in a straight on fight. I am a savage at my core, and I had heard enough from him; I knew I had to kill him. I also looked forward to doing it. In a split-second, I lowered myself and began my run at him. I hadn't gone far when I heard a shot ring out. My eyes never left Lavi, but I saw the surprise in his eyes when I was racing at him. Then, I saw shock and fear in his eyes when he realized he'd been shot.

8

PRUDENCE—SAM

I saw the mountain lion give his little speech to Tracker. I had no idea what he was saying or what he wanted, but I could see that Tracker intended to shut him up for good. Tracker can be patient, so if Tracker believed the cat needed killing, the lion must be some very unsavory character. Tracker's tough, but I knew the lion wouldn't go down easily; I didn't want Tracker to get hurt. But mainly, I believed Tracker would regret losing his temper and killing it. Whatever else may be true, the lion wasn't an ordinary lion; he was a Special. Maybe he wasn't a good one, but he was a Special, nonetheless. And other than trying to kill Dean the day before, the lion hadn't done anything yet but flap his gums.

But I did think the cat's tail was a little too long. It needed trimming. Before Tracker had run twenty yards, I stood up on a boulder, aimed, and shot a good six inches of the cat's tail clean off. It had to hurt, but there was always hope for his redemption if he lived. Still, the evil cat needed to know I could've killed him had I wanted.

Tracker was running hard when the lion screamed. With blood squirting out of the tip of his tail, the lion turned away from us and ran away at top speed. I watched the cat run until it was out of sight. Tracker stopped, turned, and looked back up at me standing on my boulder.

"Let's go," I said. "We have a party to attend."

At that point, Tracker let me have it. He turned and looked at me like he wanted to take me out. Out of him came a series of growls and barks, and it was all pure anger. I just stared back at him and let him dish it out. I had no idea what he was saying, but he said it anyway. I was glad I was up on the boulder and out of reach. Finally, after a few minutes of true anger, he quit his growling.

"Really?" I said from my perch. "I kept you from committing murder, and now, you're mad. Stop acting like a pup. Hopefully in all that growling, you complemented me for my marksmanship. That cat got trimmed a bit."

Tracker looked at me for a second, and then, his tail wagged a little. It was time to go.

REUNIONS—LIBBY

Getting home is always good. Landon and Sarah and I got to the farm before Dad and Tracker; they were about a mile behind us. On the way, Sarah talked a lot; she clearly enjoyed her freedom, and she asked endless questions of Landon and me. I was impressed with his knowledge; he knew his stuff. I liked that. I described the farm and my family, and we were all curious about the two new Specials. The black bear was interesting; I looked forward to meeting him. The ill-tempered bull, however, caused me to worry some. Landon told us nothing about his experience, but he did tell us the bull was huge, mean, strong, and perpetually angry. He was a match for Goliath, and we had no clue where Rimmy was. I truly didn't know what to expect when we got home.

Jet and Peyton picked up their pace as we made quick time toward the pastures and then home. Even though we were still about a mile away, I could see activity at the house. The east path was one of our main paths, and it led straight from the Eastern Wilderness to the area between the main barn and the back of the house. The courtyard was the big grassy area formed where the driveway circled between the barn and the back porch. I could see Kaiyo standing next to something big and black. From the distance, it looked like Gracie was standing on the big black thing. She had seen us and was pointing at us. We kicked our horses and closed the distance. In little time, I realized it was Goliath I saw, not Kaiyo. He just looked small next to the huge black thing Gracie was playing on. Then, the thing moved. And it looked at us.

We saw a massive head and enormous horns point our way. By this time, Gracie was sitting on the bull's head; her arms were outstretched from her sides as she was holding on to the horns; she looked tiny. Landon pulled Peyton to a stop; I stopped with him. Landon told us the bull had promised to kill him when they were last together. Landon also said that he told the bull he would butcher him and eat him if he tried such a thing. Sarah and I winced.

"Well," said Landon, "if he still wants to kill me, now's his chance."

Landon gave Peyton a kick, and we cantered straight toward the courtyard; the beast stood to wait for us. Gracie stayed on her perch between the horns of the massive beast, smiling and talking the whole time. I saw Kaiyo, Moose, and the black bear come out of the kitchen to meet us. Pretty soon, my mom and Miss Aliyah stepped out too. Mom loved our returns; I loved returning. Mom was smiling. The smells coming out of the kitchen were terrific. But I was nervous.

Dean, Kate, and Jack came walking up; they stood next to the great beast. Dean motioned us to come on over. We walked our horses to the driveway, and Jack came up to help Sarah off Peyton. Landon kept his eyes on the bull. I hopped off Jet and got a big hug from Kate. Sarah stood next to me. After a minute or so, Landon slid off Peyton and stood there and stared at the bull. Jack took our horses and led them into the barn.

Then, somewhat loudly, Dean said, "Okay, you guys have some mending to do. Landon, I understand you know our guest here. And you, Mr. Bull, know Landon. I don't know how you know each other, but I know you do. So I'm going to ask Goliath to take both of you over toward the side of the barn near the Southern Forest so you two can work it out."

Dean then whispered loudly in the bull's ear, "No killing on the farm, right? You good with that?"

The bull nodded, and he and Goliath walked to the edge of the Southern Forest. Landon looked at me, shrugged his shoulders, and followed them.

About three seconds later, Gracie took Sarah's hand and walked over to Mom and Miss Aliyah. Kate followed. I went to go meet the black bear. I had assumed the bear was a he, but she was a she. I liked that. For a bear, she was both beautiful and courteous. For me, it was probably shower time. I think I smelled worse than the bears. But sitting between the two bears was just too nice. We sat on the porch and talked. Occasionally, Mom or Miss Aliyah would come out and hand out goodies. They were usually meat, but there were some other delicious things too. The black bear just kept making moaning sounds as she ate the tidbits and as she watched our busy courtyard. She put an arm on me, and it was obvious she loved all of it. Sometimes, she and Kaiyo would talk. I think she liked us.

We all kept an eye on Landon and the bull. They seemed a little sheepish together. They had history. I hadn't known Landon long, but I sensed he could talk his way out of whatever predicament he was in. We got distracted when Miss Aliyah came out and asked questions about dinner. She addressed her questions directly to the black bear and to Kaiyo. Miss Aliyah understands us and the whole thing about the Specials.

Anyway, when we looked back at Landon and the bull, Landon was smiling and talking a mile a minute. Then, he started laughing hard and waving his arms and running in place. The bull was shaking his head, and it sounded to me like he was laughing. Goliath was headed back toward us. I think he was thinking about dinner. I know he saw Mom and Miss Aliyah handing out treats. I told the black bear to watch Goliath. Sure enough, he looked at us and winked as he walked up the steps and right in the kitchen. It only took a few moments before we heard Miss Aliyah and Mom yell out, "Goliath!"

The black bear was startled, and she looked at me. I was laughing. "Yeah, he's family," I told her. "There's really no difference between him or Kaiyo or Dean. He's kind of like the grown-up brother who lives nearby. He went in to steal a snack, and I think he got more than one."

Miss Aliyah shooed him out, and he wandered over and sat next to us. I think he was laughing. The black bear pushed him with a big paw and said something. She looked tiny next to him. "So," I said, "Miss black bear, what is your real name?"

We are all used to playing a strange form of charades to figure things like this, and until Landon got through mending fences with the bull, I really had nothing to do. So a game of tortured charades might be fun. Surprisingly, Kaiyo went into the house and came back with a paperback book in his mouth. I had no idea what he was up to. He and Goliath started flipping pages while the black bear leaned up and over Goliath's shoulder. In only a few minutes of page flipping, they all made bear barking noises, and the black bear motioned for me to come closer. They had my dad's guide book of birds. Dad feeds birds, and he likes to identify them. Anyway, they were pointing to a couple of pages that had pictures of doves.

"Dove?" I asked. "Your name is Dove?"

The bears gave me a few motions with their paws to show I was close. After just a few minutes of charades, I learned her name was Dovie. Names are important, and once we figured out Dovie's name, she ceased to be a stranger. Everybody inside came out to remeet Dovie. It was sweet. Sarah was extra nice to Dovie. They were once such enemies. It's amazing what Christ can do.

I looked at Sarah and said, "Let's go get showers. I need one, and you would probably love one. And I'll get you some more clothes. Ready?"

Sarah readily agreed, and we both went inside; Mom and Miss Aliyah came with us upstairs. Mom got Sarah some more clothes, and the three of them went into the guest room, each asking a ton of questions of Sarah. I went to my room. I fully intended for Landon to see me all cleaned up. The *Camper Libby* version of me was about to be past tense.

After taking a very long and wonderful shower and as I was finishing getting dressed and ready to come downstairs, I heard a few whoops and hollers with Moose barking nonstop. Dogs can bark happy, they can bark mad, and they can bark scared. Moose was barking happy. He loved Major, and he adored Dad. And for Moose, Tracker was a rock star. By the sounds of his howls, I could tell he was racing up the cart path to greet Major, Dad, and Tracker. I heard Dean whistling. It was all good.

My room looked out to the south, so I couldn't see to the north, but I understood the sounds. To me and my brothers and my sister, it meant the relief that came from knowing Dad was safe. To Goliath, it meant his best friend was back. To Dovie and the big bull, it meant another round of introductions. To Mom, it meant everything.

AYLMER'S HOME—SAM

Dogs love reunions. Whether the absence is for a few hours or a few years, dogs live for them. Moose was no different. The three of us still had to be over a mile away from the house, but Moose figured us out. He closed the distance in minutes, and he and Major tumbled into each other. Tracker enjoyed it all. Moose then came to Tracker and immediately submitted. I have taken Moose out into the wilderness, and he submits to nothing. He is ferocious, and even big bears leave Moose alone. But around Tracker, he is not the alpha, and he knows it. In fact, he likes it that way. Moose quickly fell in as we continued homeward.

As for me, I was tired and dirty. I wanted to eat, I wanted to shower, and I wanted to give my wife a big kiss on the lips—and not in that order.

After a moment, I saw Gracie riding up fast. She was looking so grown up, and she was riding like she was a part of her horse. She was already a terrific rider. Susan rode like that. In fact, all but one of my kids are good riders though Gracie seemed to be taking to it quicker than the other human kids did. My young son Kaiyo doesn't ride, but he probably could if he wanted to. He's ridden on Goliath and Peyton before, but that was over three hundred pounds ago.

Like Moose, Gracie came at us full speed. Gracie was almost always full speed, but not in the mornings; Gracie has trouble with mornings. Anyway, she raced up, and before I knew it, she had leaped from Duke's saddle and was in mine. She never even touched the ground. She hugged me hard and proceeded to tell me what was going on. After a few moments of that, she leaped down, and she and Tracker jumped all over each other. Tracker's not particularly fond of most humans, but he is family to us and us to him. But above all, Tracker absolutely adores Gracie. I think it's her heart; Tracker seems to be able to appreciate things like that.

After a few moments, Major came up and got some attention too. Right then, Gracie pulled out a leash and snapped it on Major. For the most part, dogs seem to be okay with leashes, and Major was no different.

"Dad, Dovie is here, and so is the bull. Major doesn't know them yet, so I think we need to make sure Major doesn't get hurt. And, Dad, the bull is like a small elephant!"

"So what's the name of the bull?"

"Landon told me it's Aylmer. He doesn't like the name Elmer, though."

That was one weird name. It had a serious Southern twang to it. "We'll see about that. All right, sweetheart, lead the way home."

And home was so nice. Susan met me out by the steps, and I got the kiss I was waiting for. There was a lot going on, but I needed to meet the two new Specials. Jack took our horses while Gracie led me over to the black bear. Gracie introduced us, and I told Dovie she was always welcome here. I also told her that if she ventured out into the woods during hunting season, then she must only do that if one of us were with her. I would hate for a Special to get hurt. I also told her we would take her to whatever door her home had available. But she could also stay here for as long as she wanted. Dovie looked like she was going to cry. Kaiyo said something to her, and then, he winked at me.

Then, I told Kaiyo about Lavi following us and how Tracker almost killed him. "Listen son, I may regret not killing the lion, but that would only be if he hurts one of my family. Jack and Dean told me that you and Lavi don't like each other. Is that true?"

Kaiyo nodded vigorously. "Did he threaten you?"

Kaiyo again nodded. After a few more minutes, I figured out Lavi threatened to kill Dean and Kaiyo. I suspected he would try to kill Jack too if he had a chance. I didn't know what caused such hate, but I probably should have shot him in the head instead of the tail.

When we rode up, Tracker went first to Susan; then, he greeted the other Specials, and after that, he went straight inside into the kitchen. Tracker truly thinks he owns the place. He's really part of our family, and we all loved it. I heard Aliyah swooning over him and giving him samples of dinner. He didn't come back out. Goliath was in the kitchen too. I had no idea how Susan and Aliyah were getting anything done in there, but I knew they were happy.

I then looked at the huge beast that was waiting for me in the courtyard. I have heard there were several large breeds of cattle out there, but this one was strangely big. He looked like the type of bull used in Spanish bullfights but much bigger. Landon stood next to him. I'm a little over six feet tall, and the top of Aylmer's shoulders was above eye level. His head was higher than that. When he looked at me, he was looking slightly down at me. He had to be close to four thousand pounds. He was a magnificent beast. Gracie was with me, and she held her arms up. Aylmer dipped his horns, and Gracie clambered up them onto his head. There she sat, smiling big. It was obvious the bull loved it.

"Well, Aylmer, I assume you and Landon are on the same team now?"

Landon confirmed that, and Aylmer nodded. "And with Sarah?"

Again, Aylmer nodded. I was really impressed.

Gracie then said, "Daddy, can Aylmer stay with us?"

"Of course, he can, baby."

"Forever?"

"Yes, Gracie. And yes to you, Aylmer, as long as you want."

The great bull looked at me, and I could tell he didn't believe me. "In fact," I said, "I would love to clear out another pasture, a hidden pasture, a big one, one without fences and with good grass. I want to put it over there."

I pointed over at the Southern Forest just behind our house. "Aylmer, would you help me build it? It won't be easy. What I need is a guard. Those woods are infested with watchers, and they get belligerent when we go back in there. They tried to kill me a few years back, and I haven't forgotten. If I turn my back on them, I am sure they'll throw some pretty big rocks at me—rocks big enough to kill me. I want to push them back far deeper into the forest. I'm sick and tired of them coming up to the house too. I think we could open up a huge pasture if you patrol the woods while I get the equipment in there and start clearing out the timber. I want a place that's friendly to you and to other wildlife, but not to watchers or to things that eat my livestock. And I want it to be hidden from view. We get a lot of visitors, and they don't need to be seeing you or Dovie or Goliath. I want y'all to always have a place to relax and sleep. Of course, the whole farm would be free for you to explore too. So do you think you can take on a few watchers?"

Landon told him that Benaiah was a watcher. Landon had also told me that Rimmy's real name was Benaiah on the way back today. I liked the name. While I pondered that, Aylmer almost danced in happiness at the thought of it all. "Shake on it," I said.

Aylmer looked confused. "Give me a horn."

He leaned, and I grabbed the end of his left horn. It was both sharp and huge. "Aylmer, will you help me build the pasture and help us run off the watchers? If so, let's shake."

Aylmer shook. He seemed thrilled. Gracie was smiling from ear to ear. Aylmer was a noble beast, and he desired no charity. That's why I offered him work. It was real work too. And it could be dangerous. I had meant to get Goliath over here to help me clean out this little part of the Southern Forest, but I never got around to it. As long as watchers could approach that close, I was never comfortable; though now that Kaiyo was here, we were probably safe. He may only be two and a half years old, but he's already over three hundred pounds, and he's mighty strong. Still, the watchers needed to go.

Just then, I saw two police-type SUVs coming down the driveway. From the house, our driveway went due west two miles until it entered what we called the Western Forest. From there, our driveway snaked around for another five or six miles until it reached the road. I could see Dovie and Aylmer getting nervous, but I told them to stay put. Kaiyo also said something that put them to ease. Then, a strange thing happened. Aylmer looked at me and winked. Next, he made a sound that made Kaiyo laugh. The cars were coming our way pretty fast, but they slowed when Aylmer stepped into the driveway and trotted about thirty yards toward the approaching vehicles. Aylmer stared; then, he snorted and stomped the ground with his huge hooves. Just before the vehicles got to the house, they stopped. Aylmer bellowed and tore up turf with his horns. By this time, I was behind my own truck and hidden from view. The first car honked its horn a few times. Aylmer acted as if he was infuriated and charged the car. Aylmer had a sense of humor. That was good to know.

My cell phone rang. We had a boosted Wi-Fi that worked nicely around the house and the barn. "Sam McLeod here."

"What in blazes is that thing?"

"Well, it's Sheriff Lee Tuttle! It is so good hearing your voice. Why, I do believe what you see is some sort of large bovine. You seem to have upset him. You probably shouldn't have done that. I heard he has an awful temper."

I was having fun with this. Dovie got in the game and walked over toward their trucks. Lee and Captain Troy Stahr were in the first truck, and Montana Game Warden Lowe Brigham and State Patrol captain Ed Hamby were in the second SUV. Dovie stood up and gave a roar. She looked frightening.

Just then, Troy opened the passenger door of the sheriff's car, stepped out, and threw open his arms. "Oh, I cannot wait to meet you two! I am coming over!"

The lawmen were very close friends of ours, but Troy was bold and sometimes reckless. He was almost like Dean that way; he also fully intended to match Aylmer's and Dovie's theatrics. Anyway, Troy just walked straight up to Dovie and gave her a big hug. Dovie looked back at us, but Troy didn't let go.

"He's on to you, Dovie," I said as I left my hiding spot. "Just give him some attention and hug him back. He loves the attention the most."

She did, and then, Troy stood back, looked at her, and held her head in his hands and said, "Goodness, you are a beautiful, beautiful bear! I am so glad to meet you. Did I catch the name? Is it Dovie?"

Dovie nodded. "Well, I sure hope you know the McLeods are the best of the best. If they like you, and it certainly appears that they do, then I like you too!"

Dovie looked like she had been swept right off her paws. She was obviously happy. Troy then turned and walked straight to Aylmer.

"Sam!" he said loudly. "Do you know that you have a bona fide aurochs here? They are the great grandpappies of all cattle, and they've been extinct for four hundred years. Well, the old stories were right—they were magnificent!"

Then, he spoke softer to Aylmer. "I'm right, aren't I?"

Aylmer proudly nodded his head. I figured that the country that Landon saw probably had plenty of aurochs in it, so extinction must be a this-side-of-creation sort of thing. Aylmer obviously wasn't very old.

Troy leaned in to Aylmer and said, "Trust me. Your secret is safe with us. My name is Troy Stahr. What is yours?"

"His name is Aylmer," I said.

"Elmer?"

Aylmer snorted; he didn't seem to like the name of Elmer. I thought it was a good name, but I'm sure it irritated Aylmer to hear his name mispronounced. I wouldn't want to be called Sim or Sum. Stahr was looking at me kind of funny. "No, it's Aylmer. It sounds very Southern, but it's really old English, I think."

Aylmer nodded. "Then, Aylmer it is," said Troy. "All right, Aylmer and Dovie, come meet my friends."

Then, the three of them walked over and met the sheriff, Captain Hamby, and Officer Brigham. I turned and walked back to the courtyard, and as I did, I saw Landon standing in the courtyard, staring at my back porch. His mouth was open, and he looked transfixed. I turned to see what he was looking at. What I saw on the porch was the future.

There stood Libby on the back porch; her hair was gently curled, and it fell in waves past her shoulders. She looked like she was twenty-five. I looked back at Landon; the poor guy hadn't moved. I leaned into his ear. "Take a breath son and close your mouth. Right now, you're looking foolish."

Landon breathed; he somewhat acknowledged me, and then, he bounded up on the porch to talk to Libby. Right then, the lawmen and Aylmer and Dovie came into the courtyard. I was looking forward to them meeting Landon, but we needed to get our stories straight. I strolled up the back steps and tapped Landon on his shoulder. He and Libby looked at me.

"Landon, I'm about to introduce you to those lawmen. All of them were part of the teams that tried to find you. They will press hard trying to find out everything. All I want you to say to them is you strolled way off course, and we and a few Specials rescued you. That's actually true. If they get too curious, tell them to talk to me. Can you do that?"

Landon and Libby nodded. "Feel free describing where you went and even where we found you in that cave. They may not believe you, but everybody else will. And say nothing about Sarah's little walk on the dark side. They probably won't ask anyway. Our story for her is she was also lost out there, and we got a twofer. Unfortunately, nobody was looking for Sarah, so she'll stay here for at least a while, but you will be expected to be on your way home tonight. You and I can continue our conversation when you come back to visit."

I looked at Libby and back at Landon. "And by the looks of things, that won't be very long, I'm guessing."

Landon looked confused until Libby laughed and simply said, "I hope not."

I took Landon to meet the four lawmen. They were always so pleased when a lost hunter or hiker or camper was found, and this time was no different. Troy was an acquaintance of Landon, so he was especially glad to see him. They asked him all sorts of questions, and he answered them correctly though he did leave out some big chunks of his story. Each of those lawmen was as decent as they come, and they were all friends with Tracker and Goliath. They all adored Kaiyo too, but who didn't?

Even though they were invited to stay for dinner, I was thinking that this would be over quickly and that they would be taking Landon to the hospital where his parents would meet him; that's the normal way these things go. They love it when they get to show the local press a victory or two. Finding Landon was a victory. Then, Sarah stepped outside.

OFFICER DOWN—DEAN

Kate and I were inside when Libby and Sarah came down the steps after washing up. I recognized my sister though she cleaned up nicely. She was a pretty girl, pure and simple. But what I liked about Libby was that she was so much more. She was smart, she was tough, she worked hard, she was never a complainer, and she just happened to be pretty. Some of the pretty girls in school are only that. They make the mistake of assuming their good looks will be enough. But most of them have no ambition and no appreciation for hard work. They'll probably be totally burned out by twenty-one unless they figure out life.

What surprised me was Sarah. Miss Aliyah had been upstairs helping her with her hair and makeup. What was different was she truly looked her age. When she was a demon-possessed harpy just the day before, she looked completely scary. She was filthy and joyless and could have passed for a skinny sixty-year-old drug addict. After her demon was chased off, she still looked like a mess, but her eyes came back to life. Before that, her eyes looked dead. Surprisingly, Sarah had pretty eyes. After Sarah decided to be a child of God, well she started to really change for the better. And today, one day later, Sarah was just flat-out pretty, and she looked her age. She was still too thin, but her joy showed. Dad once told me that joy, over anything else, is the most attractive thing about a person. And Sarah was proving him right. I said a quiet prayer of thanks for Benaiah. He's the one who saved her. And Landon did too. I guess I had a hand in that as well.

So there stood Sarah and Libby, and they looked terrific. Goliath was sitting with Tracker watching dinner cook, but when he saw Sarah, he gave a roar of happiness. Then, he bounded up and gave her a big hug. They understood each other.

Libby wandered on out, but Sarah stayed in the kitchen to talk to Mom, Kate, and Miss Aliyah. I went outside to see Landon talking to Libby. He was slightly out of his league, and he knew it. I was out of my league with Kate, and I have absolutely no idea why Mom picked Dad.

Anyway, after a few minutes of that, Dad took Landon to meet the officers. They all talked for a few minutes; and then, all four of the officers paused, looked up, and started staring at me. Landon was smiling at Libby and back at me. Dad was looking at me too. I was confused. They all were smiling. But Captain Stahr was looking at me in a way that made me super uncomfortable.

Then, I heard Sarah clear her throat. She was standing right next to me. I then realized that superconfident Captain Stahr was staring at Sarah, while he looked like some poor high school freshman talking to a senior. For the first time in his life, Troy Stahr had no words. But he was still quick on his feet, and he shot over to where we were standing in only a moment. I helped him out with an introduction.

"Captain Stahr, this is Sarah Tompkins. Sarah was also lost out in the Eastern Wilderness, but now, she's found."

I winked at Sarah. She snickered; she got my little play on words, but Captain Stahr probably didn't hear me. In fact, Captain Stahr pretty much ignored me. He slid underneath the rail and pulled himself up onto the porch.

"You're on your own, Sarah," I said.

She hit me on the shoulder, but she didn't look unhappy. The attention seemed welcome. In a second, Captain Stahr reintroduced himself and offered to introduce her to the other lawmen. Captain Stahr then escorted her down the steps to the others. I laughed and leaned on the railing. A few moments later, Kate came out and slid up close next to me. It was a wonderful evening. Kate was beautiful, the food smelled good, and Landon and Sarah were safe. It was good.

A few minutes later, Gunner arrived, and except for Benaiah, we were complete. I was wondering why he hadn't shown himself, but he's mighty shy. Everyone talked for another half hour as the sun was setting in the western sky. It was time. Jack and I went into the barn and brought out a large tub of grain and more than a bale of hay for Aylmer. He looked so happy. Mom, Miss Aliyah, Dad, and Gunner started bringing out steaks and chicken for the people and slab-sized cuts for the three bears and Tracker. Even the dogs knew they would be a part of it all.

Everything was placed on a big picnic table we put in the courtyard. There were tubs of potatoes cooked in salted butter and pots of steamed vegetables from our garden. Mom had also cooked breads of all types. We also had some huge salad bowls that Mom filled to the top. That didn't interest me much, but it looked good to the bears and to the females. Pies were placed in the window ledges, and Libby and Landon brought out big water bowls for the animals.

When everything was finally brought out, Dad asked me to pray. It was a big group, so I stood up on the porch and asked everybody milling around in the courtyard and driveway to form a semicircle and hold hands and paws. There was some good-natured grumbling from the officers except Captain Stahr; he was standing next to Sarah. I looked at the group. People and Specials were all mixed together. Everyone got quiet, and they all looked at me. "Let's pray," I said.

Just then, we all heard a loud howl mixed with a moan coming from the edge of the woods not fifty yards away to the south. Gracie was standing next to Tracker, and she saw his tail wag.

Gracie looked at me and said, "That's Rimmy or Bennie... Is that what we call him?"

In seconds, Benaiah broke out of the forest and joined us in our prayer circle. Libby and Gracie gave him a big hug. So did Jack. We were all so glad to see him. I guess he wanted to make sure no one else would be coming. And then I prayed. Everybody was mighty hungry, and nobody likes a too long prayer, but we had seen a few miracles. God deserved our gratitude. So I prayed a simple prayer.

"Father, we thank you so much for the miracles of Landon and Sarah. They were both lost in ways they never could have imagined. And now, here they are, found and now found forever. Your grace is amazing. Thank you for this big family because that's what we are. And finally, thank you for letting us be a part of the miracles. Amen."

Then, we ate, laughed, talked, and roughhoused for another few hours under the stars above our wonderful farm. Then, as the night came to a close, the four lawmen had to take Landon back to his family. His family was notified that he was okay, but they still wanted to see him and celebrate his rescue. I sure didn't blame them. If my son was lost like that, I would have been worried sick. Before they left, both Landon and Troy asked to return in the next few days. Libby and Sarah said *yes*.

After their departure, fatigue set in to all of us. Dad and Gunner went to the barn and laid down thick mats of straw for Benaiah, Dovie, and Goliath. Aylmer indicated he was quite happy in the courtyard. He had his cud to chew, I guess. Tracker headed straight upstairs where he took one of the two beds in the guest bedroom. He didn't ask, and nobody said no. Seriously, the wolf is like family, and he knows it.

Unfortunately, Kate had to leave too. She and her mom had worked hard today, and Jack and I had put in a long couple of days. Kate gave me a hug, and I held on tight for a long time. Jack came and tapped me on the shoulder. That kiss of hers a few days before was crossing my mind. I liked her a lot. She got in her mom's car, while Jack and Gunner loaded up Chevy in their trailer. Soon, they were gone.

Kaiyo was in the kitchen looking sleepy, while Mom and Dad cleaned up. We couldn't find Gracie, but that surprised no one except Sarah. We asked Sarah to look in the barn, and she found Gracie seated on a sleeping bag talking to Dovie, Benaiah, and Goliath. The dogs were laying on some blankets out there too. Sarah came back to report what she saw.

"So, umm, Gracie is holding court in the barn. I think she intends to sleep out there. In fact, I think the bears and Benaiah are nursing a carb hangover. Aylmer also went in to join them as I was leaving. She looks safe. Very safe, in fact."

Hearing the news, Kaiyo headed out to the barn too. Mom and Dad followed to tuck Gracie in. Gracie was certainly safe out there. She was surrounded by more sheer, explosive brawn than probably any human since the beginning of the world. Mom and Dad told Benaiah that if anybody got hungry, the kitchen would be open and to help himself and the bears if they needed it. I walked out to the barn too, said my good nights, and headed back in and upstairs. Sleep, real sleep, sounded nice.

I fell asleep thinking of what all had happened in the past few days. I awoke briefly sometime after midnight to sounds coming from the kitchen downstairs. I could hear Kaiyo's growly voice and then Benaiah and Goliath. I could also hear Dovie. They all were trying to whisper, but with animals, it just seemed louder. I heard the refrigerator doors opening and closing a few times; a couple of pie plates were rattled together. I heard meat being unwrapped and bags of potato chips being opened. They were laughing a lot too. Their little sleepover was obviously big fun. For me, it was like a lullaby; I fell back fast asleep.

PART 2

TRANSITIONS

HOMEWARD—KAIYO

It used to be when I left my farm home, everybody would get upset and cry. Not anymore. Well, Mom cries a little, and sometimes, Libby does too. Gracie just throws her arm around me and tells me she loves me and to hurry home. Dean usually peppers me with questions, like I could answer him. But they all know I'm family, and I am coming back. They all worry, but they are better than they used to be.

I suspected this trip would be longer than normal. I was so nervous. Raphael was both good and frightening at the same time, and he wanted to talk with me. I had no idea why. Raphael is a messenger, but he also has full authority in my home nation. At times, he looks human, and at other times, he looks like a creature. His role is to teach us animals right from wrong and truth from a lie. He calls it wisdom. Raphael once told Goliath wisdom is knowing why right is right and why wrong is wrong. That made sense. He also said that the beginning of wisdom is to want more of it. That would make me at least a little wise.

That morning, Benaiah left before sunrise. I imagine he slipped into the Southern Forest; it's close to the barn. He does not want to ever get caught out in the open. When he left, I checked on Gracie and tried to fall back to sleep. I couldn't sleep, so I wandered outside.

Aylmer was outside, and he motioned for me to come over. It was Aylmer who put me to ease.

"Kaiyo, this is your time to meet Raphael. But do not fear him. His role is to help carry out parts of the Master's plan. That is also your role and my role too. It's the role of all believers. But it seems you have a role in his plan that is big enough for Raphael to speak with you, so you must remember to be honored, not fearful. By the way, Tracker and Goliath are going with you. And Dovie too."

"What? I mean, that's great, but why? I can get there by myself."

"Someday, Kaiyo, you might be honored to present a new young hero to Raphael. This is their time. And they are presenting you to Raphael. Enjoy it and keep your ears open. Raphael speaks directly with the Master, so whatever he says is probably helpful, yes? And do not bow to him or do anything like that. He doesn't like it. Worship is reserved only for the Master. I know you know that, but it's easy to do when he's there in front of you for the first time."

I was so relieved. Aylmer looked at me. For a fearsome beast, he sure made me comfortable. I felt tiny next to him, but he didn't use his size to intimidate me. I thanked him and went back in the barn to try to get some sleep. Goliath, Dovie, and Gracie were sound asleep, and I just laid at the barn entrance and dozed in the dark.

After a few more hours, I saw a light go on inside. I waited only a few minutes and then went inside. Dad, Sarah, and Mom were in the kitchen when I came in to leave. Tracker was already in there. Mom knew immediately. How she could figure it out was beyond me, but she always could. Asking Mom not to worry or cry would be like asking her not to be my mother. But Mom was not a big blubberer; she was a weeper. She would weep and keep doing what she was doing. In the past, she would lecture me about roads, dogs, bigger bears, poachers, thorns, raging rivers, traps, snakes, rabies, gnats, and nearly everything that's scary. She called it all lectures one through forty-two. This time, Mom just sort of bit her lip, hugged me, and whispered in my ear, "Lectures one through forty-two, right?"

I nodded. She then wandered over to Tracker and asked if he was leaving too. Tracker nodded. "Together?" she asked.

Tracker and I both nodded. "Well," she said, "that's better. We are going to miss you a ton too, Tracker. And lectures one through forty-three for you. The extra one is to tell you to take care of Kaiyo."

She winked, and Tracker's tail wagged. "Breakfast?" she said.

Tracker barked in approval.

Dad was cooking breakfast, and he was watching Mom and me. He gave me the look and then came over and kneeled in front of me. He told me he was proud of me and that he loved me deeply. Then, we hugged. Sarah watched it all, and she started to cry.

"What about Dovie and Goliath? Are they going too?"

Tracker nodded. Sarah broke down for a few moments, and then, she caught herself. She apologized unnecessarily, but then, she said, "I will miss my new friends. They helped rescue me."

She barely got it out before she started crying again. This time, there was no stopping. I think more was going on inside of her than just a few bears and a wolf taking a trip. Tracker and I looked at each other; we didn't know what to do, so we just sat there. Mom went over and consoled her. Dad kept cooking. In a few minutes, Mom had Sarah laughing; Mom was good at that.

Gracie, Goliath, and Dovie came in and saw Sarah crying and Mom comforting her. Mom explained. Sarah then hugged Dovie and Goliath. She thanked Goliath repeatedly and asked him to be careful several times. They were good friends.

The kitchen was mighty crowded, so Mom shooed all of us into the front of the house as she and Sarah helped Dad finish cooking. Pretty soon, Dean and Libby came downstairs and joined us. Dad and Mom had cooked up a good breakfast, and Benaiah probably smelled it. Apparently, he left his spot in the forest and snuck into the back of the barn. He yelled at me to bring him some food because he wanted to stay hidden. Yeah, right, like I had hands; I didn't know what he was thinking. I yelled back and told him to man up and come inside and get real food. Then, he started whining; it went on for a while, and everyone was snickering. Finally, I felt sorry for him, and I told him to just quit complaining and wait. I went over to Dean. He acted like he didn't hear Benaiah, but we all did.

I growled at Dean until he just said, "Fine. I actually owe Benaiah a few favors."

That was true—he did. Dean grabbed a large bowl; filled it with sausages, eggs, four or five pieces of buttered toast, and a stack of waffles; and took it all into the barn. He took his own food too.

Sarah then looked at me and said, "C'mon, Kaiyo. Let's go with them. I owe Benaiah a lot too. I'll bring your breakfast."

I looked at everybody and then followed her out to the barn. The minute we got there, Benaiah stood up. Dean did too. I was interested in getting at breakfast, but I could tell Sarah had something to say. She walked up to Benaiah and stood right in front of him.

"Benaiah, I know it was Dean who asked you to catch me when I was lost and possessed, but it was you who overcame fear and brought me to this magical family. You didn't have to do it, but you did. Please, wherever you go, know I will never forget you. Your strength made it possible, but your bravery made it happen. I will miss you."

Benaiah just smiled. "Benaiah," said Dean, "I really do like that name."

Then, from out of the blue, Sarah asked Benaiah if we were headed to heaven. "Whatever Landon did when he got lost got a lot of attention, right? We wanted to catch him, and you wanted to protect him. And now you and Kaiyo and the others are leaving to go somewhere. Is it heaven?"

Benaiah just looked at her and smiled. He didn't say anything. I had no idea what she was getting at. Even Dean looked confused. "Benaiah, I am really afraid. I don't trust myself at all. I have been given another shot at everything, but what if I screw it up?"

I didn't know why she didn't ask Dean; he always had an answer for nearly everything. And he could actually talk. We couldn't. But Dean just looked at her and to Benaiah and back. Benaiah reached out, and he held each of Sarah's shoulders. His hands were huge. He towered over her. At over eight and a half feet tall and over eight hundred fifty pounds, he could have ripped her apart. Then, Benaiah spoke. From Sarah's point of view, all she heard from Benaiah was a bunch of gibberish that made no sense. Benaiah kept speaking. She had no idea what he was saying, but she listened and smiled; her eyes were wide open.

But I knew what he said. "Sarah. Do not worry. You may fail, but remember, you are a new creation. The Master loves to make things new again—things like your heart. That's what he does. Trust him, and don't try to figure out everything on your own. When you are here and when you leave, wherever you go, listen for his voice. Stay in the Book. He will keep you on the right path, I promise."

"That's beautiful, Benaiah, but she doesn't have any idea what you were talking about," I said.

"Young Kaiyo," said Benaiah sternly, "the Master's word never leaves a void. Remember that."

"So what you said, is that in the Book?"

"Yes, for the most part. Go look it up."

Dean was watching all of it. Sarah was beaming. "I know what you said! I used to talk to Lavi. I heard you! I understood you!"

Dean was stunned. "Wait! What? You got that? No way."

Sarah gave Benaiah a hug he was laughing. "I promise I will cherish those words forever."

"What in the world just happened?" I said.

Benaiah looked at me. "Kaiyo, you see miracles every day. You are a miracle. The Master gave her understanding, if only for that time. Accept it for what it is."

He patted my head, and he then sat back on the floor of the barn to eat his breakfast. I followed him with that. I hate to miss a meal.

"Sarah, did you understand what they just said to each other, just then, after Benaiah spoke to you directly?" Dean asked.

"No, that's strange. I didn't," she said. "Oh well, I guess I heard what I needed to hear. Let's go back to the kitchen."

Dean just looked stunned. That was rare; Dean is usually understanding. He was smiling big, though. I was done with breakfast and wanted more so I followed them back, while Benaiah slipped out of the back of the barn and took his position back in the woods.

After everybody had breakfast, it was time to go. Tracker told us the closest door was a long day's walk away. That was fine. Except for a few rounds of hugs for all of us and some words of wisdom to me from Dad, we really didn't have to do much to leave. We don't have pockets, so we can't bring anything. We don't ride horses, so we didn't need to deal with all that. We didn't wear clothes, so that was a good thing too. We traveled light. It takes my human family forever to gear up to go on a trip. I was made ready to go. And so we left.

Aylmer chose to stay at the farm, but the rest of us all decided to go back to our other home. I think several of them wanted to protect me too. Lavi was out there somewhere, and he was dangerous. I was happy with the company, and I remained far more concerned about Raphael. At the north end of the farm, just from in the woods, we heard a howl that told us that Benaiah was already ahead of us. Tracker responded.

We headed straight north, through a couple of miles of our farmland and then into the Northern Forest. This area wasn't like any other area around the farm. Not far from the north side of the farm, the terrain got more rugged. The mountains were only twenty miles away, and our way north was mostly uphill. We all spread out in the forest, so it didn't look like there was a herd of bears and a wolf; that would look weird. But we did make good progress. Tracker stayed well ahead of us; Benaiah was much farther ahead of us. He was so fast. We didn't lose them, though. We bears could easily follow Tracker's scent; we were better at tracking things than the best of bloodhounds. Our noses were even better than Tracker's. We also knew Tracker always knew where to go.

The three of us bears bunched up together again as we started walking along a trail that snaked its way into a box canyon. I was hoping the door would be in the canyon, but we just kept walking along the canyon floor. We made few sounds. The smells of wildlife were everywhere, but that was normal. Box canyons are a little spooky because there's usually only one way in and one way out. Regular animals seem to be able to sense the trap, but this box canyon was very big. The floor of the canyon was almost as big as the farm, and the entrance wasn't that tight. We could tell antelope, deer, and elk were used to this place. We could also tell a few bears and a couple of mountain lions had been in there. None of us were worried.

After a while, we were almost to the back of the canyon when our trail backtracked up and off the canyon floor. Soon, our trail was hugging the side of a cliff. To the left of us was a sheer drop-off to the canyon floor. I was concerned about Goliath simply because of his size; the trail wasn't very wide. But his size wasn't really much of a problem; we bears have good balance. He stuck close to the cliff wall, and we kept walking in single file. We climbed for another hour until we were above the tree line. Clouds drifted into us, and we were blinded by the thick fog several times. We came to a place where our trail neared the top of a flat, mesalike summit. There, we saw Benaiah; he was hidden, but he threw a few rocks at us. We turned to see him among some boulders not a hundred feet away. Benaiah was being serious; that meant we were close to the door. He kept his attention to our back trail, but we weren't worried. If anybody was following us, we would know. There were some bighorn sheep and mountain goats nearby, but that was expected; they like the cliffs. We knew their scents. Still, Benaiah is one of Raphael's chief guards, and I needed to respect that.

We continued until we topped the mesa. The views were beautiful, but we didn't stop to look around. We kept moving. Soon, we got to the other side, found the trail, and headed back down. A new cliff wall was again to our left, and a deadly drop-off was to our right. Our trail disappeared as it switchbacked to our left and around a foggy ledge. When we rounded the corner, we saw Tracker not very far ahead; he looked back at us, but he strayed from the trail and walked too far to the right. His next step missed and found nothing but air. He lost his balance completely and gave an anguished yelp. We saw him as he tumbled off the edge of the cliff. I was horrified and couldn't believe my eyes; Dovie gasped and let out a muffled cry. Goliath yelled out to Tracker, and then, he bolted to where Tracker was. But when he tried to stop, Goliath lost his footing on the slick bedrock. Dovie and I watched as he skidded right off the edge of the cliff and plunged out of sight. We heard a quick roar and then nothing.

What did I just see? I was about to panic. My two friends were gone and probably dead. "Think!" I said to myself. "Think!"

None of it made any sense. Dovie was paralyzed and nearly in shock; she moaned out loud. I was almost in shock too. "This can't be," I kept telling myself.

It didn't make any sense. How could this be?

And then I realized that, no, it couldn't be. There was a reason it didn't make sense. "No way," I thought to myself.

My panic disappeared. I turned and looked at Dovie and whispered, "It's a trick. At least I think it's a trick. Follow me."

She did, and we both went to where they fell. We could see nearly three thousand feet below us. If they fell, we wouldn't be able to see them in the jumble of broken boulders at the bottom. If they were there. I shifted my gaze away from the canyon floor, I was looking for something, out into the misty, foggy air. And there, my eyes focused, and I saw the door. "Look, Dovie, there's the door. See it?"

A little lower but close in front of us was the door. That's our name for it, but it's a nearly invisible, hard to see, wide oval. Looking through it was something like looking through water. It wasn't easy to spot.

"Yeah," she said, but this time, she was mad. "I see it. That wasn't funny. No, sir, that wasn't funny at all."

It took a little faith, but we both jumped into the thin air and crossed through the door together. Waiting for us were Tracker and Goliath. They looked disappointed we figured it out so quickly. Dovie was mad as a hornet, but I wasn't. We were home!

Thoughts—Tracker

Dovie was angry at us, and we probably deserved it. Still, I was so proud of Kaiyo for thinking through it. Panic didn't get ahold of him. I liked that. And we were home. I love it here—we all do—even though we still miss our humans. We were made to be with them, and when we get that rare chance to do life together, the way it was supposed to be, well that can't be matched.

Most of the citizens of this world will never have the experiences Goliath, Dovie, and Aylmer are enjoying. Benaiah is a watcher, and while he loves the McLeods, he's too much like humans to long for their company like we do. Wild, natural watchers are true monsters; they are smart, but they have no divine spark in them. That made them very dangerous.

As we traveled, I wondered if Aylmer would ever come home again. The last I saw of him, Gracie was riding her horse with Aylmer trotting right next to them. She was going to show him the farm. Aylmer looked the happiest I had ever seen him. Just before we left, he told me he intended to stay for a while. He said that he would stay at least until Kaiyo got back because, as he said, "somebody needed to keep them safe."

I laughed at that one. The McLeods are tough as nails and they're friends with every lawman in the county. But if Aylmer needed an excuse to stay with the McLeods, that was fine with me. I have also thought about living out my days with the McLeods. I still have work to do, but I like the idea. I even have my own bed in their guest room. I really don't know what's keeping me from doing it.

As for Kaiyo, he is blessed. He's a full-fledged child of a human family. That made him a star on this side. He's a mighty good bear too. He learns, and he thinks on his feet. He also has made his decision to serve the Master. And now, he meets Raphael.

There is a lot of conjecture about our home here. Most humans don't give it much thought, and if they do, they believe it was an old fable or a fairy tale. For the believers, their idea of Eden is usually a sickly view. I listened to Landon and Sam talk about it, and I could tell Sam's ideas about Eden were beyond weak. I don't blame him. For most believers, it's a kid's story, and that is probably all he has thought of it. He was surprised to learn how big it was. But Landon only saw a tiny portion of it. Eden is its own vast country. The Master did not design Eden for failure—he designed it for success.

We all know what happened here in Eden so many years ago with Adam's petty rebellion. Even though the Master knew from the beginning humanity would rebel, it had to hurt. Ingratitude is hard to accept. Still, Eden was made to be lived in by all of humanity and then to be missed if, and when, they were banished. And it was missed. For a long time, the memories lived of this amazing place, strong and vivid. But too much time has passed, and other beliefs have assaulted the ancient stories. The truth is Eden is the place that has been made for man, for us, and for the Master. Raphael has called it the heart of New Jerusalem many times. Everything is here but man and the Master. But I have heard man is coming, and then, the Master will join us. Raphael can't tell me when because he doesn't know. But he has told us to get ready.

VISITORS—DEAN

It has been only a couple of days since Kaiyo left. Just because we know he's going to come back doesn't mean we don't miss him. We do. But every time he goes away, he comes back more like a wild bear and yet more like us. It's all very hard to explain, but it's true.

Before we went out to go find Landon, I had started getting ready for football and for tenth grade in general. Football starts in mid-August around here. Living on a farm is a lot of work, and farmwork makes me strong. But football requires a lot of running, and farming doesn't. So, for the last few weeks, I have been running. In the mornings when it's cool, I run down our driveway, up into the trees of the Western Forest and back. Three miles up, three miles back. I once saw a billboard for the Marines that said something like "Pain is weakness leaving your body." That was probably true. It doesn't mean it's fun, but it is fun being strong. So the running is worth it.

Moose usually goes with me, and Major comes if Dad isn't home. That's good because we live in bear country, and I run early. There are also wolves, mountain lions, moose, elk, and some big coyotes. There are even occasional watchers too. Yesterday, Aylmer joined us. It's like having a tank for protection. I didn't even bring bear spray. And Aylmer has no problem keeping up. He's not some lazy bull who sits all day in the pasture. Captain Stahr told me that

Aylmer was an aurochs. From what I've learned, they're terrifically strong, and they can run a lot longer and a lot faster than I can.

On this day, I got up early and dressed for my run. When I came out, Aylmer was waiting for me in the courtyard. Animals, even the Specials, seem to sleep all the time and none of the time. What I mean is animals sleep very lightly. If you have a dog sleeping on the couch, open a food wrapper anywhere else in the house and the dog is up and headed your way.

"Good morning, Aylmer. Ready?"

He nodded and stomped a hoof. His hooves were tremendous. Moose was at my side. I stretched for a few minutes, and then, the three of us headed west along the driveway, away from the house. Aylmer ran alongside of me to my left. He was pure muscle, and I have never been anything but amazed at his size. He ran so his head and his horns stayed just in front of me. I was aware of those horns, so I let him take the lead.

Running was always a mind game for me. Many animals and some people seem to be made for it, but I needed to force myself to run. In the first half mile, every joint of mine was screaming for me to quit and go back to bed. After powering through that though, the steps came easy. I told Aylmer to pick up the pace, and he easily punched it up a few notches. I felt the cool breeze encourage me to run faster. Moose was right alongside of me; he was keeping to a modest trot. Aylmer was right in front of me. The next mile sped by as we neared the woods of the Western Forest.

My mind drifted to Kate. That happened a lot. She was planning on coming over today, and I was looking forward to it. She and Miss Aliyah were coming over to meet with Sarah. Sarah had some life issues that needed sorting through. She had also learned some brutal lessons about what not to do, and she wanted to share some of that with Kate. I thought that was a good idea. A lot of young people my age don't have a clue about learning from people who have lived a lot of life. Me, I want advantages. I want advantages in every part of my life. If I can learn something that makes me better, I'm all in. I know the world is competitive, and I intend to enjoy my share of victories. So I listen to what older people have to say, and I try not to forget. I have friends who mock older people; their doing so only promotes their own ignorance. That's okay; I'll gladly learn the painful lessons from somebody else who had to learn the hard way.

So if Kate avoids what Sarah ran toward, she will win that part of life. For a lot of reasons, I wanted Kate to want to be better. Not that she wasn't already wonderful, but everybody needs to make a practice of trying to be a better person. I hope she wants that for me too. Every time she sees me, I want her to see a better Dean. It won't always happen, but it's up to me. So even though I run for football, I also run for her. Frankly, thinking of her is a lot more motivating than thinking of a coach yelling at me or a bunch of smelly teammates. So, as I was running, I was thinking about Kate. Until suddenly, I wasn't.

Aylmer was bellowing, and Moose was going crazy. And I was scared again.

Mixed Reunions—Susan

Early this morning, Sarah called her mother and father. I have no doubt the Tompkins had been through their share of raw heartache as Sarah grew up. Sarah was clear she had been a wild child, and very few things were off-limits to her. Being a parent is mighty hard, and each child charts their own course. I have seen great kids with rotten parents and vice versa.

I got the impression Sarah's parents were good folks. Sarah seemed drawn to self-destructive behaviors. She didn't even understand why she was so self-destructive. Among many things missing in Sarah's life as she grew up was perspective; her parents should have filled her in on it. Somewhere along the line, Sarah failed to understand she was made by God and designed for greatness. I don't blame her or her parents; a lot of people don't understand that. Unfortunately, when they forget it, they drift. And during her short life, Sarah had been a drifter. Her life was a series of very few good decisions and a ton of bad ones. She went from one bad thing to the next and somehow always saw herself as in the right. And her journey was a mess. Each step tended to be more dangerous than the one before. My heart continued to break for her.

Sarah's parents didn't know about Sarah's recent possession by a powerful demon. They thought she had just decided to quit communicating again. Sarah told her mother she wanted to come home, but she needed to stay with us for a few more weeks. Her mother didn't quite understand, but she readily agreed. Her father got on the line to tell Sarah he loved her and missed her. Sarah beamed. She asked him if he and her mom would drive from Helena in two weeks so they could meet us and take her back home. Even I could hear his big voice over the phone happily agreeing. Then, I heard him cry and promise she could count on him to be there. The two of them had a good cry, and I walked outside to give them some privacy.

I stood outside, taking it all in. I loved the farm. Still, this place is never the same without Kaiyo. I miss him as much as I will soon miss Libby when she goes off to college. There is no question that when he is here, everything seems closer to the way things should be. Sam stepped outside.

"Do you hear that?"

Farms can be noisy places. Grain dryers and conveyors can be noisy, tractors and combines are noisy, and animals can be noisy. But this morning, except for a cow moaning in the distance, it was mostly quiet.

"Hear what?"

"I hear Moose and Aylmer."

I stepped farther out into the courtyard, and then, I heard it. The sounds were not loud, but it was obvious Aylmer and Moose were mighty upset. Then, it dawned on me that Dean was with them, and he might have been hurt or in some sort of real danger. "Let's go!"

Sam was already ahead of me. He raced into the kitchen and grabbed our rifles. I ran to the UTV, started it, and met Sam in the driveway. We had about two miles of driveway to get through, and it seemed like we would never get there. Still, our little utility vehicle was fast, and we closed the distance quickly. To our relief, we saw Dean standing behind Aylmer. Both Moose and Aylmer were riveted on something in the woods, just where the driveway went into the forest. Aylmer was bellowing, and Moose was barking, but neither of them were rushing into the woods; I thought that was very strange. We pulled to a stop, and Sam leaped out and ran toward Dean. I followed quickly.

Dean jogged over to us. "I have no idea what's going on, but Aylmer came to a quick stop, and he kept me from running past him. Then, both of them started making a lot of noise. And, Dad, I felt exactly the same fear as I did when I saw Sarah the first time. There's something over there."

I felt it too.

"They see something. Animals can sometimes see spirits. It's in the Bible, right?" asked Dean.

"Well, yeah, it is, at least sort of," said Sam.

Sam looked around and made sure everybody was safe. Then, the three of us walked up to Aylmer. We saw where he was looking, but we couldn't see what he saw. I looked at Dean and raised my voice over the noise. "You just said you were strangely afraid, like when you saw Sarah for the first time."

"Yeah," said Dean. "Just like it. Why?"

I pulled Dean and Sam back away. It was too noisy, and I had to move just to hear.

"He's back," I said. "And he wants to move back home."

Sam and Dean went white with that. It made sense. "And I bet he is bringing friends," said Sam. "We can't tell Sarah about this. At least not yet. I don't know if she can handle it."

Dean was looking back toward the house. He pointed to my SUV headed toward us. "I think it's too late for that, Dad. That's either Sarah or Libby driving this way."

Sure enough, somebody was driving my car way too fast. It skidded to a stop close to us. I saw Sam clench his jaw. The driver-side door opened, and Sarah stepped out. She looked at us and walked on over. Libby got out of the passenger seat and followed Sarah. Gracie also popped out of the back. She came over and looked at the scene.

"Geez, it's creepy here!" she said out loud.

She was right, and when she said it, heads nodded. Sarah smiled and started to walk past us toward Aylmer when Sam stepped in her way. "Sarah, I don't want you here. He, or it, is after you, and Landon's not here to cast them out again. Go back to the house. Please."

Sarah looked at Sam. She was totally confident and almost eager. I liked it, but I sure didn't expect it. She motioned all of us together. We made a circle of sorts, and Sarah spoke.

"Sam, that thing over there despises you, your wife, and your kids. I know this for a fact. I learned about you people long ago. And, Sam, we need to talk. I appreciate you being protective, but you have no faith. None. Not any. Seriously, Sam, what's gotten into you?"

Sarah stared at him. At first, she looked like a predator, but her face softened in a gentle, mirthful sort of way. Sam looked like he'd been kicked in the rear. She didn't wait for an answer, and she continued. "First of all, that thing over there is not a him or an it. It's a them. There's a bunch of them. Goliath's old oppressor and my old possessor is their leader. They think they can just stroll on in and take up residence in me again. They can't. What lives inside me now terrifies them, and that has been true ever since Dean shared the good news with me. Weren't you there, Sam? Because I thought I saw you there. Did you think I was joking? Sam, hopefully, you know it's not all about just saying a few magic words. I'm way past that now. And, Sam McLeod, you should know that."

"Well, I do. I just…"

Sarah interrupted him. "Stop it, Sam. I'm emotional, but I am not fragile. I have been through a lot, and you interpret my overwhelming gratitude as weakness. Maybe you don't think you do, but it's true. Well, your god is too small to do much of anything. But mine is plenty big to deal with this inconvenience. You, who have been blessed with all this beauty around you, should know better. Now, step aside please. I need to introduce them to the new tenant."

Sam got out of Sarah's way as ordered. Sam looked at me; he was ashamed. "I am so sorry," he said to Sarah sweetly. "Be careful. You might need our prayer cover too."

"Now you're talking," laughed Sarah. "I'll always need that."

As Sarah turned, I noticed her smile. It wasn't a happy smile. In fact, she looked more like a predator. That was our first glimpse into her true personality. We had thought of her as a victim. She never saw herself that way. She was preparing for war, and she was made for it. I loved her for it too.

We watched as Sarah strolled up to Aylmer and whispered into his ear. Immediately, Aylmer got quiet. He nuzzled her face and stamped his hooves. Sarah calmed Moose. Then, Sarah took another ten or so steps past all of us, and she simply prayed. We did too and with our eyes wide open. We watched as she commanded the spirits to leave, and she did so in the name of Jesus. She prayed for about a minute when we all heard roars that turned into panicked shrieks coming from the thin air right in front of her. She kept praying when with one big, deep growly scream, they were gone. We could feel it; it was that obvious. Libby ran over and gave Sarah a big hug. Sam was beaming. All of us cheered. Dean ran over and thanked Aylmer for sticking up for him and the rest of us.

Sarah walked back, and Sam hugged her.

"Sam," said Sarah, "to be fair, you don't know what I know. A few days ago, I was possessed by one hundred percent, poisonous, slimy filth. Now, I am indwelt with pure love. I can see the power of God so much easier than you. And don't worry about those guys. They're not coming back. They've been forever evicted."

I was so proud of her. From that day forward, Sarah was one of us. And she was right; those things never did come back for her.

2

MEGINNAH—KAIYO

It's a shame I cannot share my home with my family, but those are the rules. The cherubs would probably have to kill them if they ever tried to get in here. How Landon made it is anybody's guess, but the Master didn't want him dead. As for people coming back to this place, man had his chance here, and they blew it. Man was made with the potential for great beauty and unending accomplishment. Unfortunately, that also meant man has the potential for breathtaking evil.

I'm grateful to be a bear. I love all of it. While we bears will never be able to build a rocket, we also won't ever build a bomb to put on that rocket either. And to add to the confusion, some of those rocket and bomb builders are doing absolutely the right thing, and some are clearly not. The world of man is beyond understanding.

We came to a cherub as we approached Eden. He looked us over with his many eyes and faces, but he knew us all. Tracker and Dovie went past the cherubs a lot because they worked for Raphael. The three of them talked together, while Goliath and I waited. Dovie motioned for Goliath and me to come over. Eden is guarded by several of these cherubs. I don't know how many there are. Tracker and Dovie probably know them all, but I only have met two cherubs. Cherubs are big and especially terrifying creatures; at least they were the first few times I met them. The very first time we met, I turned and ran away. I think I screamed like the baby bear I was. Tracker had to chase me down and talk me into coming back.

Now, they're not quite so scary, but I know they're to be respected. Each time I have come here, the evidence of their fearsomeness is obvious. Old, ancient skeletons of people and creatures lay about at the sides of Eden's entrances. Seeing that is a stark reminder that Landon was mighty lucky to live.

The Book describes cherubs as living creatures, but that's only sort of right. The better interpretation is animals. Cherubs are animals, just like I am an animal. They are an ancient race, and they're smart too. Some people think the cherubs are angels, like Raphael. I know better—they are not like angels at all. They're angelic beings, but they're also animals, like me.

This cherub's name was Meginnah; at least that's what it sounded like. Goliath told me it meant *defender* in the old language. The name was appropriate. The cherubs are the perfect guards when it came to protecting us from intruders. By the looks of things, he hadn't had to slay anything in a long time. When Goliath and I walked over to see him, Meginnah looked at us. Meginnah has plenty of eyes, so when he looked at me, I knew it. He spoke first to Goliath.

"So, Goliath, tell me about our friend Mr. Haldor."

Goliath looked a little confused until Dovie said, "He means Landon."

Goliath laughed, and he proceeded to tell the whole story, and he didn't hold back. Meginnah asked a lot of questions, and all of us chipped in with answers. When we got to the part where Dean convinced Benaiah to capture demon-possessed Sarah, Meginnah started laughing hard. He's such a weird-looking creature, but watching him laugh made him seem like one of us. Goliath told him about my family's kindness to Sarah and about Landon's casting out Sarah's demons. Tracker told Meginnah about Libby's role in causing Sarah to feel safe. Tracker finished with Dean's story about the thief on the cross and about Sarah's coming to the Master.

"Too many people pay scant attention to that part of the Master's story," said Meginnah. "But the thief's story is pure power! We all heard about Sarah. Her repentance and love for the Master is a great story. She will be tested, though. Her enemy is still trying to reclaim her."

Meginnah paused to let it sink in. He changed the subject. "And this Dean, from the reports I hear, he has the heart of a lion. What else did he do besides capture a demon?"

Dovie told Meginnah about Aylmer and his capture by Goliath, me, Dean, and Jack. With his humanlike hands, he rubbed his faces. "Capturing an aurochs like Aylmer is wonderfully foolhardy! I love these stories. Knowing Aylmer, I am sure he eventually listened to reason, right?"

"Yes, he did. And he stayed back with the McLeods. He's very happy right now," said Dovie.

I filled him in on the story of Lavi. "So you and your brother were going to wrap him like a house cat?" asked Meginnah as he laughed long and deeply. "Oh, I would surely love to have seen that. That proud and evil creature deserves nothing less. He is fully lost in his narcissism."

I would have to figure out that word later. I told Meginnah of my experience with Lavi. Tracker told Meginnah about Dad shooting off the tip of Lavi's tail. Meginnah nodded his approval, but he looked back at me.

"Well, young prince, beware. Lavi is a dangerous foe, and his getting shot by a skilled shooter who happens to be your father will cause his hatred for you to burn even hotter. You have some growing up to do before you will be fully safe from him."

Meginnah stopped and looked at us all and said, "And it is good to see you, all of you and especially you, Kaiyo. I know you must be looking forward to seeing Raphael. Depart from here and go visit your kin. I will see each of you upon your next departures."

And that was the end of our little meet and greet. When Meginnah said it was time to go, then it was time to go. That was okay because going inside was like stepping into a pure, vibrant world. The colors are amazing, and everything smelled so good. Being bears, Dovie, Goliath, and I had no problem eating plant food; we do that all the time because it's good. So the first thing we did was graze on the sweetest grass ever eaten. Even Tracker loved it.

After a while, a large group of citizens came up to us to welcome us back. Eden has every type of creature that has ever lived on earth. Those types of animals that have been extinct in the world thrive here. And many of them are so strange-looking. A lot of them are huge too. Of course, regular animals were also there. It's not unusual at all to see a tiger walking down a lane discussing life with a huge, hairy rhino. We see stuff like that all the time. Unlike the world, there are no predators here. We don't really have any bullies either. The animals here know they have work to do and that the Master created them for a reason. I will always wonder why my mother ever left this place. It has worked out for me, but it sure didn't for her. I cannot curse my path, but I am free to grieve and miss her. I know what being blessed means. It means when I am here, I long for my human family; when I am there, I miss my home here. I am blessed to love both.

No matter what, when I come here, the animals I meet here all ask me about my family. I don't quite know why we animals are so attracted to people, but all of us here in Eden are. Hopefully, Raphael will let me ask him that question. Anyway, we were asked about our latest adventures. I shared some of the recent stories with them and told them about capturing Aylmer. Tracker told the story of Sarah. When he was done, all the animals gathered around us and cheered. We know something even many devout people don't understand. We realize we will all get to meet Sarah one day, and when we do, she would be hearing about the day we told her story. We animals here do not look at time with dread like people do. We look forward to the future.

Dovie talked about being with my family the day we got back and about how sweet they were to her. Earth is a very, very dangerous place for most animals, and when they heard about my family, well, they just couldn't stop with the *ooohhs* and *aaaahhs*. When Dovie spoke about Gracie, they just loved it more. All the animals here are drawn to human children because they're so cute. Every time I'm here, somebody asks me how I get along with the adult humans in my family. To them, adults are frightening.

While Dovie was entertaining the crowd, I happened to look up between mouthfuls of grass and saw several brown bears come wading through the crowd. That would be my kin. I immediately recognized my cousins and my uncle. They were terrific bears, and every time I'm here, they open their home to me. Of course, they don't really have to; this place is awesome. Sleeping outside is never a problem unless it rains.

"Make way, please," bellowed my uncle. "I want to see my nephew!"

Eden isn't quite like earth, and here brown bears are not the biggest animals around. We're not even the biggest bears. There are cave bears and short-faced bears here that make us look small. Back at the farm and in the wilderness, Goliath is the most fearsome beast around. Not in Eden. So nobody throws their weight around here. If they did, it wouldn't work; there's always somebody bigger. And it wouldn't be right to try it any way.

Still, everybody parted quickly, though probably just out of courtesy. And my bears came rushing in. My two cousins were about my size, and they came at me like torpedoes. I was ready. I have learned living in the world has only a few advantages to living here in Eden. But one of the few advantages is the learning and strength that comes from hard work and danger. Most people wouldn't think of danger as an advantage, but it is if you survive through it. So, when it came to my cousins, my senses were sharper, my reflexes were quicker, I was stronger, and I knew how to fight.

When they came at me, I dodged them as they flew past. Then I turned, leaped, and went at them. In a split-second, I had landed on both of them and smashed their heads into the grass. I roared like I was ready to kill. Then, the three of us cousins started laughing uncontrollably. I stepped off their heads, and they jumped up all over me. The animals watching us were a little bit concerned; I am a lot wilder than they are. They figured it out quickly, though, and the crowd started to thin out. It was time to see my bear folks.

Bear reunions can be a little rough, but our reunions were wonderful. I felt at home with them. My bear mom and my aunt were sisters. They say my aunt looks like her. My aunt and uncle take great care of me; they love me, and I love them right back. We talk about my bear mom a lot. Her name was Jana. It's an old Hebrew name. She must have been amazing.

Unfortunately, they do not know why my bear mom left and ended up wandering around in the Eastern Wilderness. I think her murder nearly broke my aunt's heart. My uncle gets mighty sad about it too. But both have forgiven Goliath. They think my mom was either running from something or was tricked into leaving. They also think my human family is still in danger because they rescued me. I believe them.

One day, I will find out who wanted my bear mom to die. I know it was Goliath who actually killed my mom, and he did try to kill me too. But who was it that told my mom to leave here and why didn't they tell her Goliath was a killer? Who was it that told my bear mom to get near Goliath? Whoever did that is the real killer. And one day, I will find out who it was, and there will be justice.

My bear family lived in a beautiful valley, and I was looking forward to seeing it. Goliath and Dovie walked with us until they each veered off to be with their own folks. Goliath's family is older, but his real mom and dad are still here. Since he changed, they have been so proud of him. He's come such a long way.

Tracker left our group early and went back to his pack. He's famous because he has helped many lost souls find their way back. He helped to save Goliath, and he made sure I knew about this place. I owe him a lot.

We soon got to the entrance of our valley. The valley floor was covered by miles upon miles of green grass and creeks. Birds flew about and seemed determined to prove to the world that flying is amazing and fun. The floor of the valley is longer than it is wide, but the width had to be five to ten times the size of the farm. From there, the valley was surrounded by gentle hills covered by all sorts of fruit trees and other beautiful trees. Behind the hills were steep mountains that stayed snow-covered all year. It was a bear paradise.

I was there for four wonderful days and then a messenger flew to our valley with the news. It was time. Raphael wanted me to see me.

LANDON'S BACK—LIBBY

The Fourth of July was right around the corner, and it had been a week since we got back and six days since Kaiyo left. I missed my little brother, but I knew he was safe in the odd land Landon told us about. Landon is sure the place he saw was a part of Eden. He didn't mean it was like Eden or was similar to Eden. He believes he looked into the real, ancient nation of Eden. He is confident too that God preserved it from the flood and from man. Dad was skeptical at first, but now, he's convinced. The monster that Landon saw was probably one of the cherubim described in Genesis, Ezekiel, and other Bible books. Among other things, the Cherubim were the defenders of Eden. The whole interdimensional thing at first sounded far-fetched, but a quick Internet introduction on quantum mechanics made it all sound reasonable.

Of course, my imagination has run wild thinking about it. I would love to go there, but Landon is pretty sure he was the only one to have looked at it and lived. In fact, he never went into Eden; he just stood at the threshold and looked in. I'm glad he didn't get killed—real glad—especially since he was planning to come back today.

He was coming to help us do some work on the driveway and then go into the Southern Forest to start clearing out a few hundred acres or so of forest to create habitat for wildlife. We also needed to create a buffer between us and the watchers and the other things that creep up too close to our house. A lot of people think dense forest is good animal habitat, but that's only true for a few types of forest animals like squirrels and the creatures that eat them. Basically, if the sun can't get to the forest floor, plants don't grow. And meadow-type plants provide food and cover. Without food and cover, you get a biological desert. It only looks good from a distance.

Dad also wanted to install a gate on our driveway so that if anybody wanted to come visit, they would have to push a buzzer so one of us could remotely open the gate. That way, any of the Specials lounging around here could easily slip into the forest unnoticed. We all thought that was a good idea, and we sure needed the privacy.

It's against the law to have wild animals as pets, and it's even against the law to feed certain kinds of animals. Bears are number one on the *do-not-feed list*. Those are good laws, but they weren't written with the Specials in mind. Also, since Benaiah is only a mythical beast to most people and since Aylmer is supposed to be extinct, making it easier for them to keep out of sight of the occasional visitor driving down our driveway just seemed like a good idea.

First to show up were Jack, Gunner, and Kate. Kate had been spending time with Sarah, but she also was happy to see my brother. Gunner drove his truck, but Jack and Kate rode out in front on their four-wheelers. Dean was waiting on all of them. Gunner did what he did every workday. He pulled up, parked his truck, and went into the kitchen and filled a small thermos with coffee. He loves our coffee. And since Kaiyo wasn't here, he was able to score some leftover bacon. When Kaiyo is here, there's no such thing as leftover bacon. In fact, there's no such thing as leftover anything. Kaiyo has learned good manners; but at dinner, when we are all at the table, he eats his huge meal, and then, he watches us eat. He focuses on Mom, Gracie, and me. Dad and Dean clean their plates. Kaiyo is still a growing bear, and only rarely is he not hungry. Sometimes, Gracie and I eat slowly just to tick him off. Little brothers are fun to tease.

Dean went straight to Kate first. Good call. He's learning. He used to yuk it up with Jack first thing. Now, it's the second thing. He helped her off the four-wheeler, and she acted like she needed it. She didn't of course. She's tough. I kept looking up the driveway for Landon's SUV, but the next visitor was in an unmarked police interceptor. That was Troy. He's totally smitten by Sarah. She's even met his two little girls. Troy is a single dad, and he's been taking care of his girls since they were babies. Troy is a great cop and a true friend of our family. If he and Sarah were to ever become a thing, it would be fine with me. They both come with some hefty emotional baggage, but they were so open about it that they seem healthy. Troy bounded out of the car and immediately took a verbal jab at Dean. They enjoyed the back and forth.

"Morning, Dean. Another day of you being worthless?"

"Morning, Captain. You do know I'm only fifteen, and I've already saved more people than you, and you're a cop. Dang! And I believe your girlfriend is one of them, right?"

Troy just stood there with his big smile. He had no comeback because what Dean said was true. After a moment or two, he smiled and said, "And, Dean, I am mighty glad you did."

"She's in the kitchen. Go get her," said Dean.

Troy fist pumped Dean and headed inside to see Sarah. They had a lunch date in town. And then I heard Landon driving down the driveway.

Landon had an old four-wheel drive SUV. He took great care of it, and seeing it for the first time was a treat. I was waiting for him when he parked in the grass by the front door. While we had texted and phoned each other a lot after he left, I had not seen him since the night we brought him back.

I remembered his great smile, and when he saw me, I saw it again. I waited on the porch as he bounded up the front steps and came jogging down the porch. I am sure he wanted to hug me and kiss me, but my father and brother and the rest of them were watching. I'm not real big on public displays of affection, but a quick kiss and a long hug would have been nice. I was looking at Landon as he headed my way. Landon can be a good-natured doofus, so when he got to me it was clear he had no idea what to do. Personally, I was curious too. I was looking at Landon as he was hurrying my way. I watched his eyes shift from mine to the crowd of males not fifty feet away. I saw his confidence melt. And then he tripped.

It wasn't a little trip either. The poor guy took a few quick, clumsy steps that just didn't quite catch up to his forward motion. His arms flailed briefly, and he hit the porch deck hard. A little dust flew up as he skidded to a stop right at my feet. I heard Gunner laughing, and then, the rest followed. A torrent of insults were hurled his way too. Landon groaned, rolled over, and started laughing. He looked up at me. Landon had his pride, so I had to be careful not to laugh too much or act like a doting mother. I smiled.

"Well done. I'm worth falling for."

He got up quickly and hugged me and gave me a quick kiss. And that was all right with me. That shut the men up too, except for my dad's unnecessarily loud throat clearing. Then, we both laughed as I took him by the hand into the kitchen to see Mom and Sarah and to get some coffee.

Raphael—Kaiyo

I had been walking through the countryside for several days. Home here was truly wonderful, but I was ready to get my meeting with Raphael over with. Fortunately, this is the original creation, so it has everything. There is food everywhere, the water is terrific, and the animals that live here are the best. But there is something missing, and we all know what it is. When the Master made this place, it was made for him, for us, and for man. In short, we miss the Master, and we miss the people. The divorce has been hard on all of the creatures here. Still, there is much joy here and a lot of hope. And this place is certainly not boring. It's just as amazing as it was the first time I came here. A pair of American lions joined me on my trek. They looked just like regular lions but were bigger. A group of daeodons joined us for a while too. Daeodons were fearsome creatures that looked sort of like enormous, carnivorous wild hogs. As scary as they looked, they were twice as funny. The lions and the daeodons were extinct on earth, but there were plenty of them here. There's plenty of everything here. And I am a really small.

After a while, the discussion was mostly about my family—my people family. The animals were fascinated with the thought of me having a human mom and a dad who loved me like a son and not as a pet bear. I told them about how Dad taught me about history and being careful and smart in the woods and how Mom taught me to read. They were amazed by that. Everybody up here is smart, so reading is no big deal, but it is for those of us who live on earth. When we got to talking about my brother and sisters, they just stopped right there in the grassy lane and kept asking for me to tell more stories. So I did.

I told them about the time I rescued Gracie from a pit with a rattlesnake in it and about the time when Libby and I chased off some really bad guys who were trying to sneak onto our property. Then, there was the time I fell through thin ice on one of our ponds and Dean risked his life and rescued me. I didn't exaggerate either, and they were still great stories. By the time I was done, a crowd had gathered. Standing around me were all sorts of birds, some reptiles, the lions, the daeodons, and a bear who was as big and tall as a horse.

He was a really nice bear, but I am glad I wasn't dodging those guys on earth. Male grizzlies were trouble enough. They kept asking for stories, and because I had a bunch of them, I kept talking.

After a while, it started to get dark, and I got tired of talking. Everybody left, and nearly all asked if I wanted to come to their homes. They were all so nice, but I preferred to sleep under the stars—always have, always will. I found a nice place up on a hillside because the tops of hills are usually the first to dry. My dad taught me that.

Getting ready for bed is easy; I just lay down and curl up. I wasn't on guard about anything like I would need to be at home. No hungry wild animals lived here. I could sleep deeply knowing that I would be safe. In moments, I was dreaming of home. I was starting to miss them again.

That morning, I woke up, and I wasn't alone. Raphael was sitting on the ground, staring at me. "You can sleep longer if you want to. I'm not going anywhere."

He was smiling. I was pretty sure he meant it, but seeing him there startled me; I got wide awake quick. "No, sir. I'm okay. I'm good."

He smiled again, and I felt like a tongue-tied fool. Raphael knew the Master personally—not like the rest of us did and certainly not like believers on earth. Raphael and the Master were actual friends. In addition, Raphael was powerful beyond my understanding. I was scared even though I knew he wasn't going to harm me. I started to shiver uncontrollably. I didn't want to; I just couldn't help it. Raphael stood up.

"Come, young prince. Walking will settle your soul. And you know I love you, right? And so does the Master."

"Why?" I stammered.

"Because you are worth it. Never forget that, Kaiyo. People forget that all the time. They confuse being unworthy of the Master's sacrifice with thinking they're worthless. The fact the Master did what he did proves the point that people are not worthless in the least. He knows his children are far more than worthless. Everybody is made for amazing things. They forget that part. Well, perhaps that's not true for Libby, Dean, and Gracie. I think they believe it. I like that."

He went from being serious to a gentle chuckle. "You actually know them?" I asked.

"Of course, I do," he said gently. "Kaiyo, do you know why you are so well known here? The story of your love for your human family and their love for you is both rare and a beacon of hope for all who live here. You are one of your parents' children, and you are loved no differently than your human siblings. Everyone here knows about that, and it thrills them because they know that someday, creation will be reunited. They also know they will be a part of it, and they will then share their lives with humans, the way it should be."

Raphael paused, and then, he started talking again. "Just as a young child often dreams of playing with a tiger or lion or a fearsome animal like you, the tigers and lions, bears, and crocodiles who live here dream of playing with human children too. Humans and animals are creations of God, and that means they were made for God and for one another. The divorce has been hard on all creation. So they see in you and your family a glimmer of what it once was. It is a refreshing dose of what will soon be reality. It's wonderful really. The only issue is the fallen nature of man and creation and the troubles they both bring."

I wasn't shaking anymore, but I thought of his use of *soon. How soon?* I wondered. But I held my questions.

"Kaiyo, did you know that when creation is restored, people will judge the angels, me included?"

I had heard it before, but I never understood it. "Hah, I'm sure you are looking forward to that!"

I was being sarcastic, and Raphael let me. "Kaiyo, I am indeed looking forward to it all—even the judging part. The children of God have earned it, don't you think?"

I looked at him. He was not kidding. "No, Raphael, I don't. Or maybe I can't. People are not like you. I love my family, and they are wonderful, but even my mom isn't good enough or smart enough. I'm sure even Dean would agree he's not good enough."

"You're right, Kaiyo. Dean would know he's not ready for that, and right now, both he and you would be right. But do you know why I have such admiration for so many of the believers?"

I shook my head. I had no idea. "Kaiyo, unlike people, I am not dependent on a very frightening world. Go into any cemetery, and you will see the very best face man can put on death and dying. But each grave comes at a price, and that price is paid in pain."

"Kaiyo, I have never had to bury my child or a little sister or brother. I've never suffered through all those depths of sorrow. I have never lost a parent or even a friend."

Raphael paused. "Think of what I have. I know the Master. My faith is easy. I can see what I believe. I have never lost everything to a flood or a fire, to war, to a criminal, or even to my own poor judgment. No wife has left me, no children cursed me. I have never cried out to a seemingly silent God and begged for a needed miracle. I have never doubted. And I have never been attacked or even mocked for my faith. I have never felt unloved—not even once.

"History and the present are filled with children of God who have kept their faith, who have persevered through unspeakable pain, who have lost nearly all hope, but who refused to curse God and die. Those faithful people, I will gladly serve them throughout eternity. And we will.

"Since the beginning, I watched their plight. Troubles have been with humans and the rest of creation since the fall. So when I think of myself, I know I will never have my home foreclosed or be taken to court over a debt I cannot pay. I'll never get bullied or even picked last to be on a team at school. Kaiyo, I will never even have to wear glasses. And while I have felt the searing pain from the great battle with Satan and his horde, I know death is not my destiny. I haven't even caught a common cold. Trust me on this if nothing else, the Master eagerly awaits the many reunions of the faithful, as do I.

"Kaiyo, I will happily be judged by your wonderful family and countless millions like them. So now, let's move on with our lessons."

Raphael was talking, and we kept walking. We walked and talked for hours, and except to sleep and eat, we didn't really stop. In fact, we spent the next five weeks together. Raphael spoke wisdom, and I learned much. I kept reminding myself I had an angel who knows God firsthand as my companion. I am still amazed.

He taught me about the war for the souls of man and that we would one day have victory. But he told me all wars are made of battles, and while we would win the war, we have lost battles before, and we would certainly loose battles in the future. That surprised me, but he said battles are lost and won every day. Then, he told me I would have battles of my own. I didn't quite know what he meant, but it made sense.

I loved my time with Raphael, and I grew in wisdom and in knowledge. He told me about everything that I asked about. From woodchucks to airplanes to prophesy to history, he knew it all. And he shared freely. During that short time of growth, I also grew in size. Raphael said my additional growth would come in handy because I would need it. He was right—bears need to be big, and I was still smallish for a grizzly bear. But I knew I was getting stronger here too.

Yesterday, when I woke up, Raphael greeted me and had a full breakfast ready. It was meatless, of course. Here, in Eden, meat would basically require a murder. But I did have cheese and milk and all sorts of great plant food.

"Kaiyo, you have asked me many questions, but you have never asked me why I call you a prince. Aren't you curious?"

"Yes," I said. "I am curious. I figured you would tell me when you thought I was ready to hear it."

"Good answer," Raphael laughed.

Raphael had a deep and wonderful laugh. "Of course, we have no real royalty here. That wouldn't do. But you come from a family of warriors. Because of that, the Master wants me to let you know that you are one of his princes, just like one of David's mighty men.

It's an honor he bestows on few. He sees you as his fierce and loyal child. He doesn't call many by the name of prince. Faults and all, he loves you dearly. He is your king, and you are his prince."

"Tracker is a warrior, so are Benaiah and Goliath. But war especially runs in your family. Your great-bear-grandfather was a warrior for the Master. Your human grandfather was once a warrior too. So was your bear grandfather. Your big brother Dean is a warrior now, and he will most assuredly be in the future. And, Kaiyo, your bear father was a mighty warrior."

He paused to let that sink in. I had no words. "Kaiyo, the answer to the mystery surrounding your mother and her death is not known to me. It is for you to find out. But your father was one of God's warriors who fell in battle before you were born and even before most knew he loved your mother. I knew early on because I conducted the ceremony when they committed themselves to each other.

"Rest assured, your father was a fierce warrior and as big as Goliath, if not bigger. He was guarding an open door that was attacked. He fought off an assault from the enemy's soldiers. There were several humans along with two watchers trying to force their way in. Your father held them off, but he was no match for the humans' guns and the watchers' clubs. The door was not breached, but we still look at it as a battle lost. Your mother mourned deeply, as did I."

I didn't know what to say. I was stunned at what he was saying. We were together for weeks, and there was no mention of my bear dad at all. My mind was spinning. Who were those people? Where are the watchers? But the only thing I really wanted to know, I asked. "What was his name?"

"Eli."

"Did you know him? What was he like?" I had a lot of questions like that.

For the next two hours, we talked. By the end, I was so proud of my father. He was a great bear. Just knowing about him made me feel so much more whole. I knew who I was. For whatever reason, I was a child of two families from two worlds. And I had so much to be proud about.

Raphael then looked at me and asked if I had any other questions. "Can you tell me more about my mom? And I also want your thoughts on who could've persuaded her to leave."

"Kaiyo, it is possible no one did. Jana was suffering from some severe heartache. Her life-mate was murdered. Perhaps she just wanted to get away."

I looked at Raphael. "Do you think that's likely? Because I don't."

Raphael looked at me and spoke softly. "No, Kaiyo. I do not. But for some reason, I know nothing of why your mother left. Few things escape my notice here, but that did. The Master will not share what he knows, which is everything, of course. He told me finding out is up to you. I do not want to believe any of our citizens of Eden did anything to hurt your mother. Perhaps there was a breach."

"A breach? Wait. What? Can that happen? How would anybody get past Meginnah and the others?"

"You are right about that, Kaiyo. The cherubim's role is to protect the Tree of Life and Eden from humans and all other enemies. Apparently, the serpent or something somehow got to your mother. Perhaps we had a traitor among us. Lavi came and went several times before he was banished. There could be others who escaped our vigilance. The Master had a traitor with him, so perhaps we did too. And, Kaiyo, we want you to keep in mind the goal of deceiving your bear mother may have been to kill you or to somehow use you. That's my speculation though."

That made sense. My time with my human family has only served to encourage the animals here in Eden. "So tell me about my mother."

THE GARDEN—SAM

Clearing land seems easy, but it's not. It takes years to get it right. My goal was to create spaces where wildlife could thrive and where the Specials could hide. A lot of people argue about what's best for wildlife, and none of them are totally correct. Politics, ideologies, self-interest, and ignorance plague the debates. Today's job was simply to create a hidden path, about the width of a single-lane road, that would cut east into the forest and then dogleg back west so the trees could hide the trail from view. The next goal was to clear some land in the Western Forest and add a turnaround to the driveway where the new gate was going to be installed. Then, as time allowed, we intended to bulldoze a few hundred acres deep into the south woods so our Specials could hide. If we could clear out ten acres today, that would be great.

Where's Kaiyo—Dean

That first day of clearing had gone about as I expected. We worked until we ached and couldn't see anymore. I didn't expect any trouble from watchers, and we didn't have any. Aylmer and those of us on horses headed into the forest at various places, and as we did, we spooked some black bears and a bunch of deer, elk, and some moose. Watchers may not be on our side, but they're not always on the other side either. Watchers are smart, and sometimes, they just do their own thing. I am sure they would like to grab some of our livestock, but that opportunity hasn't played out yet. Since the dogs sleep outside, sneaking onto the farm would not be easy. Now that we have Kaiyo in the family, that just made their coming onto the farm even riskier.

We didn't need Landon driving the Bobcat that day because I knew how to drive it well. But Libby wanted him here, and having him here was a good thing. If I had to guess, either Landon will be my brother-in-law someday or Libby will dump him when she gets to college next year. If she does though, she'll eventually regret it. Landon's a good one, and good guys are rare.

We made terrific progress. Gunner drove the old Ford backhoe like a master. He and Landon went into the Western Forest about a half mile from the main road and started to work. Gunner spent hours cutting into a hillside and filling a gully. Landon drove the Bobcat over it to keep it nicely compacted. By midafternoon, they had cleared out an area for a turnaround and a gate. Dad had called a company in town to install an electric gate. Since power poles went down our driveway, it would be easy to make it work. That gate would add a lot of reassurance to all of us.

Within another week, we cleared a hundred or so acres. We ultimately intended to clear out more land, but Dad had a plan for that. So, in the weeks following our work, Dad and Gunner busied themselves seeding the lanes and the new pasture in native grasses with prairie clover. At the edges, they planted serviceberry, wax currents, and rabbitbrush. Dad likes birds, so they planted enough berries, seedy grasses, and flowers to attract as many birds as western Montana supports. Planting anything in summer is tough, but we were fortunate to have had several good soaking rains in the weeks after we planted.

While all that planting was going on, Sarah's time with us came to an end. Her father and mother had come from Helena to pick her up. It was on a Saturday morning when they got here. Sarah was nervous, but a good kind of nervous. She was dressed comfortably, but her clothes didn't hide her prettiness. I was on the front porch as their car made it down the long driveway. Aylmer slipped easily out of the back of the barn and disappeared into the forest.

A few minutes later, they drove up to the front of the house, parked their car, and got out. Sarah's father looked older than his age. Sarah's mother had also aged beyond her years. I'm sure that being a parent of Sarah came with a lot stress, a lot of disappointment, and a lot of tears over the years. She'd been a problem child for probably most of her life. I stood up to greet them as they walked up the stairs to the front porch. Sarah's father spoke first.

"Hello there, young man. I'm Kurt Tompkins, and this is my wife and Sarah's mother, Linda."

He reached out and gave me a strong handshake. Mrs. Tompkins could give a strong handshake too. "Welcome to the farm. We've been looking forward to your visit."

Libby came out and introduced herself and so did Gracie. I could tell the Tompkinses were enjoying themselves, but they must have been mighty curious about their daughter. Mom opened the door and invited them in. They introduced themselves to Mom and Dad. Mom immediately told them how much our family has loved their daughter. On cue, Gracie came out of the kitchen leading Sarah by the hand. I kept my eyes on Sarah's father. I intended on being a father someday, and I always looked for examples of good fatherhood. I watched as his eyes caught Sarah's, and I saw a dad find his lost, little girl. He gave a muffled moan and ran to Sarah.

He was crying. That was one good dad. They embraced. Sarah's mom was right behind him, and she joined into a small group hug. Sarah was both laughing and crying. I think I saw my own dad wipe away a few tears; I know I had a few tears too. There wasn't a dry eye in the place. Mom led them to our dining room for some privacy. She brought them coffee and treats, and we gave them their space; they had a lot of catching up to do.

I went back to my chores, and a couple of hours later, we all ate out on the picnic table on the back porch. A Sheriff's Department SUV pulled up right as we were finishing lunch, and Captain Stahr hopped out. He's usually overconfident, but today, he looked a little nervous. Sarah went out and grabbed his hand and brought him over. Less than an hour later, Captain Stahr loaded up Sarah's few belongings in the Tompkins' car, and Sarah and her parents drove off with Captain Stahr escorting them to the county line. I think we all felt her loss. Sarah had turned into an awesome lady, and she would be missed. Her absence somehow also made us all wish Kaiyo would come home soon. I hated it when he stayed away too long.

By mid-August, the new hidden pasture was really developing into a beautiful meadow. Both Gunner and Dad intended to make the cleared-out area look like a park, and they were close to it. Each day, after football practice, Jack and I would go out there to just take it all in. Aylmer had apparently fallen in love with the place. He knew we made it for him. He spent a lot of time in the barn and anywhere else on the farm he wanted, but several times, we saw him just standing in the middle of the pasture just taking it all in. Jack and I would go talk to him and bring him some treats. So far, there were no watchers, but he showed us tracks showing where he had run off a few black bears and a grizzly.

The only thing we worried about were wolves. Aylmer was big, but a pack of wolves is deadly when it wants to be. Twice, he got attacked by the same pack, and we heard him bellowing. The first time, Moose and Major bolted out to help him, and the three of them held off the pack long enough for Gunner to ride up and shoot a few shots in the air. The other time happened yesterday. Tracker had come to visit us. We were all outside to see him, but before we could get in three words, we heard Aylmer cry out from deep in the hidden pasture. Tracker took off, and the dogs were right with him. I grabbed my rifle and ran after them. Gunner had gone for the day, so Dad ran for the UTV. If a golf cart and a small pickup truck had a baby, it would look like a UTV. We depend on our two UTVs.

Anyway, I was running down the path when Dad caught up to me. We both arrived in time to see Tracker crash through the pack and right into the biggest wolf. Tracker didn't even bite him; he just ran into him and knocked him down and back a ways. Dad and I kept our distance. We watched Tracker stand over the poor cowering beast, while Aylmer walked up and stood over him. The rest of the wolf pack, about nine other wolves, stood back. They were totally confused. Tracker was all wolf and nearly twice the size of the alpha wolf. And, to further confuse the wolves, he was with the big bull and with the dogs. The wolves took it in, and they seemed to decide to be submissive. The dogs were barking, but a few growls from Tracker shut them up. The tables had totally turned on the pack, but I had to give the wolf pack credit for not running.

Tracker let the alpha wolf up, and then, he gave it a quick chase to force it to submit again. He then released the wolf and turned to Aylmer, and they both turned away from the pack and started to walk away. Tracker stopped, turned, looked back at the pack, and the pack ran off. I wasn't quite sure what had transpired, but Tracker and Aylmer had taken the fight right out of them. The wolves were not frightened by Moose and Major even though dogs are often more aggressive than wolves and a little crazy at times, especially Moose.

But Tracker had them totally intimidated. Aylmer was dangerous, but I suspect the wolves still looked at him as fresh meat on the hoof.

Before long, the foursome came up to us on the way to the house. Dad made Aylmer agree to sleep in the barn or the courtyard until the wolves moved on out of the area. Aylmer agreed, but I could tell he and Tracker were distracted. They mumbled to each other, and they double-timed it back to the farmhouse. The dogs thought it was all fun, and they happily ran along. Dad looked at me.

"Something is going on with those two. Any ideas?"

"Kaiyo, maybe?" I said. "I could tell when Tracker first got to the house, he wasn't quite right. Like he was trying to sniff up something."

"Yeah, I noticed that too. Let's hustle back. I think we got an issue."

In grown-up speak, an issue is the same as a problem. And Dad was right—we had a problem. By the time we got back to the house, Tracker was already in the kitchen greeting the family, but he made it quick. Dad and I walked in, and Tracker whined. Communicating with the Specials, especially when they want something, is frustrating. Mom asked questions like *what's wrong* and things like that. Unfortunately, that sort of question requires much more than a *yes* or a *no*; it requires the ability to speak English. Dad cut to the chase. "Are you looking for Kaiyo?

Tracker nodded to say, "Yes."

That was a problem, and everybody started talking. Questions were flying all around, and Tracker was trying to answer the questions he could. This wasn't our first time with the Q and A. In short order, we learned from Tracker what was bugging him. Kaiyo had left Eden days before, and nobody knew where he was. We had a real issue.

Worst of all, we didn't have a clue what to do. Kaiyo had vanished.

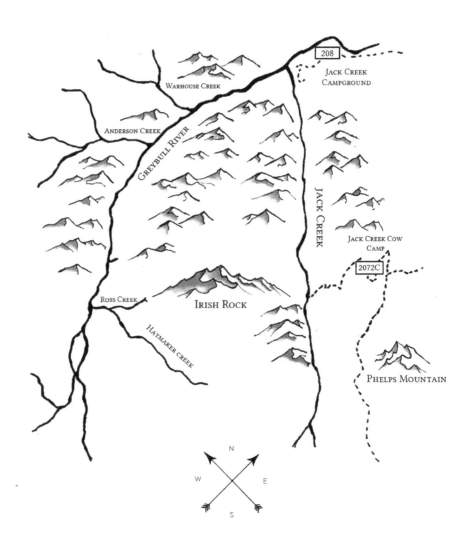

3

COMING HOME—KAIYO

I was lost, and nobody knew it. The doors that bridge the way between the worlds don't always open to the place where we expect them to. It is our responsibility to look around and get our bearings once we step outside. If we don't like what we see, we can always make our way back through the door. But this time, I and several magpies and a raven came out, and I was thinking of home while they were discussing their missions and what they needed to do. We have magpies and ravens in Montana, so I just guessed we were all headed to the same place. We weren't. After about ten minutes of walking down a mountain, a mountain that looked the same as any other mountain in Montana, they flew off. It was then I noticed, slowly, that the air didn't smell quite right; it wasn't like home. I looked around and realized I had no idea where I was. As far as I knew, I could have been in Mongolia. I knew then I was in big trouble.

Panic is not a grizzly bear problem. We don't panic. We can fly into a rage quickly, but we don't panic—at least not often. But I wanted to panic. I was scared and mad and embarrassed at the same time. How could I have made such a sloppy mistake? I immediately headed back up the mountain, but this time, I was running hard. If I was lucky, the door would still be open. I ran fast and got to the spot in less than five minutes. The door was gone; I searched everywhere. All I heard was the breeze and a few twittering birds.

I have long heard my human family say everything happens for a reason. Right about then, I had a hard time believing them. We were supposed to acquire wisdom so we didn't do stupid things. At that point, I had little comfort in that thought. I had showed no wisdom, and because of that, I was lost, and I had absolutely no idea what to do.

I spent the next ten or fifteen minutes feeling sorry for myself. But finally, I accepted my lot. I was a midsized grizzly alone in the forest. That's a normal life for most grizzlies. We're somewhat grumpy anyway, and we like being alone most of the time. Then, I prayed hard for deliverance, wisdom, and strength. Then, I prayed that if I died, I would have courage and die a good death. I had God waiting for me on the other side, so why shouldn't I go out in a blaze of glory? At least, I sounded tough.

Anyway, after that, I looked around and smelled everything on the wind. I needed a look around, so I decided to climb higher. There, I could get above the tree line and maybe get a clue where my home was. Also, I could grab any scent that floated by. At least it was something to do.

People who don't live in mountains don't understand how mountains are more than big hills. Mountains can have their own valleys, cliffs, creeks, glaciers, forests, and tundra, plus some. A mountain can have different climates and different weather, all at the same time. And mountains, at least the ones I know, are big. I had hope too because the mountains in the range I found myself in were big, just like the ones near home. My hope was they would lead me home.

Normally, I would watch my back trail, but I didn't really have one. So I got very still and watched all around me. After a few minutes of that, I picked myself up and walked up toward the tree line.

I made sure I was working the wind. My nose was telling me nothing new, and that was a good thing. That meant I probably wasn't too far from home. The tree smells were basically the same, and I caught the vague scents of elk, deer, porcupines, and other things that I was used to. The good news was I didn't detect anything strange. Seriously, in the situation I was in, *strange* was something I just didn't need to deal with. Being totally lost was strange enough.

I made my way up the slope, but I took my time. An animal in a hurry gets a lot of attention, and I didn't want to attract any unnecessary attention. So I just acted like an ordinary grizzly. If something smelled interesting, I would check it out. I stayed alert. After an hour of wandering up the slopes, the trees gave way to a dryer landscape of grassy areas with low plant cover. I saw a few patches of snow stubbornly clinging to the shadows. I climbed still higher.

I came to a peak that allowed me to see in every direction. To the east, I saw miles of lower mountains that fell off to a vast plain that went to some far distant mountains. I could see a few towns, a lake, and the telltale green ribbon of a creek or river that flowed out of the endless mountains that were to my north and west. Mountains seemed to be in every direction but east. I saw a road near that far creek or river too. I needed to be making my way home, and a road might help me figure out where I was. And I was hungry too. That was where I needed to be.

I stayed hidden in some rocks and shifted so I could see better to the north and west. I figured I was probably in the Rocky Mountains, and I needed to know which way to go. At the base of the mountain was a dirt road. That was great news. I liked seeing that road, but I didn't need to act too quickly and get shot at or get crossways with a bigger bear or a moose.

After an hour, I spotted some movement. Three dirt roads came together at the north base of my mountain; I watched as a mother black bear and her two cubs took the road that headed south. They walked right down the middle of it, so I guessed the roads weren't used much. Still, I decided to take a different road; mother bears are always trouble. I began to make my descent.

After a few hours coming off the slope, I made my way to the crossroads using trees and rocks for cover. I saw a road sign and prayed it was in English. Shuffling over, the sign said FS 207 2C. I knew that meant the road was a Forest Service road. Bingo! Now, I knew I was in America.

My mood jumped to positive again. Happier, I quickly crossed the road and kept it to my right. I wasn't so bold as to walk in the middle of the road. I went mostly west, taking advantage of whatever cover was available. Wherever I was, it was pretty country. I passed an empty cabin nestled in some trees on the other side of the road to my right, but I was not interested in an empty building.

It didn't take long until I descended a few long slopes to a point where I could see that the road ended at a dusty parking area. There were a few vehicles and trucks with horse trailers parked there so I stayed out of sight. Parking lots in the middle of nowhere don't just happen, so I knew there was a reason.

I took a few steps out of my cover when the breeze shifted, and I caught the wonderful smell of clean water. I had passed a few little ponds on the way, so I wasn't thirsty. But a creek means fish, and fish are food. I thought about staying to the south of the dirt parking lot to get on the other side of the creek, but I needed some information.

I didn't see any people, so I gathered my courage and strolled boldly into the little dirt parking lot. I quickly looked at the car tags. Of the five vehicles, four had Wyoming car tags. The other one had an Iowa tag. I figured I was in Wyoming, and that made my heart leap. Wyoming was super close to my home in Montana, and I was thrilled. Libby and Mom had taught me to read and write with my paws. They also showed me maps of the country and the world, so I kinda knew where I was. I also knew I could walk home from here, and I had no doubt about that at all. It might take a month, but I could do it if I had to.

Since there were people here, they would be used to seeing bears because we were in wild country. If my nose was right, and it always was, there were plenty of bears where I was. So I came up with a plan.

I looked around the parking lot for footprints, the smaller the better. Finding prints was easy; all I had to do was to look at the ground near the car and truck doors. I moseyed up to the cars, and yep, just as I thought, a lady and a couple children were here, so was a man. Their tracks were proof enough. Perfect. Even better was that they were from Iowa. I like Iowans. My mom's family is from Iowa, and my cousins visited once when I was a cub. They're great folks.

But I wasn't looking for great Iowans. I needed people without guns, and travelers usually don't carry them.

My plan was first to score some food. Not just some roadkill, which is good, but I was thinking sandwiches, trail mix, and cookies. This area looked like a place where people hiked and rode horses. I even saw tire tracks. People always seem to travel with great food, and Iowans are great eaters. So I wandered north along the right side of the creek looking for some Iowans.

It wasn't long before I heard children laughing and splashing in the creek. There, about two hundred yards away, I saw them. I went wide right, but not too wide, and kept walking until I was right behind the picnicking family. Their backs were to me as they watched their kids play in the water. They were fun to watch, but it was time to turn on some charm. A bear out here, especially a grizzly bear, can be scary. I didn't want to scare anybody. Scared people may give up their food to a scary bear, but they bring back other people with dogs and guns. I didn't need any of that.

I was probably about a hundred feet from the parents. I sat and rested on my butt and waited. Sure enough, one of the kids climbed the creek bank and saw me. He was probably about eleven years old, and he froze in fear. So I waved. He wasn't expecting that. I waved again, this time with some up and down paw movement. And I stayed seated. That was the key. In a second, he was pointing at me and telling his parents. The dad leaped to his feet, and he unholstered his bear spray. That was good. If he had unholstered a pistol, I would be running away fast. But I sure didn't want him to get closer and use the bear spray either. Bear spray is pure pain.

The mom ordered their little girl up and out of the creek. She stood there protecting her children. I liked that. So I waved again. We bears have good wrists so we can give a pretty sweet wave with our paws. They just looked at me. I gave them another paw wave that looked extra cute. Then, I waited and stayed seated.

The dad lowered his spray, and he waved back with his left arm. I mimicked his wave as good as I could. He smiled and looked at his wife. She wasn't smiling; she was a mama bear in her own right. But the dad told her to wave at me. She gave me a quick, silly wave, like she was embarrassed. I did the same thing right back. The mom's mouth nearly dropped to the dirt. I mimicked that too. After a few more minutes of me mocking and copying their motions, she was laughing. The dad was having a time of it all. Then, I went in for the kill.

I pointed to my mouth and then rubbed my tummy. I even tried to make a sad face. They all started looking around them like they were being filmed by some hidden cameras. They even looked up for drones. I expected this, but it was still fun to watch.

Then, the dad yelled out something like "Are you hungry, big guy?"

Oh yes. Yes, I was. I nodded vigorously. He turned back, and I could see he and his wife were quietly arguing. Men sometimes do truly dumb things, and sometimes, women do too. But women with young children are usually smart enough not to feed grizzly bears. People get killed that way. Even getting too close to grizzly bears can be fatal. Ordinary grizzly bears can fly into a rage without provocation. So feeding bears is way up there on the stupid meter.

It was time for me to push this one over the edge. I cried. Yeah, I faked it, but I needed to get my point across. Then, I pointed to my mouth again. The mom melted. I watched as the dad reached into his sack and grabbed a sub sandwich. Too bad it wasn't an Iowa fried pork tenderloin with pickles, but a sub sandwich would work just fine. But this was the hard part. I didn't want him throwing the sandwich out of fear of getting too close. That could ruin a perfectly good sandwich. So I motioned him over with both arms. He pointed to himself and then back to me. I nodded excessively. He took out his bear spray and took a few tentative steps my way.

Seeing that bear spray gave me an idea. I put one paw over my eyes while I motioned him to keep coming. I saw him smiling at that. He covered that hundred feet with great caution; I didn't blame him. When he got closer to me, I held out both paws, pads up.

I got to give it to the dad; he wasn't too bright, but he had guts. He laid that sub sandwich right on my paws. It was probably the bravest and certainly the dumbest thing he had ever done in his life. Mom over there was filming everything with her phone. I pulled in the sandwich and left one paw sticking out. He shook it. When he did, I nodded a few times. Then, I proceeded to eat my turkey club sub sandwich with loads of cheese and peppers. It was terrific.

When he went back over to his family, I saw him scrambling to get more food. "Can I bring one of the kids? You won't hurt him, will you?"

What fool talks to a bear? Seriously, talking to bears is just crazy. Anyway, I kept eating my sandwich and motioned with a paw to bring the kid on over. "You sure?"

I looked up and nodded. The mother was wearing out her cell phone to film it all. The dad brought over the boy, and he shakily gave me his peanut butter sandwich. He was smiling big, but he was still scared. I let him touch my paw. He squealed in joy. By then, their little girl was practically climbing on her mother to let her feed the cute bear. Mom relented. This had to be as weird to her as anything she had ever imagined. I wondered if she knew feeding the bears in heaven would be a commonplace thing. Raphael told me that, and I look forward to it. Hopefully, she knew the way to heaven.

Mom led the little girl over to us. I was glad because she brought the sack that held their food. When she got there, I sat back and held out my paws. The little girl laid a nice peanut butter and jelly sandwich right on them. Of course, I ate it. They kept bringing stuff out of that sack and feeding me. They even gave me some loose mints that had probably been laying on the bottom of the sack for years. The mother forgot all reason and asked for a picture. I nodded.

While I'm smallish for a male grizzly, I'm still a good-sized bear, so getting everybody in the picture was not working. But I needed them to take that picture. The mother looked frustrated and took charge of the situation.

"Can the kids hop on your back so we can all be in the picture?"

Good judgment wasn't their strong suit. People have been killed by bears a lot smaller than me. But I nodded my head and got back on my four feet. They stepped back out of fear. I motioned for the kids to hop up on my back. The father was loving everything.

"Oh man! Honey, this has to be the best trained bear ever! He's done this before. I wonder what he's doing out here in the wild?"

"Eating our food!" said the laughing mother.

She was filming everything. When the kids got up on me, the two adults squeezed in next to me, and we took a selfie. Then, more selfies. I smiled every time. When the pictures were taken, the kids got off. They thanked me profusely, as if a bear would understand. But I did. I gave the family a bear salute, and I walked off, downstream, and to the north. I knew there were more people downstream, and right now, I needed more people.

The family said their goodbyes. I heard the dad say, "No one would ever believe what just happened. I can't wait until I post this."

And that's what I wanted to hear. Once they got their videos in circulation, it would probably only take about a day for them to get reposted around the world. I felt certain Gracie would see it. And when Gracie saw me, she would tell Mom and Dad, and then, they would come get me and bring me home. As it turned out, I was nearly right. Gracie didn't see it first. A day later, Sarah up in Helena did. She called my mom just as Gracie came racing downstairs screaming and holding her cell phone.

To the Greybull—Dean

Libby was waiting to pick up me and Jack from football practice. It was late, and I was tired and beat up. I may be big for my age, but I'm not close to the biggest kid on the team. I'm a little over six feet tall, but there are a dozen kids on the team taller than me. Only a few of them are stronger than me, so that matters for something.

Grown-ups always say a particularly dumb thing that bugs me to no end. After they find out I play football, they say something like "Well, are you having a lot of fun?"

Whoever says that has never had to deal with football practice in the summer or they forgot everything about it. What is fun about football practice? It's hot, the coaches are always mad, and football literally hurts. I love the games. I like the duels. I like the attention from the girls, and I love my team. But football practice is not close to fun. And today was even less fun than usual. It was hot, and for some reason, the coach decided to practice longer and run us more. Fortunately for us, it was Friday, and I was done for the week.

When I came out of the locker room, I saw Libby waiting in her truck. Jack was right there with me. Libby saw me and immediately started waiving me to hurry. Well, Jack and I had no hurry left in us. And we were carrying our gear. She became even more emphatic, but all I could do was to trudge on.

"It's Kaiyo!" she yelled.

"Oh geez," said Jack.

We broke into a full sprint. She had the truck pulled out in a *go* position. We threw our smelly gear in the truck bed, and I all but flew into the front seat. We started asking questions, but Libby motioned for us to be quiet. When we got out of the school lot and on the road, Libby filled us in.

Somehow Kaiyo had pulled a rabbit out of the hat and figured out a way for us to find out where he was. It started with a few videos of a Midwestern family picnicking in Wyoming. They even posted selfies with my little brother, cheezing it up, front and center with their family. All I had to do was search my phone, and there was my little brother trending heavy. There were about ten other videos of Kaiyo taken by six or seven different people at a place called Jack Creek Campground in Wyoming. I had never heard of that place, but he made sure he got some pictures of him next to the sign. The campground was along a stream called the Greybull River. That river's name was familiar to me, but I didn't quite remember why.

Libby told us Tracker and Aylmer were shown the videos. They shook their heads in disbelief. A short time later, the two raced off the farm and were last seen making time for the northeast. Landon had talked about a door of sorts that led to Eden, and we suspected they were headed to one of those doors.

Libby laid out the plan. Mom, Dad, and Gracie were taking the four-horse trailer with them. Gunner was going to drive his truck taking me, Libby, Jack, and our horses in another four-horse trailer. Landon volunteered to stay at the house and watch the farm. Captain Stahr and Sheriff Tuttle were notified, but they couldn't help because they weren't Wyoming lawmen. They were on standby to vouch for us if necessary.

We drove straight through the night and arrived in Meeteetse, Wyoming, right at sunup. We found a nice little restaurant and were able to park our rigs on the street. After stretching our legs, we went inside and ordered breakfast. Just as we were finishing and as Dad was paying the bill, we watched a Wyoming Highway Patrol officer walk around our rigs, check out our tags, and inspect the horses. That got our attention because there was nothing unusual about us being here. Trucks and horse trailers have always been common in the West. She lingered around the trucks, and since we were done, we exited and walked to our rigs. Upon seeing us, she waited by the trucks as we approached.

She spoke first. "Where are you Montanans headed today with those beautiful horses?"

At first, the trooper spoke like a cop. I can't describe it, but all law enforcement types tend to talk the same way. She was in her thirties, pretty, somewhat short with dark hair. She seemed confident. Libby told her we were headed to Jack Creek Campground to ride the trails. The trooper looked at each of us and said, "And to see the amazing grizzly bear, I bet," she said.

That caught us a little off guard, but Gunner was quick. "What bear? Are they having bear trouble?"

Gunner looked sincere, but the trooper showed no emotion. She was obviously unconvinced. Mom told Dad out loud that we don't need to go where there's bear trouble. She was faking and only mildly convincing. The trooper looked at us slowly. She looked at Gunner again and asked for his identification. This was getting weird, and there was no reason for her to stop us. The trooper was wasting our time, and I was getting mad. She had no right to detain us or even to ask for identification. Dad was getting mad too.

Gunner was cool, though. "Of course, ma'am."

Gunner shot a glance over at Dad as if to tell him to watch his temper. Dad could be cool under fire, but Dad is no pushover. He didn't appreciate what was going on at all. The trooper looked at Gunner's driver's license, and then, she handed it back to him.

"So"—she said matter of fact like—"is your name actually Steven Gibbs or do your friends just call you Gunner?"

We weren't expecting that. She looked at us. "And I suppose the rest of you are the McLeods?"

We weren't expecting that either. "Uh, not all of us. I'm with him," said Jack pointing to his dad.

That broke the ice, but we all truly relaxed only when she smiled. "No worries, folks. My brother is Justin Martinez. I believe you know him."

All of us gasped. We knew Sergeant Martinez. Goliath had nearly mauled him to death a few years back. Martinez has some severe scars to prove it. Since then, he often comes out to the farm when he patrols our sector. When Goliath visits, we let Sergeant Martinez know. They're good friends now. Several times, he would bring lunch, and the two of them would go sit in the grass or on the back porch and have lunch together. Kaiyo would join in sometimes too.

"He told me that you people could use some help down this way. He also told me you guys know a certain bear that saved his life. He calls him Goliath, right?

"Well, yes," said Mom. She was confused. "But Goliath tried to kill him, not save him."

"That's not the way he sees it, ma'am. And yes, I visited him in the hospital, so I saw him all torn up. But he later told me, in confidence, that the bear had somehow 'repented' and became a really good bear and the McLeods made it happen. I have never seen a repentant bear, and I sure don't know how anyone turns a killer bear into something good. But what I do know is after Justin got out of the hospital, he's been the best man he's ever been. He loves his family, and he's always joyful. So when he called me last night, he said you guys were on a rescue mission and that I needed to do whatever I could to help. It was either you people or the giant miracle bear who somehow saved my brother, so I am indebted to you. And I have information you need. I saw Kaiyo yesterday. He's quite amazing."

"Wait. You know Kaiyo?" Pretty much everybody said that.

"Yep. Let me go get some breakfast, and I'll be back out, and we can talk."

"Oh, that's not going to happen!" said Dad. He was excited. "You tell us what you want for breakfast, and we'll go get it for you. We can sit outside at the picnic table."

Dad looked at the trooper's badge. "Dean, take Trooper Garcia's order and go get her whatever she wants."

One hour later, we were driving west out of town to the Jack Creek Campground. Trooper Garcia had given us her contact information so we could call her if we needed help in any way. She was amazing. Unfortunately, the news she gave us wasn't all good. Apparently, Kaiyo had moved on from that first family, and he strolled right up to the campground. Within a few hours, he had stolen everybody's hearts. He ate like a king, and he even gave some little kids rides around the campground. I knew that was true because we had seen some of the same stuff online. His videos were everywhere. Well, word got out, and the rangers came into the campground late yesterday afternoon to capture him. I can't blame the rangers; bears in general and grizzly bears especially can be killers, sometimes on a whim.

But before all that, Trooper Garcia went to the campground yesterday after she got the call from her brother. She leaned against her SUV and watched as Kaiyo mingled with the campers. The campground is a big one, and Kaiyo kept his distance from her. Several times, she waved at Kaiyo, and at first, Kaiyo ignored her. By the third wave, Kaiyo waved back. Garcia motioned Kaiyo to come over. He took his time, but he came within ten feet of her.

"Well, well, it's the famous Kaiyo McLeod."

Trooper Garcia said Kaiyo did a double take and a total jaw drop. Then, she told him about her brother's call. Kaiyo loosened up. She told him we were on the way to come get him. Kaiyo jumped up and down when he heard that. Then, she told him the bad news;

Forest Service rangers were on their way, and they were going to bring trouble. They deal with problem bears frequently, and they wouldn't have a clue that Kaiyo wasn't one. She then told Kaiyo that if the rangers got serious, he must run away fast to the west past the campground. Then, she told him to climb the slopes and get off the valley floor. The campground was the end of the road, literally, and the ranger's trucks couldn't handle the rugged terrain or the slopes. She then told him he should stay south of the Greybull and that she would figure out a way to let his family know where he was hiding. Minutes later, two Forest Service vehicles came into the campground.

Garcia watched as the rangers did their thing. The first thing they did was grab their catchpoles and advance on Kaiyo. Kaiyo played a great game of *catch me if you can*. When they tried to sneak a loop over his head, he would just swat it away. Then, they tried to herd him into a trailer cage. He would get close and then run away in fun. Apparently, some of the campers helped hide him behind their tents.

The rangers got serious and brought out their tranquilizer rifles. He would stay just out of range but still close. He would even hide behind people and use them as shields. He was having fun until one of the rangers traded his tranquilizer rifle for a real rifle. When that happened, Kaiyo let out a bawl and ran off fast. That bonehead move caused a near riot from the campers. They were furious that the rangers were going to kill their sweet, tame bear. The campers were so angry the rangers called in for backup. As for Kaiyo, he was last seen running west along the south side of the Greybull, and then, he was spotted climbing the slopes to the south and into high, rugged country. Trooper Garcia watched him until he was out of sight.

The rangers gave up and became more concerned with the campers' anger than about capturing Kaiyo. But all the anger melted away when a family came into camp screaming for help. Their little girl had somehow gotten separated from them and was missing. It had been hours. According to Trooper Garcia, the rangers and everybody at the campground quickly forgot about Kaiyo, and they started searching. Shortly after that, the Park County Sheriff sent deputies and his search and rescue teams. Garcia was called away, and that was all she could tell us about the goings on at Jack Creek Campground.

We studied the campground while we drove there. The campground is nothing special; it's like many other Forest Service campgrounds in the Shoshone National Forest. It's rather Spartan. There's no water, no power, and no reliable cell coverage. But, if somebody comes prepared, it's a nice place. People go there to fish and relax and also to hike the network of trails around it. There are some very good and popular hiking and riding trails that start at a trailhead at the west end of the campground. The trails run west along the river and then go in many directions. And there are a lot of them. It's mostly open country, so getting lost is not easy to understand, but there are plenty of trees on some of the slopes. As for us, we needed to get Kaiyo out of there and go home. But things were not that simple.

When we got near the campground, we quickly realized that staying there overnight was out of the question. There were vehicles everywhere. Some were official, but most were from the good citizens of Wyoming who were volunteering to help find the lost little girl. There was no room in the camp, and they were turning away vehicles. But because we had horses, we were asked by a sheriff's deputy if we could participate in the search and rescue. We readily agreed. We parked a half mile east from the actual campground and got ourselves ready to find Kaiyo. Dad and Gunner hitched a ride on an ATV to a command post to let the authorities know where we would be searching.

While they were gone, the rest of us saddled up our horses, and we led them to the Greybull River. Calling the Greybull a river was generous. It was, at best, a big stream, but that was normal for these parts. It ran cold and fast, and depending on where it was, it went from thirty to seventy feet wide. It was shallow too. Once we got there, the horses enjoyed stretching their legs and drinking the cool, clean water. After the horses had their fill, we rode them back to the trailers. Dad and Gunner had just returned.

They looked grim. According to the sheriff's man in charge, Major Alan Osbourne, the little girl's name was Danielle Klein. She was nine years old and was with her family when she went missing.

They had hiked west along the Greybull; then, they went north and west following the Anderson Creek trail. That trail went by more timbered areas than other trails. Because of it, hikers were a lot more likely to see moose, elk, deer, and bears.

Danielle's dog, a big mutt named Luke, heard or smelled something so he ran down a short trail toward the timber. Danielle followed him, and the Klein family stayed on the main trail and waited for them to come back. But they didn't. Noticing she must be hidden by the trees, the girl's parents called for her and Luke to come back. When neither responded, the parents searched the area in a near panic, but they found nothing. One minute she was there, and the next minute she wasn't. They heard a dog bark, but he sounded too far away to be Luke. And that was all anybody knew.

For the parents, it was a horrible nightmare. For law enforcement, it was a huge task, and most of them had children too. We saw real worry and fear on the faces of the searchers. For us, our role was to find Kaiyo, and while we were doing that, we could also help be a part of the search team. We would be looking for her as diligently as we would for Kaiyo. We were comforted by the fact my little brother was a midsized bear with great bear skills. He would be fine. Danielle, though, was in danger, perhaps even mortal danger.

ANDERSON CREEK—SUSAN

Our horses were ready to get going. Just to get the edge off, we rode them hard until we got right next to the campground. At that point, we fell in line. We were riding, mostly single file, through the campground. It was busy, so we rode slowly. A helicopter landed somewhere behind us, and we saw several small groups of people, volunteer searchers probably, being briefed by men and women in uniforms of varying sorts. Two men were assembling a drone for surveillance. We also rode past the tent of the parents of the missing little girl. Their daughter had been missing overnight, and they knew that for every minute she was missing, the likelihood of her being found diminished. The area where she went missing was thoroughly searched, and nothing, not even a footprint, was found. To make a horrible situation even worse, if their daughter couldn't be found, as far as law enforcement goes, those two parents would be at the top of their list of suspects. The whole thing was awful.

As we rode past, all I could think of was that another poor person got swallowed up in a forest, and now, they're gone. It happens with some regularity in our national parks and national forests, but private lands also have their share of disappearances. Books have been written about such odd disappearances that have been occurring for centuries. I have long understood that the nation's forests are not safe places to be. We have had our own issues in the forest south of our farm.

Each year, people get lost in the woods or near the woods. That makes some sense; a lot of people live in forests, hike in forests, hunt and fish in forests, and otherwise enjoy the forests. When that happens, a few people are bound to get separated from friends or family while others simply lose their way and end up lost. But some end up dying; some are never found.

Sam and I believe the easiest and most likely answer is usually the right answer. That principle is called Occam's razor. A person may hear a barred owl as it makes its crazy, spooky sounds in the dead of night, and immediately, they think it can only be a bigfoot. While there is a remote possibility it's a bigfoot, the most likely answer by far is it's something quite common, like a barred owl.

So that brings us to this place. In a forest, there are many true dangers. People can fall to their deaths, they can get bitten by poisonous snakes, they can break a leg, and they can be killed by bad people or by ordinary predators. They can die of exposure; they can even starve or die of thirst. Each year, lightning kills people in our national forests. The list of ways to die in a forest is lengthy, so jumping to conclusions is unwise. Those searchers will probably find that little girl's tracks, and our hope is she will be found healthy and quickly. But all of us here know she had very few places to go, and she should have been found by now.

Both Sam and I know strange things happen. The whole Kaiyo situation is stranger than strange, but here we are. My adopted son is a bear who thinks like the rest of us. Landon was taken to another dimension, and he peered into another world. Gracie was able to hear him when we couldn't. We all knew Christ had appeared in a locked room and was there, talking and being touched by his disciples. He wasn't there as a hologram; he was fully there. None of that was magic either.

For us to assume that evil cannot move within their own dimensions is probably shortsighted. And if evil things can move between dimensions, then kidnappings, for whatever reason, are unlikely but still a possibility. On more than one instance, Sam has told me stories of being in the woods and experiencing terror he just can't explain. Usually, he feels perfectly normal in the woods, but not always.

When we first moved out to Montana, he once talked to an old hunter who told him a story we thought was pure crazy talk. The hunter said that he was working his way through timber following a well-used game trail. As he was walking on the trail, he saw, but didn't really notice, a dull waterlike shimmer hover over the path. He walked through it and the timber to either side changed with each step until it appeared to be granite boulders. Suddenly, a creature, big and humanlike, but still not human, jumped in front of him, smiled, and yelled out something that he didn't understand.

Then, it raised a sharpened club and started for him. The old hunter said that he was terrified, but he didn't panic. He raised his rifle and shot the thing right in the chest and dropped it dead. He then heard a world of angry screams as he casually walked backward and out of that place. As he did, the boulders became trees and forest once again. He said that it was only then he saw the shimmering doorway clearly. He told Sam that he stood there, thought about it, and fired a couple of shots into the doorway for good measure. He wanted whatever else was in there to think twice about following him out. After that, the door vanished, and the hunter fled. That story is no longer hard for me to believe.

Our plan was to find Kaiyo and to help search for Danielle. But first things first—we headed out of the campground to find Kaiyo. Everybody but Gracie was armed, and all of us had walkie-talkies set to the same channels. Once we cleared the campground fence, we were able to pick up our speed. Trooper Garcia estimated Kaiyo probably ran about a mile before he raced up and into the mountains. Finding his tracks was something we were confident we could do.

The helicopter flew overhead as did a small, single-engine plane a few minutes later. The plane flew higher than the helicopter as it searched a much broader area. That told us Danielle had not been found and they were expanding the search area. That wasn't good.

After crossing Jack Creek, we fanned out and headed generally westward. The farther west we went, the more rugged and sloped the terrain got. Pretty soon, we were riding almost single file again along the Greybull. Anderson Creek was about two more miles upstream, but searchers had been all around both sides of the river looking for her. Any hopes of finding bear tracks were dashed. The mudflats and flatter areas were covered in ATV, horse, dog, and human tracks. We talked to a few searchers who were heading back to the campground. They told us there were no reports, good or bad.

We rode farther west when we noticed the helicopter turn and go back to the campground. The airplane, farther away to the west but still visible, turned, gained altitude, and flew north where it disappeared behind the mountains.

Gunner turned to us and said, "That's a development. Somebody found something, or they found her. There's no reason for both of the air assets to leave the area where she was last spotted unless something changed."

That made sense. But it changed nothing for us. Our job was to find Kaiyo, so we kept riding. A short time later, we came to a little creek that drained into the river. It ran south to north through a nice gap as it emptied on the opposite side of the Greybull from Anderson Creek. The slopes next to the Greybull were steep, but at the 9,000-foot level, it flattened out a bit. We decided that Gunner, Jack, and Libby would ride up the little creek and use the gap to get to higher ground. Sam, Gracie, Dean, and I would ride past Anderson Creek and follow the Greybull upstream. Before we got to the first creek, a Park County sheriff's deputy with a dog came toward us on his way back to the campground. We asked if his dog was helpful. His answer caused Sam and I to grimace.

"No," he said. "Not today. Toby's been a great tracker for several years, but today, he was off his game."

The deputy handling the tracking dog was a man in his early thirties. His dog looked like a German shepherd. He was proud of his dog, but he was confused. I asked him where he had been searching.

"The little girl got separated from her family a distance past where Vick Creek came into Anderson Creek. It's mighty rugged country, but I've seen younger kids than her out here. From what I heard, she was already an experienced trail hiker. The family is from Lander, and they love the outdoors. Anyway, Toby tracked her scent all the way to the banks of Anderson Creek. He picked it up again on the other side, but then, nothing. We circled all around the timber, but it was like she got to the other side of the creek and flew off somewhere. Then, some hikers up Vick Creek, not too far from the Anderson Lodge, found hiking boots that match those the girl was wearing. I guess she backtracked and headed in a different direction. How nobody saw her is beyond me though. Those boots were a long way from where she disappeared. I got ordered to go back to the campground to give Toby a rest, and if they don't find her right away, then our chopper will come and get us."

The deputy looked tired. "One more question," I asked. "Did Toby ever track onto something today but refuse to follow it?"

"Well, yeah, come to think of it, he did. On the south side of Anderson Creek, where Toby found her scent again, there was one game trail that led up through the timber, and Toby refused to go up the trail. He was okay when we cut across it, but he refused to budge when I stopped to go up the trail. That was odd behavior from him. Why do you ask?"

I lied. "That may mean a grizzly or something was up the path. Maybe that scared him."

"Hah!" he said. "Nothing scares Toby."

"Something did, Deputy."

I let that hang there for a moment. Then, I finished, "My suggestion is the next time Toby refuses to follow a scent, you ought to take the latch off your sidearm."

"Seriously?"

His question was sincere. So was mine. "Maybe the girl was carried. So, yes, we're serious."

The deputy looked at me and then at each of us. He was about to ask a question when Gunner asked, "One more question, Deputy. Has anyone found her dog?"

"No, we're all hoping she's still with the dog."

"Good point," said a smiling Gunner. "We're gonna check out this sector. If we don't come back, send Toby."

We all laughed and said goodbye to the deputy. Then, we split up. It was time to move on.

Gunner, Jack, and Libby turned left and up a path through long-standing sentinels of rock. They were going to climb the slopes and go due south for a while and then turn west. Our plan was to ride alongside the river where it bends to the south. A creek called Haymaker Creek emptied into the Greybull upstream. If we got to it before Libby's group, then we would continue riding up the Greybull, and they were to follow us. If they got there first, they were to explore up the creek and cut north and east at the base of the peak known as Irish Rock. All the while, we would be looking for Kaiyo.

As we parted with them and rode up the Greybull, Sam rode up next to me, "Geez, honey, you probably scared that deputy to death!"

We laughed, but there was no room up here for being too casual. The deputy wasn't thinking things through. Once we passed Anderson Creek, we saw no other sign that searchers had been where we were. We saw tracks of people, but they were old. There was a well-used trail that meandered along one side of the river and then the other. We had only three miles or so before we got to Haymaker Creek, so we took our time. The other group would have a much tougher ride.

We were determined to find our bear-child. After a mile and a half or so of following well-used trails, Gracie found the first track. "Bear!" said Gracie. "Grizzly too. And just about the right size and fresh."

Dean was on it in a moment. "Proud of you, Gracie. You are spot on. Good tracking. Keep following."

Gracie did. Our trail took us to the river's edge, and we waded across the river. Once we got to the other side of the river, we had a long, clear view to the south. The river here was slower with frequent sandbars, and we could see for miles. The view was beautiful. Irish Rock was a couple of miles to our southeast, and a long north-south ridge of 10,000 feet was to our right. With us observing the beautiful valley, we didn't pay attention to the river next to us. Gracie got my attention when I heard her laugh. Then, Dean joined in the laughter. I had no idea what they were laughing at and didn't really care at first.

"Mom," said Gracie, "you need to see this."

She was pointing to a sandbar in the river. It was messy, and there were some dead fish lying on it. They were mostly skeletons. "The fish?" I asked.

"No," said Gracie. "Dead fish aren't funny. Read the sand, Mom."

Sam and I both gasped at the same time. There, scratched in the sandbar in some awful handwriting, was a clear. "Hi Mom!"

It was written with bear claws. I was so excited I almost screamed. I told Sam to fire a shot. Sam wisely refused. A shot might bring a lot of searchers hoping we had found the lost girl. Periodically, we could hear helicopters, so we figured she had yet to be found. "Then whistle," I said.

Sam let out an ear splitter, even the horses flinched. And then I heard him. There was a patch of timber a few hundred yards away up on the slopes to the right. We looked up in time to see my Kaiyo running downhill fast. It always amazed me how fast bears were, and Kaiyo was faster than most. He went straight off the hillside into the river, and then, he turned and came our way. We all kicked our horses into high gear, and we all came together in seconds. Gracie pulled back on Duke and swung a leg over the saddle in one fluid motion. She was off her horse before any of us. She hit the sand running right into Kaiyo with a scream and a giggle.

He had grown so much. It had been almost two months since I had last seen him, and he looked so good. He bawled and roared and whimpered. We were all so happy. We were all group hugging and just telling him how much we loved him and missed him. I cried some. Why not? My son was lost, but now he was found.

WAR PARTIES—SAM

All the things that happen when a family member goes missing, we experienced. We were scared most of all, but the worst was feeling helpless. Most people want to be able to do something, but when a loved one vanishes, the sense of helplessness is overwhelming. And until Kaiyo figured out how to be a social media star, we were helpless. As I look back on everything, finding Kaiyo was one of the best moments of my life. He was my son, and I loved him.

I looked over at Susan, and she was a wreck, but a happy wreck. She cried, and the relief was obvious. Gracie, Kaiyo, and Dean were roughhousing together. It was fun to watch. As strong as Dean was, he was nothing compared to Kaiyo. Kaiyo tossed him around with ease. Gracie just kept talking while she was hugging on Kaiyo. When they all tired of it, Kaiyo gently greeted each of the horses. They all liked him. He was their pasture buddy, and Kaiyo had been on several adventures with most of them.

Then, Kaiyo went to Dean to talk. Kaiyo doesn't speak English on this side of the world. According to Landon, once they go through their door, Eden's animals talk quite freely. Because of that, Kaiyo lets us know when and to whom he wants to talk. We are all getting good at it. Kaiyo can write, so that helps too. He can't hold a pen, so he scribbles in the dirt. Kaiyo took Dean aside and sat him down. We watched. After a few moments, Kaiyo wrote a word in the dirt. Dean tried to read it, but he had to ask questions. Then, I heard Dean whisper, "Lavi?"

Kaiyo nodded. "Here? Is that it? Lavi's here? Kaiyo, wait. Are you telling me Lavi's here? How?"

Kaiyo was never a conversationalist. He didn't like questions like *why* and *how*. I guess that if you can't talk, it's too hard to answer.

"Is that the lion who wants to hurt you?" asked Susan.

To be honest, Lavi wanted to kill Kaiyo, not just hurt him, but I didn't bring that up. Kaiyo nodded and then pointed to Dean. After a few tries, we confirmed Lavi had it in for Dean too. Then, he pointed at me. Well, that was useful information. So Lavi hated the three of us. That made sense. He hated Kaiyo because he is a Special on our side. He hated Dean because of whatever happened when they were together about two months ago. If I know Dean, he insulted Lavi more than once. And he hated me because I shot off the end of his tail. Lavi was filled with pride, but I understood him hating me. I probably should've killed him when I had a chance.

"Well, he's outnumbered here," I said. "I don't know how he got here, but Kaiyo is bigger, and Dean and I are loaded for bear. No offense, Kaiyo. He will keep his distance."

On the inside, though, I was mighty concerned. Lavi somehow followed him. I am sure Kaiyo's celebrity status and his pictures gave him and his location away to somebody who saw the videos who then told somebody who then told Lavi. And if Lavi was here, he could figure out that we would be looking for Kaiyo too. That meant he would be trying to trick us.

"Dad?" asked Gracie. "Do you think Lavi had anything to do with that little girl being lost?"

I thought about that for a few moments. It was a good question.

Susan was buried in thought too. Kaiyo was acting excited. She looked at Kaiyo. "Kaiyo, was Lavi alone?"

Kaiyo shook his head to indicate no. "Was there a little girl with him?"

Kaiyo nodded. That was not good, and it complicated things a lot. We were hoping we could just sneak Kaiyo out of here and go home. We didn't ever think we would come across any sign of the girl. She got lost only a few miles away from us, but that was as the crow flies. There was a long ridge of 10,000 feet between us and the place on Anderson Creek where she disappeared. She could not walk up and over that. Few things could. Susan was right when she was talking to the deputy earlier. It dawned on me then. She didn't walk over the mountains—she was carried. I learned later that a trail, the Boulder Basin Trail, crossed the ridges. While a little girl probably couldn't walk it, experienced hikers regularly used the trail. And it went right to Anderson Creek.

"Kaiyo, the little girl...was there a dog with her?"

Kaiyo shook his head.

"Was a watcher carrying her?"

Kaiyo looked at me and again shook his head. That was not the answer I expected. "Was anything else with them?"

Kaiyo nodded. Everybody looked at one another. When asked about normal things like a horse or people, Kaiyo shook his head.

"Did you know what it was?" asked Dean.

Kaiyo again shook his head.

"What was it like?"

Kaiyo sniffed in the air and walked up and then down the slope for a few moments. He walked a few wide circles and then came to a jumble of large rocks about thirty feet away from us. He looked and then huffed. That was his way of telling us to come, so we did. We were there in a few steps even though we had no idea what he was up to. He pointed to something in the rocks. Susan saw it first. It was a horned toad. Technically, it was a short-horned lizard, but everybody called them horned toads.

"Wait," said Dean, "you saw a horned toad?

Kaiyo looked sort of frustrated. He then sniffed up a little race-runner lizard and pointed it out. It quickly scooted away.

Dean looked confused, and so did Gracie. But Susan looked at me and frowned. We knew.

"Kaiyo, did you see some sort of big, two-legged lizard?"

Kaiyo nodded vigorously. Dean and Gracie started asking a bunch of questions. "How tall?" I asked.

Kaiyo stood up. Then, he pointed to Dean. After some more questions, we guessed the reptile thing Kaiyo saw was over six feet tall.

"Okay, Dad," said Gracie, "you and Mom seem to know what that thing is, so can you tell us?"

She said it sweetly, and Kaiyo obviously agreed. Dean's expression showed he was still perplexed. I couldn't blame him.

"Okay, do you want a dad answer or a quick answer?"

I always ask that because the kids usually want to know things but not in depth; they just want a quick answer. Sometimes, a quick answer is good enough. Sometimes though, it's not possible to give a quick answer.

Dean, Kaiyo, and Gracie all agreed. They wanted a dad answer.

"All right. Sometimes, those things are just garden-variety demons. They appear that way sometimes. But there are others that are actual flesh-and-blood creatures, like the Lizard Man. The thing Kaiyo saw is one of those. They're a prehistoric race. As for the one Kaiyo saw, he's up to something. Maybe they're just stealing a child. That happens from time to time, but we don't know why. But I suspect they are going to use the little girl to try to kill us. Maybe they are going to try to lure us into an ambush. Kaiyo, did they see you?"

Kaiyo shook his head. "Did they come across your tracks?"

Again, Kaiyo said *no*. "Guys, I really don't think they know exactly where Kaiyo is, and I doubt they know we're here yet. Maybe they just want to kill Kaiyo. They know he would try to rescue the little girl."

"Dad?" said Dean. "Lavi would love it if we searched for Kaiyo and found Kaiyo dead. The cat is clever, but I don't think he's being very smart. He's out for revenge. Patience is not a virtue to him. And, Dad, you shot the tip of his tail off. I think he won't rest until he kills the three of us. I say we go get him. Is the reptilian demon thing dangerous?"

That was a good question. "Those things are hard to pin down. We don't know much. Sometimes, they are real flesh and blood. Sometimes, they're just evil spirits. They even masquerade as space aliens from time to time. Still, I'm sure they're very dangerous. If it crosses back into its world, I suppose it would be mighty dangerous. But here, this time, it's probably here to help Lavi. Maybe he owes Lavi a few favors. Plus, those reptilian things truly hate us Christian types anyway. It probably wasn't hard for Lavi to get help."

We filled Kaiyo in on who the lost girl was and what we heard about her getting snatched away from her parents and family. Kaiyo remembered her from his time at the campground. We knew we had no choice. We couldn't just rescue Kaiyo and go home. That would make us terrible people. We would need to save her or die trying. Everybody else was miles away looking for her in places she had never been. It seemed that it was up to us.

The new plan was to go south along the river as far as Haymaker Creek and wait for Libby, Jack, and Gunner. Once there, we would track down the bad guys and hopefully save the girl. We rode to fight. What we didn't know was that we were headed into a real battle.

Pursuits—Dean

Haymaker Creek was only a mile or two away, so we got there quickly. The creek flowed out of a wide drainage basin made by mountains to our left. Irish Rock was the most obvious mountain at 11,000 feet. Haymaker Creek tumbled off a low cliff to make a pretty, little waterfall before it meandered to the Greybull. This area was beautiful, and normally, I would be loving all of it, especially after the happiness we experienced when we found my little brother. Instead, we were all grim. This was all new ground for us, but we were determined to rescue the lost girl. I was convinced we had all the advantages. The biggest advantage was the bad guys didn't know Kaiyo had us to help him. We were also well armed, and we had numbers. What could go wrong?

Kaiyo caught a scent, and he led me past the waterfall to another trail. The hiker trails seemed to crisscross this entire wilderness. This one led up and out of the river basin and headed toward Irish Rock. We scouted about, and in the sand by the river, we saw clear tracks of Lavi and his pal. In fact, they were so obvious it seemed like they intended to be found. The girl's tracks were there too. While everyone waited for the rest of our group, Kaiyo and I backtracked the prints to the other side of the river. The little axis of evil had apparently taken a trail from Anderson Creek over the ridge, and it looked like they were headed east for some reason. Their motives were hard to decipher, but their tracks weren't. They had come through here only a few hours beforehand, and they were going to be dealing with us. Just then, Kaiyo ran toward Gracie right before she cried out.

Visions—Gracie

I was seated on Duke, hugging the side of the little cliff where the creek fell onto the flatland by the river. It was hot, and the shade was nice. We were just talking and watching my brothers track the kidnappers when I started to hear her. Kaiyo immediately knew something was going on. I saw him splashing across the shallow river to get to me. I looked at my parents; they had quit talking and were staring at me.

I was just like when Landon spoke to me when he was trapped. She could see us, but only I could hear her. "Help me. I'm scared. They're going to hurt me. I want my mom!"

The last part was her crying. "Can you hear me?" I asked.

I was surprised when she said she could. Everybody was around me now. Nobody spoke. "Where are you? Are the kidnappers still there?"

She said that they went back outside after leaving her in a scary place filled with terrible things. When I asked where she was, she said she walked through the side of a big mountain.

"Please hurry," she said. "They want to kill your bear. They like to kill things."

I told her we were coming to get her. Then, she was gone. Just like that.

Everybody started asking questions, and Dad hushed everybody up. When he did, I told everybody what she said.

Dad thought for a minute. "Walked into a mountain? That's like the old Anasazi Indians. Legend says that they disappeared forever when they lined up and walked into a mountain and never came back. I don't believe it, though. I read they were cannibals. I think warfare, drought, and maybe eating the neighbors caused them to disappear from memory."

"Well, Dad," I said, "Danielle walked into a mountain. It's not impossible, right?"

Dad looked at me and smiled. "Good point, sweetie. It is definitely possible. I guess our issue is how we can do it too."

Dean suggested we get off the floor of the valley and follow the tracks for a while. Besides, the others were coming, and we needed to get something done. Waiting here was a waste of time.

Dean took the lead, and Dad was the last to follow. We followed the tracks to the south, staying on the flats of the river valley. We found where Lavi's group followed a trail that led up onto higher ground. Irish Rock was about two miles away, but it looked a lot closer than that. Once we left the river valley floor, the tracks of the snatchers disappeared on the rocky soil. I was proud of my little brother. The soil was dry and rocky, but Kaiyo followed their trail easily.

Mom and I volunteered to cross the creek and ride north up into more mountains to meet up with Libby and the Gibbses. We didn't need them making a lot of noise. Mom spurred Cali, and Duke got the message. We flew across the creek and climbed into the barren hills to the north. As I was leaving, I saw a crow come and land near Kaiyo. That had to be about something.

Air Spies—Kaiyo

One of the many things Raphael taught me was that even the enemy had to face rebellions against him from time to time. His kingdom has never been of one mind. When one third of the angelic beings decided to side with Satan, they permanently separated themselves from God. But some of the demons let their own huge prides test their loyalties. When that would happen, they would go their own way. Only a few of them were ever brave enough to challenge Satan directly, and they were smashed quickly. Others, though, have wandered off, looking for their own little kingdoms. I wondered why the reptile was helping Lavi and who was encouraging it.

With Mom and Gracie gone, it was time to get moving. I wanted to go home, but we weren't going home until we rescued the girl. Fortunately, we had help. A few days ago, when I got here, I was talking to a few magpies and a raven. The same raven landed about twenty feet from us and was cawing up a storm. I gave Dad and Dean a stern look telling them to stay, and they did.

The news had gotten back to Raphael how I had gotten lost and that little Danielle Klein had been snatched away. The raven was told to stay and help. Anyway, a mostly dry creek called Ross Creek ran east to west through the main basin downstream of Irish Rock. It turned and ran into Haymaker Creek not far from us. The raven told me Lavi was waiting for me to follow Ross Creek upstream. He had hidden himself on a ledge. The raven also told me he had seen a little girl near a small cliff. He thought a door might be there because she disappeared and there were no places she could have been hiding. The raven then told me that Raphael put me in charge and that he was ready for my orders. I wasn't really that type of leader, but I was glad to have the authority. I told him to stay put.

I had to think. First, if there was a door, then it was a door into a miniature hell. Raphael had mentioned reptilian creatures that lived in another world. Maybe Danielle was taken into some demon's version of home. It didn't matter, but I felt for the little girl; she was in a very bad place. A fight was brewing. Fighters die sometimes, and if that was going to be the case, then so be it. I knew where I was going if I died, and dying was a lot better than suffering through the poisonous regret of cowardice. But I was still scared.

Ross Creek ran from the slopes of Irish Rock, and its banks were steep. It was made for an ambush, and Lavi was clever. All mountain lions are ambush killers. Lavi was probably better than them all. It was time to go and end this thing.

I asked the raven if there was a way for Dean and Dad to outflank Lavi and surprise him. Between the two creeks was a lone, low mountain just to the west of Irish Rock. My gut told me that they shouldn't follow me. I needed whatever element of surprise we could muster to our advantage. The raven hopped up on my shoulder and said that there were trails that led from Haymaker Creek up and over the summit and then down through the little mountain's heavily forested north slope. If Lavi was waiting for me along Ross Creek, anybody that snuck up and over the mountain could look from the high ground and see Lavi first. We could ambush the ambusher. I liked the plan.

I was ready to go when the other riders joined us. It was so good seeing Gunner and Jack. Libby jumped off Jet and raced into me. My human family is amazing, and I couldn't have asked for a better army. We celebrated briefly as Dad and Gunner spoke. Gunner and Jack are two of my best friends. Seeing them here was a celebration and just what I needed. They were almost like my real human family. I felt like we were unstoppable. But thinking of the little girl, used as a hostage, gave me a cold chill, though.

I made motions to Dean and the others to follow the raven. The raven jumped up and flew along Haymaker Creek. Everybody caught on and turned their horses southeast along the Haymaker Creek Trail. Dad gave orders for Mom and Libby to stay back and guard Gracie.

"What?" said Gracie. "I don't need a guard. We need to be with Kaiyo, we just found him, and he's going alone? That's crazy. That mountain lion wants to kill him. We can't leave him alone. And if I get another contact from Danielle, how can I let you know?"

Well, she had a good point on the last part. The part about being with me was foolishness, but I had no doubt Gracie believed it. The part about Gracie having contact with the girl though, well, that made a lot of sense. Dad looked at Gracie, Libby, and Mom. The raven had flown back and landed on my back. Gracie giggled when she saw it. Dad was thinking about what Gracie said when Dean broke the silence.

"Dad, I know what you're thinking. You are concerned that with everybody going southeast along Haymaker Creek, there would be nobody guarding Kaiyo from anything coming from the west or the north, right?"

He didn't let Dad answer, but that was Dean's style. He kept going. "So anyway, if you have Libby and Gunner, you have the two best shots in the family with you. They could cover Kaiyo or the door from hundreds of yards away. Libby has her .270, and I noticed Gunner brought his .300 Winchester Magnum sniper rifle. That rifle is good at a thousand yards. Dad, you need them with you."

The raven was taking it all in. Gunner was leaning on the horn of his saddle watching me. When we caught eyes, he winked. He knew Dean was right. Libby was smiling. Mom was not smiling, but she was listening. Dean was making his points and was getting to them quickly. I was getting antsy to go.

"Next, Libby and Mom can guard Gracie if there's a problem. If those lizard things figure out that Danielle is speaking to Gracie, they're gonna send a watcher or something to come for Gracie. Both of them are armed, and all three have bear spray. If they had to get away, Libby could cover them. Cali is only second to Solo in being sure-footed and quick, and with Gracie riding Duke, that's two quick-turning horses with some good speed. But as for me and Jack, all we have are shotguns loaded with slugs. It would be better if we followed Kaiyo from a distance, so somebody has his back trail. Plus, if Lavi starts to get the best of him, Jack and I can come save his bacon."

I liked the plan and nodded. Gunner spoke next. "This stuff about doors and demons is new ground for me, but it seems to me that Dean's plan makes some sense. As for the creatures who took the girl, if they breathe, they bleed. We can kill them. There's nothing down there we can't handle. What do we know about doors? What's on the other side of those things?"

Susan then shared with everybody the story of an old hunter who somehow walked through a door and ended up shooting some sort of creature that menaced him. The story was creepy, but Raphael had told me similar stories; some of them didn't end up nicely either. Raphael hunts those doors and destroys them when he finds them. God has been restraining evil for thousands of years, and destroying evil doors was all part of it.

"I've heard enough," said Gunner. "If Jack wants to follow Kaiyo, it's okay with me."

Dad looked at Dean. "All right, Dean. That's a good plan. Keep in mind this is grizzly country, and there are tons of black bears here. Moose and elk too. Not everything out here is a Special or a demon or a lizard. The regular animals can be dangerous enough. Keep your bear spray handy. And, Kaiyo, I trust you. But I sure as all heck don't like you going alone. Is there any other way?"

Nothing came to mind.

I am a grizzly bear, and clever tricks aren't our style. We tend to go straight into the action. Coyotes are clever; bears are smart; mountain lions are mean—everybody knew that. I went over to Dad, stood up, and leaned on Hershel. I was getting tall. I buried my head in his shirt. I was scared, and that surprised me. Then, I went to everybody, but Jack and Dean and said goodbye. The raven took to the air. It was time to go.

Sniper—Libby

We rode quickly to the east with Haymaker Creek usually to our right. The slopes to our left were steep, but the trail we were on was well used by people, horses, and all sorts of game. The raven guided us as we rode. Several times, we saw campers on the grassy flats on the other side of the creek, and we even passed an empty cabin. We waved at the campers, but we were in a hurry and rode on.

Soon, the raven flew north and encouraged us to climb up the mountain. It cawed and flew back to us, encouraging us to do what seemed impossible. It wanted us to follow, but the hill was too steep. We had to trust the raven. We all turned our horses and followed him. Out of nowhere, a dry streambed appeared, and we followed it up. At a point, the raven landed on a game trail we never would have noticed. We used that trail as a switchback and followed the game trail as it climbed, tacking back and forth, until we reached the ridgeline.

Crossing the ridge, we were pleased to see that the north slope of the mountain was not nearly as steep as the slope we had just scaled. From up high, we had a commanding view of the other side. We could see down the north slope to much of Ross Creek. The raven urged us to keep moving so we could hide in the nearby timber that hugged the long slope between us and the creek.

As we made our way down the north slope and to the edge of the forest, Gunner dismounted and walked back up toward the ridge to a tumble of boulders. He slipped in between boulders and was able to crawl up on top of a wide flat boulder. He surveyed the creek, slid off the boulder, and came back to us.

We all yielded to the wisdom of Gunner's years of military experience. "Sam, you and I need to get down there. Libby, your .270 has a range of eight hundred yards. If you want my rifle, you can have it. It shoots farther, and the slug is bigger. The distance is about five hundred yards downhill. Which gun do you want?"

I told him that I was comfortable with my rifle because I was. I could hit a teacup at four hundred yards. Learning how to shoot a new rifle at this point seemed like a bad idea. Everybody agreed.

"Susan, you and Gracie will guard Libby while she acts as the team sniper. Stay out of sight if you can. If Libby takes a shot, expect something to come after her."

Mom thanked Gunner; she was a capable shot herself. She carried a 30.06 that fired a big round. The gun was heavier than my .270, but it didn't seem to bother Mom. Mom also had a pistol in a holster lashed to her leg just in case.

Gunner then spoke to Gracie. "And, Gracie, that bear spray is mighty effective. Use it if you think you need to. And if the little lost girl reaches out to you, let us know."

But Gracie wasn't listening; she was staring at nothing. What Gracie said next put us in a near panic. "She told me they were going to kill the bear, and they were laughing about it. She told us to hurry because they could see the bear coming."

Dad looked at Gunner. "Let's ride."

They leaped onto their horses and rode down into the timber. In a few seconds, they were lost from view. We tied up our horses just inside the timber, out of view of everyone but us. Then, the three of us ran back toward the ridge to get into the boulders. I needed to get my scope downhill. Within a few moments, I was on the flat boulder. Gracie and Mom were next to me, glassing up and down the creek with their binoculars.

After a few more minutes of trying to see movement, Mom spoke up first. "I see Lavi. Five hundred fifty yards-ish."

"Me too," said Gracie. "On a ledge, just where the creek splits."

I put my scope on that spot. Unfortunately, the moment Lavi came into my crosshairs, he smoothly slithered over the edge of its perch. I couldn't see him after that.

"He's slippery," whispered Mom.

I agreed. That was a lost opportunity.

"Kaiyo. Eight hundred yards downstream to the west."

That was Mom again. I brought my rifle over, careful not to put him in the center of my scope. I didn't want to shoot my own little brother. We saw no sign of Dean or Jack. I moved my scope back upstream when I heard Gracie gasp. "He's running!"

Mom and Gracie watched as Kaiyo raced upstream toward the low cliff at the intersection of two creeks. He came in and out of sight, hidden by rocks, timber, and a few of the creek's high banks. He covered the distance in seconds. He was so fast. Then, I saw Lavi and Kaiyo collide. Lavi was knocked back. He struggled to regain his footing when Kaiyo swung a vicious paw that caught him on the shoulder. Blood exploded in a fine, red mist. Lavi was flipped almost out of the creek. Lavi turned and leaped back to the fight. Kaiyo swung again but missed as the two circled each other. Kaiyo charged again, and they fought viciously. Lavi was in the fight for his life. Then, Kaiyo was smashed in the face and muzzle by Lavi's razor-sharp claws. He was cut and bloodied, but Kaiyo was stronger and faster. Lavi tried every trick to get his jaws into Kaiyo's throat or skull, but Kaiyo would dodge and then connect with powerful bites and blows to Lavi's shoulder and head. Kaiyo was fully in bear rage.

Lavi lunged again, but he missed and fell. Kaiyo was on him. He grabbed Lavi in his jaws, stood, and shook the big mountain lion like a stuffed animal. He meant to break Lavi's neck, but Lavi got tossed back to the low cliff. Lavi crashed and slumped to the rocky floor of the dry creek. I thought it was over. Kaiyo was the better fighter, and he was winning. Kaiyo lunged at Lavi, but somehow, the big cat leaped straight up and over him. Kaiyo's momentum took him right to edge of the door. It shimmered like water. Suddenly, before Kaiyo could turn and chase Lavi and kill him, we watched helplessly as six thick, scaly arms reached through the door. They grabbed Kaiyo's fur and body and dragged him back, through the door.

Then, he was gone. Disappeared. "They took him! They took him. Shoot the lion. Now!" cried Gracie.

I was one step behind her. I centered the crosshairs on Lavi's head as Lavi looked at the still shimmering door. I squeezed the trigger; the noise echoed throughout the basin. I watched as the bullet exploded into the creek bank behind Lavi. The lion's head snapped to his left at the sound of my bullet as it crashed into the shale next to him. I cursed myself for forgetting to aim low. I was shooting at a steep angle downhill. I had the distance right, but I made a beginner's mistake. My round went high because I didn't correct for downhill shots. I was supposed to aim low, and I didn't. And I should have known better.

Just then, at the same time, I saw Lavi turn to look back downstream. He appeared fully alarmed. I heard Gracie say something like "They're coming."

Lavi looked panicked. He turned and leaped up and on top of the low cliff, and he ran straight up a dry streambed that was on the west slope of Irish Rock. I kept watching him, but he was clearly running away. He seemed bloody and badly hurt. While I was watching Lavi, I heard Mom say something like "Oh dear God!"

I scoped the creek bed by the low cliff where the door was still visible. In less than a second, we watched as Dean and then Jack rode at top speed through the door. I muffled a scream, but Gracie didn't muffle hers. Neither did Mom. Just like Kaiyo, Dean and Jack were there, and then, they weren't. Mom and Gracie kept their binoculars riveted to the scene; I used my scope. Nothing happened for thirty seconds; then, a few more minutes passed; it was quiet. I wondered where my father was.

Gracie saw them first. "I see Dad and Gunner."

We watched Dad and Gunner race out of the timber and into the creek bed. "Oh no! Oh no!"

That was Mom. Helpless, we saw Dad and Gunner spur their mounts. They were in full gallop. Both Dad and Gunner had their horses' reins in one hand and rifles in another. They followed Dean's path right to the doorway, and they never slowed down. And then they were gone too. And we were surrounded with silence. There was nothing I could do about every male in our group disappearing, but at least, I could look for Lavi and kill him.

While Mom kept her eyes on the door, Gracie and I scanned the slopes of Irish Rock for any sign of Lavi. Gracie saw the raven flying high up the slopes. He was helping us find him. He would dive and pull up and dive again. Sure enough, we finally saw Lavi. He was getting out of the area though it was obvious he was injured. He seemed to be limping, but the distance kept me from being clear on that. In minutes, he reached the far, high ridge and disappeared on the other side. The three of us were stunned. Mom sat up and looked at us.

"All right ladies, this is grim, and I have no idea what to do, but I think we need to get down there."

I wanted off the boulder and going down the mountain to the door was at least doing something. Gracie agreed with me and Mom. Just then, deep in the timber below us, we heard howls. Not like from a pack of wolves, but from very angry creatures.

Gracie spoke first. "We need to bring our horses back. Whatever animals are down there, they sound like horse eaters."

Or worse.

THE BATTLE OF ROSS CREEK—KAIYO

I was a long way from the door, but I could still see Lavi reclining on the ledge of a small cliff. I could see the door shimmer right by him. Lavi saw me making my way up the creek, but I had the wind in my favor. I smelled Lavi well before he saw me. I knew where he was. My plan was to continue moseying up the creek so Lavi would believe I hadn't seen him. But when one of those lizard things walked out holding the little girl, I lost my temper and bolted for the door. Lavi was such a hideous beast. He may have looked like he had a lion's heart, but he was rotten on the inside. That he would intentionally terrify and maybe kill a little girl just to get to me pushed my temper into rage. Well fine, he would have me.

In a flash, I was at top speed and closing the distance when Lavi stupidly decided to run straight at me. Lions are fast, and our closing speed approached eighty miles per hour. Right before we collided, I leaped on the hunch that Lavi would try to leap over me. He leaped, and we collided head on. I had grown since last seeing Lavi, and I was now almost twice Lavi's weight, and because of that, I got the best of him. He was thrown backward, and I hurt him. Lavi was slow getting his footing, and I was on him. I smashed his left shoulder with a swing from my right paw. Before he ricocheted from the blast, my claws raked his shoulder and neck; a cloud of blood exploded away from me.

Lavi was strong though, and he shook his head and came at me. But Lavi wasn't prepared for my strength or quickness. He tried to sink his sharp claws in me to get some advantage, but each time, he had to deal with me biting and pounding his head and sides and raking him with my claws. My face was bleeding from a smashing hit, but he was far bloodier. He jumped on me repeatedly to bite my neck and sever my spine, but each time, I batted him down and bit him wherever I could.

Lavi's hatred made him stupid, and he lunged again. I caught him and brought him down. He was stunned, and I leaped on him and bit him savagely about his neck and shoulders. Holding him tight in my jaws, I stood and shook him. I was surprised I didn't snap his neck, but I sure tried. He was a strong beast. Then, I tossed him near the door. I had no plans on giving him another chance at terrorizing me, my family, or another innocent child; so I lunged for him. I intended to finish him off.

Lavi saw the rage in my eyes, and I saw fear in his. But Lavi was clever and still immensely powerful. Just before I was on him, he leaped almost straight up and over me. My momentum took me to the edge of the door. Then, the next thing I knew, I was grabbed by powerful, clawed hands and pulled through the door. Those disgusting, other-world creatures used my momentum to pull me in.

I really didn't know what they were thinking, but at the time, I was a medium-sized grizzly in a state of full rage. It's common sense to never corner anything meaner than you. I was in no mood to cower before those creatures, and they thought they had me cornered.

I had been through doors before, so this was not new or frightening. And seeing these things, I knew what they were. Among other crazy things, Raphael had prepared me for the creatures who were attacking me. He called them Sobeks. Some looked like snakes with legs, and others were much more robust. They were flesh and blood throwbacks to the time of the fall, and their anger and hatred of man led them to side with Satan. Sobeks were a lot like reptilian versions of watchers. Their home was a poor counterfeit of Eden where they believed they were in charge.

Roaming demons would sometimes use a mercenary band of them to sack a village, prop up some mystical despot, or act as some sort of local or national god. The Mayans, Egyptians, and other ancient societies worshiped Sobeks. They even masquerade as space aliens from time to time. Except for the alien thing, the modern world seems to have forced them back into their world where they belong. Satan is described as a dragon, and the Sobeks are just smaller versions of the dragons of old.

This door led to a dry, hot valley surrounded by low, barren mountains. Because it was a counterfeit world, it didn't feel right. But there was plenty of room for fighting, and I was surrounded by the sharp-toothed reptilians. The first thing I did was attack one of the Sobeks who still had pieces of my fur and some of my blood on its claws. His disgusting smile melted as I turned on him and bit deeply into his shoulder and through his armor. The other Sobeks that had first grabbed me were not prepared for me fighting back. They were used to terrorizing others, but I had no sense of fear in me then. I did later, but not then.

The Sobek fell screaming, and I swung hard with my left and nearly tore his scaly face off his bony skull. Instead of finishing him off, I pounced on one of the others who had earlier grabbed me and dragged me into his hellhole of a country. I swatted him hard, and he flew back. I didn't check to see if he lived because other Sobeks were recovering from their shock and started to advance upon me.

So instead of me trying to get back out, which is what they had prepared for, I ran deeper into their country and then turned to face them. When I did, I was not expecting to see the small horde of creatures barring my way out. There had to have been at least thirty of them. They faced me with clubs and machetes. I roared and stood. I would certainly die but not alone.

I dropped to my feet as the Sobeks advanced. They started to come at me when Dean and then Jack miraculously appeared through the door charging on their horses at full speed. They were yelling and firing their shotguns. Two of the Sobeks were killed outright, while several others were badly wounded. Dean and Jack ran through them trampling a few with their horses. The Sobeks scattered out of their way.

Dean and Jack rode past me and yelled for me to follow. I did, and deeper into the country we ran. By then, the three of us were nearly two hundred fifty yards from the door when we turned again to fight.

We ran to the crest of a low hill that gave us a clear view of the countryside. It looked like a cheap copy of somebody else's work of art. From our vantage, we watched the creatures regroup, and their numbers somehow increased. The country was vast, so I knew there were tens of thousands of others somewhere else. I doubt they all knew what was going on here though.

The Sobeks carried off their wounded, and then, they focused back on us. They seethed in anger and chanted loud, annoying, repetitive chants. They were consumed with jealously and rage. I stood to get a better view, while Dean and Jack sat on their saddles and calmly reloaded when the chants turned into more screams. Sobeks were running and confused. Shots rang out as Sobeks scattered to the right and to the left. Then, we saw Dad and Gunner charging through their lines, both firing as they rode. We cheered. Several Sobeks fell, and like before, others were wounded and trampled. We waved, and they raced over to join us. Again, the Sobeks regrouped and stood between us and the door. But I knew it didn't really matter. The kidnapped little girl was in here somewhere nearby, and we would never leave her in this horrible place. We had to find her.

We waited for Dad and Gunner to run to us. The three of us stood together, out in the open. Dad and Gunner had to dodge a series of rocks and clubs thrown their way, but they were moving fast.

Out of the blue and while we were waiting for Dad and Gunner, Jack looked at me and said, "Geez Kaiyo, you were a beast out there. I seriously had no idea you could fight like that. I knew you were strong, but you tossed Lavi like he was a stuffed toy. Lavi was a mess. And we nearly ran over two of those dead creatures when we stormed in. Did you kill them too?"

I nodded. Then, Dean said, "First, what are those things? They look like Sleestaks mixed with Zorgons. And throw in some crocodile too."

Except for the crocodile part, I had no idea what he was talking about. "Second, little brother, you are a true fighter. I am so impressed and proud of you. You're going to have some awesome face scars too."

Jack agreed. Dean went on. "Thanks for holding back when you and I fight. I knew you did, but I didn't know you could kill me so easily. Kaiyo, I will be proud of you till the day I die. Of course, by the way things are going, that will probably be today. Unfortunately, I see no way to win here. There are just too many of them."

Then, Dean's mood picked up a little bit. "But God is with us, right? What are we worried about? The worst thing is we die fighting, and then, we get to see God up close and in person. And we won't have to wait long because we didn't bring enough ammo."

Then, Dean laughed. Dean is weird that way, but I didn't think any of it was funny. Everyone knew he was crazy brave. Jack wasn't smiling either, but Dean looked pleased with himself and no more ruffled about dying than he would be about not getting seconds at dinner. I hate it when I don't get seconds. Dean just laughs at me.

But as for today, Dean may have made his peace with being dead, but I really hadn't planned on dying yet. I just didn't feel like today was my last day. I don't know why, but I didn't. In seconds, Dad and Gunner came cantering up to us. They turned to face the angry crowd that was still several hundred yards away from us.

"Okay, said Dad, "we are so proud of you boys. And, Kaiyo, just dang! You fought like a cave bear."

That was a major compliment. I knew some cave bears, and they're tough. I just smiled and said, "Thank you, Dad!"

Now that was weird. Very weird. I talked. I talked to my family. In English. The four of them stared at me. Jack was first. "Did you guys hear that?"

"Oh my gosh," I said. "You understand me! First, if we die, I love you Dad. And, Dean, I love you too. Thank you both for having me as a part of our family. Gunner, you are probably my best friend. And, Jack, you are too. Thank you for helping us here. And I am so sorry that I got us into this…"

When I said that, they all came around me to make me feel better. But it was true. If I hadn't gotten out of the door on the wrong mountain, we wouldn't be here. Gunner hopped off his horse and threw his arm around my shoulder. "Well, thanks, Kaiyo. I feel the same way. We've been buds ever since we met at the school bus stop. But let's talk about what you just said. I liked the first part, and I can't wait to talk to you more. But, Kaiyo, the last part was a bunch of pure crap. None of this is your fault. This whole thing was going to go down here or somewhere else. Lavi wasn't going to give up, right? By the way, you have a damn fine voice."

Gunner was an occasional curser, but I was glad to hear I had a nice voice. I had always wondered. Gunner looked up again. "And we need to focus on getting Danielle and fighting our way out of here. I have only ten rounds left, total. What do you guys have?"

Dad had twenty rounds in his saddlebags and six rounds in his rifle, Dean had twelve shells left, and Jack had thirteen. That wasn't enough unless none of them didn't miss. And those creatures were good at not getting shot. Still, if it wasn't for Danielle, I was sure we could have bunched up and fought our way out of there. But there are things worth dying for. Getting that little girl back with her mama was one of them.

"Pray Up!" said Dad.

But we didn't get to praying because we saw a miracle.

SOLDIERS—GRACIE

I may only be ten years old, but sometimes, I can be so mad I can quit being afraid. Me sitting on that mountain was one of those times. My dad was gone and so were my brothers. Our friends disappeared into a hole that came from nowhere. A girl was taken and may now be dead. And evil things caused it all. I didn't like sitting here. Neither did my mom nor my sister.

We were listening to some crazy animal sounds, but they stayed lower down the mountain. Mom was thinking about getting off the rock when I saw movement far down the slope near the creek bed. At first, it was a pack of wolves running out of the timber. A watcher was with them. They were following Dad's tracks, but they were running hard. We could see them howl, but it took a while before we could hear them.

"What in the world is going on?" said Mom.

As Mom talked, we watched as several grizzlies came out of the timber all spread out. They stormed the creek bed and were running just behind the wolves. No one would ever believe this.

I was looking through my binoculars when a wolf and the watcher stopped as the others disappeared through the door. The wolf howled and then looked up at us. I knew them! "It's Tracker and Benaiah!"

Benaiah waved, and then the two of them ran through the door. While we were watching, some monster pigs ran by them and into the door. Then, we saw Aylmer and others like him. He stopped and looked our way too, before he went through the door. I couldn't move. None of us said anything. We watched as more animals came into view. We saw a few more watchers and even some terrifying ostrich-sized dinosaurs with big heads and lots of teeth. They looked ferocious as they charged through the door.

I saw something move by our horses about thirty yards from us. It was a black bear. Libby swung her rifle toward it.

"Careful, Libby," said my Mom. "We have friends around."

It was Dovie! I didn't wait. I jumped off the boulder and tumbled into some sharp rocks. I got a little scraped up, but I ignored it and ran. Dovie stepped out of the timber, and we met in the middle. She wasn't expecting me to come flying at her, but I did. She was a big black bear, but I almost knocked her down "Dovie!" I screamed. "What is happening?"

Then, I started crying. I buried my face in her fur, and I cried so hard it was hard to breathe. Dovie patted my back and made little cooing sounds. Pretty soon, Mom and Libby came up to us. I looked at Dovie and kissed her snout and then turned to look at Mom. "Sorry, Mom. I just had to get that out of me. I needed a good cry."

"Oh, baby," said Mom. "No apologies needed."

Moments later, after we all swarmed around Dovie, she motioned us toward the horses. We got the message and got on our horses with Dovie leading the way. Within a few minutes, we were by the dry creek. The horses were jumpy with the smells of so many dangerous animals about, so we had to sweet-talk them. When we were close to the door, Dovie made us stop. She wouldn't let us go in. We didn't have long to wait, when suddenly a bright light appeared from the west and came past us like a rocket. It went straight into and through the door. It shook us all. The horses got startled, and the three of us screamed. But Dovie didn't move a muscle. Well, she kind of closed her eyes because of the brightness, but that was all.

"Was that a good thing, Dovie?" Libby asked.

Dovie nodded and gave us a bear smile. What we saw and heard next was even more amazing.

VICTORY—DEAN

The wolves were first through the door along with Benaiah. The minute I saw them, I knew the tables would be turned on the lizards. I let out a yell and was about to kick Solo when Dad yelled, "No, Dean!"

I couldn't believe it. This was our fight too, and Dad was playing it safe. I started to protest, but the look on Dad's face said it all. Gunner was equally grim.

Kaiyo spoke at me. "Dean, you'll just get in the way. The door is going to be closed for good. The wolves are just the beginning. Just wait, and you will understand."

Waiting wasn't pleasant. I wanted in the fight, and from where I was, the wolves and Benaiah were fighting for their lives. "Dad," I said, "Benaiah saved your life once, and now, we're just going to sit here on our butts and watch him fight for his life? We have guns. We can make a difference."

"I agree," said Jack.

"I told you to wait!" snarled Kaiyo. "This is not Montana, and you will be helping nobody. You don't even know the rules."

Rules? What rules? And why was Kaiyo so mad at me. I admit to wanting to wade into the fight, but I was confused.

"And now the bears," said Kaiyo.

I turned back, and a sea of brown and blond fur came racing through the door. They charged into the confused Sobeks. My mouth dropped. "Yeah, that's why I told you to wait," said Kaiyo.

Then, behind the bears came Aylmer and more of his kind. They were spreading out in the country attacking groups of Sobeks. Then, the scene was filled with things I had never seen before. Huge carnivorous pigs came onto the scene and creatures that looked like *Jurassic Park* raptors stormed into the Sobeks.

Kaiyo was so right. Those creatures on our side looked like they hated everybody. "Okay, so everybody was right but me. And Jack."

After a few more minutes, we saw a blinding flash of light. Kaiyo let out a cheer, but I had no idea why. Anyway, the situation with the lizards appeared to turn into a mopping-up action. I could see some additional dead Sobeks and more wounded ones, but the others were being rounded up and herded together by the wolves and the raptors. They were leading Sobeks away from the door and off to the southeast. Some of the aurochs and bears went with them.

Dad said that it looked like the party had ended, and he and Gunner took the lead to take us off the hill. We started riding back toward the door, but we all knew we needed to find Danielle. From the distance, we saw Mom and my sisters ride through the door. Their horses were easy to recognize. A man was walking alongside of them and so was a black bear. I assumed it was Dovie. Kaiyo gasped and broke into a run. Dad told us not to run but to let Kaiyo surprise them. We also decided we needed to go to some of the animals to thank them and show respect. That was easy to do; they saved our bacon. Without them, we would have been killed or tortured first and then killed. Jack and I headed over to the killer-looking pigs.

Voices—Susan

"Mommm! Mommm!" I heard it, but it didn't register. "Mom! It's me, Kaiyo!"

Kaiyo? What? I looked out, and I saw Kaiyo about a hundred yards away, and he was running our way.

"Oh my gosh!" said Gracie. "He's talking!"

I saw it, but I didn't believe it. "Mommm!"

It was Kaiyo! I jumped off Cali, and I ran, but Kaiyo got to me immediately. Libby was at my side. So was Gracie; Kaiyo hugged us all. He stood up and hugged me and told me how much he loved me and missed me. He was so much taller than me, so I just hugged and held on. He needed a bath, and he was cut up by Lavi's claws, but I didn't care. I was finally talking to Kaiyo, and it was amazing.

And he talked. And talked. It was the purest music my ears had ever heard. And he sounded so grown-up. It amazed me how quickly it all became normal. I was able to focus on what Kaiyo was saying, not just the fact he was talking.

After a few minutes with a lot more *I love yous* being said by all four of us, Kaiyo asked, "So I see you've met Raphael."

I looked back to see the man. "Well, not really."

Raphael came up to us and smiled. I extended my hand and introduced myself. "Wait," said Kaiyo. "Have you two not met yet?"

"Mom, this is Raphael. He's the angel that takes care of Eden. And lots of other things. He's been teaching me amazing things."

I was flabbergasted. Raphael kept his eyes on me. He knew I was a proud mom. He spoke with a common voice. I don't know what I was expecting, but he seemed so human.

"Well, truths are amazing things. I wish I had more time with Kaiyo. He's a surprisingly good student."

"Wait," said Kaiyo, "why are you surprised?"

Raphael smiled and ignored Kaiyo. "We have work to do now, but I want you to know that your love for Kaiyo, and his for you, is a glimpse of what God had made for man to experience long ago. I also want you to know the Father is pleased with your family. He is also very pleased you love him back. In fact, it makes him happy."

I had no words—at least no smart-sounding words. "Thank you, sir," was all I got out.

Raphael smiled at that one.

"What about me?" asked Gracie.

Raphael laughed and got on a knee. "Yes, dear child, you too are loved deeply. So is Libby and your brothers and father. I do not know everything, sweet child. Only the Father does, but I understand he has plans for both you and your sister. And right now is one of those times. I have a mission for you. There is a dwelling to the north of us about two miles away. These poor, misguided creatures have imprisoned Danielle there. Libby, take your little sister and little brother and retrieve her. Please be on guard. I suggest you hurry."

Libby reached over and gave Raphael a sweet hug. She thanked him for Kaiyo and for being here. For some reason, I expected Raphael to pull back, but he seemed to appreciate the gesture. Gracie joined in.

"Follow the dry creek bed?" asked Libby.

Raphael confirmed it and told them to hurry. I started to hop up on Cali to go with them when Raphael told me to stay. That confused me. "As for you, Susan, you have extended family to attend to. Show them how you love Kaiyo and then love them as well. Having friends in Eden is a good thing. Having family is even better. Susan, I must get back to work now. We have a door to destroy."

He winked as I thanked him. He left us to confer with a small group of animals that looked like they had authority. I could not understand the language. I started thinking about what Raphael meant about *family*. He clearly didn't mean Sam or Dean.

"Mom, I am so excited," said Kaiyo. "My uncle and cousins are here. I'll be back and make the intros once we get Danielle."

I watched them race off to the north and felt helpless. I had to pause to take it all in. Somehow, we rode into a different world that was populated with lizard people who seemed to hate us and were kidnappers. My family and the Gibbses barged our way in and then got rescued by a small army of dangerous, talking animals who were led by an angel. If I told anybody that story, they would think I was crazy or just plain stupid. Only a handful of people like Aliyah Gibbs or Officer Brigham would believe me.

Thinking about Aliyah caused me to look over at Gunner. He was on his knees in front of Raphael with his head down. Whatever Raphael said caused him to jump to his feet. That made sense. The good angels don't like to be treated like God; it makes them mad. And Raphael looked mad. He softened up and patted Gunner on the back. Sam seemed to be enjoying it all.

I rode over to them. Dean and Jack seemed no worse for the wear. Within a few minutes, Goliath came over leading three other grizzlies. At this point, we were far past having to adjust to talking animals. Landon had told us the animals could talk to him, and here we were. Goliath looked a little bloodied, but he seemed to be in great spirits. He then proceeded to introduce us to Kaiyo's family. Now, they were our family too.

DANIELLE—LIBBY

We rode quickly, and about fifteen minutes later, we spotted several small, plaster-sided buildings just where Raphael indicated Danielle would be. This country reminded me of pictures I had seen of North Africa or the Holy Land. It was sparse, and there wasn't much water. We spotted several Sobeks in the distance to our right and to our left, but they seemed content to avoid us. Kaiyo was loping alongside of us when I noticed he caught a scent.

"She's there," Kaiyo said. "But she's not alone. She's with a lizard."

Gracie looked at me. Her hair was blowing back, and she started looking so grown-up. She really had turned into a good rider. "Libby, make sure you're locked and loaded."

"No, problem, little sis. Hey, Kaiyo, got an update?"

"Yep. It's just her and one lizard so far."

In moments, we pulled up in front of the little low buildings that surrounded a small, dusty center courtyard. I admit I was scared. Gracie was too. Kaiyo was cautious.

"Call for her, Gracie," said Kaiyo. "She knows you."

I thought of how much I would miss Kaiyo's talking. I had forgotten about that. I was also so wrapped up in feeling responsible for Gracie that I overlooked the fact Raphael sent her with us for a reason. Gracie looked straight ahead.

"Danielle! It's me, Gracie. Where are you? We're going to take you home."

After a few moments, we heard shuffling. In a hutlike building to my right, I saw a green-clawed hand pull back the cloth door. A Sobek stepped into the doorway. It looked female. Kaiyo's hair was on end.

"Steady, Kaiyo. Let's see what she wants."

"Fine," Kaiyo growled.

The Sobek stood there. She wore a brown smock, and she appeared older. She motioned us to come in, and then, she turned back inside.

"Me first," said Kaiyo.

Gracie hopped off Duke, and I dismounted from Jet. I tied them up to a nearby shade tree, grabbed my rifle, and the three of us went inside. I had to duck a little in the doorway. When my eyes adjusted to being inside, I saw Danielle in the center of the small structure. She was dirty, but she looked unhurt. Directly behind her was the Sobek guard. They were holding hands.

Well, that surprised us. Gracie spoke first. Slowly, she asked, "Are you ready to go home, Danielle?"

Gracie walked up to her and gave her a hug. "And who is this?" asked Gracie pointing to the Sobek.

Danielle spoke. "Yes, I want to go home. But I want Annag to come home with me. She rescued me from the bad ones. We've been hiding here. I've been waiting for you, Gracie. I knew you would come."

Raphael knew what he was doing by sending Gracie. Gracie then looked at Annag, and we all noted a softness in the Sobek. To think I was ready to shoot her minutes before bothered me. Gracie looked past me to Kaiyo.

"What do you think, Kaiyo? Can we keep her?"

Then, we laughed. "Of course," said Kaiyo. "Annag, there are others like you where I'm from. They all felt the oppression here, and they knew there had to be something better. Somehow, they made their way to us. And I promise, there is something far better."

Gracie looked at me. "Of course!" I said.

Danielle let out a little cheer, and Annag clapped her hands and stomped her feet in joy. She spoke with a bit of a hiss. "I have waited for thisss day. Danielle ressscued me, you know."

I started to cry at that one. Annag and Danielle grabbed a few things as they chatted to themselves. Annag was so happy. Danielle comforted her as their joy was obvious.

Danielle turned and asked if we had her dog, Luke. She said the mountain lion tried to kill it, but it got away. "No, baby, we didn't see it. But I bet the searchers found him."

She described Luke as a midsized mutt, a mix of a pit and a cattle dog with a splotchy coat and several large black patches. I couldn't really think of what a dog like that looked like, but it probably wasn't pretty. Regardless, it would have been no match for Lavi. I wondered if he was even still alive. I needed to change the subject. "Danielle and Annag, have you ever ridden a horse? Because you're about to."

We stepped out of the little building, eager to head back. The light was blinding but, in the glare, I could see trouble. Seven or eight Sobeks were blocking the way to our horses. When we stepped out, they stepped back. Except one. He was bigger than the others, and he looked like any one of the warriors we saw on the battlefield. He wore full armor, and he had a weapon at his side. Kaiyo growled. From behind us, we heard Annag say, "Fam-i-leee."

Family or not, the strong one looked unpleasant. He walked to Kaiyo. Slowly, he pulled out his weapon and handed it to Kaiyo. Kaiyo reached out, touched it, and pushed it back to the Sobek. This was the warrior way for surrender and respect. The Sobek bowed to Gracie and me; then, he barked a few commands to the group. Danielle was placed on Duke by the tall one, and then, he helped Annag get up on Jet behind me. The other Sobeks gave their version of *oohs* and *aahs*. Well, this was amazingly new to all of us.

Kaiyo spoke to the warrior, and they agreed to take up positions on the outside with the other Sobeks in the middle. Gracie would lead, and I would be last. It made sense. I had a rifle. I couldn't tell if I had prisoners or refugees, so I knew I should keep my eyes on them. But they seemed so happy. *Joyful* was a better word to describe them. Kaiyo seemed unconcerned, and Gracie and Danielle were chatting up a storm. And I had an aging Sobek riding behind me and holding on to my waist with scaly, green hands with some big, sharp, nasty-looking claws that could probably still do some damage. She was laying her head on my back. In the craziness of the situation, it was wonderful.

It turned out having her ride with me on the way back was pure treasure. Her story was stunning. She was somehow drawn to God in this hellhole. There were no churches, no pastors, no Bibles; there was nothing. But God found her. And she listened and waited. And she shared what she knew with her family. The big Sobek guarding us was her son. His name was Haydar, and he gave up everything to escape. I had no clue what future these Sobeks had, but I didn't doubt the extent of God's grace. I'd happily take Annag to Montana, and I had a strong suspicion we were here to rescue her and her family just as much as we were here to rescue Danielle and Kaiyo.

Getting back took a little longer because the Sobeks had to walk, but they were excited, and they walked quickly. It wasn't very long before we walked up and over a rise, and before us was a sight to see. We all stopped. The *ooohs* and *aahhs* began again. There on the arid plain was a gathering of life I would probably never see again. I could see my family off their horses surrounded by grizzlies, a few wolves, Benaiah, and two other watchers. Overhead were eagles and some flying dinosaurs. Many Sobeks were running off to the south, but I saw ten or eleven Sobeks standing in the middle of it all with Raphael smiling and holding his arms out wide. The fighting was over.

"Annag," I said, "would it be okay if I introduced you and your family to a real angel?"

Annag's voice was breathy, and her words were drawn out. "A reeeeal an-gellll?"

"Yes, Annag. A real one. And don't be afraid. He won't hurt you."

Kaiyo ran over to Haydar. The two spoke briefly. Then, Kaiyo came over to me and told me to drop off the Sobeks and join the rest of the family. He then ran off.

We rode into the gathering and went straight to Raphael. Haydar took the lead. When we got close, the other Sobeks showed what appeared to be fear. Raphael spoke first. "Haydar, Haydar, God has heard your prayers. Annag, you are blessed. Are you ready to come to the land you were made for?"

Raphael's voice boomed, and many heard him. Haydar picked up his mother and ran to Raphael with the rest of his little group of Sobeks in tow.

It dawned on me how this whole story here wasn't as much about us and Kaiyo as I had first thought. I marveled at how countless, different stories get woven together into a bigger, better story. Danielle's story, ours, and the Sobeks', both good and bad, contributed. Even Lavi played a role in this amazing story.

It was time to introduce Danielle to Raphael and for us to go meet some amazing creatures. Most importantly, Gracie and I needed to meet some bears. Somehow, we were related to them. Who gets to say something like that?

6

THE GATHERING—SAM

My head was swimming at the events that had occurred over the prior eight hours. Having Kaiyo had opened my eyes over the years to a lot of things I never dreamed possible. But today was beyond anything I could have imagined. And the day wasn't over.

We sat on our horses not far down the creek from where Kaiyo battled Lavi. From our vantage, we watched a stream of courageous animals, some wounded, calmly exit through a bizarre rip in space and leave that strange, awful country. As they appeared out of thin air, they made their way out of the creek bed and up into the timber. Their spirits were high. They were going to go through another rip in the fabric of space to a different country and a better country. I hoped to see it someday.

We watched the procession. The small group of Sobek defectors came out and waved at us. We all waved back. Libby, Danielle, Gracie, and Kaiyo raced over to say goodbye to Annag and Haydar and the others. Time was short, and the Sobeks had to move on. They were so happy.

The strange parade of even stranger creatures passed by. Aylmer, Tracker, Benaiah, Dovie, and Goliath came over and said goodbye. They promised to be waiting for us at the farm when we got there. Then, they too slipped into the timber. More of our animal rescuers continued to exit out of Sobek-land and vanish into the timber.

Raphael then appeared among us. He told us to expect the door to be destroyed. He thanked us and whispered to each of us individual messages that will be treasures in our hearts. Saying goodbye, he vanished when the last of his troops walked into the timber. Then, a silent but brilliant flash of light seared the door shut. All of it was burned in our memories.

Kaiyo stood and leaned against my horse. I had my left arm draped on his huge right shoulder and was so glad to have my youngest back with us. I will miss being able to talk to him, but at least, we would have him back at the farm. Gunner just kept looking at Jack and smiling. The Gibbses have been blessings to my family. I couldn't help but notice how Susan was looking so pretty while she looked at a map. Dean was next to her, and the two of them were already planning our exit out of here. Danielle was on Gracie's horse next to me.

After a few moments, Danielle caught my eye and asked, "Mr. Sam, nobody is going to believe me. What do I tell my parents? They don't even believe in God or anything. What do I say?"

I wished she had asked somebody else. That was a tough question. Everybody turned to see how I answered. Kaiyo cleared his throat and raised an eyebrow at me. But starting with the truth made things easier.

"Well, Danielle, they may not believe you. We saw all this, and we were all, somehow, in a different world. You were kidnapped by a Sobek and a mountain lion, rescued by a Sobek, and then met a real angel. It already seems kind of unreal, right?"

Danielle smiled and nodded. "What happened to you today is an amazing treasure that is to be stored in your heart. Most people won't believe either you or us, and I couldn't blame them. But, as you go through life, you will never have to doubt that God is real or that you are loved. That's a priceless gift. You saw a tiny part of God's team in action today. That's another priceless gift. Very few people are blessed with such proof. So when you tell your parents this story, forgive them if they don't believe you. They probably won't, and they probably can't. What happened here is beyond the ability for most people to believe. Does that make sense?"

I looked at Kaiyo. He gave me his look of approval. "Yes. It does," said Danielle. "But what do we tell everybody when we get back? They're going to want to know what happened to me."

That was a harder question. She was a smart nine-year-old. I had some problems with this one too. I didn't really want to tell her to lie, but the full truth was not remotely believable. But the truth was all we had. "Well, how about the truth?"

Everybody, even Kaiyo looked at me like I was crazy. Danielle's face was all twisted up. Everybody was thinking this out.

"Okay, hear me out. The minute we try to concoct some sort of story, the details will unravel, and the fact we're lying will create even worse problems. They might even think we had a hand in Danielle's disappearance. But except for the rangers and the police, we shouldn't talk to the press or to anybody else. We don't have to. I wouldn't be surprised if the rangers don't want this story getting out. It's just a hunch."

The group debated my idea, but one by one, they all concluded that truth was our only defense. My hope was law enforcement didn't ask very many questions. We just went through an amazing ordeal. Trying to also remember a complicated and bogus story was asking too much. And it wouldn't work.

"So now what? Where to?" said Gracie.

Jack Creek Campground was going to be a circus. There were people and cops all over the place there. I had no plans to waltz in there with our group. We needed to control the situation. Susan kept looking at her map. It showed hiking trails in this part of Wyoming, and there were dozens of them. Looking at her map, Susan said, "There's a trail to a Forest Service road. It's the Haymaker Timber Creek Trail, and it goes to a parking lot on Jack Creek. It's pretty remote, but it might be a good place to meet the sheriff."

Kaiyo went nuts. He ran over and looked at the map. I sure missed him not being able to talk. He gestured wildly. Dean, though, communicated with Kaiyo beautifully. In short order, we learned

Kaiyo had been there. That was terrific news. Susan said that as the crow flies, it wasn't very far, maybe two miles.

After some more discussion, we had a plan. Susan would take the group over the high ridge even though it wouldn't be easy. The mountains here are higher than ours at home, and we were concerned about altitude sickness. Gunner and I decided to go back to the campground, load up our horses, and meet everybody somewhere on the Forest Service road.

"Susan, when you get to the crest of the ridge, see if you can get a signal. If so, call Trooper Garcia. We're going to need her."

Susan agreed and kissed me goodbye. I told everybody to remember Mom's lectures one through forty-two and to keep a lookout for Lavi. Kaiyo snorted at that one. Last, I recommended Danielle ride on Kaiyo's back from time to time, especially if the trails got a little too sketchy. Kaiyo was sure-footed and safe. Danielle squealed. I understood. That probably sounded like a lot more fun than riding behind Gracie. I kissed Susan goodbye. Gunner and I watched them climb and follow Ross Creek up toward the massive ridgeline to the east.

Trails in the West last far longer than the East. Rain and the rapidly growing vegetation overcome even frequently used trails in the South. But here, trails are almost permanent. I had little doubt that the trail Susan saw on the map was still there. We guessed only the one big ridge separated us from the parking lot on Jack Creek. I would have preferred it if Gunner went with them, but Gunner needed to drive his truck and horse trailer, and I needed to drive mine. Susan has pulled a trailer before, but she didn't like doing it. So we compromised. Fortunately, Susan, Libby, Dean, Jack, and Kaiyo were dangerous alone and extremely dangerous together. I know I didn't need to worry about the group, but I did anyway.

Gunner and I followed Ross Creek downstream to Haymarket Creek, and then, we followed the short trail to the flats of the Greybull River valley. We were in a hurry, so once we got to the river, we pushed hard to the north. The river valley was like a postcard. The water was crystalline, the sky was a beautiful blue, and the ridges around us spoke to our souls. It was hard to believe how earlier that morning, we ate breakfast in Meeteetse. Jack Creek Campground was less than ten miles away, and the terrain allowed for quick travel. I was hoping to be on the road within the hour.

Gunner and I were tired, so we didn't talk much, but we travelled quickly. That's why I was surprised when I heard him call out. "Dog!"

He pointed to a dog sniffing around the river where we found Kaiyo. It was holding up its back leg. When it saw us, it slinked away. We were convinced it was probably Danielle's dog. We rode up to it but stopped short. Gunner hopped of his horse and stood in the sand. Very few people have a way with animals like Gunner does. My own farm animals like him better than me. Every time we hunt together, he has a hard time pulling the trigger. I don't, but he does. I stayed seated on Hershel and held the reins of his horse. Gunner walked toward the timid dog and just started talking gently and kindly. Then, he got on his knees. It didn't take long for the frightened dog to go to him. After calming the dog, Gunner inspected his wound and then read the name on the dog's tag. "It's Luke. This is her dog."

Gunner picked up the dog and kept speaking to him. He took his horse's reins and walked over to some rocks. He was smart; he used them as a mounting block. He held onto the dog and crawled right onto the saddle. He draped the injured dog over his saddle and held onto the dog's collar. By this time, the dog trusted him. We rode slowly at first, but then, we picked up the pace as it appeared Luke was content with the ride.

We passed Anderson Creek and then Warhouse Creek. The foot traffic had picked up, and we started passing searchers coming and going. A helicopter passed us overhead. In front of us, the path was full of people. We used the less-travelled trails and headed straight into the campground. Even though we were carrying Luke, no one really noticed us. A lot of the search and rescue teams had dogs, so we fit in. That was good because we rode into the middle of what had become a small town.

The Sheriff's Mobile Command Post was there; vehicles were parked everywhere. A few more official tents had popped up. Most of the recreational campers had packed up and gone, but there were four or five different search and rescue teams coming and going that took their spaces. There were horses and ATVs everywhere. It was dusty. I saw almost no one smile. Unless a lost child is found quickly, these situations do not normally turn out well, and everybody involved knew it. They were grim-faced, and I understood why. Little did they know, all of them would get to go home that very evening.

The press was everywhere. Several TV trucks were there from stations in Billings, Casper, and Riverton. That was the group we needed to ignore. I took the lead, and we walked our horses to the command post where we spoke with Major Osbourne early that morning. As we were helping Luke off the saddle, several people came up to us and asked if Luke was the girl's dog. We nodded and said nothing as we carried Luke into the tented area. Danielle's mom and dad, Robin and Chris Klein, were seated there holding hands. They looked terrible. When they turned and saw Luke, we didn't want to string them along. We knew they were going through hell.

"This is Luke. He's been clawed by a mountain lion, but he'll be okay."

The news of a mountain lion attacking Danielle's dog sounded awful, and Gunner and I knew it. I cut to the chase. "And, Ms. Klein, Danielle is fine. We found her. She's unhurt, and she's safe."

The two of them burst into tears and hugged both of us. They immediately started asking a bunch of questions. I looked at the Kleins and said, "She is safe and doing well. She's also super smart. You should be so proud of that little girl. Right now, she's with my wife and children. They are riding to a nearby road."

Major Osbourne had stepped inside, and he listened to the conversation. "You two are the folks from Montana. Where did you find her?"

I could tell he was skeptical. "We found her at the base of Irish Rock."

"That's impossible. There's no way she could have gotten over there all by herself. Where'd you find the dog?"

He had a tone, and I didn't like it. Several other lawmen stepped into the tent. I started to get angry. Once again, Gunner stepped in. "Major, I understand the questions you have, and I know you and your men are tired. The good news is we found her, right? But here we are, two strangers who walk in with her dog. We're strangers who haven't even been searching for Danielle a full day? So you're skeptical, right?"

"Definitely," said the major. "Why didn't you bring her here?"

The Kleins were watching. I had no doubt they were wondering the same thing. "Major," I said, "there's a State Patrol Officer named Emma Garcia. Perhaps you know her. Gunner and I are also close friends with Sheriff Lee Tuttle in Madison County Montana. He and his second-in-command, Captain Troy Stahr, can vouch for us."

"Yeah, we know Emma. She's a good cop. I'll check with the sheriff in Montana. Don't go anywhere."

When the Major stepped away, Robin asked, "So why didn't you just bring her here? Is she all right?"

"Good questions. First, Danielle is doing great!" said Gunner. "So we're just gonna level with you. The day before Danielle vanished, do you remember that young grizzly that hung around camp here for a few days?"

They did. "What did you think about that bear?" asked Gunner.

They looked confused. Gunner asked again. Chris spoke, "Uh, it was remarkably well-behaved. Kids climbed all over it, and he gave them rides. He ate well because of it. And he loved to get his picture taken. Danielle wasn't allowed to get close, but the two would wave to one another. It was very strange, actually. Why?"

I answered. "Because he's my son. He's not a pet—he's my son."

I paused briefly to let that sink in. "His name is Kaiyo, and he somehow got lost down here. We came to rescue him. Of course, all of that sounds mighty strange, but what you folks are going to hear about your daughter's ordeal will be far more unbelievable. And you will probably not believe her because both of you are closed-minded people. At least, Danielle implied it."

269

They looked at each other and protested, but I kept going. "But her story will be true. You will have to let your biases not get in the way. That's why Danielle decided not to come here with all these people around. She wants you and the major and the rangers who chased Kaiyo to hear the whole story. And once the good major contacts our friends in law enforcement, he's going to come running in here and tell you guys to get on a helicopter. Danielle should be five or so air miles away right now."

The two confused parents looked both hopeful and skeptical at the same time. I understood. Dashed hopes are especially painful, and they were trying to guard themselves. Just then, the major barged in. "Yeah, you two are solid. Sheriff Tuttle is no nonsense, and he loves you guys. And Trooper Garcia somehow got a text from your son to meet at the Jack Creek Cow Camp. She's almost there now. You are free to go. Okay, Kleins, the chopper is coming back, and it ought to be here in about three minutes. Bring the dog too. She'll want to see him. You're going to be holding your daughter soon! She's not far. And let's keep the destination confidential until we are ready."

The Kleins' nightmare was over. And so was ours. The Kleins found their daughter, and we found our son.

TRUTH—DEAN

The trip back was as beautiful as it was uneventful. We all got slight cases of altitude sickness when we crossed over the ridge just south of Irish Rock. Everybody but Kaiyo had a headache. Thankfully, the headaches went away as we descended toward Jack Creek. Danielle rode Kaiyo most of the time. She tended to lay down on his back. Even with her headaches, she would just giggle. Sometimes, Kaiyo would laugh too.

When we got to Jack Creek, we walked right into the water. Our horses drank as Mom pulled out a baggie of snack crackers to share, and Kaiyo almost threw Danielle in the creek to get at them.

She had to hold on tight. He's a Cheez-It fiend. How do you share with a grizzly? It's not like he's a regular bear—he's family. How do you say no to an eating machine? Plus, he was still growing. So we have learned to yield. It's worth it. Kaiyo is awesome. Still, Mom wouldn't intentionally favor Kaiyo so she divvies out food and snacks by weight. That was fair, but Kaiyo always acts like he's getting gypped.

Once the horses were watered and rested and Kaiyo got everybody else's crackers, we crossed the creek and rode up into the sandy parking lot. Back in the world of the Sobeks, Kaiyo told me about what he did here when he realized he was lost. I loved his story. The stunt with the Iowans was a gutsy move.

Just then, a van full of young campers pulled into the lot. They came to a quick stop upon seeing Kaiyo. Until Danielle got snatched, Kaiyo was quite the famous bear around here. Of course, people walking with any grizzly would be a car-stopper. They poured out of the van and just watched as we proceeded through the parking lot. We were dirty, well-armed, and rough-looking; and a young grizzly carrying a nine-year-old girl led the group. They would never see that sight again in their life.

"Is that the bear of Jack Creek?" one of them yelled out.

"The one and only," I replied.

They asked if they could get their pictures taken with Kaiyo. "No, the time is no longer right for that. But heads up, you're about to be involved in one massive police action. If you're clean, no worries. If not, you might want to leave."

"Hah," said one, "thanks for the warning, but we're okay. Is that the lost little girl?"

Even though Danielle had passed them, she yelled out, "Yep! And they found me."

They applauded and thrust fingers in the air. "We've been praying! Thank you!"

Well that changed everything. "Okay," said Mom, "Danielle's parents will be ready to see their little girl. Just a few pictures of the bear but it will cost you in crackers."

Kaiyo heard it all, and he and Danielle turned abruptly and happily rode into the group. The girls among them screamed, but they all laughed. After a few moments of adjustment, they crowded around Kaiyo and Danielle while Gracie took pictures from seven different cell phones. It was fun watching Kaiyo. He really enjoyed being with people. And, in front of the camera, Kaiyo could really cheese it up. Danielle just looked precious. Within moments after the last picture was taken, a low-flying helicopter buzzed overhead and flew on to the east. With a quick group prayer, which was wonderful, we mounted up and continued up the road. The helicopter and our little caravan were headed to the same place.

Trooper Garcia had given us directions to a place called the Jack Creek Cow Camp. It was about a mile and a half up the Forest Service road from Jack Creek. The cow camp was a cabin and a corral first set up when the area was a ranch in the late 1800s. I heard it's still used from time to time for cattle ranching. Once we got away from the creek, we were in in the Jack Creek Flats. It was named that because the area was flatter, and the cattle could graze easily. For us, it meant that a helicopter can land there.

"Miss Susan," said Danielle, "if it's all the same to you, can I stay on Kaiyo? It will make my story more believable."

"Of course!" said Mom. "I agree. I know your family will be waiting, but that's good thinking. Let's hurry!"

After a few more minutes, we could see the camp in the distance. The helicopter lifted and flew by us. I assumed it was going back to get more people. We could see activity around the camp. There were at least three police vehicles, and people were milling around, waiting for us.

We closed the distance quickly and were better able to see who was at the camp. Waiting were the Kleins and a dog. They were standing next to a sheriff's deputy. We let Danielle and Kaiyo take the upfront position. She was so excited Kaiyo practically sprinted to get there. The Kleins were scared of Kaiyo, but their joy overcame their fear, and they rushed to hold their daughter. Kaiyo let them take Danielle off his back. The dog and Danielle rolled on the ground in pure joy. It was fun to watch.

Kaiyo spotted Trooper Garcia standing to the left of the Kleins, and he hurried over to her. The two deputies drew their sidearms, but Garcia yelled at them to stand down. She and Kaiyo just hugged on each other as she talked to him the entire time.

This situation with Danielle could have gone poorly. I imagine that until Dad and Gunner made it to the campground and gave them the good news, the parents and the lawmen were all bracing for the worst. But today, their joy was evident.

We pulled up to the camp, and Jack and I staked the horses to rest and graze. Trooper Garcia and Kaiyo joined the girls. She hugged my mom and my sisters, and they spoke briefly. Jack and I joined them. She briefed us.

"Expect Major Osbourne to ask a lot of questions. The USFS rangers who tried to capture Kaiyo will be coming here on the next helicopter. They'll want to know everything. And expect them to still want to capture Kaiyo. So what are you going to tell them?"

"The truth," said Mom. "Just the truth."

Mom winked at Trooper Garcia. "Really? Interesting approach. Well, I have no idea what happened or how you folks found the girl, so I will definitely listen in."

"I hope so," said Mom. "We would prefer you attend our inquisitions."

"There's no reason to be concerned with the Park County deputies or even Major Osbourne. They're good folks. The rangers? I don't know about them. The State Patrol works with the sheriff all the time, but with the USFS? Not so much, at least not for me. We'll see. That is going to happen soon too. Chopper's coming."

Whoever flew the helicopter understood horses. Instead of acting like some jerk and flaring right near the cabin, he landed over two hundred yards away. The horses barely noticed.

I expected to see other family members come out of the helicopter, but only rangers came out. Kaiyo barked and pointed at the rangers. He laughed his gravely laugh. "Yeah," said Trooper Garcia, "you made them look foolish. But remember, the young one pulled out his rifle. Be careful, Kaiyo. They probably think you are a problem bear, and that's not a good thing. Let the humans do your talking."

That was good advice, especially since Kaiyo couldn't talk. Our family was stuck here as we waited for Dad and Gunner to bring the trailers. We wanted to go home. We had been up all night driving here, and the day was about as stressful as a day could get. With the rangers here, it was probably a good idea Dad wasn't here too. Not that he's a problem, it's just Mom is a quick-thinking, smooth-talker, and she's pretty. Dad can be a little short-tempered at times.

Major Osbourne and two deputies were with the Kleins. The rangers went straight to them. We watched as they were clearly happy with the rescue. They shook hands, and we saw lots of smiles. They all sat at a picnic table and started trying to figure out what had happened. Trooper Garcia joined them. She wanted to hear the story too. They spoke to Danielle, and Danielle talked. A lot. From time to time, they would look back at us.

That went on for about thirty more minutes when Dad and Gunner drove down the dirt road to the camp. In no time, the two of them had backed up the trailers onto the driveway. We intended on leaving, and we didn't wait for permission. Jack and I unstaked the horses, and we all took our horses past the lawmen and the Kleins. Danielle was in the middle of telling her story to her parents and to the lawmen. The deputies and the rangers were taking some serious notes.

The parents were lost in Danielle's story. The rangers were look-ing at one another. Kaiyo walked over to their group and listened. No one paid him any attention. Danielle was doing all the talking.

We wanted out of here, and we really didn't want to give any statements, so the quicker we loaded up, the quicker we hoped to leave. Unfortunately, loading up horses is not always a quick thing. Saddles, pads, and blankets needed to be removed. The horses needed some brushing and TLC. Bridles needed to be replaced with hal-ters, and everything had to be properly stowed. Only then would the horses be loaded. That usually takes some time. Because everybody just wanted to get home, we were all extra efficient. Then, one of the deputies came over and told us not to leave because they would need statements. We all groaned; that could take hours.

Once all the horses were put in their stalls, the rangers walked up with Trooper Garcia. She introduced us to the rangers. The older ranger identified himself as Ranger Kent Thomas. The other ranger was Bill Adams. Kaiyo growled when Adams spoke.

"So," said Dad, "you must have been the one who was going to shoot Kaiyo."

Ranger Adams blushed and said, "Well, if half of what the girl said is true, then I would've been guilty of murder, right? I'm mighty glad I didn't. Sorry, Kaiyo. But in my defense, you have to admit you do look like an ordinary bear."

Kaiyo raised an eyebrow and nodded. Ranger Thomas then spoke. "We just informed Major Osbourne that we would be responsible for taking in the evidence. He was pleased with our assertion of jurisdiction, and he will not be asking you for statements."

That was terrific and surprising news. He continued. "Folks, we don't know what exactly happened out there, but we will not be taking any statements either or even notes from you. Whatever notes any of us jotted down will be destroyed. I am guessing you all are going to tell me the same story the girl just told. So let me summarize to save you some time."

Ranger Thomas then looked at his notes. "You guys were looking for your youngest son, Kaiyo the bear, when you realized the girl was nearby and had been taken by a lizard man and a smart mountain lion. Danielle didn't have a phone but somehow she was able to communicate with this young lady named Gracie."

He looked up from his notes, pointed to Gracie, and kept going. "Then, Danielle was dragged into another world, and Kaiyo came in that world after being dragged in too. But first, he had to fight the mean mountain lion who got away. Kaiyo killed a few of the lizard people, and then, he was rescued by Dean and Jack, who also killed a few of the lizard people. The three of them then were rescued by their fathers who also killed a few of the lizard people when they charged in. You all were fighting a bunch of lizard people when that world was invaded by animals like Kaiyo, including some dinosaurs, and an angel. How am I doing so far?"

We all said he was doing well. "Good," said Ranger Thomas. "Okay. Next, you ladies rode in. And after that, Kaiyo, Libby, and Gracie actually rescued Danielle. But Danielle was being sheltered by some rebellious lizard people. Not too long after that, you all came back to Wyoming from wherever you were, and the door into the other world was destroyed by the angel. Then, you people decided to meet us here to get away from the crowds. And thank you for that, by the way. And, finally, the two fathers rescued Luke the dog. And now, we're all here. Anything else?"

We looked at each other. "That's about all, I guess," said Dad. "There's more of course, but I suspect you have heard enough."

Ranger Adams laughed. "Yeah, that's plenty. Was she right about the door being destroyed?"

"Yep," said Gunner. "The angel seemed to have destroyed it. Why?"

Ranger Thomas responded. "We have had some odd occurrences here that concern us. Adams chased a lizard man one night a few months back. Other districts have had their own problems, but not with lizard people. Other things, but not lizard people. And yes, any experienced ranger is fully aware that sometimes, there are things in the woods, swamps, and deserts that are unusual and sometimes very dangerous."

"I think your lizard people problem is over for a while," I said.

Ranger Thomas looked at Kaiyo and then back to us. "Good. When it comes to your story, let's just say you all found her near Irish Rock and brought her back. As for the details, please just say something like *no comment*. And then give them our contact number for details. We will say it's still an active investigation, so no comments will be made, but we will make it known absolutely no foul play was involved. This will be hard to contain, but let's try. Typically, these things get forgotten in a few days. Does that work for you guys?"

It did indeed. Dad asked if there was anything else they needed. "Yeah," said Ranger Adams. "Can all of us lawmen and the Kleins take some pictures with Danielle and Kaiyo? I need a picture of Kaiyo to remind me that I can be wrong. He's basically a walking miracle, and somehow, I couldn't see how he was obviously different when I saw him at the campground. Sorry, Kaiyo."

The pictures were taken, and we said our goodbyes. In less than an hour, we were on the road and headed home. Kaiyo had refused to get in the trailer. He had a point. We initially thought we would have to smuggle Kaiyo out of here, but that wasn't the case anymore. He made it clear he wanted in the truck with the rest of us. Dad agreed. The bed of the pickup had a shell on it so Kaiyo could stay hidden. We emptied it of our stuff and piled it all in an empty horse stall. Kaiyo crawled in the truck, and we slid open the back window. We were, finally, together again.

Once we ate, Kaiyo promptly fell asleep. He'd been through a lot. We were so proud of him. But I knew, or feared, Kaiyo would be destined to fight and battle again. Gracie wanted to crawl back in the truck bed and snuggle up next to him, but we believe in seatbelts. She fell asleep instantly anyway. Neither of them woke up until we pulled up in the courtyard of the farm many hours later. When we did, Landon came out of the house and met us. He had been asleep, and he was sporting some major bedhead.

"That was a nice, quick trip. Looks like everything went well. Did anything interesting happen down there?"

GRACE—KAIYO

It's been nearly three weeks since we came back from Wyoming. I sometimes wake up thinking I'm lost. Or I dream I'm still fighting. Those dreams are more like nightmares than dreams. Dean has the same bad dreams. Jack does too. I'm sure Danielle struggles with her own night terrors.

My friends are here. Sarah's been here for a week, and it's been so nice. Landon's been here a lot too. Best of all, Aylmer asked me if he could live with us permanently. Of course, I agreed. And my parents loved the idea. He comes and goes, but he loves the hidden southern pastures.

I was gone when the pastures were cleared and crafted. Dad and Gunner sure created a beautiful place. We have had some wolf problems too, but Tracker's visits seem to keep them away.

Benaiah also comes by from time to time. At first, he really didn't like the pastures, but once he learned how hidden they were, I often see him and Aylmer sitting in the grass together. Dovie likes to patrol the farm with the dogs and sleep on the porch. She's going to go home for the winter, but we'll have a few more months with her. Every few days, it seems Officer Brigham brings us some tasty roadkill. Dovie and I, and sometimes Benaiah, eat like kings.

I have wondered about Lavi. I think it's Lavi who truly haunts my dreams. He must know he cannot threaten me anymore. I am simply too fast and powerful for him. But I fear for my family; they are all targets of his hatred.

Today, Aylmer had chosen to lay in the center of the grassy courtyard and chew his cud. We like it when he's here around the farm, and he does too. He isn't much a talker when he's working on the cud. Personally, it sounds disgusting. Food doesn't need to be eaten and swallowed twice to be good. But he adores the family, and we love him right back.

The wind had been coming out of the east most of the day, but in the afternoon, it shifted to a south wind. Every wind brings a thousand scents. To a human, those scents converge to become a smell. To us bears, scents are just like sounds. A human can hear a bird sing, a door close, a starting car, and a dog barking at the same time and identify each sound. Bears can do that with scents. Each scent can be the subject of our focus, and each one is distinct. By their scent, I know who is near me and who is not. And I can smell hundreds of different scents at the same time. And one of those scents was Lavi's. He was here.

I eased off the ground because I didn't want Aylmer to follow me. Silently, I walked through to the back of the barn and then out the back. From there, I made my way to the edge of forest and took the hidden lane into the new pasture. Lavi's scent was strong, and I was downwind. He would not know I was coming. At last, I would find Lavi and put an end to him and his threats to my family. He had apparently healed from our last fight, and now, he was back. That was a bad mistake. I would soon be dragging Lavi's lifeless carcass to our back porch. It was time for my nightmares to end.

Following the scent was not hard. Even a house dog could have located Lavi. Just at the far edge of the pasture, into the timber, Dad had piled up a jumble of tree trunks and boulders. Lavi was in there. No worries; I could wait him out. I wasn't going to wade in that mess and give him a chance to pin me down. So I made my way across the pasture and stopped thirty feet away. I didn't need stealth. Instead, I roared a challenge. After a few moments, I saw movement in the shadows, and out slinked Lavi.

Gone was the regal, arrogant, cat. What I saw was skin, bones, and pain. His coat was scruffy, and he limped badly. "Hello, Kaiyo. Surprised to see me?"

I didn't answer. I couldn't tell if he was faking his pain. "Well, I suppose you are. It seems the cat's got your tongue, and I would be the cat, right?"

He sounded like his old self. "Ah, I see that rage bubbling up in you. I saw that rage recently, and it nearly killed me. So please, young Kaiyo, hear me out and try to resist your primal urge to kill me, at least for a few minutes. Can you do that for me?"

I had to think about it. Then, I said, "All right, Lavi. I'm curious."

"Of course, you are. I look like hell, and I'm not trying to kill you. That must be new for you, right?"

He paused, took a breath, and said, "Kaiyo, you have bested me. I never expected to think or, especially, to say those words. The fight wasn't even fair, but as you know, I never planned on a fair fight. I don't like fair fights. That's why I used the Sobeks. They were supposed to kill you. That's why they took the little girl. They do things like that. Even I thought that was excessive, but I hated you with such vigor, blinding vigor apparently, it seemed to be acceptable. Collateral damage, you know."

Lavi settled into the grass and winced as he took the weight off his shoulder. "That's better. Bear with me, bear."

He chuckled to himself and continued. "It seems the Sobeks are as inept as they are ruthless. And I never suspected your humans would risk their own lives to save you or any one of us, for that matter. That surprised me. And the Sobeks certainly never expected an invasion of gun-toting cowboys. I was glad to have gotten away, but I would have loved to have seen that. Sobeks are truly disgusting creatures."

"Anyway, back to you. Kaiyo, I was simply not prepared for your speed and strength. My pride fueled my disdain for nearly all others and especially for you. My judgment was worthless because of it. You were on me and killing me before I knew what was happening. When I clawed your face, I hoped you would cower, but I seemed to have dredged up even more of your rage, if it were possible. You wear your scars like the champion you are. How I ever thought I could defeat you was lost on me when you shook me in your merciless jaws like some pitiful play toy. I had nothing. In my despair, I prayed. I did. Who would have thought, right?"

I had no clue where Lavi was headed with his admissions. He still seemed despicable though somewhat less so. "I am broken, Kaiyo. I know you can smell this. You bears can smell practically anything. Don't look so confused. That's a compliment. Look at my shoulder. It's broken, infected, and it stinks. It was hard to get here, Kaiyo, and it will be impossible for me to get to where I need to go. To get here, I nearly starved. In fact, I am still starving and well on my way to death. I was lucky to occasionally find worked-over roadkill, and when I got really lucky, some rare dog food left out on porches. Getting across streets and highways was an adventure in pure pain."

Lavi laughed hoarsely. He sounded bad. "You know what I learned, Kaiyo? Whatever was dead, I ate it. I could kill nothing, of course. I learned if I'm hungry enough, roadkill so old it was ignored by disgusting scavengers is somehow still edible. But, to get to the point of my conversation here, you have humbled me. It appears all I ever had was my strength and my pride. Oh, and my hatred for so many things. I don't want to leave that out."

"Now, those things are gone. I am no use to my old masters or to anyone else. And during these weeks, I kept trying to remember why I hated you so much. All I could come up with was jealousy. I was jealous of you getting to go home whenever you want. I was jealous of your human family. To be frank, I was jealous of everything about you, Kaiyo. Jealousy, my young friend, looks a lot like hate. And I was more than sure that I hated you. But perhaps not."

I was surprised at his confession, but I was still wary. "So what can I do for you? Do you need food?"

"Of course, I do, Kaiyo. I'm a bag of bones. Look at me. But what I really need is to go home. And I want you to take me."

I was stunned. Why would I help him? "Yes, I expected that look. Young bear, you are so predictable. Well, perhaps not. I certainly didn't predict your strength, right? Or your blinding speed.

You bears still manage to look stupidly clumsy even when you're running faster than a deer. That's not fair to those of us that harbor contempt for nearly everything.

"Anyway, I have had something of an epiphany. What else is there if you have nothing? If that stinking, lowlife, thief on the cross could swallow his pride and seek forgiveness, perhaps I could too. The other fool, the second thief, he kept his pride. And what did that get him? He's probably wandering around, alone, in eternal darkness while being tortured by lightless flames.

"I am tired, Kaiyo. I am tired of nearly everything that I am. I want more. In short, I miss Yeshua. He is all I seem to be able to think about. I dreamed of him as a kit and even prayed to him. That was so long ago. But I never forgot that he offers redemption to man and to those of us from Eden. But I somehow got turned around. In essence, I have spit on Yeshua's face. Frequently, I blamed him and man. Kaiyo, it's remarkably easy to blame everybody else for everything bad in your life. Don't go there. There's a never-ending amount of blame available to excuse any flaw or failure.

"So back to my story, which I'm assuming is good because you haven't killed me yet, right? Anyway, in my misery, I called out. It was hard to do so. Even as I was dying, and I am dying now, I was embarrassed. How preposterous though. I didn't really have any friends that cared about me. I was embarrassed for myself.

"So as I escaped from your rage and limped and crawled for weeks to get here, I asked those awful questions about myself that I had managed to avoid confronting before. And because of that, I have made my peace with God. And you, Kaiyo, are going to teach me all about him while you take me home. I don't want to die here on earth. It's not my home."

He didn't stop. "Meginnah and his ilk know me, and they know I'm a traitor. You must vouch for me, or I won't get in. Will you do this for me? If not, then kill me now. I will understand if you do. I am truly at the end of my frayed, miserable rope."

Lavi missed his calling. His life was theater. I didn't doubt his sincerity, but he just used a thousand words when fifty or so would have worked just fine. And he was still a little annoying. But he was

282

trying hard, and I appreciated the effort. And I was far more thrilled than I wanted to let on. Finally, I couldn't contain it, so I bounced around in joy. Lavi told me to quit carrying on and to behave, but the news was just too good.

For the next three weeks, Lavi lived in the barn. Dovie didn't trust him at first, but he won her over quickly. Dr. Cindy visited him several times and gave him some shots to deaden the pain and a jar of pills to heal the infection. My brother and Jack spent hours talking to him, and my sisters and Kate fawned all over him. So did Sarah, Miss Aliyah, and Mom. At first, he weakly resisted. But after a few days of Sarah, Kate, Gracie, and Libby cradling his head and talking to him, he came to love it. He would even order me to go bring them back to the barn to do it all over again. He would start purring at the sight of them.

He especially loved Sarah. They had history together, and they had both found their own ways home. She, Libby, and Gracie spent several nights in the barn. Several times, I would come to the barn and see the dogs and Lavi asleep in one bundle of fur and the girls in their sleeping bags watching over him. It was good.

Mom and Dad and sometimes Gunner would check on Lavi and clean his wounds. I had injured him badly. His shoulder was shattered, ribs were broken, and his bite wounds were extensive. I came to respect Lavi for getting here from Wyoming as hurt as he was. Hi cuts and bites were deep, and they needed cleaning. That had to hurt. But, to his credit, Lavi accepted the pain. Dad even looked at Lavi's tail and talked about it. He told Lavi he was mighty glad he didn't kill him. Lavi purred like a motor the whole time.

That doesn't mean everything was great. Lavi was still irritating at times, and he tended to talk down to all of us and treat us like his personal servants. For the most part, we called him on it even though we enjoyed serving him. Goliath came to visit for a few days, and Lavi ordered Goliath to go get him a snack. Goliath told all of us to leave, and he closed the barn doors and had a real come-to-Jesus meeting with Lavi. It was noisy and took a while, but even Lavi admitted he needed it. I did notice that he still got Dovie and others to do his bidding. Goliath was just the wrong bear to order around.

Weeks later, when the day came, Aylmer volunteered to let Lavi ride his back on the way home. Lavi had recovered some of his strength and the infection was gone, so he was well enough to travel. His shoulder was still badly broken, and he knew he might be crippled for the rest of his life, but he was okay with it. The whole day, he ordered us around and fretted about things that didn't matter—all of which was normal for him. Despite Goliath's lecture, during the entire three weeks, we were his nursemaids. He was still Lavi, but this time, he was our Lavi. And that changed everything.

There were the expected goodbyes and the tears that came along with it, especially from Sarah. Miss Aliyah, Kate, Mom, Libby, and Gracie were upset too. Even Jack got a little misty. Everyone knew they would never see Lavi again. Lavi cried like a kitten. It took him so long to get ahold of himself that Dean and Jack started to snicker. I had to tell Lavi he needed to pull it together. Lavi agreed, but this love stuff was too new for him to take for granted. He was a melodramatic wreck.

Then, it was time. Dean placed thick saddle blankets on Aylmer's back, and then Dad and Gunner helped Lavi leap up on Aylmer and get settled. As the sun was setting, Dovie, Lavi, Aylmer, and I left the farm to journey back home where Lavi now belonged. In the distance, we heard a wolf howl. That was Tracker, and we would follow his howl all the way home.

Like Lavi, I wonder if I should just go home to stay. At least, it's safe there. But I know I will never choose to abandon my family. All the troubles that go with living on earth are worth it.

Man lost so much more than just easy living in Eden. Man has been cursed. With just a few exceptions like dogs to remind man of what he lost, man will rarely ever be close with creation. Animals are wild; their understanding has been taken away. They do not desire closeness with man, and because of that, both man and creation are cursed.

There's also the slightly disturbing fact that both man and the meat-eaters like me love steak, burgers, fried chicken, and barbecue. Sometimes, it's just impossible to have much in common with creation when you're busy killing and eating it. Every time I get philosophical, I keep coming up with conundrums, and I remember that one day, all my questions will be answered.

In the meantime, I'll just be a grizzly bear with a God who loves me, a family I love, and a wilderness to enjoy. I would be living the dream except for one thing. I've been wondering who really killed my bear mother. Even Raphael didn't know, but he believed that whoever killed my mother probably wanted to kill me too. I have wanted justice ever since my bear family and Raphael told me about my bear parents.

And I don't know where to begin.

The end

POSTSCRIPT

TWO AND A HALF YEARS LATER

RUN—KAIYO

I tracked the bear killer for a week. What I didn't know was he had been tracking me even longer. Over a few weeks, he had killed two grizzlies and left their carcasses to freeze. The tracks in the mud and snow told me he had a method. Each time, he chased a panicked bear and shot it at close range. The first time, he used a dirt bike. When the first bear was killed, the killer's boot prints showed that he left the bike and walked up to the bear and then around it. The second time, he used a snowmobile. The tracks in the snow told the same story except the second time, he had a big dog with him. He wasn't a poacher killing for profit; their handiwork is easy to spot. But this shooter confused me. All he did was look at the dead bears. Then, he moved on.

Autumn had been unusually warm and wet, and normally, those bears would have been hibernating. The first one was killed right around Thanksgiving; the second one was killed a few weeks later. Though smaller than me, they were both large male grizzlies.

Because of the warmer weather, just after Thanksgiving dinner, I left the farm to get in a quick visit to my Eden home before Christmas. Christmas is wonderful there, and it was good to see everybody again. After a week, I began my return journey back to the farm. On the way back, the cold had broken through, and the wind howled. It was then I found the first bear.

Seeing that poor dead bear brought out my temper. I should have controlled my temper and gone home. But I didn't. I hate poachers, so I checked it out. I had plenty of time. Within a few days, I

287

had followed the poacher back to a small Forest Service campground that was at the end of miles of dirt road. With elk and deer seasons over, the campground was empty, and the poacher had moved on. I decided to keep looking. I wondered, though, what I would do if I found the poacher. I had no good answers to that question.

I decided to follow my nose and not go home just yet. A few days later, I was much farther east when I heard gunfire miles away. It was still hunting season for wolves and mountain lions, but that type of hunting was rare in the Eastern Wilderness. I headed toward the sound and found the fresh tracks of a snowmobile. I didn't want to be found, so I left the open spaces and kept to the timbered slopes close by to the north. A few miles later, the scent led me to the second bear. He was chased down before he could get into cover.

I waited in the timber. We are told to be wise as serpents, so I waited to make sure the poacher had gone. From my position in the woods, I could see the tracks left by the poacher as he rode away from his kill, to the southwest. After an hour, I came down onto the flat, snowy plain. The dead bear was cold, and only the wind kept the snow from covering him up. I recognized him. He wasn't like me; he was just a normal bear, but I had come across him many times. For a grizzly, he was always friendly and good-natured, and he was part of the wilderness.

The wind was gusting hard, and I caught no scent of the poacher, but I was upwind of where the poacher had gone. But he had been here; his tracks were everywhere. By chance, I looked up and saw a muzzle flash about a half mile away. I knew immediately what that was. The poacher had hidden himself and shot at me. Before I heard a sound, the bullet passed through me, up high where my neck met my shoulder. The bullet went too high to kill me, but too low to miss me. The pain was blinding. I felt my bear rage begin to race out of control, but I knew I needed to think. I turned and broke hard for the timber behind me and ran at top speed away from the shooter. I knew what I had to do.

I saw snow and dirt kick up around me well before I heard the cracks of his rifle. I tumbled into a frozen creek bed and kept running. I hit the timbered slopes right about the same time I heard his snowmobile. I was being hunted. And I was leaving a bright red trail of blood.

About the Author

Author Cliff Cochran sees life as a collection of countless sagas that somehow weave themselves together to form God's plan for creation, redemption, and completion. From Jesus' parables to Shakespeare to modern theater, the draw is always the story. He focuses on the power of story as an attorney, as a husband, and as a father of three because life is often best learned that way.

Raphael is the second book of the Kaiyo Stories trilogy. The first book, *Kaiyo: The Lost Nation*, set the stage for Kaiyo to find his strength and courage and discover his love for his amazing human family. The *Kaiyo Stories* arose out of the many requests from Cliff's now adult children to build on years of fascinating bedtime and campfire stories. Those stories were told to strengthen their faiths, feed their limitless imaginations, provide insights to their own potentials, and encourage them to see life as an adventure.

To find out more and to be a part of the Lost Nation go to: www.kaiyobooks.com and follow us on Facebook @Kaiyobooks and Instagram @kaiyo_books

For book clubs/reading groups: See study questions and more info at www.kaiyobooks.com. Also, if your book club/reading group would like to schedule a phone call with Cliff, please reach out to his assistant at: hello@kaiyobooks.com.

CPSIA information can be obtained
at www.ICGtesting.com
Printed in the USA
JSHW020012151220
10261JS00003B/43